UNBUTTONED

"I loved *Unbuttoned* by Maisey Yates in a big way. . . . I love a feisty heroine and a charismatic hero, especially when they clash. The scenes where they duked it out verbally, all the while undressing each other mentally, were so delicious. . . . Lots of fun."　　—Smart Bitches Trashy Books

"A sexy, compelling read. . . . It's a great start to what looks to be a promising new small-town contemporary series and has introduced me to a new-to-me author who writes enjoyable characters with great emotional depth, witty dialogue and steamy love scenes."　　—Ramblings from This Chick

"A lot of fun to read. . . . I look forward to reading the next installment. She provided humor, tension, smexy times, twisted family dynamics and a re-enjoyment of life."
—The Book Pushers

"Maisey Yates is a very talented author and has created the perfect small-town romance about two people that found love once they learned to take a leap of faith. . . . I can't wait to see what is in store for the residents of Silver Creek."
—Books-n-Kisses

Titles by Maisey Yates

Silver Creek Romance Novels
UNEXPECTED
UNTOUCHED
UNBROKEN

Silver Creek Romance Novellas
UNBUTTONED
REKINDLED
UNWRAPPED

$\mathcal{U}$NEXPECTED

MAISEY YATES

BERKLEY ROMANCE
New York

BERKLEY ROMANCE
Published by Berkley
An imprint of Penguin Random House LLC
penguinrandomhouse.com

ISBN: 9780593641705

InterMix eBook edition / August 2013
Berkley Romance mass-market edition / January 2024

Printed in the United States of America
1 3 5 7 9 10 8 6 4 2

Book design by Kristin del Rosario

For my husband. Maker of many meals, washer of many dishes. Hero of my heart. I love you always.

CHAPTER

One

So, when are you getting married?

"So, Kelsey, when are you getting married?"

Kelsey fought the urge to stab her own thigh with one of the fancy forks that her sister had selected so carefully for her special day. She could see the question forming in all of her well-meaning relatives' eyes before the words made it from their minds to their lips.

Well, Aunt Addy, I've set the date for five years from now. With any luck, I'll have sunk my claws into some unwitting victim in just enough time to pick out china patterns.

"Someday," she said, pasting a smile on her face. One she hoped looked happy and not like she was contemplating homicide.

It was such an idyllic setting. Her family's eastern Oregon ranch, the field bright with grass and yellow flowers. And she was as miserable as she could ever remember being.

She looked back up at her aunt, who was contemplating her a bit too carefully.

Don't say "on the shelf." Don't say "on the shelf."

"You're nearly on the shelf, dear," her aunt said with a chuckle.

Kelsey eyed her fork. "I like the view from up here," she said.

She was thirty. Thirty wasn't old. Thirty was just starting to come down from the postcollege, young-professionals club scene. Thirty wasn't even remotely ready to shackle yourself to someone until divorce did you part. Or so she'd heard. She hadn't made it to the divorce. She hadn't made it down the aisle. She'd made it into the bedroom she'd shared with her then fiancé to find him doing some very inappropriate things with another woman—but no one was giving her any credit for that.

She'd been too young then anyway. There were a lot of women who married older, and statistics suggested those marriages were likely to be more successful. She knew that. Heck, she clung to that.

But something in the water in her rural Oregon town had compelled most of her friends to get married right out of high school. The other stragglers had been caught up sometime before their mid-twenties had hit, and she felt like the odd one out in a big way.

Even more now that the last of her younger sisters had just done the deed. At twenty. Bitch.

Okay, she didn't really think her sister was a bitch. But she was feeling a little bit bitter as the reception wore on. Plus, the bridesmaid dresses were yellow, and she looked horrible in yellow. Kailey knew that and she'd picked it anyway.

"You look . . . I was going to say 'great,' but you actually look really grumpy."

Kelsey looked over her shoulder and up at the broad frame of her very best, and last, single friend, Alexa Lambert. "Thanks, Alex," she snarked. "Shouldn't you be over there trying to catch a bouquet?"

"Hell no!" Alexa, dressed in black pants and a black top, looking so out of place, sat in the chair beside her.

"Avoidance, huh?"

"Why do you think I moved across the country? To get away from this kind of thing. Honestly, none of my friends in New York are married yet. Shacking up, maybe. But married, no."

"I moved."

"To Portland. Glamour central," Alexa said wryly.

"I want to be close enough to visit still. All my sisters started having babies, and—"

"Yeah, the baby thing doesn't get me gooey like it seems to do for most women. I'm avoiding babies."

Kelsey wasn't in baby-avoidance mode. Babies did make her gooey. She wished they didn't. She wished that holding her niece and smelling her baby-soft head didn't make her stomach cramp with the worst kind of futile longing imaginable.

"I'm not anti-marriage. I'm . . . without and fine with it. That's all. Somehow that makes me 'on the shelf.'"

She didn't need to get married. She had bad taste in men anyway. But what she did want was a family, which made all of this an awful tease. Children. She wanted crayon pictures all over her fridge and juice stains on her carpet. Okay, she didn't *want* juice stains on her carpet, but she was ready to deal with them.

She thought about the brochures buried in her desk back at her house. Brochures she'd stuffed in a drawer six months ago and tried to forget about. Artificial insemination. The chance to have what she wanted without the part she didn't want.

To have her own child. To feel her baby move inside of her.

Her ob-gyn had reminded her just recently that her fertility wasn't getting better with age. Yet another person out to make her feel like the world was passing her by while she worked and aged. Except that her doctor had a valid medical point. A scary one.

She looked at all her nieces and nephews running around in the grass, barefoot, filthy, and adorable. Her sister Jacie was hugely pregnant and trying to chase her three-year-old son, who was holding a dirt clod and most likely had evil intentions.

Kelsey envied her in that moment. So much she nearly choked on it.

Alexa leaned forward and hooted, effectively breaking her out of her moment of self-pity. "'On the shelf'? Sounds like something a maiden aunt would say."

"It *was* my maiden aunt."

"Figures."

"Doesn't it?" She looked down at her hands. Even her French manicure was yellow tipped. She looked like a freaking daisy. "It's worse because of the whole Michael thing." If she'd never been engaged, maybe they would all just assume she didn't want to get married.

No, that wouldn't really help. But it would have helped *her*. It would have made her feel less . . . like a failure.

"That was, like . . . five years ago."

"Six," Kelsey said. "Six years ago."

"I'm sort of glad it didn't work out," Alexa said.

"Why is that exactly? Don't make me take back that other half of our best friends heart necklace."

"Because he was a jackass who was screwing another girl behind your back."

"Kinda in front of me at the end."

Alexa nodded. "But also, I think if you would have gotten married that long ago, you would have put me in a bridesmaid dress that was even worse than the one you're wearing now. That's one point for marrying older. Better fashion sense, minus the Cinderella princess complex."

"True that," Kelsey said, leaning forward, resting her arms on the table. "I'm happy." But she didn't even convince herself.

"Clearly."

"Well, I'm happy when I'm not sitting at the family table by myself, fielding questions from well-meaning relatives. I have a career. I get to work from home. In my pj's. I win the game of life."

"This is probably why you haven't met a guy."

Kelsey smacked the table with her palm, sitting up straighter. "That, and I don't need one. I've been there, done that. Didn't make me happy, did it?"

"No. Because he was a jackass."

"Yes, he was. But my point is, I'm living my life. I'm not buying into this whole 'your life doesn't start until your trip down the aisle' thing. I'm living in the here and now, baby."

Except you aren't. You're living in the someday, wishing for things you don't have because you're too afraid of what your family might think.

"Have you been drinking?" Alexa asked, one eyebrow raised. "When you start calling me baby, I assume you've been drinking."

Kelsey frowned. "There's no alcohol here."

"Your sister really does hate you."

"She doesn't. I'm happy for Kailey. I am. I just . . ."

"Wish you were happier for you?"

Wasn't that too keen an observation? "Darn skippy."

"Ah, look . . . bouquet toss!" Alexa said, false enthusiasm all the way.

"I'm staying over here. It would be adding insult to injury to get up there and try to mow over a bunch of teenagers to catch that thing. It would completely negate the cool facade of disinterest I have going on."

"Is that what you have going on?"

"Yes. That's exactly what I have going on."

"Ah. Yeah, I don't believe you," Alexa said, her lips curved into a smirk.

Kelsey watched her sister—her baby sister—stand in the middle of the lawn, her white dress making her look like an angel. All blond hair, blue eyes and big grin. She just hoped that Kailey knew what she was doing, that David was going to treat her right.

Even though she'd spent the last hour of the reception engaged in a pity party, she still just wanted Kailey to be happy. Blissfully so. The kind of happiness that would make her feel jealous forever and ever was fine with her. As long as her sister never knew what it was like to be betrayed by someone she loved.

Those scars didn't heal as easily as Kelsey wished they would. Trust was sort of hard for her to find these days.

A gaggle of women dressed in pastel spring colors crowded behind Kailey. Oh, yes, there was pushing and shoving. Desperation to grab that bouquet and secure a spot on the next-to-wed list.

Were any of these girls even out of high school?

Kailey turned and slung the bouquet over her back, the yellow daisies sailing through the air and over the teeming mass of estrogen. And onto the table right in front of Kelsey.

Alexa scooted back, her evil grin barely suppressed. "It's a sign," she whispered.

"I hope not." Kelsey picked the bouquet up and stood, waving to the remaining guests, who were clapping for her. Some of them clapping a bit too enthusiastically for her liking. Like the bouquet was going to fix something they all thought was broken about her.

Kelsey forced a smile and held the flowers up over her head, pretending triumph. Inside, she focused on trying not to die from what had to be the most humiliating thing that had ever happened to her.

She wasn't getting married next. Not even close. She'd barely had a date since the whole Michael fiasco. Sad? Yes. But it was just . . . too hard. She had trusted him, wholly and completely. More than anyone else in her life. She'd slept with him, lived with him, been prepared to make vows to him that she would be with him forever and ever. And he'd been lying.

If he could lie to her, trick her, anyone could. She was always conscious of that. She kind of wished she weren't.

"Want me to give it to one of the sad little girls?" Alexa motioned in the direction of the women who had been vying for the bouquet. "One of them could wear it as a corsage to prom."

"You are evil."

"It's been said."

"Kelsey?" Kelsey's second sister, Jacie, approached, baby in her arms. "Can you hold Delia? Aiden is up in the loft in the barn, and I need both hands to climb up and get him down." Her sister sounded more angry than wildly frightened, but having five kids had given her a high shenanigan threshold.

"Sure." Kelsey took her tiniest niece in her arms and found herself fighting the urge to smell the soft baby head. The sweet smell of shampoo and that other fresh smell that was impossible to re-create. It was its own thing: unique, and probably existing for the sole purpose of tying her ovaries in knots.

Alexa grimaced as Jacie ran up toward the barn. "Really, those are the sorts of problems I don't want. I doubt you want them. Anyway, isn't your job really intense right now?"

Kelsey's health-and-wellness column was syndicated in newspapers across the country, and she'd been doing more and more special features for magazines and blogs as she became more well-known. There had been a couple of major talk shows too.

"Yeah, it is. And it's great. But . . . I don't know. I don't know why I'm not happy, Alex. I'm just . . . not."

It was the truth. Unvarnished. One she hadn't even admitted to herself before that moment.

"You need to come back to New York and visit me again."

"I was just there a couple of months ago for *Good Morning America*."

"Yeah, but not for long. We didn't get to do very much."

"We stayed in. We drank martinis. I felt fancy."

"Your fancy standard is dangerously low," Alexa said.

"Well, neither of us like the club scene," Kelsey said. Alexa grimaced and shook her head. "And say what you will about me, but you don't date much either. We're both more involved with our jobs than we are with real people and . . . it's not what I want. It's not how I saw my life. I want . . . more." She looked down at Delia. "I want this."

"Kind of moot since you don't want a guy, though."

Kelsey nodded absently. She thought about asking Alexa what she thought about artificial insemination. About choosing to be a single mom. But she couldn't voice the words. They stuck in her throat.

You don't want her to tell you you're crazy.

She didn't want to hear how crazy she was; that was true. Even if she was slightly unhinged for contemplating it. Maybe she was.

But she'd set out to be successful in her career, and she'd done that. She had her house—a house with a gorgeous backyard that no one ever used. She had financial stability, a job that let her work at home. So many things that people would give their right eyeballs for, she had.

But she felt alone. And the only reason she'd stuck the clinic brochures in a drawer and tried to forget about them was fear of what her family and friends might think. She was still trapped in this little bubble of other people's expectations, sacrificing her own happiness for it.

No more. It was her life. She was the one who had to live it.

She rested her cheek on Delia's head and just let herself feel all of the longing. For a baby of her own; for all the mess and chaos and love that went with it.

"Maybe I don't need the guy," Kelsey said.

CHAPTER

Two

"What the hell do you mean, you don't have it anymore?"

"That's just what I'm saying, Mr. Mitchell. We don't have the sample. I've . . . I've looked, and I can't find it."

"Check your computer again." Cole leaned over the counter and gave his hardest glare to the man sitting behind it.

"I . . . did." His brow furrowed, and his lips tugged down into a frown. "This can't be right."

"What can't be right?" Cole hated this place and everything it stood for. A shining city on a hill of his youthful stupidity. A grand reminder of what a jackass he'd been for love. And today, he'd come to face it, end it, stop being such a damned coward about it and ignoring it like it didn't exist.

"It looks like your sample was . . . purchased."

"Excuse me?"

"It's what I have in here when I enter the code that was linked to your name. It shows the sample was used for several conception attempts by the same patient. I don't know why your sample was placed in the general bank, only that it must have been."

Cole felt like a blood vessel in his forehead was going to

pop. It had been stressful enough making the trip to Portland from his ranch in Silver Creek. He was already dealing with the unpleasantness of trying to settle some of his father's old debts—debts he didn't really want his brother or sister finding out about—and he'd decided to tack on the joy of dealing with the last remaining evidence of his extremely short, extremely stupid marriage. Now this.

He blew out a long breath. "Attempts? Not actual . . . success?"

"I can't give you any more information about the client, Mr. Mitchell. It's . . . This has never happened. Well, it's happened, but not here. And at this point I have to honor patient confidentiality."

Cole took his Stetson off and set it on the high counter, squeezing the felt top, trying not to imagine it was the other man's neck. "You're telling me some woman ended up with my sperm. That she possibly conceived my baby. And your concern is patient confidentiality?"

"She signed paperwork guaranteeing her anonymity. Under normal circumstances a donor would have done the same."

"I'm not a donor. I was paying you monthly to bank the stuff, and you don't even have it. It was supposed to be here so I could have children someday. With my wife." A wife he no longer had. Thank God. But he'd work the angle if it would help.

"And you were here to ask us to discard it today. I don't know what difference it makes."

"Listen"—he looked down at the guy's name tag—"Troy. It makes a whole hell of a lot of difference. Because I'm not a donor."

A baby. He couldn't imagine himself holding a baby. Never had been able to. But Shawna had wanted babies someday, and since he'd been unwilling to have them right away, she'd come up with the bright idea of banking it for their future. She'd done eggs too. Because they were better off doing it young for genetic reasons, or something. And she was pretty sure he was going to damage his count riding all those horses.

And because he'd been a freaking moron for love, he'd done it. For her; for him, maybe. To keep the peace in his house and try to keep alive a marriage that he should have staked in the heart on sight. Because he'd been a complete ass who had still trusted that people were who they showed the world they were.

Too bad it had taken him a full two years to figure out that it wasn't meant to be. Two years of hell and "Yes, dear" and sleeping on the damned couch. No wonder she'd needed him to bank his sperm. She never slept with him.

Not that he was complaining. Better a couch by yourself than a bed with a shrew.

Even so, after he'd cut the woman loose, he'd just sort of ignored that it had ever happened. And that meant ignoring the fact that she'd goaded him into the sperm-banking thing. While he continued to pay for the storage of the stuff.

"It isn't that I'm not sympathetic to your situation, Mr. Mitchell; I am. And it isn't as though we won't act. But there will have to be attorneys, and it's going to be a whole legal thing. We'll contact you when . . . Wait, what are you . . . You can't come back here."

Cole rounded the counter and put his foot on the rolling office chair the man was sitting on, pushing it backward three feet so he could lean down over the computer.

"You're welcome to remove me," Cole said, scanning the information that was up on the screen. Damn it. *Damn it.* He needed something to write it down with. "It's nothing personal, but I don't really like the waiting that comes with the court system. Any sort of bureaucracy, really. You understand?"

"Uh . . . it's not a matter of not understanding . . ." Troy's voice faded out. He must have realized arguing was futile. Either that or he was trying to reach a silent alarm beneath the counter.

Cole hunted for the print icon and hoped that the printer

the computer was linked to wasn't hidden in a back office somewhere. He didn't have a major problem shoving Troy out of the way, but he didn't exactly want to storm the clinic.

Not that he wouldn't.

He heard a printer kick into gear to his left and he turned and held his hand out, ready to catch the paper when it hit the tray.

He grabbed it and nodded at the man who was still sitting, openmouthed, in the rolling chair. "Thanks, Troy. Tell them you tried to fight me off." He pulled his hat from the counter and put it on his head, touching the brim and tipping it slightly. Because otherwise, he'd just flip him off.

Or haul off and punch him in the face. Missing sperm was one thing—a baby was another. He had to find out if there was a baby.

And then he had to figure out what, if anything, he wanted to do about it.

He looked like the type who might take his hat off and call her ma'am. But he didn't. The tall stranger just looked at her, black Stetson firmly on his head, dark eyes fixed on her, brown brows locked tight together. As though he were angry with her.

He was supposed to be her Chinese takeout. He was not Chinese takeout. He wasn't even bearing Chinese takeout, and he hadn't been worth getting up off the couch for.

Kelsey gripped the doorjamb and tried to hide the fact that her legs were shaking. She also hoped he couldn't tell she'd just held a second viewing of her lunch in her hall bathroom only half an hour before. She was pretty sure she still had that just-vomited sweat sheen people were constantly confusing for a pregnant glow.

Not that she looked pregnant yet. Not that anyone in her life knew she was pregnant. Telling people was one of those things that was on her ever-increasing, very ignored to-do list. Right up there with dusting the top of the ceiling fan.

"Can I help you?"

"Kelsey Noble?"

"Yeah," she said, closing the door a tiny bit. Anything to put more of a buffer between herself and the very big man on her doorstep.

Then he did take his hat off, his large, masculine hands gripping the top, holding it to his chest. She found herself fixating on his hands, mostly because focusing on a stationary point helped ward off the weird dizziness that always seemed to come with standing up these days. And also because the Willamette River was just out her front door, behind him, and looking at the water would most certainly have her losing her balance.

Morning sickness, people said. They didn't say morning, noon and night sickness with crippling vertigo and the inability to get off the couch for more than five minutes at a time.

Forget making it upstairs to her bedroom. The couch was her home now. Her shining beacon of comfort and stability.

"I just came from the, uh . . . fertility clinic."

"What?" She took a step back. No one knew about that. She hadn't told anyone. Not even Alexa. No one should know she'd been there except for the employees, and he didn't work there.

She would have remembered a great, hulking cowboy with big calloused hands and a strong square jaw. He was handsome. She was almost totally sure. Mostly, right now, he looked like walking testosterone. Which was her most hated enemy just at the moment.

Since the father of her baby was anonymous, pretty much any man was in danger of getting a glare from her. The cause of all her pain and suffering. Men and their sperm. Yes, she'd chosen it. And yes, she was happy with her decision. But she was due for a good whine.

"Yeah, I know, patient confidentiality. But I . . . bypassed that."

"How?"

"Moved the receptionist out of the way. He's a little guy."

"Uh . . . yeah. And why?"

"Are you pregnant?"

She swallowed hard. She couldn't throw up. Her dinner wasn't here yet and her stomach was empty. "I think you should just go. I don't know who you are or why you have a belt buckle the size of a dinner plate or why you want to know if I'm pregnant, and I just think—"

"It's kind of a long story, but when I went to the clinic today to collect my . . . sample . . ."

She was pretty sure the cowboy looked uncomfortable bringing up the clinic. Well, good. She didn't really want to stand around talking about any of that with a stranger either.

"Right. Okay."

He put his hand out and gripped the edge of the door. "It's not okay. When I went . . . they couldn't find it. They checked the log, my name, my Social Security number. They found it eventually, and found that it had been . . . moved. Miscategorized somehow. And that it had been used. By you."

She felt the floor tilt under her feet. She was sure it did, because her sight went wiggly and she was having a hard time focusing on anything. Even the stranger's hands.

Miscategorized? What the hell was that supposed to mean? A donor was a donor. As far as she was concerned, there was no way to categorize them wrong. He left the sperm; she picked the sperm. She never saw him.

So why was she seeing him?

"You all right?" he asked.

He didn't touch her. Which was good. She didn't want him to. She wanted him to go away.

"No. Nope. Not all right." She tightened her hold on the doorframe. "I haven't been all right since this stupid 'morning sickness' crap hit two weeks ago. I can't drive. I can't sit at my computer. I can't work. I can't eat anything. Morning sickness, my ass! It's all the time and I'm so tired of it. And now . . . now my *anonymous* donor is here, at my house, on my doorstep, trying to give me a heart attack. Does it sound like I'm all right?"

"No . . . maybe not."

She was shaking, every part of her trembling from the inside out. She didn't need this. Didn't need this added complication. She needed a nap. And to feel human and not on the verge of death. She needed to figure out what he was doing here. What he wanted. And then she needed to get rid of him.

"I am." She took a breath. "I mean, I'm not, but I am. I'm doing it by myself. So I don't know what you came by for except maybe out of some misguided Old West sense of chivalry or something. But I don't need it. Thanks anyway."

"That's not why I'm here."

"Why else would you be here?"

"You're pregnant with my baby."

"It's not your baby," she said, annoyance clawing its way through the crippling sickness, fighting for front-row status.

He handed her a sheet of paper, along with his driver's license. And her knees just about buckled beneath her. Right there on the paper, there was his name, and the number of his sperm sample. She knew the number. He was donor #456. And now he had a name. And a face. And, it turned out, a cowboy hat.

"You look younger in this picture," she said, holding up the driver's license.

"It's been a hell of a few years. But it is me."

"Yeah." She looked at his name: Cole Mitchell. On the license and on the printout from the doctor. She read further on this time. And she saw her name. The printout showed her as the recipient of his donation. "Did you . . . How did you get this? It was supposed to be anonymous."

He shrugged. "In light of the situation, they felt it best to give me the information."

"You took it."

"Yes. I did."

She handed the license and paper back to him. "I don't care what this says. It's not your baby. It's my baby. I'm the one who's carrying it. I went to the clinic. I mean . . . we didn't have sex or anything . . . anything intimate like that. It was just your sperm. It's not . . . you."

"My genes. My baby."

She shook her head. "No. Please go away. Oh, just go away, because I'm going to be sick again. And I'm dizzy. And I'm pretty sure I hate you."

She put her hand on her head and tried to stop the growing, pulsing pain that never really went away. And she hoped that maybe if she closed her eyes long enough, Mr. Tall, Dark and Stetson would disappear.

"You don't look good."

Her eyes snapped open, annoyance coursing through her. "I know. I'm pathetic."

"You're sick," he said. "That's different from pathetic. You need to rest."

Kelsey just wanted to cry now. Because it was what she needed. It was what she'd deprived herself of receiving from friends or family, because she hadn't told anyone that she was pregnant. And now she had to take comfort from a stranger.

A stranger who was apparently, according to him, the father of her baby.

"I don't want to rest," she said. "I want to throw up. But I'm pretty sure that's impossible since my stomach is empty from all the vomiting that happened earlier."

Cole didn't have a clue what he was doing, only that Kelsey Noble looked exhausted and half starved. She had dark circles under her eyes and pale skin, and she seemed far too thin to be pregnant.

Why the hell wasn't someone here taking care of her? Did she have a boyfriend? A girlfriend? Parents?

"Seriously . . . I have to . . ." She turned and ran from the door, leaving it wide open, disappearing from his view.

He just stood there on the front step, not sure what in hell he was supposed to do.

"Expecting dinner?"

He turned and saw a girl standing at the bottom of the steps, holding a large paper bag.

"Probably." He peered back into the house but didn't see a sign of Kelsey. "Not sure if anyone's eating, though." He walked down the stairs and took the bag. "Keep the change," he said, handing the girl a fifty. He would probably regret that later, but now wasn't the time to worry about it.

He walked back up the steps and looked again. The kitchen was still empty. Well, great. He hesitated for a second, then went inside, closed the door and shoved his wallet back into his pocket. He walked back toward where Kelsey had disappeared and saw a closed door with a shaft of light shining beneath it. He paced back into the kitchen. And then he just stood in the middle of a house that wasn't his, a house he hadn't been invited into, and tried to decide what he was doing. Was he going to be a father in seven months? Would she let him? Did he care?

Number one on the agenda was making sure Ms. Kelsey Noble didn't languish and die. Everything after that . . . he could figure out later. At least that directive gave him immediate purpose.

He set the paper bag on the table and reached into his pocket, pulling out his phone.

Hopefully his dumbass brother would answer. It rang five times. A lot more times than he'd like it to ring if potential guests were calling.

"Hello."

"Cade, you have to say 'Elk Haven Stables.' "

"Why? You know who you called, don't you?"

"I don't have time to listen to you run your mouth. I won't be home tonight."

"Did you look at the tractor?"

The story for why he'd come to Portland. To look at a tractor. Why his brother had fallen for it, he didn't know. Or maybe he hadn't, and he didn't want to know just what Cole was up to or why he'd felt the need to lie. If Cole had the option, he wouldn't want to know.

"Yeah, I'm gonna take a pass on it. The condition wasn't as good as they made it seem like it might be." He looked back in the direction of the bathroom again.

"And why won't you be home?"

"I'm, ah . . . busy."

"You are a terrible liar. You getting laid?"

He heard the toilet flush, followed by a heavy sigh and the sound of running water.

"Yeah, maybe," he said.

It was all Cade thought about. Getting some. Moving on to the next woman. That was another thing, in addition to his mother's quilts, that his ex had stolen from him. His libido. Or maybe she had just killed it stone-cold dead. Because, thanks to her, he knew now that what started out as a simple fling could easily morph into a road trip to Vegas with a hangover that lingered for years.

"Good for you. I'll tell them the news. The not-getting-the-tractor news, not the getting-laid thing. I'll make up a story that's not about you getting some when I tell them you aren't coming home."

"Great. Make sure the guests are taken care of and—"

"Cole, I do know how to keep things moving around here. I'm planning on doing a bronc-busting demonstration later."

"Oh, good. Just don't tell the insurance company."

"I'm not letting the guests do it."

"Well, clearly you aren't able to ride, so I was confused."

His brother was silent for a second, and Cole felt a twinge of guilt for bringing up his limitations. "Give me a little credit for not being a total moron."

"Working off of your track record, I'm not sure I can."

Cade's response was filled with color and with words that started with *F*. Cole held the phone away from his ear and let him rant for a minute. "Finished?" he asked when the line went silent.

"Hell no. But I'll let you hear the rest when you get back home."

"Yeah, in the meantime, don't blow anything up."

"Shouldn't be too hard. Hopefully there's blowing where you are."

"Shut up, asshole." He hit the end-call button and put his phone down on the table.

He let out a breath and surveyed the small kitchen. The house was so feminine. So obviously lacking in male influence. Or at least lacking the influence of a man who had any input on his surroundings. A bowl of dried flowers and some other useless, purely decorative crap were in the center of the table. The pink kitchen rugs matched the pot holders and the lace curtains.

The sink was filled with forks. Only forks.

He looked over to the trash can and saw that it was over-flowing with white cartons. Her entire diet seemed to consist of Chinese takeout eaten straight from the box.

He looked at the door. It would be easy to walk out the door. To go back to Elk Haven and get back to work. Forget that some woman was pregnant with his baby. She didn't want him anyway. He didn't know if he wanted kids. He had no desire to ever get married. That was a hell he wouldn't visit willingly again. Anyway, his whole inspiration for keeping that marriage together had been his parents' marriage. And then it turned out that had been a lie too.

No. Marriage was not for him. And in that case, kids weren't either.

One of his siblings would have kids, and he could be the favorite uncle. That was fine with him. It was really all he could handle at this point in his life.

But there was a baby. And, genetically, it would be his baby. Which kind of took the "should he have kids" question right off the table and moved it into completely different territory.

He rummaged through the take-out bag and took out a paper carton and a plastic fork. He opened the carton and his stomach growled in appreciation. Chow mein. Good. He was starving. And since he'd had no appetite for a good portion of the day, he had catching up to do now.

He pushed the fork down into the noodles, and it snapped in half. He snorted. That explained the sink full of forks. He went to the sink and gave one of the real forks a quick rinse, then returned to his position at the kitchen table.

He had no idea what he was doing. The only thing he was sure about was that he was staying until they came to some kind of understanding.

Walking away wasn't an option.

Three

"Oh, you're still here," Kelsey said. "And you're in my kitchen." She'd stayed an extra few minutes in the bathroom, running cold water on her wrists, hoping that her problem in cowboy boots would magically disappear by the time she came out.

No such luck.

"I am."

"Why?"

"It seemed like the right thing to do."

"You know what? It seems like maybe you could have gone with the 'my host seems indisposed, so perhaps I should show myself out' right thing to do."

"Bear with me here, Kelsey," he said, his voice rough. "I just found out you're carrying my baby, and you're sick as a dog. I'm supposed to walk out the door and pretend that I didn't see any of it? That I don't know? I can't do that."

"What do you want?"

He shook his head, hands on his lean hips. "I don't know."

"Then why—"

"Because. Now go sit at the table." He was ordering her

around. In her own house. Like he belonged there. The strangest thing was, it didn't feel as bizarre as it should. He did feel like he belonged, and she couldn't fathom how that could be.

Strangely comfortable feelings aside, she still had to deal with him. She would talk to him. They would get it straightened out. Things would go back to the wonky kind of normal she'd been living for the past couple of months.

For some reason, that thought brought her very little comfort.

She curled her lip into a sneer, made sure he saw it and walked the rest of the way down the hall and into the kitchen. The table was set. With actual dishes. And her dinner was hot.

"Can I hire you?" she asked.

"Sorry. I have a job."

"What do you do?" she asked, sitting in front of her previously desired Chinese food. She wasn't sure she could muster up an appetite now, recent vomiting and unexpected cowboy considered.

"I work at a ranch. I own it. With my brother and sister. It's one of those old family ranches. Passed down and all."

She bit her lip, trying to keep the emotion that was rising in her chest back down where it belonged. She was pretty sure it was emotion anyway; otherwise, she was about to be sick again.

"That's . . . You'll pass it down to your kids, or . . ."

"Yeah," he said, his voice rough. "That's the theory."

"Don't you have a wife?" she asked. "Girlfriend? Boyfriend?"

"None of the above," he said. "You?"

"No. I'm . . . doing this alone," she said. Then she laughed. "Not doing very well, am I? I should have . . . I haven't told anyone yet. I kept thinking I would, and then I got the morning sickness, and I've just been concentrating on surviving. I'm alive, so points for me."

"Barely. You don't look like you've been sleeping."

"It's hard to sleep on the couch."

His eyes widened.

"Well," she said, "it's more trouble than it's worth to go up and down the stairs half the time, so a lot of the day, I'm in the living room."

"That doesn't seem . . . healthy."

"This is stupid." She put her face in her hands. "I don't even know you."

"Does anyone know you right now? You haven't told your family you're having a baby."

"Fine." She lifted her head. "I suppose, at the moment, you know me, since you know something no one, not even my best friend, knows. So, let's pretend, then. Yes, I have been sleeping on the couch."

"Are you eating?"

She lifted up her fork and raised her eyebrows.

His lip curled. "Are you eating anything that's staying down? You look thin."

"I'm always thin," she said.

"Shouldn't you . . . not be so thin right now?"

"I'm not quite ten weeks pregnant. I'm not supposed to look different."

"I don't know anything about pregnant women."

She speared a piece of chicken with her fork and put all of her energy into examining it, and not Mr. Cole Mitchell: 6'3"; Sex: Male. Per his driver's license, but also, obviously. "In some ways I find that comforting."

"That there aren't a lot of women currently pregnant with my babies?"

"Yeah. So you don't have any kids, then?"

He shook his head, and some of his slightly overlong hair fell into his eyes. "No. I wasn't sure I was going to either, but this . . . changes some things."

"Why was your sperm at the bank? I mean, if you weren't a donor, and you're no longer sure you even want kids."

A muscle in his jaw ticked, and he averted his eyes. "It was a thing. With my ex. Something about optimum fertility. But she's my ex, so it didn't need to be there anymore, and I went to unbank it."

It was pretty obvious he didn't want to give details. And she didn't really want them. She felt weighted down, wholly and completely, by her situation. By the facts that work was piling up, that she was keeping a major secret from her family, that she couldn't seem to keep any food in her stomach for more than a half an hour. She didn't think she could handle the weight of Cole's burdens too.

So she didn't press.

"Oh."

"So what is it you want me to do, Kelsey? Walk out of here and pretend this didn't happen?" he asked, voice rough. He sounded just as tired as she felt.

"I don't know," she said.

Because it was one thing to have a baby alone, to ignore the father of her baby when he was just a nameless, faceless nobody. She didn't feel like she was depriving her child of anything. But knowing his face . . . she wasn't sure she could forget him. She wasn't sure if she should.

"I don't know you at all," she said. "You might be a psycho stalker who saw me at Voodoo Donut a couple of weeks ago and traced me back here."

"A possibility. But I'm not."

"No. I know. So, why are you still here? I mean . . . what do you think we're going to do?"

"I don't know why I came in the first place. Not really. Because I haven't figured out what the right thing to do is. Thing is, I'm not the kind of guy who gets a woman pregnant and walks away, and this . . . feels the same."

"It's not."

"But it feels the same. And as much as I wasn't counting on it or asking for it, walking away still feels like the wrong thing to do."

"And doing the right thing is important to you? Because I'm not asking for a Boy Scout to come and help me cross the street and change diapers. I can handle this on my own. If I couldn't, I wouldn't have pursued the pregnancy. You caught me at a low point, but I promise I'm not usually this pathetic."

Cole looked down at his hands. His heart was pounding hard in his head, his entire body tense. He didn't know which argument to take. The one for him leaving, or the one that meant staying and facing this whole thing. This thing that he hadn't asked for, that he hadn't had any real involvement in, but that he felt just as connected to as if they had conceived during a one-night stand.

He swallowed. "It's not about being a Boy Scout. It's about . . . if I walked away, whether I would think about him. How old he was. If he looked like me. If he ever missed having a dad."

His chest hurt just thinking about it, a kind of deep, intense emotion he wasn't used to anymore. The kind that he'd lost along with his youth and optimism a few years ago. Actually, he wasn't sure it was like anything he'd ever felt before. It made his hands shake.

She looked at him, her eyes glistening in the dim light. "Those are pretty scary questions."

"Scariest I've ever asked myself." And that included questions about his childhood, his father, things he'd defined his whole life by. But this seemed worse somehow. This was about whether or not he could abandon a child, his child. About whether or not he could make the mistakes he'd discovered his father had made. And no, maybe this wasn't exactly the same, but knowing it had come about differently didn't make him feel absolved.

"I don't . . . This wasn't supposed to happen," Kelsey said.

"I know."

"I don't know what to tell you."

"I don't know what to tell you either, so I guess we're even," he said.

She put her fork down and stared at her mostly untouched dinner. He wished she would eat something. "I'm tired again."

"Can I help you upstairs?"

"Uh . . . probably not. I know you could have . . . I mean, if you wanted to hurt me, you could have done it by now, but still, probably best not to let a strange man carry me to my bedroom."

"For some women, that's just Saturday night."

"Good point. But it's never been my Saturday night."

He nodded and stood from the table. "Can I at least bring you something?"

"No. I'm fine. Well, I'm not fine. I'm actually deathly ill—but you know."

"I'm going to come over tomorrow morning."

She nodded. "I kind of accepted that as inevitable."

"We have a lot to talk about."

"I know." Her words were choked.

He'd never done well with emotions, and now was no exception. His chest felt tight and he was ready to walk out the door. Walk right out and never come back. But he also felt rooted to the spot.

"Or maybe we won't talk that much. Maybe I'll just bring . . . herbal tea. What can you have?"

"Usually nothing."

"Well, I'll figure something out."

"I hope so," she said.

And he knew perfectly well that she wasn't talking about breakfast.

Cole didn't know why he'd come back. He didn't know why he hadn't run the hell away from the whole thing. Of course, then he remembered that image, the one that had compelled him to stay at her house and make sure she was okay in the first place.

An image of a little boy with dark hair holding a baseball. There wasn't anyone there to throw it to him.

His own father had been tough. Limited hugs, no praise unless they'd really done something spectacular. But he'd been there. He'd supported them in his quiet, steady way, and never once had Cole doubted that he would be there for him. Always.

At least that was the treatment he and Lark and Cade had

gotten. The other family, the one he'd just found out about a year ago, hadn't been so lucky. But he didn't have the time to think about that right now.

He knocked on Kelsey's door as best he could with a tray of drinks in one hand and a bag of breakfast food in the other. He'd had no clue what to get her at the coffeehouse, so he'd gone with sweet and savory, healthy and greasy, with beverages hot, cold, caffeinated and decaf.

Just covering the bases.

He knocked again. If she didn't answer, he was just going to walk in, because the image of her curled up in the fetal position on the bathroom floor made his gut tighten.

He was about to knock again when the door swung open. She was in the same clothes she'd been wearing the night before. Those stupid sweats that had writing on the butt. Her blond hair was pulled back into a limp ponytail, and her face was pale.

"You came," she said, not sounding particularly excited or surprised.

"Yeah. I said I would."

She shrugged her small shoulders. "That doesn't necessarily mean anything."

"It does when I say it. Count on it."

"Shall I be Miss Kitty to your stalwart sheriff?"

"Was that a crack about the Stetson?" He walked past her into the house and set the food items, and his hat, on the counter.

"Yeah. And the belt buckle."

"I won this," he said, touching the intricate silver buckle.

"Doing?"

"Calf roping."

"Cute."

"I don't think I've ever heard it called 'cute' before, Miss Kitty. That's a first."

"Have mercy," she said, rolling her eyes, her tone pitched into a breathy Southern lilt. At least he thought that might have been what she was going for. She let out a long breath and leaned against the counter. "You're here."

"Yes."

"And does that mean what I think it might mean?"

"That I think I should be involved in my child's life? Yes. I don't know in what capacity, but . . . now I know, Kelsey. Now I know you're having my baby. I can't forget that. I can't walk away from that."

"I should probably get a paternity test done."

"Probably," he said.

"I never thought I would be in the position to need one of those. Not a big Saturday-night-out girl, as I mentioned."

"Well, I wouldn't expect you to be. At least not now."

"Funny." She opened the paper bag he'd brought and grimaced, but rummaged through the contents. "I guess I could get one at the clinic. We should sue them, by the way."

"Probably. But that's not really my number one priority at the moment."

"And what is, Sheriff?"

"You."

"Me?" She arched one pale eyebrow and pulled a bran muffin from the bag.

"That's right. You, who are too sick to get upstairs and look like you haven't had a decent meal in weeks. You."

She looked away. "I'm fine."

"You are not. You're alone."

"But I don't have to be."

"But you are."

"I could call my parents anytime. I could call Alexa. My friend Alexa. She lives in New York, but her job is pretty flexible."

"Then why haven't you called them?"

She picked at a raisin that was half exposed on the top of the muffin. "Because. Because they would say I was crazy. And if not crazy, then maybe just irresponsible, or plain wrong, to have a baby when I'm not married."

"And why are you having a baby by yourself? Are you a . . . Do you not like men?"

Her eyes widened. "Oh, no. I like men. JTT posters all over my room in junior high. Definitely a man liker."

"Then why?"

"Because there's not a particular man I like right now. And I don't see there being one in the near future. And I'm independent. Apart from this whole sickness fiasco, which, have I mentioned, is not just inconvenient but pretty freaking humiliating? I'm a very well-respected columnist. I write about health and wellness, ironically, and I've been on *GMA*. And I have this house, and I have the finances. I wanted kids. I want kids."

"You were just done waiting."

"Everything I've ever wanted I've gone out and gotten for myself. My sisters all got married right out of high school, and it's what they wanted, so that's fine. But I wanted more. And I moved away, and I got more. But I'm ready for the next phase now, and . . . the rest of it hadn't fallen into place yet. I was at my sister's wedding and I was watching my other sisters with their kids and I thought . . . that part of life is passing me by. I didn't want that to happen. I didn't want to wake up one morning and realize I'd left it too late."

"Better than jumping the gun." And he was speaking from experience.

"True. I had a near brush with gun jumping. But this is different. This is . . . You have goals, don't you, Sheriff?"

He thought of Elk Haven Stables. Of the way things were really getting up and running there. How they were taking a business that had been failing and turning it into something successful. Unless his father's newly discovered debts screwed things up. "Yeah, I have a few."

"So you have to understand, then. The importance of meeting goals."

"I get it."

"And I doubt anyone I'm related to would. They're so traditional, and I'm already the wild one because I moved to the big city and went to college."

"Clearly a fallen woman of Babylonian proportions."

"Yuh-huh."

"And you think they won't notice when you have a baby?"

"No, I'm going to tell them. But I don't think I could

stomach my mom putting a cold cloth on my forehead while she was shaking her head, asking me what on earth I was thinking. And Alexa would just cuss me out. And then she'd put chick flicks on and ignore me until I needed something. Maybe I should call Alexa."

"Sounds like a peach."

"She is, actually."

"I meant it."

"So what do you propose we do, Cole?"

She turned her blue eyes on him, sharp now, not glassy. And he saw the businesswoman she was. The keen mind. The woman who had been determined enough to go after what she wanted whether she had the support of everyone or no one.

And he had no clue what to tell her.

"Come to my ranch."

Apparently his mouth had more of a clue than his brain.

"Your ranch?"

"It's a guest ranch. Well, not entirely—we have horses. But the majority of our income is in the guest cabins. It would be private, but we have a chef there who could cook for you. We also have maid service."

"I am so tempted to get in the car with a stranger right now. Could you offer me candy and make it sound a bit more sweet and sinister?"

"Sorry. No candy. But I'm being honest with you about who I am."

"Somehow I believe you, Mr. Cole Mitchell. And it might be the Stetson."

"Got a computer with Internet?"

"That's like asking if I have my right arm handy."

"So yes."

"Yeah. Through there." She gestured into the living room.

"Can you make it?"

"I'm upright, aren't I?"

"Lead on, then."

He followed her into the living room and chuckled when he saw the letters on her ass again. "'Juicy,' huh?"

"Don't read my butt. I did not give you permission to look there."

"You're broadcasting, darlin'."

"Well, I didn't expect to have an audience when I dressed."

"Pants like that are begging for commentary."

She turned and shot him a glare that could have singed a lesser man's arm hair clean off. "I'm not begging for anything, I assure you."

"Now, I wouldn't dream of being so presumptuous."

"Ten-dollar word, Sheriff."

"We have schools out in the Wild West."

She snorted and kicked a black leather office chair out of the way with her foot before leaning over the computer desk and opening up a web browser on her laptop. "What am I looking for?"

"Elk Haven Stables."

She put in the keywords and hit ENTER. The top result was the right one, thanks to Lark and her brilliant skills at search engine optimization.

"This is you?" she asked, scrolling through pictures of vast, painterly scenery.

"Purple mountain majesties and all. Click on the cabins."

She did, and her mouth dropped open slightly.

"Every modern convenience you could ever want, with a little luxury, right out in the pristine Oregon wilderness."

"So it says right in the tagline," she said.

"It's real. Interested?"

"I could write a piece on retreats to cleanse the body and soul," she mused.

"And you could rest."

"Yeah, that. I'm bored of that. I like doing things. Thinking of new things."

"Then yes, work. Whatever makes you happy. And maybe we can . . . figure this out."

"I'm not letting you drive me there."

"Fine with me."

"And I'm paying for it."

"No."

"Uh . . . yes."

He put his hand on her arm, and her eyes widened. "You aren't paying me. And if you try, I'll tear the check."

"Take Visa?"

"I'll cut your card."

Their eyes locked, and he felt his stomach get tighter, his heart racing. Not really like attraction; more like the way he used to feel when he did roping competitions. When he knew he was going to get a serious fight from the calf.

"I'm not an easy woman to control, Cole Mitchell. When I set my mind to something, I do it."

"Then it's going to be interesting, Kelsey Noble, because I'm not the kind of man who backs down. I've got one hell of a hard head, and I have no problem butting it against yours."

She pursed her lips and pulled them to the side. "Hmm. Well, this is going to be interesting."

"Sure is."

Four

"So the only place you can write about rest and relaxation is at this ranch out in BFE, Oregon?"

Kelsey turned her head slightly, grateful that she had managed to keep the vomiting under control since Alexa had come to pick her up. She'd made it to the car with her suitcase and loaded it into the trunk herself.

And now they were twenty miles outside of Portland, headed into the sticks. If Kelsey thought about it too much, she started to feel a little bit nauseous again. Thankfully, her friend had managed to finagle more vacation time so she could come spend a couple of weeks up at Elk Haven with her.

It made it seem slightly less insane. They were using the buddy system. That was just good sense. And this way, she would have someone to hold her hair if she started retching uncontrollably en route.

"I got an offer I couldn't refuse." Or at least one she hadn't been able to turn down lightly. What a mess. She wanted to hide and pretend this wasn't happening, but seeing the man in person—the father of her baby—had made it feel so real. Made her aware of what she would be denying her child, specifically, if she chose not to have him involved.

He was the kind of man a small child would see as a hero. Tough, larger than life . . .

Alexa took her eyes off the road for a second to offer her an arched eyebrow. "Oh, really?"

"What's 'Oh, really'?"

"Just the way you said it. It sounded mysterious. You don't usually do mysterious."

"It's not mysterious. I met this guy, and it's his ranch, and—"

"Is this a backwoods booty call?" Alexa asked, her voice pitched higher than normal.

"What does that even mean? And no. No, it's not. I'm just saying, he showed me the website for his ranch and offered to let me stay there and write a piece and I said yes because— Well, who couldn't use rest and relaxation? And anyway, I'm a health-and-wellness columnist, and this falls under the heading."

"Was that all one sentence? That's a sure sign you're lying. You're going to this ranch to hook up with some guy. You want to save a horse and ride a cowboy."

Kelsey tried not to let the image of riding that particular cowboy linger in her mind's eye for too long. She hadn't really studied Cole's features, since she'd been lost in a haze of sickness and fatigue, but what she remembered of him was pure masculine goodness. And no, she hadn't seen him in anything that gave too much information on his physique, but it was easy to imagine what it might look like. Tanned and toned and . . . well, darn if her mind's eye hadn't added a little glossy sheen of sweat to those muscles. And a little bit of chest hair.

Saddle up indeed.

She blinked. Nope. She wasn't riding anyone. She could barely ride in a car without succumbing to dizzying nausea, so the very idea of dealing with motion sickness while she was . . . Oh, no, it didn't even bear thinking about. Not even for a second.

And she hadn't really pictured riding Cole. Not really. It was Alexa and her stupid dirty jokes. That was all. It had forced the image on her, really. There was no choice but to picture it. Anyone would have. Her mother, the most restrained, least scandalous woman alive, would have had to picture it. And then she would have washed Alexa's mouth out with soap.

"There will be no riding." She glared at the side of Alexa's head. "None. This is rest and relaxation. For work. I said 'for work,' right? Because this is for work. Anyway, if I wanted to hook up, why would I bring you?"

"Because he has an equally hot friend and you pitied me in my long single state and thought I might benefit from a little 'relaxation' of my own?"

"I'm not that nice."

"Stone-cold."

She was going to have to tell Alexa eventually. But putting it off meant less time in the car with a friend who was screaming at her. Also, the closer they got to Silver Creek, the less likely it was that Alexa would turn the car around and take her back to Portland and straight to a mental health institution.

"That's me."

"Hungry?"

Hell to the no. "Sure. Yeah, I could eat."

"Great. There's a place up here that does pie and ice cream. Sundaes so huge they need to be eaten with a ladle. They show them on Food Network all the time."

"I thought you meant lunch. Something sensible."

"Ugh. You and your whole grains. I want pie. It has dairy, eggs and fruit. Healthy."

Kelsey laughed. Probably for the first time in weeks. Oh, yes, it was a very good thing she'd brought Alexa along. "Nice try. Very nice try. You have earned your pie, even though your logic is as faulty as a condom that's been in some guy's wallet for three years."

Bad analogy, all things considered. But Alexa appreciated it. As Kelsey had known she would.

"Blech. Can you imagine? One impromptu hookup and you get knocked up by some doofus with expired condoms?"

Actually, Kelsey could well imagine. And she hadn't even gotten to hook up with anyone. Though the pregnancy had been intentional, the baby-daddy drama had not been.

"A new thing to worry about," she said.

Alexa maneuvered the car off of the main road and into the parking lot of a grubby-looking diner with a bright yellow sign that, at one time, had likely boasted of the tasty treats inside. Now it just had peeling letters that made the message unreadable.

"This doesn't really look promising."

"It's going to be amazing," Alexa said. "Pie slices as big as dinner plates."

Kelsey's stomach rolled over. "Mmm."

"Right?"

Kelsey followed Alexa's bouncy brown ponytail into the diner and tried to ignore the faint tacky feeling of the floor as they walked over to a red vinyl booth. It smelled like grease. French fry grease and a hot griddle top. Which normally wouldn't be a bad thing, but given the current state of things, it was very bad.

"It smells like a deep fryer in here."

"So good," Alexa said, picking up the single-page menu and reading the list of offerings.

Kelsey glanced at the menu, unwilling to pick it up in case it was as sticky as it appeared, and looked for the most innocuous item she could find. When the waitress came by, Alexa dropped the menu.

"Can I get a burger? And then I'll have a slice of the marionberry pie after."

The woman nodded and looked at Kelsey.

"Green salad. No dressing. Water?"

Both Alexa and the waitress raised their eyebrows at her.

"Sure, honey," the waitress said, taking the menus and walking away from the table.

"Don't tell me you're on some kind of weird cleansing diet."

"How would iceberg lettuce cleanse you?" Kelsey asked.

"I don't know. I don't do stupid things like that. I eat. Food sustains us, after all."

Kelsey rolled her eyes. "Yeah, french fries are the side dish of champions."

"You look thinner than you did at your sister's wedding. No one needs to be that thin."

Kelsey was sort of nourishment deprived against her will, but she didn't really want to have that conversation yet. She didn't really want to have it ever. Alexa was going to flip out. And Alexa's reaction was the least of her worries. She really, really wished she could crawl into a hole.

Not face her friend. Not face her family. Not face the decision she'd made a few months ago. And most especially not face Cole, the father of that decision.

"I just don't feel very well. The car ride and all."

Alexa frowned. "Yeah, you look pale."

"Thanks."

The waitress returned a few minutes later with Kelsey's salad and Alexa's grease fest. Alexa picked up one of the yellow plastic bottles and squeezed a blob of mustard onto her hamburger.

The tangy, bitter scent of the mustard hit Kelsey with a force that was shocking for a condiment. Her stomach turned over, a vile flavor filling her mouth.

"Excuse me." She jumped up from the table and dashed into the diner's bathroom, where she lost what little she'd eaten that day. She bent over and slapped her hand on the side of the bathroom stall, a tear rolling down her cheek.

This wasn't what she'd signed on for. None of it. Not the nausea, or the weight loss, or Cole. Most especially not Cole.

"What's wrong with you?" Alexa pushed open the stall door, and Kelsey cringed. She didn't really want anyone seeing her right now, on her knees on the grimy tile floor of a diner bathroom.

"I'm sick."

"Obviously. How sick are you? Holy crap. Are you dying

or something? Is that why you're going on a retreat and eating only lettuce?"

"I'm not dying." Kelsey stood up, her legs wobbly, her muscles feeling more like gelatin than anything else. "Even if I feel like I am most days."

Alexa breathed out an expletive that probably could have shocked the two biker guys sitting at the counter in the dining area. "Are you pregnant?"

Kelsey rested her head against the cool wall and breathed out slowly. "Yes," she said. "Move over. I need out of the stall. And I need a toothbrush."

Alexa stood to the side and Kelsey bent over the sink, washing her hands and face, blotting at her clammy neck with a paper towel.

Alexa stood, arms crossed, eyebrows drawn together. "So you already rode the cowboy."

Kelsey sighed. "It's more complicated than that."

"Sex isn't really that complicated."

Kelsey arched a brow. "That's a lie. A lie from the pit of hell. Sex is nothing but a complication. On that you can trust me. Michael having sex with another woman was complicated."

"And I suppose when one gets pregnant, that also makes sex complicated?"

"Yeah." She held back the truth. Because how could Alexa, who had a severe aversion to all things baby, understand the sort of driving ache that had made Kelsey make the decision to have a child? Even now, that ache, that desire, was what kept her sane. It was what reminded her why she was doing this. Her own baby. And not just a baby—a child.

"So . . . are we going to beat child support out of him with a stick or what?"

"No." Kelsey ran cold water over her wrists. "No, I think he's more than willing to pay child support."

They hadn't discussed money, but there had been no reason Cole needed to track her down. He wanted to be involved. If he didn't, she would have been able to continue on, blissfully unaware of who the owner of half of her baby's genes was. But he had come looking for her. For his child.

She shut the water off and braced her hands on the countertop. "He wants to get to know me. To decide what we're going to . . . do."

"Are you keeping the baby?" Alexa asked.

"No matter what." Even if she puked her guts out from now until she was in labor, she was keeping her baby. "It's just . . . It's the complicated thing again. We don't really have a relationship. And we really weren't planning on having any sort of connection." That was the truth. Sort of. "And a baby is a connection, no matter how much we both want to pretend that it's not."

"So you broke your dating moratorium by hooking up with a random guy?"

"No. And who said I was on a dating moratorium?"

"You have been, though, right? You haven't had a date since Michael. Admit it."

"No. I won't admit it. Because it's not true. I've had a date. And a half."

"Half?"

"He was nice. But the waitress spilled a drink in my lap during dinner, and then I noticed he had a piece of spinach in his teeth, and . . . you know. There's nowhere to go but down from there."

"And then what?"

"I faked a work emergency."

"Do newspaper columnists have work emergencies?"

"I might have led him to believe I was an ace reporter. And that there was a robbery somewhere . . ."

"Shameless. So, what about the cowboy?" Alexa asked.

"I'd rather not talk about Cole in the women's room. Can we . . . No, I don't want to go back and smell your lunch either."

"I had the waitress clear it. And I paid."

Kelsey tried her best to keep her lip from wobbling. "I love you."

"Why didn't you tell me, then?" Alexa pushed open the

bathroom door, and they both walked out into the diner, ignoring the looks they got from the burly guys at the counter.

Kelsey sucked in a breath when they were outside, grateful for the fresh air. "I didn't tell you because . . . I thought you'd think I was crazy."

She opened the door to her little green sedan and settled into the passenger side, even more grateful now that she had a driver.

"Why?" Alexa settled into the driver's seat and jammed the key into the ignition. "For having ill-advised sex? Most of us have been there and done that. I don't want to drag skeletons out of my own closet but there was this guy at my work a couple years back. He was an intern, for heaven's sake. An *intern*. He was like barely twenty. It doesn't get much more ill-advised, or fast, than that."

"No. I know you wouldn't think I was crazy for that reason. You're more likely to think I'm crazy because I've never had anything other than 'stable-relationship, we have a commitment' sex."

Alexa pulled the car out onto the highway and leaned forward, her forearms draped over the steering wheel. "'Splain, Lucy," she said, her tone exasperated now, which was fair enough, since Kelsey was talking in circles and she knew it.

"I think you'll think it's crazy that . . . I got pregnant on purpose."

Alexa turned to face her, her green eyes round, her lips pressed tightly together, like she was holding a string of very foul expletives back. Which she probably was.

"See! You're judging me. Your face is all . . . judgy."

"I'm not . . . No, wait. . . . Hell yes, I'm judging you! That's . . . crazy. . . . What, did you pick him out because you saw him in a bar and liked his genes? And I'm not talking Wranglers here."

"No! You make it sound like I'm one step away from sending him pieces of my hair in the mail. Gah. No. I . . . I spent a lot of time thinking about it, and a few months after the wedding, I went to a clinic and I did hormone treatments and started the process of getting inseminated. It took a couple of tries, but in February . . . it was successful."

"These are the kinds of life decisions you talk to your friends about!" Alexa nearly shrieked it. "You wouldn't decide on a scrunchie for prom until I gave you my opinion! Why would you do this without consulting me?"

"Because the decision to have a child really shouldn't include your friends. I'm the one who wants this. I'm the one who feels like there's . . . a hole in my chest because I'm missing something I want so badly. I'm the one who will be doing midnight feedings. I'm the one who has to give birth and pay for college, and suddenly it doesn't seem like there's as big of a gap between those two things as I would like. It's all me. At least it was supposed to be. Now it's me, but it's also Cole, because they used his sample on accident, and he's the father. So what was I supposed to do? Tell him that's too bad. Sorry I'm going to have your baby, and I get that you're a victim here too, but I'm just going to double-victimize you and make sure you'll never get to be a part of his life?"

Alexa turned her focus entirely back to the road, and Kelsey looked out her window at the broad expanse of sky and the snowcapped mountains. Maybe she could count pine trees on the way to Silver Creek. That would eat up some time.

"Sorry," Alexa said.

"What?"

"I'm sorry. You're right. This was your decision, not mine. And a baby is a bigger deal than a scrunchie."

"A bit."

Alexa continued. "And of course you had to consider Cole. Because you wouldn't be you if you hadn't."

"You wouldn't have?"

"I would have told him it was my baby, so eff off."

"I pretty much did. But it didn't work. And then it turned out, he seems pretty decent. It feels like I owe it to the baby to . . . find out. So now away we go to the ranch."

Alexa shook her head. "This is just . . . It's like romantic-comedy material. Only it's neither romantic nor funny."

"Neither are a lot of romantic comedies."

"Touché."

"But romance isn't really a factor here," Kelsey said, writing off the fluttery feeling in her stomach as more nausea. "Because the really important thing is the baby. It's the fact that if my son or daughter asks me about their father one day, I won't feel right if I have to lie or tell them that I wouldn't let him be involved in their life."

That reminder, at least, was a tiny bit bolstering. Because as scary as all of this was, she knew she had to at least try. Try to work out some sort of relationship. For his sake. For the sake of their child.

It would be wrong to do anything else. And she did still care about the whole right-and-wrong thing. Inconvenient.

"No. You can't do that," Alexa said. "You really can't."

"I know."

"Anyway, how bad can it be? Millions of people have to deal with custody arrangements and all the stuff that comes with ex-husbands and -wives every day."

"Yeah, but those people have the benefit of actually having liked each other at some point. Or, if not that, the benefit of liking to jump on each other's bodies."

Alexa pressed the gas down a bit, and the car's engine revved. "Well, I suppose if your cowboy is jumpable, that will put you in the same position."

The trouble was, he really was jumpable. She hadn't actually noticed the first time she saw him, since she'd been dizzy and generally blech at the time. But now that she had some restored equilibrium . . . yes. Yes, he was pretty darn good to look at. Even from her limited view of him through the windshield, with him standing across the driveway, she could tell.

Even in the broad, open expanse of the landscape, he looked big and masculine. And she was starting to think maybe testosterone wasn't the enemy, after all. The snow-dusted mountains behind him and the vast expanse of field backed by an endless evergreen forest only added to the picture. He was at home here. This was his natural habitat. Not her sweet little suburb. There he looked big and rugged too, but out of place. Here . . . here the tight jeans and belt buckle didn't look silly. They looked . . . they looked something else entirely. Something not altogether unpleasant.

The building directly behind Cole was a little more rustic than she'd anticipated. She was starting to wonder if the pictures on his website had lied.

Kelsey opened the passenger door of the car, and Cole started taking long strides in her direction. She ignored the rapid up-tempo of her heartbeat and put her foot down, then sank into thick, oozing mud, her tennis shoe sliding out from beneath her. She swore and pitched forward, gripping the top of the door as tightly as she could.

A warm weight settled on her fingers and she looked up, her eyes locking with Cole's. Cole, who was no longer standing across the yard. Cole, whose eyes looked a bit like chocolate. Not sweet, though. Dark, a little bit bitter. But tempting all the same.

"Careful," he said, his tone so . . . paternal . . . it made her bristle.

"I thought this was a guest ranch? I didn't expect for there to be mud in the driveway." She slipped her hand out from beneath his and stuffed it into her hoodie pocket, trying to ignore the hot, tingling sensation he'd left across her knuckles.

"Apologies." He inclined his head and stepped back.

She wondered if she'd imagined the warmth in his hand. Because there was no warmth in him now.

"Right. Um . . . this is my friend Alexa."

Kelsey looked over her shoulder at Alexa, who was half out of the car, one leg on the driver's seat still, as though she were ready to make a quick break for it if necessary. She offered Cole a half wave. "Hi. You must be Cole."

He regarded Alexa for a minute. "How'd you guess?"

"Lucky," she said, green eyes narrowed.

He looked back at Kelsey and she felt his gaze hit her—felt it down to her toes.

"Good. Now we've all met," Kelsey said, afraid Alexa would start snarling at any moment.

"Do you have any bags?" Cole asked, looking at Kelsey and ignoring Alexa.

"Several," Kelsey said, gesturing toward the trunk.

"I'll get them and show you up to your cabin."

That was good. If he was showing them up to the cabin, that meant some time without him. She'd been in his presence for only two minutes and she needed a break already. Annoyance, discomfort, trepidation . . . those were feelings she'd been prepared to deal with. But those feelings coupled with the heavy knot in her stomach of . . . She didn't want to call it attraction; it was more like appreciation. Well, that she was not prepared for.

"We can't . . . drive up?"

"No road access to the cabins."

"Quaint," she said, annoyance coursing through her. She hadn't planned on roughing it for the next few weeks.

"You can park down by the front of the main lodge area." He gestured across the field to a large log-cabin-style structure with honey-colored wood and a green roof. "Or I can move the car there for you later."

"Where are we now?" Kelsey asked, her eyes on the closer building, which looked more like Lincoln Logs than luxury accommodations.

"You came in on an access road. This is just an equipment shed. My barns are in better shape than this."

"Well, that's a relief. Seriously, though, signage would be nice."

Cole's eyes lingered on hers, dark and compelling. She just wanted to keep looking at him. And she wanted to turn away at the same time. She wasn't sure how he managed that. "Whatever you could possibly want, I'll make sure you get it."

Her cheeks heated, her stomach tightening a little as she

thought of all the things she might need from a man like
him . . . of all the things he would be able to give her. Oh,
no, that didn't even bear thinking about.

Because there were bigger things happening. The baby.
Their stranger-than-fiction situation. They had serious issues
to deal with, and they had nothing to do with how nice he
looked in a pair of jeans. So while she wasn't above noticing,
she wasn't going to dwell.

Not on that, or his husky voice, or how strong he was or
how warm his touch was. Nope. None of it.

Alexa leaned in and pulled the lever to the trunk. They
had at least six bags between them. And Kelsey was suddenly a little bit embarrassed that hers were pink and
flowered.

"Do you have one of those . . . bag trollies like at hotels?"
Alexa asked.

"I'll make another trip." Cole said, rounding to the back
of the car and pulling out one of the suitcases, hauling it up
onto his shoulder and curving his forearm over it in one fluid
motion. Then he reached down and did the same to another
one, stacking it on top of the first. He took a third one out
and held it by the handle, like a sane person would do.

"Close the trunk for me?"

Alexa nodded, a little bit dumbly in Kelsey's opinion,
obvious and blatant in her appreciation of the male form.
She looked gauche, really. Then Alexa stepped forward to
oblige Cole.

"This way," he said, jerking his head to the left.

Kelsey noticed the casual flick down that Alexa did with
her eyes when Cole stepped in front of them. Which meant
she had to do the same. Yes, he looked good in denim. Yes,
he had a tight, muscular butt. And yes, it had been too long
since she'd simply enjoyed the sight of a man's backside.

So she'd remedy that—just for a few minutes.

She breathed a sigh of relief when they stepped out of
the graveled lot and onto a paved path that wound through
the grove of pine trees that surrounded the main structure.

The path wound around the equipment shed and behind the lodge they'd seen in the distance.

"Are we taking the long way?" she asked, her legs feeling a bit unsteady.

"Yes." He stopped and turned to face her. "Do you need help getting there?"

"No, this is . . . good. The air smells good. Although, why didn't you tell us we were going to take the longest route possible?"

"I didn't really think about it. Big property like this lends itself to walking a lot."

"Why didn't you ask if I need help?" Alexa asked.

"Because your comfort isn't my primary concern," Cole said.

"That's almost touching," Alexa said.

"It wasn't meant to be." The chill on Cole's words was as pronounced as the biting cold in the air blowing off the mountaintops.

Kelsey hadn't really seen this side of him—this sort of grumpy, snarly side—when he'd been at her house. Typical. Hiding his bad behavior so he could draw her in. Very male move. Fortunately, she was wise to that. And it didn't matter how nice he looked in a pair of tight jeans.

"So, tell me about the ranch," she said, desperate to pull the conversation onto something she didn't care about so she could stop overthinking every interaction.

"When my dad was running it, it was mainly a cattle ranch. Now we board horses, and we've just started a breeding program, but that's still in the early stages. And, of course, we're taking guests now. Either for a chance to enjoy luxury accommodations or to give you a little ranch and rodeo experience. The rodeo part of it is my brother's job. If you can call it that."

"Why wouldn't you call it that?" she asked.

Cole turned, a half smile curving his lips. "Because Cade doesn't work if Cade doesn't have to."

"I have a brother like that," Alexa said.

Cole ignored her comment.

The path forked, and Cole took the one on the far left. The uphill incline grew more pronounced, and the trees thinned, giving way to a mossy clearing with a cabin set into the hillside and made from the same knotted, honey-colored wood that the lodge was built out of.

Kelsey turned and looked behind them. The view was spectacular: green mountains fading into a hazy blue, stretching on forever.

"Beautiful," she said. She had seen views like this every day growing up, and part of her missed that. Portland was a city surrounded by greenery and mountains, an urban life that didn't require a total sacrifice of nature. But this was different.

The sky stretched on forever without being interrupted by gray steel. There was no noise. There were no car horns or engines to break the thick silence—nothing but the occasional bird. For just a moment, the sense of yearning and homesickness was so pronounced, it was painful.

"There's another, smaller bedroom through there. Bathroom next to it. There's a path behind the cabin that will take you the short route to the lodge." Cole walked up the steps and pushed the door open, depositing the luggage just inside.

Kelsey and Alexa both followed him in. The cabin was warm, with pristine wood floors and a plush bed. There was nothing rustic about it. It was luxurious in a way she hadn't anticipated. Cinnamon-hued drapes hung from the windows, and the bedding was made of a heavy satin in chocolate brown. She sort of wanted to curl up in the middle of the bed and go to sleep.

"I'll bring the rest of your bags up later. But if you want a moment to settle in . . ."

"Yes. Thank you. That would be good," Kelsey said, the strange sense of vulnerability still clinging to her like an unwanted mist wrapping itself around her skin.

Cole nodded and walked out, shutting the door behind him.

"What a jackass," Alexa said.

"Didn't stop you from looking at his butt."

"Consider that a public service. So I could let you know if it was worth it."

"What makes you think I didn't look?"

"Did you?"

She tried to play it off, even though she was slightly ashamed of herself. "Of course I did. I'm pregnant, not blind."

"So was he that big of a jerk when you first met him?"

Kelsey shook her head and sat on the edge of the bed, the down comforter fluffing up around her. "No. He was nicer. I don't think he likes you."

"A sure sign of a faulty character."

"Maybe."

Alexa came and sat down next to her. "Hey, in all seriousness . . . what are we doing here? What do you expect to happen?"

Kelsey was a planner. She'd always been one. She'd had dreams; she'd chased them. Even better, she'd caught them. Because she'd always believed that it was in a person's power to make her own life what she wanted it to be.

Now she wondered if that was even close to the truth.

"I'm trying to figure it out."

"So, we have guests in four?" Lark, Cole's younger sister, looked up from the computer screen.

"Yes," he said, settling onto the leather sectional that stretched across the open public foyer that served as the lobby of the lodge. The lodge was also his family home. The downstairs was mainly dedicated to guests, with a large dining and lounge area. The kitchen was private, with a small dining area. But other than that, the upstairs was where he, Lark and, most recently, Cade lived.

"How long are they staying?" Lark turned her focus back to her computer, a lock of dark hair falling into her face. Lark ran everything administrative on the ranch, and she was their webmaster. Most of the time she still looked like a kid to him.

"Don't know."

"Cole, I have to know."

"Well, I don't know. Kelsey is a writer. . . . She's here to do a piece." *Sort of.* "And she'll be here until it's done."

"Kelsey?"

"Kelsey who?" Cade walked through the front door and straight into the room.

"Back up and wipe your boots, Cade," Cole said.

Cade took another step forward. "Kelsey who?"

"A guest," Cole growled.

"He knows her name," Lark put in.

"Why do you know her name?" Cade turned to him and arched one brow.

"I met her," he said, standing up and wandering into the kitchen. He jerked open the fridge door and pulled out a bottle of beer. He positioned the lip of the cap on the edge of the counter and smacked it with his palm, popping it off. He raised the bottle to his lips, ready for a little bit of stress relief.

"Where did you meet her?" Lark asked.

She and Cade were standing in the kitchen doorway, peering at him more like a couple of overeager kids than like the adults they were supposed to be.

"Portland," he said. The truth would work until a lie became necessary.

"She's the girl you banged?" Cade asked.

"Cade, ew, don't," Lark said.

"What she said." Cole gestured to his sister with the hand that was gripping the bottle.

"Well, is she?" Cade pressed.

"No." The truth again.

His brother, to his credit, dropped it. "But you know her name."

"A common courtesy, introductions. Maybe they didn't teach you that on the circuit?"

"I may not have asked every woman her name before"—he cast Lark a look—"but I am familiar with introductions. You, Cole, are usually short on friendliness, especially these days, and especially with women, so it stood out."

"I know her friend's name too." Except as soon as he said it, he realized he didn't. He did, though. He had to. He'd met her some twenty minutes ago. She'd said it. Or Kelsey had. But he didn't really remember which one. All he could really remember was that her friend had given him the evil eye. If looks could castrate, he'd have been a soprano.

Lark smiled. "This is some sort of a record! You talked to two guests in one day."

"Are you both saying I'm—"

"Aloof?" Lark asked.

"An asshole?" Cade put in.

"Rude?" Lark again.

"I'm not. I just don't have time to be social. There's a lot of work to do around here. Work that doesn't involve an Internet connection, and work"—he looked at Cade—"that doesn't involve strutting around, hitting on every woman that comes into the area. Don't," he said, pointing his finger at his brother, "even think about hitting on Kelsey or her friend, by the way."

"First off, I don't strut, not these days," Cade said, smacking his thigh muscle. "I believe they call that a gimp. Second, you aren't in charge of who I hit on."

"In this instance, I am. If I see you looking at them wrong, I'll make the other leg gimpy too."

"You can't have both of them, Cole. Unless . . ." He shot his sister, who was crimson, a sideways glance. "Well, you could have both of them."

"That's it!" Lark said. "The testosterone is too thick in here." She turned and walked out of the kitchen.

"Don't be such a dog," Cole said to Cade, following Lark out of the room.

He stopped cold when he saw Kelsey standing in the center of the common area, looking up at the high ceiling and the collection of antlers on the wall.

"My dad's," he said.

"Oh." She looked at him. "Hi. Look, I just wanted to . . . I'm glad you're here because . . . I was thinking maybe I should go."

"No, don't go."

"Kelsey?" Lark asked, taking a step forward, her hand outstretched.

Kelsey blinked and shook his sister's hand. "Yes. And you are?"

"I'm Cole's sister, Lark Mitchell, and this is our brother, Cade."

Cade inclined his head and touched the brim of his hat. "Charmed."

It took all of Cole's restraint not to thump his brother for that. Cade was just as at home on a subway as he was on the back of a horse. The folksy thing was a total put-on he used to get women into bed. It seemed to work for him too.

"Nice to meet you both," Kelsey said.

"Can we talk?" Cole ignored the owlish look he was getting from Lark.

Kelsey's eyes darted to his siblings. "Sure."

"Out front." He put his hand on her lower back, and she jerked away from him like he'd burned her.

It had been too long since he'd touched a woman. Since he'd interacted with one that wasn't family. He was losing his mojo, apparently. Although, considering his past selection, it could be argued that he had never had mojo but had just been scraping the bottom of a very desperate barrel.

He lowered his hand and flexed his fingers, tried to ignore the faint heat that lingered there from the brief contact.

He opened the door for her, and she breezed out in front of him, her focus on the fields in the distance and definitely not on him.

"I'm sorry."

Her head whipped around, pale blond hair shimmering over her shoulder. "You are?"

"I was a jerk. I'm not . . . My brother and sister have accused me of not being real personable. I expect they're a little bit right. I work a lot and I get focused."

Plus, he was just out of practice. Things had changed a lot in the past five years. The loss of his dad, too soon. The loss of his wife, not soon enough. He'd assumed operation of the ranch, and life had just sort of filled up with busy.

He just hadn't wanted to see people. His sister had been

too sweet to let him push her away, his brother too damned stubborn.

"Right. I get that. I guess this is the start of our getting to know each other," she said.

"Sorry again."

"It's fair. It's how you are."

"It's how I can be. I hope it's not who I am."

But he wondered if it was whom he had become. Life had pretty well kicked the idealism out of him, and it had stung. He'd never thought of himself as an idealist until he'd become a cynic and seen Cole: Premarriage for who he really was. An idiot who thought good intentions fixed it all. Who thought all it took was love. Who thought when someone said "I love you," that was it, and they meant it. Who thought everyone was who they said they were.

Yep. That guy was a damned idiot.

Kelsey shrugged. "I suppose we all have those moments."

"Right. Tell your friend I'm sorry."

"Alexa," she said.

"Right." He would try to remember the name of the friend who wanted him dead or incapacitated. "If you want, I can give you the tour," he said, stepping off the porch and looking back at her.

She looked over her shoulder. "Sure. That would be . . . cool. I guess."

"Do you think you can handle a ride in the pickup?" From the moment she'd stepped out of her car and into the mud, she'd looked decidedly underwhelmed by the whole ranch experience, so he wasn't really sure what to expect.

"Look, Sheriff, I might live in the city now, but I'm a country girl born and bred. I may not like getting dirt under my fingernails, but I'm capable of it, all right?"

"Okay, then. Come with me."

Kelsey climbed into the pickup and slammed the door shut. It was familiar in a strange way. Like part of another life. She was starting to wonder if all ranch trucks smelled the same. Like sweat and hay and men.

Although she had to confess that Cole smelled better than

most men she associated with hard work and dirt. He smelled like leather and aftershave. And, yes, a little like sweat—but she was surprised to find that it didn't make her want to gag.

Maybe she was showing progress on the morning-sickness front. She was going to celebrate that victory rather than dwell on her disturbing appreciation of his scent.

She cleared her throat. "Your brother and sister don't know, do they?"

"Nope."

"I thought not. Based on the lack of abject horror or shock on their faces when I walked in." She worried her lip between her teeth. "Are you going to tell them?"

"Eventually."

"If you decide you want to be involved?"

He nodded slowly. "That's the plan."

She let out a breath. "I'd better let Alexa know to keep quiet."

"Does she do quiet?"

"Not well. But she will if I tell her it's really important. She's a good friend like that. And after sixteen years of friendship, we're sort of stuck together for better or for worse."

"I can tell you right now, she expects this situation to be a 'for worse.'"

He was observant. Or maybe he wasn't, so much. Alexa wasn't known for subtlety. "With Alex, you're always guilty until proven innocent. She's sort of a born cynic. It's part of her charm." She put her elbow on the armrest and looked out at the wide expanse of green. "So, explain it all," she said as he turned the key.

She jumped when the engine turned over, the roar of eight cylinders filling the cab. She gripped the door handle and shot him a bland look.

He smiled. That sort of half-cocked grin that made her want to hit him. Or something. "The ranch? Or is this extending to the mysteries of the universe?"

"Just the ranch will do, pilgrim."

"Well, like I told you earlier, mostly we raise horses, and ideally, those horses compete in the ProRodeo circuit. My dad had beef, but I think cows, in mass quantities, are too much trouble."

"And horses aren't?"

"Oh, no, it's a pain in the ass, but basically, all ranch work is."

"Then why do you do it?"

His smile spread, a genuine one this time. "Because I love it." He maneuvered the truck onto a dirt access road, and she gripped the handle tighter as her side of the cab pitched up when the front tire on the driver's side dipped into a pothole. "We do still raise beef cows, but on a small scale. It goes out locally, unadvertised, so we don't have to deal with certifications."

"Is that legal?"

"Yeah. Technically."

"Oh. Nice."

"As long as they buy the cow while it's alive."

"Oh, ranch life. How I haven't missed it," she said.

"Right, you're a country girl. So, tell me about it."

"About being a country girl? Are you trying to form a milkmaid fantasy? Because I don't milk cows, and I really wouldn't do it in a minidress."

"Hardly. Just curious. Since you're the mother of my baby and all."

His words hung in the air, awkward and intimate in a way that made her shift in her seat. She didn't know him well enough to be the mother of his baby. It made her head hurt.

"Right. That." Talking about her childhood was preferable to thinking too hard about their current situation. "I was born and raised in Oregon. In Bonanza, actually. My parents own a ranch. It's not commercial or anything, but we had ducks and chickens. Horses. One cow, which we couldn't eat because Jacie named it. Actually, she became a vegetarian over that friendship."

"Sounds like she's a good friend to have."

"She is. All of my sisters are."

"How many?"

"Four."

He looked at her, his eyebrows raised. "You don't want that many kids, do you?"

"So what if I do? They won't be yours."

"No, they won't."

She regretted her choice of words right after they'd slipped out of her mouth, because they just sounded bitchy. Really, though, she was right, and it wasn't his business how many kids she wanted. "Not because you aren't a fine specimen of a man who I'm sure has fantastic genes, but mainly because I barely know you, and I'm not really enjoying gestating this baby all that much. My original statement stands."

"I'm not offended," he said.

"Good. I wasn't . . . I didn't mean to offend you."

"Have you wondered at all why I left the deposit? Details, I mean, not vague generalizations."

She breathed out, long and slow. Good yoga breathing. Thought-clearing breathing. Except it wasn't working. "I don't really want to think about it, actually."

"Why is that?"

"It might humanize you, and I'd rather be pissed at you. I'd rather blame you for this somehow, but I know you're just as much of a victim as I am."

"I don't know about that. I don't have to give birth."

"But I chose this."

"And I could have chosen to walk away," he said.

"That's true. So why haven't you?"

Cole pulled his truck up in front of a long, narrow building painted dark red with natural wood trim. He threw it into first, killing the engine. "I don't know. Is that a good enough answer?" Kelsey shook her head. "I didn't think it was; it isn't good enough for me. All I know is . . . I can't walk away. Because like I told you already, if we'd had a one-night stand, I wouldn't walk away, and it feels . . ."

"It's not the same."

He took a deep breath, the lines around his mouth deepening. "It feels the same."

"Except you truly had no part in this. You didn't make the choice to . . . to sleep with me. You didn't make any choice."

"No," he said slowly. "I did. I chose to bank the sperm."

"Why?"

"I don't like talking about it. And it's not because it's serious or anything, not really. It's because it's stupid. It's because I made a stupid choice and I married a woman I had no business even going on a date with, and the list of things I let her talk me into is long and it's ridiculous. And banking the sperm so that we had premium biological material was just one of the insane things. And now it's turned into about the biggest, most long-lasting repercussion of that marriage. Answer your question?"

She looked down at her hands, her heart pounding hard. "Sorry. About the marriage thing." If there was one thing she knew about love and marriage, it was that it could suck bad when it went wrong.

"Well, you know, everyone makes mistakes. I happen to make giant-ass mistakes that are harder to get rid of than they should be." He opened his door and got out of the truck, his movements easy, slow, giving her plenty of time to admire the view of his denim-clad butt as he made his way over to the barn. That view was fist-bitingly good.

She stifled a whimper and opened her door, hopping down onto the soft ground.

It took her a moment to notice she'd managed to scramble. "I didn't puke," she said when she entered the barn.

"I'm glad to hear it," he said, not turning to face her.

"I'm sorry, but . . . you know this mistake doesn't have to last for you."

"Yeah, Kelsey, it does. Whether I walk away or not doesn't change that a child of mine exists. It just changes how big of a douche I am. It changes whether or not I've abandoned my child for my own comfort." He turned away again, kept walking.

She let out an exasperated breath and increased her pace, pleasantly surprised by the continued lack of nausea. "So, these are your horses?" She walked along the row of stables, looking through the window in one of the doors. There was a large bay standing there, his brown eyes assessing Kelsey. He seemed to find her acceptable. He raised his nose and nickered, and Kelsey put her hand through the opening in the stall door, letting him sniff her, letting his lips brush over her palm.

"Yeah. That's Ol' Trigger," he said, affecting a slow, folksy drawl.

She turned to face him, her eyebrow raised. "You're joking."

He stuffed his hands into his pockets and offered her a smile. "Yeah. And this one's Simon Says Stop, but we call him Simon. Then we have Coal Black over there; my brother named him for the satisfaction of calling him Coal when he's a pain in the ass. Then there're Miss Kitty, Captain Kangaroo and Jumpin' Jack Flash."

"Fancy names, cowboy."

"They're retired rodeo horses. Now they just live here and get spoiled rotten. Miss Kitty and the captain are our barrel racers. They go easy enough that guests can ride them, learn a few tricks."

"Sounds fun."

"Can pregnant women ride horses?" he asked, looking down at her stomach.

She put her hand over it, covering his view. It seemed invasive, having him look at her like that. She wasn't sure why. "Uh . . . I think it's all right if you're already a rider, but I'm not, so I definitely won't start now."

"You didn't ride horses back in the day?"

She rolled her eyes. "Well, back in the day, sure. But it's been . . . years."

"You don't ride when you go back home?"

She snorted a laugh and tucked a strand of hair behind her ear, moving from Ol' Trigger's stall down to Coal Black's. "I don't stay home long when I go. Like this last time, I went to my sister's wedding, but I didn't stay any longer than I needed to."

"Just long enough to catch the bouquet?"

"More like dodge it."

"And run to the nearest fertility clinic?"

"I didn't run straight there," she said dryly.

"You regret it?"

"The vomiting, the cowboy, the feeling like the inside of my mouth is carpeted in roadkill, yes. Those things I regret. The baby? No. When I think about the baby, I'm sure I did the right thing."

Cole looked down at Kelsey, at her determined face. She looked sure. Surer than he could remember feeling about anything in a long time. After Shawna and the big bad divorce and his finding out his dad—his hero—wasn't the man he'd always thought he was, Cole's life hadn't made a lick of sense. He'd just been trying his best to hold it all together, to keep the ranch moving. To keep Lark and Cade from ever finding out that their dad had feet of clay.

"What about you, Cole? Are you sure this is what you want?"

He shook his head. "Nope. Not even close. But it's happening, right? Not to compare the more joyous event of conceiving a child to finding out your wife is a master manipulator who loves your money a hell of a lot more than she loves you, but in some ways, it's like my divorce. No matter what, it's going to happen. And whether you want it to or not, whether you want to deal with it or not, doesn't matter. It's happening. All you can do is do the best you can with the situation you're in."

Talking about the whole ex-wife thing ranked right up there with getting his scrotum caught in his horse's reins and getting dragged across the Oregon mountains by his balls. Actually, at the moment, the thing with his balls seemed less awkward than this.

Because why even bother getting to know each other? They had nothing in common. Nothing but a baby.

A heavy weight settled in his gut. Not for the first time,

he wondered what the hell he was doing. There was a piece of him, a small corner of his mind, that could imagine what it would be like to have a kid. To be a father. That part of himself pictured sweet, homey scenes. Pictured him teaching his child how to ride a horse.

But that was a very small part of himself. The rest of him . . . The idea of a baby in his arms seemed so strange and foreign. Scary, mostly. He didn't have any experience with kids. He'd spent his adult years working hard and playing hard. At least until his dad had died. Till he'd gotten married. Now playtime was . . . nonexistent. But just the thought of getting hammered on a Saturday night didn't seem worth the hangover that would be there at sunrise. He had too much responsibility to sleep in. And as far as getting laid went . . .

He didn't even seem to care about that anymore.

His focus was squarely on the ranch: on restoring its former glory, then improving it further. An eventual wife and children hadn't even been on the radar. He'd put all that way behind him.

Now, though, it wasn't just a distant thought. Wasn't just something he could say he didn't want to do. It wasn't even a "someday." There was a due date involved. He couldn't imagine turning his back on a real child, one with his DNA. That was where he got stuck. That was why Kelsey was here.

"Ready to see the rest?" he asked.

Kelsey turned and smiled at him. It made his stomach tighten. Her entire face lit up when she smiled, a dimple creasing one of her cheeks. He'd never seen her smile before. Not really.

It turned out, she was beautiful.

"Ready," she said.

Alexa turned right at the fork in the path that led from the cabin and found herself out in a pasture. A fricking pasture.

It was so open, it made her dizzy. The silence—the thick, oppressive silence—was foreign now. Give her the concrete jungle any day of the week. Sure, she was from the Beaver State, but she'd adopted New York with extreme enthusiasm.

"You can't even order pizza out here," she muttered, tromping through the tall grass. She should have stayed back at the cabin. She was supposed to be giving Kelsey alone time with her accidental baby daddy. But Kelsey had clearly gone dangerously insane, so leaving her alone might not be the best idea.

The roar of an engine broke the silence, ricocheting off the mountains as it drew closer.

Alexa put her hand up to block the sun from her eyes and watched the faded blue truck pitch and bump its way through the field.

The driver must have seen her, because the truck braked, the abrupt motion rocking the iron beast, stopping it about thirty feet away from her. The driver's-side door opened, and one denim-clad leg appeared before the rest of a tall, muscular, young ranch hand. He was hot. Broad shoulders, broad chest, trim waist and hips.

But damn, he was young. Maybe twenty-two or twenty-three. Maybe.

"You lost, ma'am?"

"I know you didn't just call me ma'am, cowpoke. Not if you value your"—she let her gaze drift beneath his garish belt buckle—"valuables."

"Shucks," he said dryly. "You staying in one of the cabins? Lark mentioned we had guests."

"Yes, I am staying in one of the cabins, which blessedly has Wi-Fi, or I would be hitchhiking back to civilization."

"Lark can't live without Internet," he said. "She figures no one else can either."

"And you can?"

He shrugged. "I've never minded not having it."

"Do you have a name? And please don't say Slim or Tater or I will vomit."

"Tyler."

"Acceptable. I'm Alexa." He stuck out his hand, and she

looked at it. "Do people shake hands out of the office these days?"

He leaned back, hip cocked, thumb hooked through his belt loop. "Would you prefer that I tipped my hat?" He put his hand on the brim of his suede cowboy hat. "Ma'am?" He drawled the last part, a total put-on just to piss her off. She loved it.

"Wouldn't hurt. Give it a try, Tyler. I might swoon."

A slow smile spread over his face. He was so cute. Like a shiny, sexy poster of a cowboy model. "Now that would be something." His blue eyes flickered over her curves. He was quite obviously checking her out. It had been a while since she'd bothered to play the "I'm hot, you're hot, let's get naked" game, but she remembered it.

And right then she realized she missed it.

She was also very much not going there. She'd done the younger-guy thing. Once. And then she'd been only two years her partner's senior. But it had been the lamest, most why-bother sex of all time. Life was too short to get sweaty with a guy who didn't push all the right buttons.

"I'm thirty," she said. That ought to scare him.

"And?" He arched a pale eyebrow.

"The least you could have done was act surprised."

"Sorry. I'll practice it and get back to you. So you're thirty and . . . ?"

"And nothing. When I was in high school, you would have been young enough for me to babysit. I would have given you crackers and a juice box and set you in front of *Power Rangers.*"

"I'm twenty-four."

A good year older than she'd guessed. Still. Not happening. "Yikes."

"Good yikes or bad yikes?"

"Not-getting-into-my-pants yikes," she said. "You can give me a ride back to the main house, though, so I don't have to wander around out here until I'm eaten by wolves."

To his credit, he didn't blush or anything, like she might

have done when she was his age. Gads. Just that thought made her feel old.

"I think I could arrange that. You need any special assistance getting into the vehicle?" His mouth quirked into a smile. A darn charming smile.

"Too cute, Tyler. I'll take the ride without commentary."

He walked over to where she was standing and put his hand on the top of his hat, which he put over his heart. "Now that's too bad, ma'am." He leaned in, close enough that she could smell his aftershave and very fresh minty breath. *Oh, my.* "Because I give good commentary."

He was messing with her. And flirting with her. And it was working.

"I'll be the judge of that."

From the stables with the retirees, Kelsey and Cole moved on to the main stable, where the Mitchells kept the stud horses and the horses that were being trained to compete in the rodeo circuit.

"There's big money in this. I mean, potentially," Cole said, indicating one of the stalls. "If you can breed a winner—and by that, I mean one that's good at shaking riders off his back—you're looking at serious dollars."

"And this is the main thing you're doing?"

"Mainly. It's fun. I got into it because Cade made some good connections back when he was riding pro. Things are really starting to take off there. We need it, because the whole hotel portion is good, but it's still growing. And to keep growing it, we need other sources of income."

"He's not competing now?"

"He can't ride anymore. Which, honestly, sucks. He broke his femur. Bad enough that he can hardly walk a straight line. Plus, he's got some back problems. I think. He doesn't like to talk about it, not in depth."

"Runs in the family, I'll bet."

"We're the strong, silent type," he said.

"What happened to him?"

"To Cade? He was thrown off the horse he was riding, which isn't that unusual, but his boot got caught in the saddle. So he was on the horse, sort of, hanging by one leg, and every step that horse took landed on him first."

"That sounds horrible," she said, putting her hand on her stomach, trying to quell the rising nausea.

"It was bad. Is bad. It ended his career. Plus . . . it wasn't exactly an accident. They found a spike under the horse's saddle. One of the other riders, Quinn Parker, he put it there. That someone did that to him on purpose just made it worse. That someone would do it for the money, the prestige. He's just lucky he can walk at all. He could have been killed."

"Oh . . . geez."

"Yeah."

"I'll bet he misses it."

"Almost as much as I miss him being on the road."

She frowned. "You don't really mean that."

"Mostly not."

"Good. But I do sort of get it," she said slowly. "The siblings-driving-you-crazy thing. My sisters . . . well, they're perfect. As far as my parents are concerned."

"Yeah?"

"Yeah. They're married."

"And that's perfect, huh? What about you? You're successful, right? Your column is pretty big."

"Oh, it's huge," she said, her tone overdramatic, earning a chuckle from Cole. "I'm kind of a big deal. But I don't have a husband, so . . . my parents think maybe I'm not such a big deal."

"So, you're the black sheep."

"Baaaaa."

"Nice."

"Thanks." Kelsey pulled a piece of hay from a bale that was wedged into a massive stack and twisted it between her fingers. "Yeah, I'm the strange one. Kelsey, the Noble who went to college. The last single sister." She threw the piece of hay down onto the ground. "It doesn't help that I'm the oldest. I'm like this major oddity. I go back home and I think people are watching me to see if I'm morphing into a cat lady."

"Your friend . . ."

"Alexa."

"Right. She's not married, is she?"

"No. But she moved away too. She's living in New York City. Her family's not quite as conventional as mine either, so she doesn't catch half the crap I do over being single. Or being a 'career girl,' as my mom puts it."

"A career girl?"

"Condescending, yes?"

"You actually get grief for being successful?"

"Oh, tons. But the thing is, in their world, I'm not successful. It's subtle, but I just . . . I know my mom doesn't get it. She doesn't get how it makes me happy. That I love what I do. She doesn't understand why I want things outside the 'natural' order. Which I think to her has something to do with being barefoot in the kitchen."

"And the baby?"

"She's going to get that even less." Kelsey sighed and looked down at her stomach. It was still flat. Her family wouldn't even guess for a while. But she would have to tell them eventually. It sucked to have anxiety about something like this. To hold in something she was honestly happy about. Not the Cole disaster, but the baby. "Oh, this is a mess."

"But it's what you want."

"Yes. It is."

"Then who cares what they think?"

"Well, sadly, I do."

That earned her another chuckle. "Yeah, I get that. My mom would be on me about getting married again. For real this time, and not in Vegas like a godless heathen. Yeah, she would have said that."

Kelsey laughed. "She and my mom could have been friends."

"Oh, Lord, no. They would have encouraged each other too much."

"So . . . do you want to? Get married again, I mean." After the words left her mouth, she wished she could call them back and reorder them. Or just not say them at all. Because they sounded a whole lot more like a marriage proposal than she'd intended for them to.

But she was curious. She needed to know *something* about him. Although she wasn't really sure why. That was the real mystery. Why she was looking for a connection with him at all. They had an accidental connection, one that might very well last them all of their lives. But they didn't really need anything deeper. More personal. Because none of this was about who he was beyond whether or not he would be a good father.

She chewed her lip.

Maybe it did matter who he was. Because if he decided he wanted to pursue a custody agreement, that meant her son or daughter would be spending weekends on the ranch.

A solid ball of emotion formed in her chest and melted, spreading through her, making her feel shaky. That wasn't what she wanted. It certainly wasn't what she'd imagined when she'd thought about having a baby.

"I'm not all that interested in revisiting the institution, no."

"Why? Not all marriages are bad, you know." She was just digging herself in deeper.

"Maybe not. But it's hard to tell. Some look fine when . . . when they aren't. So, since we're playing twenty damn questions, why aren't you getting married?"

She sighed, long and slow. "That's a whole . . . story. I doubt you want to go there."

"Probably not." He looked down at his watch. "It's about time for dinner. Do you want to come down and eat in the lodge? We deliver up to the cabins too, but we also do a family-style dinner."

"Um . . ." Did she really want to spend more time with Cole today? Strangely, she found she did. "That sounds great."

Six

Kelsey couldn't remember the last time food seemed appealing. But it did now. She could have kissed someone. Preferably the cook.

There were mashed potatoes, which looked like starchy heaven, and there was pork. She had no idea why, but as soon as she saw it, she knew she needed the strong, salty flavor for her life to be complete. There was a green salad that looked so crisp and amazing, she wanted to weep with gratitude.

Blessedly, there was no poultry.

Pregnancy didn't make sense.

Kelsey was sitting next to Alexa on one end of the table, with a few ranch hands she had yet to meet in between her and Cole and his siblings. It was pretty obvious she and Cole had some sort of connection, and sitting at opposite ends of the table wasn't really going to disguise it, but still.

She wasn't ready to explain the situation, and if Cole wasn't either, it was fine by her.

"So, Kelsey, Alexa," Lark, straightening her glasses, addressed them both, her dark ponytail swinging as she did, "are you enjoying everything? Did Cole show you everything?"

A slow grin spread over Cade's face. "Yeah. Did he show you *everything*, Kelsey?"

Lark turned and shot him a dirty look while Cole pretended to miss the innuendo. Then she continued. "Did you get to try any barrel racing?"

Kelsey coughed. "Uh, no. I don't think I'll do much riding. I'm not . . ."

"Oh, it's easy," Lark said, her enthusiasm so sparkly that Kelsey felt like she needed sunglasses. "It's not like professional-level barrel racing or anything. Just basics. And it's really fun."

"She said no, Lark," Cole said, his eyes meeting Kelsey's.

Kelsey felt her stomach flutter. And it wasn't from nausea.

Lark looked slightly crushed. "I know. I just wanted to make sure she knew it was . . . tourist level."

"Thank you," Kelsey said, feeling like she'd been involved in a puppy-kicking incident. Lark radiated youth and naïveté. It was very likely that the whole situation would shock her if she knew. "I really did enjoy seeing everything"—she shot Cade a look—"at the ranch today. The horses are beautiful."

Lark turned her focus on one of the ranch hands, a cute blond. "Did you have a good day, Tyler?"

"I did." Tyler gave Alexa a look that could be described only as smoldering. Kelsey tried very hard not to feel jealous.

What was there to be jealous of? Flirtation? Sex? Yeah, it had been a long time since she'd had sex. And yeah, she missed it. Of course she did. But now was not the time. Her only real option would be Cole, and that would be stupid. She looked across the table at him: at his square jaw dusted with dark stubble; at his lips, firm-looking and sexy. . . .

Yes. *Stupid.*

Alexa looked away and sighed. There would be questioning later. Big, serious questioning in which Kelsey demanded to know exactly what was going on.

Lark looked down at her plate and nearly pushed a lump of potatoes off onto the table. "I'm going to go work on . . . I have a thing." She stood and walked out of the room.

"I hope that wasn't because of what I said about the barrel racing," Kelsey said.

"Probably me," Cole said. "She's sensitive. And I'm not. I'll apologize later."

Over dinner, Kelsey and Alexa met Dave, Tex, Mike and Tyler, whom Alexa clearly already knew. They chatted for a while about their jobs on the ranch and also treated their guests to a gruesome story about Mike and a horseshoe nail.

Kelsey quietly celebrated the victory of not vomiting at the end of the story.

Dinner got loud and boisterous, and Kelsey just sat back and listened to the guys swap stories. She laughed and looked over at Cole, finding his gaze on her. Her stomach dropped that time. She took a sharp breath and did her best to ignore it. Best to pretend it hadn't happened, really. Because there was no point. None at all.

That was really just a direct result of watching the brief flirtation between Alexa and Tyler. A little jealousy mixed in with a vague longing for her own flirtation. At least that was what she was telling herself.

Because she didn't really want a flirtation. She didn't.

When the plates were cleared, Cole offered coffee.

"No, thanks," she said, standing as fatigue washed over her suddenly and completely. "I think I'm going to sleep. Maybe now if I don't hurry back to the cabin."

"I'll go with you," Alexa said.

"I'll walk you to the path." Cole stood too and followed them out of the dining room and into the common area of the lodge.

"How do you feel?" he asked when they were out of earshot.

"Great. Fine. For the first time in . . . forever, pretty much. It's a miracle. I ate and it stayed in."

"Should we make up a certificate?" Alexa asked.

"Maybe. With gold stars would be nice," Kelsey said.

"All right, this way," Cole said, his tone reminiscent of someone trying to get unruly children under control.

He closed the front door of the lodge behind them.

"That was parental of you," she said.

"Yeah, well, it was a fluke," he said, his voice rough.

Kelsey breathed deep, taking in the clean mountain air. Portland was a small city, as they went, but still, the air was different here. "It really is gorgeous."

"I could never leave," Cole said.

Her stomach tightened. He could never leave. And the ranch was six hours from Portland. It would be a long commute. But then, at least they weren't bitter exes. Maybe she could even stay on the ranch during weekends. A little part-time family. And a dude ranch for her son or daughter to play on. It would be . . . neat.

It might work. Maybe.

"I could," Alexa said.

He turned to her. "Now you're just trying to annoy me."

"You can't order Thai food at midnight," Alexa said like he hadn't spoken.

"A shame." He grabbed a flashlight from a shelf on the side of the lodge and handed it to Kelsey. "You're in charge of this. I don't trust her."

Kelsey took the flashlight and tossed Alexa a mock-haughty look. "I'm in charge." She looked back at Cole. "Is this official?"

"Just for the walk up," he said.

"Yeah, don't get too excited." Alexa gave Kelsey an elbow nudge.

"Too late. Drunk with power. And I wield the flashlight." Kelsey waved it around in a circle, casting the light on Cole's chest. She cocked her head to the side. Wow. He had a nice chest. He could be the feature photo for her health-and-wellness article on the ranch.

Man candy.

She shook her head and dropped the focus of the light down to the ground. "Well, thanks for . . . everything. Dinner. And stuff. Showing me the ranch."

Why were things so awkward with him?

"Sure." He put his hands in his pockets. "See you to-morrow?"

"Yeah. Tomorrow."

"Should I step back and allow for a good-night kiss?" Alexa asked.

Both Kelsey and Cole looked at Alexa. "No," they said in unison.

"Sorry. I had to break the tension; it was making me uncomfortable. It reminded me a lot of some of my dates in high school. Just before the guy copped a feel."

"Sorry," Kelsey said, her apology directed at Cole. "She doesn't interact with people very often. It's . . . like a puppy that gets locked in the laundry room all day."

"Should I get her a treat?" he asked.

"Hey," Alexa said, her tone defensive. "Is the treat bacon?"

"Milk-Bone," he said.

"Then I'll pass and head to bed." She looped her arm through Kelsey's, and they turned, stepping off the porch.

"Good night," Kelsey said, turning back for one more ill-advised look at Cole.

He was already halfway into the house, the door closing firmly behind him.

"He's an ass," Alexa said.

"A sexy ass," Kelsey added.

"Well, aren't they all?"

She snorted. "If I'd met one that wasn't, I might have settled down by now."

"Did you see that Tyler guy?"

"The one who was looking at you like you were dessert?" Alexa cleared her throat. "Yeah. That one. Subtle, isn't he?"

"Not so much."

"Ah, the enthusiasm of youth."

"I take it you met him earlier?"

"Yeah," Alexa said. "He gave me a ride in his truck."

"Is that a euphemism for something dirty? Because if it is, I want details."

They both tromped up the wooden steps to the cabin, and Alexa pulled the key out of her pocket. She shoved it in the lock and then pushed the door open. It was warm inside, and now it seemed more cozy than small. It definitely had its appeal.

"Would you really want details of . . . whatever 'gave me a ride in his truck' would translate to in sex lingo?"

Kelsey walked over to the bed and sat on the edge of it. "I have to get my kicks somehow."

"Get them with a man."

"Now? Like . . . while I'm gestating a human being? That would go over well."

"How long has it been, Kels?"

"Too long."

"There hasn't been anyone since Michael, has there?"

Her secret shame. "No."

"Why?" Alexa asked. "I would . . . explode if I went that long without sex. I can't even . . . How?"

"Believe me, I've been close to exploding several times. But I don't . . . I can't. I'm not a one-night-stand girl. You know that. And . . . look, if the guy that supposedly loved me enough to marry me had to satisfy his sex drive somewhere else . . . I don't have a lot of confidence in my appeal."

"You cannot let one rat-bastard ex make you doubt that you're hot."

"Sure I can. Can and have. And do."

Alexa plopped down on one of the dining room chairs. "It's ridiculous, Kelsey. He was stupid. It has nothing to do with you."

"Easy for you to say. You got . . . felt up in high school. No one felt me up. You remember—I was kind of a loser. And then . . . Michael liked me, and I felt validated."

"And losing him . . . unvalidated you?"

Kelsey sucked in a deep breath. "Kind of." It was embarrassing to admit. Lame. And until that moment, she hadn't realized how true it was. "But he was, like . . . the one, and then it turned out he wasn't, and so . . ."

"And so what?" Alexa shrugged.

"And that's . . . I was set. I wanted to be with him forever, and I knew it. I was so sure about it. Look where that got me."

"You were wrong. *So what?* I've been wrong about a lot of guys. I've also been right about a lot of guys, knew that it would never last and went for it anyway. I'm still standing."

"Well, I let it knock me down for a while. But I was just starting to get a handle on the personal stuff, and now there's . . . Cole. So yeah, instead of talking about my screwed-up life, can we talk about Tyler and you *riding in his truck*?"

Alexa made a face. "I don't even want to know what you're thinking. I really did just ride in his truck, over to the lodge. He showed me around. That's all."

"Did you flirt with him?"

"Yes. And I told him we're not having sex."

"Why?"

"Because! Look, I know I talk a big game, but I haven't done that wham-bam-one-time-only stuff in a long time. It's just not . . . appealing anymore. 'Cuz I'm all mature now and crap. Anyway, he's twenty-four."

That sort of surprised Kelsey. Alexa had always been a gleeful hedonist in her mind. Seeing her showing restraint was . . . odd. "I'm a little disappointed."

"Sorry, babe. I'll try harder to live up to your expectations of me as a wild heathen some other night." She stood and stretched. "Which bed do I get?"

"The kiddie one in the other room. I get the princess bed." She lay back on the downy mattress. "I'm pregnant and weak."

"It is going to be a very long nine months," Alexa said, turning and walking into the small bedroom.

"Pffft. It'll feel a lot longer to me!" Kelsey shouted after her.

Yeah. A lot longer. And now, with Cole involved, morning sickness wasn't even the half of it.

* * *

"Can I come in?" Cole called through Lark's closed door, guilt tightening his stomach. He hadn't been as nice to her as he could have been. The whole situation had put him on edge. Hell, life in general had had him on edge for the past few years.

But Lark was only twenty-one. She'd been a teenager when their father died. She'd been a child when they lost their mother. And he'd tried, in his clumsy, ham-handed manner, to step up in some way. More often than not, though, he'd screwed the pooch where she was concerned.

Like he had tonight.

"Yes." Her voice was muffled.

He opened the door and saw her lying facedown on her bed. She sat up and wiped at her cheeks.

"Damn, Lark, I'm sorry. I shouldn't have snapped at you."

She looked at him, blinking her owlish eyes. "You think I'm crying because of you?"

"I was a bastard."

"Well, yeah, but you're my brother. I'm used to it."

"Then why are you upset?"

This wasn't his forte. He kept the ranch going, made sure they could afford to put food on the table. He worked hard. He showed his caring that way rather than via conversation. It was easier for him. But he couldn't just leave her like she was.

"I really, really would rather have my toenails pulled out with a pair of pliers than discuss this with you."

He took a step back. "Are you PMSing or something? Because you're right. I don't want to talk about that. But I could. It's not like I'm not familiar with women and—"

She held up a hand. "For the love of all that is holy, stop now before you embarrass us both. It's not that. I can handle that on my own."

"Then what's up?"

"Did you ever really like someone? And they very

obviously didn't like you back? Shawna excluded. I need you to think of a real human-being-type person for the scenario."

He tried to think. Tried to remember a time in his life when he had referred to sexual attraction as "liking someone." Back before he'd seen the ugly, complicated side of love. "I'm sure . . . I did."

"Oh . . . never. It never happened to you, did it? I'm a genetic oddity."

"Why would you say that?"

"Because you and Cade have . . . women. Lots of them. They buzz around you like flies."

"Nice."

"It's true! Well, not you so much anymore, but that's your choice."

He cleared his throat. "You noticed."

"And guys just don't seem to notice me at all!"

"Forgive me for not being too broken up about that."

"It's Tyler."

"Oh, hell." He leaned back against the wall.

"I just really thought that there was something between us, but he's ogling Alexa like she's the hottest thing he's ever seen. And I just don't get what happened, because everything was really great between us. He's . . . fantastic and . . ."

A knot started to form in Cole's stomach. "Stop right there. He's fired. You're not pregnant or anything, are you? Because I will—"

Lark recoiled. "What? How did I get pregnant in this scenario?"

Cole could see violence in his future. Lots of it. Violence and blood and mayhem and no remorse at all. "I just wanted to be sure before I kicked his ass off the ranch. Possibly ran him out of town on a rail, whatever the hell that means."

"I've never slept with him!"

"But you said . . ." He played everything over slowly. "You didn't say you'd slept with him."

"No."

"I assumed because . . . well, you made it sound like you had something going with him, and in my mind—"

She cut him off. "We did! I mean, he would come in and talk to me while I worked sometimes. And he let me walk through doors first. And he treated me like I was . . . special."

He really had forgotten what it was like to be that young. To be that innocent. That they'd lived through all they had with Lark staying so darn sweet was . . . It had nothing to do with him. He wanted to protect her from everything just then. The truth about life and love.

The truth about their dad.

"You are special, Lark," he said, his chest tightening. "And just because some dumbass doesn't see it doesn't mean it's not true. Anyway, he was just looking. Guys look. All the time."

Lark started gnawing her thumbnail. "I wouldn't know."

"Don't stress about it. You're young. You'll meet someone."

"You haven't met someone. Not a real, good someone anyway. Unless . . . Did you really hook up with Kelsey in Portland?"

"Not your business, kid," he said. "But no."

"You seem to like her a lot."

"She's . . . nice." *And I'm stuck with her.* And he still hadn't figured out quite how to handle it. He needed to handle it. Fix it.

"Maybe you could ask her out."

"You're cute."

She frowned. "That's patronizing."

"I was being sincere. Hold on to it as long as you can, Lark. Life knocks the stuffing out of you eventually. Look at me. Look at Cade. As long as things are simple, keep them that way. As long as unrequited liking is the least of your worries . . . it's not so bad."

"It feels bad."

"I know. Take comfort in the fact that that actually makes you pretty normal."

"Not comforted."

He laughed. "That's normal too."

"Shut up."

"Love you too." He didn't say it often enough. But it had never been easy for him to say.

That earned him a smile. "I do. Love you, you know. Thanks for trying. And thanks for . . . being willing to kill someone for me."

"It's what brothers are for. Night." He turned and walked out of the room, trying to breathe around the tightness in his chest.

Maybe he wouldn't be the world's worst dad, after all. Maybe he could actually do this.

Health and wellness are particularly important during pregnancy. It's important to take time for yourself. Time to puke your guts out. Time to brush your teeth after. Time to have the flavor of the toothpaste permeate your mouth with its overly strong, false minty taste. Time to run back to the toilet and retch your guts out for the second time in ten minutes.

Don't forget to eat a light meal afterward. You'll need something to vomit up later.

Yeah. That wasn't going to print. "Delete, delete, delete," Kelsey mumbled as she highlighted and killed every word she'd just written. Maybe it was too soon to write about pregnancy stuff for the column.

Still, she needed something. The ranch column wouldn't run until the following month, and she needed something in the meantime. Frankly, with her lack of wellness, she wasn't sure what to write. Yes, she felt better now than she had, but only marginally.

She'd managed to eat breakfast, at least.

Lark had shown up at the cabin bright and early with a tray laden with eggs, toast and bacon. Of course, Alexa had inhaled most of it on her way out not to flirt with the sexy, younger ranch hand she was so not going to have sex with.

Kelsey had managed only the toast, but it had actually been good. And it had stayed where it belonged, which was the most important thing.

The baby needed to eat.

Her heart stuttered. It was crazy, but sometimes she forgot about the baby. It was so easy to focus on the insanity of being pregnant. Of finding out that the father wasn't just an anonymous donor but a man who very likely wanted his child.

Sometimes the realization that there was a little life inside of her got lost in all of that.

She put her hand flat on her stomach. Sort of hard to believe it was real. That she would have a baby in just a few months. Would it ever feel real? Maybe when her stomach started getting rounder, when she could feel the baby move. Maybe then. Maybe.

She stood and stretched. She wasn't going to get anything done on the column until she had a topic. Thank God she had a couple of emergency columns finished just in case she ever had trouble coming up with something.

There was a knock at the cabin door, and she closed her laptop and walked across the tiny kitchenette. "Coming."

The little curtain that was there to cover the cut-glass window on the door was swept to the side, and she could make out height and broad shoulders. Which meant it was Cade or Cole. And her money was on Cole.

She opened the door and tried not to let her heart race out of her chest at the sight of him. Cole was basically a stone-cold hottie. And the less sick she felt, the more she noticed.

"Hi."

He inclined his head. "Can I come in?"

"Sure."

He walked into the cabin and filled it up completely. It

wasn't just his height and breadth; it was his presence. She'd noticed that at her house, even through the green haze of illness she'd been lost in.

"I'm going into town today," he said, palms flat on the counter, looking large and masculine and so good, the muscles in his forearms flexing. Her mouth dried.

"Uh-huh."

He looked tastier than toast. Which was a compliment, considering she could eat toast without regretting it later. She was certain tasting Cole would come with quite a bit of regret, though. She really, really couldn't. It would be a disaster. Tasting him. Although, if she wanted to get rid of the guy, sex with her for a few weeks would probably do it.

Men seemed to find her boring.

"I thought you might want to come with me. It would give us a chance to . . . talk more."

"Right."

"Lark was upset about a guy thing. I didn't hurt her feelings. You didn't either."

"Oh. That's really good to know, actually. I felt bad. She seems . . . well, she seems really sweet."

"I'm not entirely sure how she managed to stay sweet, considering she was basically raised by Cade, my dad and me, but yeah, she is. She's special."

The way he talked about Lark . . . it made her chest feel all tight. Made her imagine he would be a really great dad for their child.

"Do you want to get dressed?" he asked.

She looked down at her bright blue-and-gray polka-dot pants. Heat flooded her cheeks. That she hadn't realized what she was wearing was a testament to just how out of it she'd been socially the past couple months. "Oh, yeah. I should get on that. Shocking that I had to use a fertility clinic to have a baby, right? Guys are usually all over this." She rolled her eyes as she turned and headed for the bedroom.

Cole watched her saunter off with an exaggerated shake of her hips. She certainly seemed to be feeling better. He was starting to see some life in her personality. Some color in her cheeks. She was actually sexy, baggy pajama pants aside.

It had just seemed beyond pervy to look while she was so sick. But now that she was feeling better, he felt free to look. She had a damn fine figure. Her tight, long-sleeved gray top had been molded to her full breasts. And his body had noticed.

He hadn't really noticed a woman in a long time, not with more than a brief, passing interest. The whole idea had just turned him off since his marriage and the death of said marriage, followed closely by the slow unraveling of all his father's lies.

Sex had just seemed like too damn much of a complication. A dangerous one. He'd proven he couldn't be trusted to make good judgment calls when his dick was doing the thinking.

But he wasn't feeling immune to Kelsey. Not by a long shot.

She returned a few moments later wrapped in a pair of skinny jeans and a plain pink T-shirt. It was stretched tight over her breasts—a sight he was enjoying way more than he should.

Her thick blond hair was tied back in a ponytail, and her face was bare of any makeup. Which was just fine with him. He liked women. A lot. Made up, dressed down, in a pair of jeans, in nothing. Blond, brunette. He'd never had a type.

At the moment, Kelsey felt a lot like his type.

Hell no. He repeated that mentally more than once so his body would get the message. This was all complicated enough. He was not going to confuse it all more by dwelling on his attraction to her—or by acting on it. Which would be stupid beyond reason.

"Ready," she said, grabbing her purse off a hook by the door. "Let's ride, cowboy."

It was a short trip from Elk Haven Stables to the main street of Silver Creek. The town was small, but clean and lively.

Tourists were everywhere, taking pictures of historic buildings, eating at the quaint restaurants that lined the streets, and in the shops buying crap that they'd never find a practical use for once they returned to their real lives. There were restored classic cars, all parked in a row—a club on a cruise, she imagined. All of it added an air of nostalgia and comfort to the surroundings.

It was different from Bonanza, which, in her opinion, had little to no tourist appeal and an extreme lack of culture.

"This is great," she said as Cole parked his truck on the curb along the main drag. "Different from what I imagined. Because when I think 'small town,' I think . . . depressing. Nothing but greasy spoons and mills."

"Which we have. Trust me. But Silver Creek has sort of become big with retirees. And tourists too. A good thing, because Elk Haven has really benefited from that."

"Do you get a lot of guests?"

"Yes. But we're still just hanging on in the slow season. It warms up in June, so next month we'll start getting guests and then some through ski season. It's cold and miserable here if you aren't into winter sports, but those that are tend to be pretty die-hard. Which works for me."

"Do you ski?" she asked.

"No. I hate snow. It's cold. It's wet. It's hell to try and wade through to get ranch work done in the winter."

"You're not in a great place to hate snow, Mr. Mitchell," she said, getting out of the truck and looking up and down the street. There was a bronze-cast statue of a frolicking foal in front of the post office, and down behind that was a cowboy, frozen in metal, his rope above his head, his horse captured midstride.

"No. But it's home." He smiled, and she felt it echo through her body, a tightening response she couldn't control or stop. The way he said "home." The way he so clearly felt it. And how sexy he looked thinking about it. It made her feel all warm inside. And warm in . . . places.

Not okay, Kelsey. Not okay.

She cleared her throat and looked up at the mountains

that surrounded the town, blue peaks blending into the sky. "I'd love to feel that way about a place."

"You don't feel that way about Portland?"

She followed him down the sidewalk, working to keep up with his long strides. "I like Portland. It's quirky and it's fun. You can get donuts twenty-four hours a day. And there are these little cafés that are word-of-mouth only. One of them makes you feel like you're underwater. Anything you want, they have it, weirder than you could have imagined. It's just . . . It's different from how I grew up. And I love that. But I don't know if it feels like home. But then, home doesn't feel like home either, because I don't really fit in there."

"Why is that? Did your mother drop you on your head, or . . . ?"

She snorted a laugh. "The other theory is that I was delivered by FedEx. Either is plausible."

"Maybe FedEx dropped you in transit." Another one of those smiles.

"Ah, yeah. Funny. Never heard that one."

"Expectation is a funny thing. It either pushes you to try harder so you don't disappoint, or it pushes you in the opposite direction. So, how do you even know what to do with a kid?" he asked, his tone serious.

"I don't know," she said, frowning. "My parents—and I love them dearly—drive me crazy."

"Mine were the best," he said, an odd note in his tone. "My dad was hard. He expected the best from us, but we knew it was because he knew we were capable of greatness. Cade especially. He lived his dream. He went pro. That came from being pushed. At least, that's how I remember him. That's how I knew him when he was alive."

There was something more there, something more he wasn't saying, and not on accident. "I, on the other hand, got pushed in the other direction," she said. "What about your mom?"

"She was the support. She was . . . She made us all strong.

She made sure we knew we were loved. And when she got . . ." He paused, looking past her, his eyes unfocused. "When she died, everything went to hell. We all wish we could have had longer with her. But Lark . . . I really wish Lark could have had longer with both of our parents. She was too young to lose them."

"There's never a good time."

He stopped walking and turned to face her. "We're not going to screw our kid up, are we?"

His face, the seriousness, the depth of concern, stole her breath straight from her lungs. "Do you . . . I mean . . . have you made a decision for sure, or . . . ?"

"I haven't stopped thinking about it. Not since I found out you were pregnant. In some ways it would be simpler to just walk away, but . . . there's not really anything simple about knowing you have a son or daughter somewhere. One you'll never know. I don't think I could live with that, Kelsey." His gaze was intense, his jaw locked tight, a muscle twitching in his cheek.

"I won't ask you to, Cole. I know . . . I know you'll be a good father. I don't know how we're going to do the rest of this, but I do know you'll do a good job. However big of a part you play."

"We have time," he said, turning and walking down the sidewalk again.

She nodded slowly, trying to remember to breathe. "Yes. We do."

"I'm going to the post office. And to get the spider gear I ordered, over at John's."

"I'm not even going to ask you what that is."

He laughed, breaking some of the tension. "Fine."

"Because I don't care."

"I assumed as much." He opened the door to the post office and waited.

She looked at him. "Chivalry."

"Manners. My mom taught me those. My dad taught me to spit."

"How is it you're single?"

"One of the great mysteries of our time."

She walked along behind him, touching the row of PO boxes that lined the wall. Everything in Silver Creek had a sort of rustic charm. Even the gilded, old-fashioned post office boxes.

Cole took his keys out of his pocket and opened his box, pulling out a thick stack of mail before shutting it again. "Exciting times. Looks like Lark got her new *Tech Gear* magazine."

"She's big into computers, huh?"

"Yeah."

"Were either of your parents into computers?"

He frowned and shook his head, turning and walking back to the front door of the post office. "No. We didn't even get one until Lark was maybe . . . seven or so. And then Dad had someone from town come and help out because he didn't want anything to do with it. But Lark learned on her own. She was doing all kinds of cool things with spreadsheets when she was ten. She's always kept us organized."

"And your parents encouraged her?" He held the door open, and she paused, standing beneath his arm.

"They did," he said slowly, "because they recognized that she was good at it."

"So maybe that's the key, then," she said, "encouraging your kids and pushing them, but . . . noticing what they want too."

"A parenting mystery solved. And it's not even noon."

"Maybe we don't suck at this."

"Maybe."

He released the door and they both continued down the street. "Just so you know, John will probably hit on you. He's harmless, but he tries to pick up anything that moves."

"I'm sort of insulted by that. If you're going to tell me that a guy is going to hit on me, follow it up with something like 'He only tries to boink the classiest women he meets.' You know, something to make a girl feel special."

He turned and huffed out a laugh. "You're funny."

"Thanks. I get paid to write my witticisms down, actually. Quite well."

"I know, but you weren't very funny when I first met you."

"Throwing up for fourteen straight days will do that to a girl." She cleared her throat, trying to stop it from tightening with the emotion that was rising in her chest. "And I felt . . . really alone. I don't so much now. It's nice."

Cole cleared his throat. "Good."

The hardware store was just another cute fixture of the town. Every piece of trim was painted a crisp white, while the rest was dark red. It was clean. Cleaner than anything in the city, and certainly cleaner than anything in her hometown.

"This is a bit Stepfordian," she said, wandering through a row of gleaming tools on their way to the counter in the back, which was made from old-fashioned cracker barrels with a slab of marble counter on top of them.

"It adds to the charm," he said. "Actually, in truth, this is becoming a top-dollar place to live. A ranch like Elk Haven would be worth a few million dollars if we decided to sell."

"Really?"

"But we won't. It's been in our family about ninety years. It's more than money. It's . . . it's a legacy."

"So you really aren't just stuck here."

"No. Not even close."

"I guess I tend to picture people as being stuck in small towns. Not . . . choosing to live in them."

"I would feel more stuck in the city. I like having the option to drive to one, but I can't imagine living in one."

"Hmm."

A man walked out from the back room, looking every bit as clean and neat as the store. He was about Cole's age and in good enough shape that she looked a couple times.

"Hey, Cole. Here for the spider gear?"

"Yeah."

"Are you related to this man, miss? Because I can't imagine any other reason you'd be hanging out with an ass like

him." The man—John, she assumed—directed that statement toward her.

"Thankfully no. Not related." The idea made her cringe,
all things considered.

"She's staying at the ranch. Her and a friend. I thought
I'd show her around town. Kelsey Noble, John Campbell."

"Pleasure," he said, sticking out his hand. He gave her
thumb an extra sweep with his when she shook his hand, a
clear invitation to flirtation. Even as out of practice as she
was, she recognized it. And she was pretty proud that
she had.

"Nice to meet you," she said, putting her hand back at
her side, unable to resist wiping off the impression of his
touch on her jeans.

He was cute, but she wasn't even tempted.

He bent beneath the counter and pulled out a small brown
box. "Here you go," he said, sliding it over to Cole. "That
should fix it. Do you need anything else?"

"Lark mentioned putting some pansies in the boxes out
front. Do you have pansies?"

"We just got a bunch of flats in. They're out back if you
want to take a look."

"That'd be good. I should probably call her and find out
what color she wants."

Cole pulled his phone out of his pocket and headed out
the back door. Kelsey made a move to follow him, but John
intercepted her.

"So, where are you from?"

Blah. He was actually chatting her up. And so obviously
too. Did this ever work for men? It must, or they wouldn't
bother.

"I'm from Portland. Well, not *from* from there, but that's
where I live now."

"Yeah?" He smiled, that slow, "don't you want me, baby?"
kind of smile. "What do you do?"

"I write."

"Novels?" he asked, his eyebrows arching.

"No. A column."

He deflated visibly. "Oh. That's interesting."

"It actually is."

"No, no. It is," he said, attempting a recovery. "What do you write about?"

"I'm due in November," she said, the tart words slipping out without her permission.

His eyes widened and he took a physical step away. "Pardon?"

"The baby's due in November."

"Well . . ." He cleared his throat. "Congratulations." He walked quickly back behind the counter and feigned interest in something she couldn't see from where she was standing.

She fought the urge to laugh. That had been . . . way more fun than it should have been.

Cole walked back through a second later with a flat of deep purple pansies and a scowl on his handsome face. "I thought you were behind me."

She smirked and shot a quick glance at John, who was still not looking in her direction. "I was."

"Put it on my tab," Cole said.

John nodded in agreement; at least, she thought he did. It was hard to tell when he was still keeping his head intently focused down so he wouldn't have to look her in the eye again.

She bit her lip and followed Cole as he exited the store. The minute the door swung closed behind them, her laugh escaped, along with an inelegant snort.

"What?" Cole asked.

"You should . . . Oh . . . you were right," she said, wiping her eyes.

"About?"

"He hit on me."

"And?"

"And I told him I was due in November."

Cole looked like she'd slapped him across the face with a fish. His mouth went slack, his eyes wide. An expletive that made a woman walking down the street do a double take escaped his lips.

"I didn't tell him it was yours," she said, rolling her eyes.

"Well, he'll assume."

"Why? I'm a guest at your ranch. As far as he knows I have a husband. And I have a feeling *that* wouldn't have bothered him." She looked away from Cole, focusing on the bronze cowboy. "Anyway, everyone will have to know eventually, won't they?"

"Yeah, eventually," he said. "But not like that."

"I know." She sighed. "I'm not really looking forward to everyone finding out. Well, not your family so much as mine. But I already weathered Alexa's judgment, and I lived."

"She doesn't seem to like me much."

"She's protective."

He let out a breath. "Sorry. About freaking out."

"You're allowed a few freak-outs. This is big."

"It is. But I've made my choice. Yeah. I have. I've made it. I want to be involved. Not just a little bit, but as much as I can be."

Kelsey's stomach tightened. "I . . . I don't know how it's all going to work out."

"I don't either. But I think we can figure something out."

"We can go to the truck if you want. So you're not holding the pansies."

He looked down, like he was surprised to still see the flat of flowers there. "Right."

She followed him back to the truck and climbed into the passenger side, waiting while he deposited the flowers in the bed. He got into the driver's side and closed the door. He put the key in the ignition but didn't turn it on.

"We'll make it work," he said, not looking at her.

She looked down at her hands, a lump forming in her chest. "I . . ." And she realized that they had to. Because he was her child's father. It didn't work to pretend that he didn't have a link. Not for her. Because she felt a connection, an attachment, already. And she knew he felt something too. "Yeah. We'll make it work."

They would figure out a way. They would be mature and

rational. She wouldn't think about the way his smile made her stomach tighten and made it hard for her to breathe. Because this whole thing was bigger than they were, and she had to remember that.

Yes, they would make it work. And hopefully they wouldn't kill each other in the process.

CHAPTER

Eight

"You look nice today."

Alexa turned, scowl at the ready, and treated Tyler to a deadly glare. "Not happening."

She was already unnerved in all the wide-open space, and having him sneak up on her like that when she'd dared to venture out into the corral area just seemed cruel.

"I can't compliment you?" he asked, arching one eyebrow.

"Not with that tone, you can't. I've been around, little boy. I know the games. I know exactly what a man means when he says 'You look nice today.' And I'm not falling for it."

He cocked his head to the side, a half smile curving his lips, blue eyes that were too damn enticing for her own good glinting. "Maybe that's how it's been in your experience. I'm sure you know more than I do, simple country boy that I am." He said it dryly, none of that put-on cowboy charm from the day before. "But where I come from, a man tells a woman she looks nice when she does. Because not doing it would be a crime. Especially when the woman looks as beautiful as you do."

That successfully sucked her retort right out of her brain.

Alexa couldn't remember the last time a man had left her speechless, if ever. She was the alpha female. If she wanted a guy, she got him. If she didn't or shouldn't, she pushed him away. And he listened.

But Tyler was . . . charming. And it was doing something to her. She didn't get it. Not in the least.

"Then I accept," she said when she could finally grab hold of enough words to form a sentence. "At face value. So, if you're keeping score or trying to . . . you know, well, don't think that it worked. Because I am taking it as is and not . . . um. You know."

"Got it," he said.

"So, what is there to do around here?" she asked, surveying the corral, which was surrounded by stables. And dust. Dust that she bet, with the first few raindrops, turned into deep, slick mud. The thought should have totally squicked her out. Not filled her head with images of Tyler with mud on his jeans up to his thighs . . . his shirt inexplicably discarded, muscular chest splattered with just a little bit of—

"Seriously," she said, desperate to drag her mind out of the gutter. "Is there anything to do?"

"I manage to fill my days up. But then, I have to work."

"I work."

"What do you do?"

"Advertising. In New York."

"You work on concepts for commercials?" he asked.

"Print ads, online ads, television, buses, billboards. Anywhere you can stick an ad, I can figure out how to make people want to look at it and buy the product."

"Sounds interesting."

"It is. I love it."

"And you like living in the city."

"Love it." She looked around the corral. "I mean, this is its own thing. There's nothing wrong with it, but it's really not . . . me."

"Want to see something cool?"

She narrowed her eyes. "If this has anything to do with you undoing that belt buckle . . . I've seen it all before."

"Nope. Sorry to disappoint you. You seem to think about that sort of thing a lot when I'm around. Interesting." He turned and started walking toward the stable.

She sputtered and followed behind him, trying to dodge the soft spots on the ground out of fear for her leather boots, which were more suited to sidewalks than dirt. "Now wait a minute. You're the one thinking about . . . about sex."

He stopped and turned, frowning. "I don't think I've brought it up once. You, on the other hand . . ."

"Well . . . well . . . hell." She stopped walking. She'd assumed . . . Her stomach curled in, humiliation assaulting her. She'd been attracted to him. Wildly so, from the moment she'd first seen him, and she'd jumped to conclusions. Conclusions that had apparently been way off the mark.

Or he was screwing with her. Either way, she was the one with her foot in her mouth. Bastard.

"Don't be embarrassed." He reached out and brushed his thumb over her burning cheek.

She backed away. "I'm not. I don't do embarrassed."

"Could have fooled me." He turned away again. "Now, do you want to see something cool or not?"

She was grateful for the reprieve. And annoyed that she was grateful. "It'd better be really good, Tyler."

"Oh, it is."

"Oh. My. Is Alexa on a horse?" Kelsey's jaw dropped when they pulled up to the corral.

"It appears that she is." Cole put the truck in park and killed the engine. "Is she not into horses?"

"She's not into nature so much. Or animals of any kind. Or babies. Anything that could possibly get her dirty or wake her up in the middle of the night. Men excluded."

Cole laughed. "Well, she seems to be doing all right now."

They both got out of the truck and walked over to the corral. Tyler was in there with her, keeping an eye on things as Alexa maneuvered Miss Kitty around a few widely spaced barrels, her lips pursed, her concentration intense.

Cole leaned against the fence, dropping his arms over the top rail. That simple action was more interesting than watching Alexa engage in the world's slowest barrel race. There was something about Cole. From his tight jeans to his belt buckle, his buttoned-up shirt tucked in. His muscular build and strong profile. He looked like he belonged. Like he was a part of the land, the ranch.

She'd never felt at home like that anywhere. She was starting to wonder if Kelseys had no natural habitat.

"Ride 'em, cowgirl," he called out, a grin, a real one, brightening his face. Her stomach tightened. He was the father of her baby.

Would their baby look like him? If he was a boy, she hoped he did. Cole was so handsome, tall, broad shouldered. And Cole could teach him things. Things she couldn't.

For the first time, she was glad about the mix-up. Glad there was someone else. Which seemed chicken and wimpy. Because she'd made the decision on her own, and now she didn't have to follow through on her own.

And part of her was relieved. A part of her that was getting bigger.

Cole looked at her. "What?"

She blinked rapidly, realizing she'd been caught staring. "Nothing. Well, not nothing. I was wondering . . . who the baby would look like."

He swallowed visibly, his Adam's apple bobbing with the motion. "Oh."

"Yeah. I'm . . . getting ahead of things a little bit."

"I think that's normal," he said, keeping his voice low. "If we had . . . planned it together, wouldn't we be wondering about things like that?"

Her eyes caught his and held, sending a wave of heat through her body, all the way down to her toes. "Yeah." She turned her focus to Alexa. "They're going to hook up."

"You think?"

Yes. Focus on them. Not on Cole. Not on all the handsome. "She got on a horse for the man. She wants him."

"Poor Lark."

"What about her?"

Cole smiled ruefully. "She has a thing for Tyler. But please, don't tell Alexa. Because honestly, if he wants to hook up, I don't want it to be with my sister. She's too . . . innocent."

"Plus, she's your sister."

"Well, there's that. But honestly, she's sweet. She's not . . . She's managed to come through losing her parents, watching Cade and me go through the crap we've gone through. Hell, she had to share a house with my ex for two years, and she was . . . she was a bitch. Not just to me, to Lark. Lark lived through all of that without losing her optimism, her ability to see good in people. I don't want anyone to take that from her. A minor heartbreak would be better than one that happened after some big love affair."

Kelsey snorted a laugh. "Yeah. Those suck."

"Not one for big love affairs, huh?"

"No. Not exactly."

"I'll stand with you on that one. Love's just a kind of crazy they make Hallmark cards for."

"Another thing we have in common." A good thing too. He was practical like she was. Not to be swayed by feelings or attraction or . . . anything. Except he was looking at her very intently, and it was making her feel all languid and weak-kneed and . . .

"Check that out!" Alexa crowed as she dismounted the horse. "I barrel raced."

Thank God.

"Against no clock. Really slowly." Kelsey gave her two thumbs-up. "I think you won."

Alexa responded with a bright smile and a different, one-fingered signal. "Whatever. I did awesome."

Tyler smiled at her. "You did."

"See?" Alexa shot back. "I did."

"Well, I'm not getting on a horse, so you beat me by a long shot."

Alexa did a small, uncoordinated dance in place. "I kicked butt!"

"You're insane," Kelsey said.

"So what? I rode a horse."

"All right, enjoy your moment of contentment."

Alexa sauntered over to the fence. "So, where have you two been?"

"Town," Kelsey and Cole answered together.

Alexa's eyes widened. "There's a town? Are there sidewalks? I miss sidewalks."

"Drama queen," Kelsey said.

"So? It's part of my charm."

"It is." Tyler walked up to stand beside Alexa, and Kelsey was shocked to see a flush of color stain her friend's cheeks.

"Well, Tyler, if you think so . . . you're welcome to babysit her anytime you like," Kelsey said.

"Noted."

There was a strange sort of normalcy to the whole exchange. And Cole appreciated it, given how weird and upside down everything had been for the past few years. Starting with Shawna, to the revelations about his father and on to the baby.

"Hey." Cole turned at the sound of Cade's voice coming from behind him.

"Hey."

"Got a minute?"

He looked at Kelsey and Alexa, who were busy engaging in banter with Tyler. "Yeah." He touched Kelsey's arm and felt a shock, like static electricity. But this went deeper, beneath his skin. "I'm going to go see what Cade needs. See you later?"

She licked her lips, the action sending a different kind of electricity down south. What a time for his libido to make a reappearance. "Yeah. See you later."

Cole followed Cade around behind the truck. "What's up?"

"I was looking at the books, and there's like fifteen thousand dollars missing. I don't know what it went to. It's just gone." Cade held out the printed sheet of paper, evidence of the discrepancy. Which Cole didn't need to see, because he knew it was gone.

His mouth went dry. The money he'd used to start paying off his father's debts. The house his father's bit on the side had lived in had already been repossessed. All that was left was for the collectors to start in on the estate in Silver Creek. Unless Cole could get it paid off. And he didn't want Cade to know how bad it was. To know that the dad they'd looked up to, the dad they'd loved more than anything, had been a lying, cheating, gambling bastard.

"What were you doing looking at the books?"

"I know you think I'm half illiterate, but the fall from the horse broke my leg, not my head. I wanted to check and see how things were going. This is my inheritance too."

"Why didn't you just ask if you wanted to see the financials?"

"Look, Cole, the money stuff has always been you; it's really not my thing. If the ranch needs money—"

"It doesn't. We have money."

"Then what's this about?"

"Nothing. Shit gets lost sometimes."

"Fifteen thousand dollars? It gets lost? Cole, you would drop-kick my ass to Idaho if I lost fifteen grand. Now be straight with me."

"I messed up." It was a lie. "I must have made a mistake in the accounting. I'm sorry. I'm sure it's there, or never was, or something."

Cade crossed his arms over his chest. "This is a big operation. If you need some help keeping track of things—"

"I don't need help. I have a bunch of new contracts lined up with the rodeo association. New stock to get put into the circuit. And whatever this discrepancy is . . . it's just a paper mistake. It's nothing big." He grabbed the papers out of Cade's hand and stalked back to the house. He would get the truck later. For now he needed the walk.

Shit.

He opened the door to his office and slammed it shut for good measure, throwing the paper and pen down onto the floor. He should have known there was no way to keep it from Cade, but damn it, he wanted to. Why did everyone have to have their childhood crash down around their ears? Why should everyone know what a lie their lives had been?

Why should everyone know that the man who had been there for them, who had loved them and guided them, had abandoned another child? Had barely sent them cards for Christmas. That the man had betrayed their mother with another woman for at least ten years of their marriage.

A marriage that had been Cole's inspiration to try to do right by his wife. That had led him to allowing himself, and his family, to get walked all over by that same wife so he could try to keep some peace. The wife who was the reason for the sperm mix-up fiasco.

Man, people tried to blame a lot of crazy stuff on their parents, but he really had a right to.

He swore and pressed his fingers into his temples. He would have to tell Cade eventually. It was one of the many things that sucked about having his brother living in his pocket. He was right; this was his inheritance too.

That meant he'd inherited the cosmic disaster their dad had left behind, same as Cole. It meant they would have to have some sort of honest talk about it.

But not yet. Not just yet.

Kelsey and Alexa had dinner in the lodge every night that week. But Kelsey didn't talk to Cole very much. After he'd left the corral the other day, he'd come back in a surly mood, and he had been distant ever since.

On the bright side, though, she'd been able to eat every day that week, and she was wondering if the morning sickness had run its course. Sure, there was the odd fit of nausea if the wind kicked up when she walked by the feed barn that held the silage for the cows, but otherwise, she was starting to feel like herself again.

Like herself, but not. Because she doubted if she would ever feel like she had before she'd gotten pregnant. Because everything was changing. Everything in her and around her.

She looked up from her chicken potpie—chicken that

she could eat without dire consequences—and at Cole, who was content to let the ranch hands BS and tell stories while he said nothing. Just as he'd done at dinner every night recently.

"Dessert?" Jason, the man behind the fabulous food, came out of the kitchen with a tray laden with cobbler.

There was a round of yeses, but Kelsey's stomach rebelled. She was at the end point of her happy eating. Any more and she would be sorry. Of course, she'd be hungry five minutes after she left the dining room, but she'd bought a bag of cookies the day she and Cole had gone to town, so now she was armed with sugar for emergencies.

"I'm going to get some fresh air," she whispered to Alexa, who was engaging Tyler in conversation. Alexa had been talking almost exclusively to Tyler all night. And Kelsey had a feeling it had been the cause of Lark's early departure from dinner.

It made her feel bad for poor Lark. But if a guy wasn't that into you, there was no point trying to force it. That just led to broken engagements and ugly fights that just weren't worth the hassle.

"Do you need me to come with you?" Her friend looked genuinely concerned.

"No. I'm fine. Stay and flirt."

"I'm not flirting," Alexa hissed.

"Yeah, you are. But it's okay. I'll look the other way and pretend it's not happening." Kelsey stood from the table and walked out of the dining room. There was so much activity, she doubted anyone would really notice if she slipped out for a while.

That was one of the things she liked about the ranch. There was so much activity. So many people. She was from a big family, so she was used to that to a certain degree, but in her family, it was different.

This "family"—because whether they were blood related to one another or not, they felt like a family—was populated with people who came from all kinds of different backgrounds. People who were headed in different directions but who were together for now. And who accepted one another just as they were.

There was no crushing weight of expectation. No sense of feeling odd or out of place. Somehow, everyone at the Mitchells' dining table managed to be different from her without ever making her feel like their differences were wrong.

So unlike her family.

She wandered through the living area of the lodge and through the back doors onto an expansive wooden deck that overlooked the pastures. It was dark out, nothing visible but the inky black shape of the mountains backing the deep blue sky, which was dotted with big, bright stars.

She breathed in deep, feeling the air wash through her. The simple act of breathing here was like a baptism. It made her feel clean, refreshed. Like she was starting over every time.

She liked it. It made all the baggage she'd carried around for so long seem lighter. Seem unimportant.

"You okay?"

She turned and saw Cole standing in the doorway, his broad frame silhouetted by the lights shining from the house. "Fine. Just . . . wanted to get out for a minute."

"I smell rain," he said, walking out onto the deck and coming to stand beside her, leaning against the rail. "It's coming soon. Do you smell it?"

She closed her eyes and breathed in again. "I actually do."

"I actually like rain. I don't really like the heat. Fall is one of my favorite times of year. The leaves don't turn dramatically. Most of the trees just stay green. But it reminds me of my mom baking pie, of cold mornings, before snow, with frost on the ground."

"That's how it was for us too," Kelsey said. "Well, all of us girls would bake pie with our mom. I always managed to mess it up. Like, I'd put the apple on the peeler-corer thing kind of wonky and then seeds would get in it, and I wouldn't notice because I was always thinking about something else."

"A daydreamer?"

"Guilty," she said.

"What were you dreaming about?" he asked.

She looked at him, her breath catching when she saw his expression. Serious. Intent. "I . . . At the time, I was dreaming of a lot of things. Moving to Portland. Being a writer. Wearing black."

He laughed. "Wearing black?"

"Yes, wearing black. Because I thought of it as being very dramatic and artistic. Don't laugh. My mom said I looked like a Goth, and she always made me wear one article of clothing with color."

He shook his head.

"Right?" she said. She hesitated. "And then of course I was dreaming a lot about marrying Michael."

"And who was Michael?"

"My boyfriend. I started dating him my last year of high school. We moved to Portland together after graduation. We went to college instead of getting married, which my parents thought was . . . crazy. Then we moved in together, which my parents thought was even crazier. We got engaged. And everything was going just how I wanted it."

"Obviously it didn't keep going how you wanted it, or you'd be married to him."

She snorted. "Yeah. Obviously. Well, I might have thrown my diamond engagement ring at him when I came home early from work to find him in our bed with another woman. Very naked, very sweaty and doing something he never seemed to want to do for me."

"Did the ring hit him?"

"Right in the ass. Less satisfying than it sounds, since I was pretty distraught and the ring was so pitifully small, it didn't have enough weight to do much of anything. But I kicked him out, because hey, it was my house. I was the only one of the two of us who'd managed to get a good job after college, and the house was in my name. Thankfully."

"I'm sorry."

"It's not my favorite memory, but I've moved on." *Liar.* "I'm really, really glad I didn't marry him." That was true.

She didn't regret the loss of him. But the fact that she hadn't had a relationship since definitely meant she hadn't moved on.

Cole studied Kelsey's face. She didn't look sad talking about her ex. Talking about her family made her look sad, wistful. Talking about him just seemed to irritate her.

"He was an idiot."

He heard himself say the words before he realized he'd even thought them. But they were true. Any man who had Kelsey in his bed and couldn't keep it in his pants around another woman was definitely an idiot. He'd had his faults as a husband, but staying faithful hadn't been a problem. And Kelsey—she was the kind of woman male fantasies were made of. At least his. At least now that she didn't look like she was on death's door. Not that it mattered, since he wasn't ever going to go there. But it was the truth, and while he *was* abstaining, he wasn't blind.

"Or he was unhappy and he was doing what he could do to try to get out of it. Either way, we weren't meant to be. Which is great, because when I am at the point in my life that requires me to clean orange Cheetos fingerprints off of my couch, they'd better be from kids and not my husband. With Michael, there was no guarantee."

"I know a little something about ill-fated romance," he said, looking down at his hands. "I met Shawna when I was twenty-six. And I was nuts for her from moment one. She was . . . fun and wild and all these things I'd never really been. Growing up on the ranch, being the oldest, I'd always had a lot of responsibility. Not much time for crazy. Not like . . ."

"Not like Cade."

"Yeah. Anyway . . . I met Shawna and I was done. After dating for a full two weeks, I thought . . . 'Why not be crazy for once?' I was just . . . consumed by her, you know? By attraction, lust, but I thought it was love. So we drove to Vegas and got married. I pretty much knew it was a dumbass move a couple months in, but . . . marriage. It was important. Sacred. So I tried to make it work. Slept on the couch a lot. Banked some sperm to try to keep her happy while I delayed having kids. Then my dad died and things got really busy for me running the ranch. She got mean and possessive of the estate, which she thought should have been ours—code for *hers*—since I was the oldest."

He let out a long breath. "About the time she screamed at Lark for 'taking' something that had belonged to my mother—a necklace Shawna felt entitled to—I kicked her ass out of my house and told her I never wanted to see her again."

"Wow. What a—"

"Yeah. I know."

"And right after your dad died, that—"

"Yeah, I know. Anyway, I had my family. They're all I need."

"Speaking of your family . . . when are we going to tell them?"

"Soon," he said, his gut seizing up at the thought.

It was quiet for a moment, then he felt Kelsey shift beside him. "Do they know . . . do they know you banked your sperm?"

"Did I tell them that I banked my sperm to keep my crazy-ass wife happy? No," he said. "There is no easy way to start that conversation with your brother and sister."

Kelsey laughed and the sound moved through him, made the hairs on his arms stand up, made his heart beat faster.

"No. I guess not. Sidenote: I've never used the word 'sperm' in polite, or impolite, conversation so many times in my life as I have with you over the past few weeks."

"It's not really the best focal point for a conversation."

She wrinkled her nose. "No. Not really."

She turned away from the view and leaned up against the rail. Her breasts pushed against her top, round and so very enticing. She made him feel. Made him feel lust, desire. She made him feel like a man again. Reminded him why being a man was so damn good.

The realization made his chest knot up tight.

After the confrontation with Cade about the money, after the years of trying to just hold everything together, trying to get through the day, she made him feel like he might want to do something crazy again.

Nothing very honorable. Nothing that extended too far beyond wanting to see her naked. And that just couldn't happen. There was no ignoring the complications, the circumstances. Circumstances that were bound to create some heightened feelings. Heightened desires, which he had a feeling were his problem.

"Your fiancé was a moron," he said, because it was true, regardless of whether or not he could ever act on his attraction to her.

She looked up at him, blue eyes wide, full lips parted. "How do you know that?"

"Because that's a jackass way to behave. Cowardly. I don't have any respect for a man who cheats on a woman he's made a commitment to. You're smart. You're . . . probably really funny when you're not sick and grumpy."

"Thanks."

"You're probably prettier than she was."

"You don't know that."

"Well, I'm not blind."

He let himself look at her curves. Really look. Her breasts—breasts that made his body ache—her slim waist, rounded hips. It was easy to imagine just how perfectly they would fit in his hands. He could grip her hips, pull her to him, let her feel the effect she was having on his body.

And damn, was she having an effect. And just for a moment, he wanted to enjoy it. Not deny it. Just for a little bit. He wouldn't do anything. He would just look. He would just let himself feel the effect she was having on him.

Harmless.

She blushed—actually blushed—the light from the house revealing the spots of pink as they bled across her cheeks.

"Thank you. I appreciate the compliment. I've felt . . . well, less than attractive lately," she said, biting her lip. He wanted to be the one biting that lip.

The desire was suddenly so strong, and he'd spent so long denying that part of himself, that he nearly lost every ounce of his control then and there. He tightened his hands into fists, holding them firmly at his sides.

Control. He wasn't some horny teenage kid. He was thirty-three years old, and he ought to have control over his body. He knew what happened when people lost control. They married the first person who came along. Or they cheated on their wife. And he was not that guy.

But damn. She made him forget all that.

He relaxed his hands, lifted one and tucked a strand of wispy blond hair behind her ear. She didn't move; she only looked at him. He wondered if she felt it too. The attraction. He couldn't feel anything else. His body was wound so tight, he was afraid he would explode then and there. If she touched him . . . he would be gone.

His cock hardened and he shifted, trying to relieve the pressure as the seam on his jeans bit into his erection.

She swallowed, her eyes dropping to his lips. And he knew she felt it too.

It was tempting. It was very tempting. To lean in and taste those lips. To press her soft body against his. To find that part of himself that he'd been missing for so long. For once, when he thought of sex, he didn't automatically think of getting yelled at or manipulated. Didn't think of where that road had led in the past. Everything, every other experience, seemed to be gone. He just thought of how soft Kelsey's skin would be.

But it was stupid too. Because she was pregnant with his baby. Because about the only thing that made that situation tenable was the fact that they were able to be civil to each other. The fact that, unlike most people who had children together and weren't couples, they didn't have baggage. They didn't have a flame of love or desire that had burned out.

They had the potential to be friends. To be partners in the raising of their child. And sex would screw it up. Big-time.

He lowered his hand and took a step back. "Are you ready to go back inside?"

She shook her head and blinked as if she were coming out

of a trance. He imagined he looked a lot the same. Only maybe a bit more like he'd been smacked upside the head with a two-by-four.

"Yeah. That's . . . fine. I . . ." She clasped her hands in front of her. "Are you okay?"

"What?" he asked, ignoring the throbbing in his body. "Fine."

"You've been . . . I've barely talked to you over the past few days. And I'm leaving on Sunday."

"I know."

"So, I just wanted to make sure you . . . that you hadn't changed your mind."

"About?"

"About the baby."

The arousal that had been coursing through his veins abated.

Hello, reality. "Do you want me to change my mind?"

"I . . . no."

That was progress. "Good. And no. No, I won't change my mind. Ever. A child isn't like a puppy. I won't ever just decide that being a dad's not for me. Because"—his throat tightened—"because I realized that whether or not I choose to be in his life, I am this baby's father. Not being around . . . I would still be his dad. Just his deadbeat dad that was too damned scared and selfish to be there for him." Like his father had done to the other child. The other child he'd never known. Who was younger than him and Cade, older than Lark. A kid his father had ignored because he'd been too afraid to face up to his mistakes.

She shook her head. "I wouldn't have seen it that way. But now that you've decided to do this . . . I'm really glad. To have your support. To have your help. I think I'll need it. And I think you're going to be a really good dad."

He snorted. "Don't speak too soon. There will be plenty of chances for me to screw things up."

"So, I'll see you tomorrow, then."

"Yeah." His heart rate picked up. She really did make him feel more like a kid than a grown man. Although the desire she made him feel was certainly a man's desire. "Do you want to have lunch with me tomorrow?"

"Lunch?"

"Yeah. A picnic. I want to show you this place . . . I'll show you. What sounds good to you?"

She puckered her lips and twisted them to the side. "Hmm . . . roast beef sandwiches? Doable?"

"More than. Beef we've got."

"Then it's a date," she said. "I mean . . . not a *date* date. Clearly we don't need . . . There's no need for that. That's not what I meant."

"No, I know. But yeah, it's . . . a plan."

"A plan."

"See you then."

"Yeah."

And as long as he could keep his body in check, things might keep going smoothly between them.

"You're leaving soon," Tyler said.

Alexa stiffened as Tyler moved behind her. Her entire body was on red alert. How did he do it? How did he make her react the way he did? She liked men. She liked sex. But she always had control over herself. Over whom she wanted and when.

He took it from her. This stupid twenty-four-year-old kid who really, really didn't seem like a kid at all.

She turned from where she was standing on the front porch. She was holding the flashlight, ready to head back to the cabin, hoping Kelsey would be joining her at some point. But she'd seen Cole follow her friend out onto the back deck, and she wasn't about to interrupt that.

"Yeah, I know we are."

"I'll be sorry to see you go."

"Aha. So it wasn't all in my mind."

He wasn't detoured by her joke. His face stayed serious, his eyes intent on hers. "Of course it wasn't. I'm going to kiss you now, all right?"

"Uh . . ." All of the breath left her body. "No. No, it's really not all right."

He backed away. "Suit yourself."

"No! I mean . . . Oh, please, just kiss me."

He leaned in, his lips touching hers. Heat exploded in her stomach—that desire, that intense, uncontrollable desire burning like a gasoline-fueled fire.

When they parted, they were both breathing hard.

"Do you have a room? Somewhere private? I don't have . . . I don't know when Kelsey will come back to the cabin."

He nodded. "Yes. I do. But not tonight." He tipped his hat and smiled, turning away from her.

"What?"

He turned back to her. "I said 'not tonight.' I haven't even taken you out to dinner; I'm not taking you to bed. And if the men you usually date would be willing to do something like that . . . I'd reevaluate."

"What if I want to?"

"I don't," he said, shrugging.

"Liar."

"Not lying. I don't do casual sex. But I do like you. A lot. So if you want to have dinner with me tomorrow, away from the ranch, I'd love to take you out."

"I . . ." Alexa's stomach fluttered, and she had no idea when her stomach had learned a trick like that. "Yes. I'd . . . I'll have dinner with you."

"Then I'll see you tomorrow." He inclined his head and walked away from her, leaving her standing there, gripping the flashlight.

"Son of a bitch," she whispered.

CHAPTER

Ten

"I didn't know they made picnic baskets like that," Kelsey said when Cole showed up at the cabin the next day.

"Huh." He lifted the wicker basket up to his eye level. "What else would you bring on a picnic?"

"Tupperware? I don't know. That's what my mom did."

"Well, my mom had to bring bigger containers for food when the family ate outdoors. But she used this when she and Dad . . ."

He trailed off, his stomach tightening at both the memory and the unintended comparison. He wasn't trying to force himself and Kelsey into a version of his family. Not even close. They just needed to be able to figure something out. Just . . . anything would do for now.

Anyway, that wasn't real. It had all been a lie, a facade. He wondered if his mother had ever known. He hoped not. Damn, but he hoped not.

"I like it," she said, reaching out and brushing her fingers along the braided wood. "It's nice. Although, as long as you brought roast beef, you could have wrapped it in a brown paper bag and it would have looked good to me."

"Wrapped in brown paper, huh? Like porn?"

"Food porn. I'm hungry."

"It's an improvement from how sick you were when we first met."

"I don't think I'll ever live that down. I was such a disgusting blob. And you witnessed it." She grimaced and stepped off the porch. "Not my finest moment."

"I felt bad for you; I wasn't really thinking about how you looked."

"Even worse. I was reduced to a pitiable creature instead of a sexual object. No woman likes to hear that."

"I didn't think women liked being treated like sex objects either."

"It's nice to be considered a sexual being, though."

"Ah. Well . . ." He cleared his throat, a strange kind of heated discomfort filling him. "How about we start with 'person currently incubating my child' and work our way up from there?"

She laughed. "Yeah, all things considered, maybe we should begin there."

"If we just walk around through here, there's a picnic table set up with a nice view. Does that work for you?"

"I follow the meat. And by that I mean the actual meat and not a clumsy euphemism for . . ." Her cheeks flushed. "Well, you get the idea. I'm hungry."

"Right. This way."

He turned and followed the path that ran behind the cabins, winding around the mountain and stopping at a clearing. The picnic table was set in a flat space, overlooking the fields and mountains. He loved this place. It was his legacy, the legacy of his family. And for most of his life, he'd believed his family history to be as idyllic as the setting.

Ah, well, at least he still had the mountains.

Kelsey sat down on the bench, her head tilted back, blond hair spilling over her shoulders. "Gorgeous," she said, bathing in the sun. The picture she made, the light casting a glow over her skin, was much more enticing than the scenery.

He looked away and turned his focus back to the food.

"Yeah, it's not bad." He set the picnic basket on the table and opened it, taking out sandwiches and cans of soda. "Diet?"

She tilted her head and arched an eyebrow. "You saying I'm fat, Mitchell?"

"There is no good way for me to answer that question," he said. "So I'm not going to." He sat across from her and picked his sandwich up, filling his mouth with a bite and giving himself even more of an excuse to ignore her question.

"Sneaky."

He swallowed. "It's been said."

"By?"

"No one. But I suppose it's applicable since I've had a woman staying here for two weeks who happens to be carrying my baby and only you, me and Alexa know about it."

"That's not all that sneaky, Cole. I asked you to keep it to yourself."

Cole rubbed the back of his neck, thinking of his earlier confrontation with Cade. He was getting to be a professional omitter of the truth. And that wasn't who he wanted to be. It wasn't who he'd been raised to be, which was a man of integrity, a man of purpose who saw to his commitments and kept his word.

At this point, it was just a joke. Everything he'd been raised to believe was possible about a man and his integrity was a lie.

"If that was the beginning and end of it, it wouldn't be so bad."

"What else?" she asked.

Anger, unreasonable and hot, shot through him, and because Kelsey was the only person there, because his father was dead and he was trying to protect Lark and Cade, and because it was better than the tightening in his groin he felt when she was near, he unleashed it on her. "I didn't ask you for hand-holding and therapy, Kelsey. You don't really need my life's story, do you?"

"No. I don't need it, but I thought you might give it."

"Why?"

She let out a long breath. "I don't know, Cole, maybe because we're in this . . . unreal position, because we've been forced together. But then, here's the beauty of the situation. I don't expect a damn thing from you. I don't know you. I don't know who you're supposed to be, who you want to be. So, if you want to vent and just let it out, why not do it with me? Lord knows I've done it with you. I'll do it more. I'm scared. I'm sick. I want to cry, like . . . all the time. I'm so afraid of what my family is going to say when they find out. I'm afraid I'm going to screw this up. I'm afraid I might be ruining your life and mine and it's too damn late to do anything about it. There. Honesty. You go."

He cleared his throat and shifted his weight, looking down at a spot on the table. "There's just . . . There's a lot of stuff left over from my dad's death that no one knows I'm dealing with and it's getting to be . . . it's getting to be too much."

"Ask for help," she said. Like it was that simple.

He looked back up at her. "Because you're so good at asking for help?"

She shook her head. "No. I suck at asking for help. But I'm outside the situation looking in, so it's easy for me to tell you to do it."

He laughed, a bitter, hollow sound. "Well, you're honest, Kelsey Noble. I'll give you that. You're a pain, but you're honest."

"I *am* honest. And I'm serious. Cole, there's no shame in needing some help. It sounds like when you lost your dad, you lost . . . It sounds like you lost a lot."

"We did. Lark was only seventeen. Cade was on the circuit at the time, and I think he felt a lot of guilt over being gone. Way more than he should have."

"And you were left holding it all up."

"Yeah. But that's not the hard part, Kelsey." He stood, pacing in front of the table. It wasn't easy to talk about this. Which was why he never did it. "I was . . . I was left as the executor of my father's estate. Everything was in order at first—at least it seemed like it was. We got the ranch divided equally between us, though we all decided we wouldn't sell. We got a decent-size chunk of change, which we all decided to reinvest and use to reinvigorate the ranch. Another thing that pissed my wife off."

"She wanted money."

"Yeah."

"And losing her while you were going through all that—"

"Was the best thing that ever happened to me."

"Then why did you stay married to her for so long?"

He shook his head. "That's the other thing about my dad. My dad taught me that a man honored his commitments. A man never walked away. A real man to me was my dad. He stayed with my mom until she died. Then he finished raising us. He was tough, but he was fair. He was my hero, Kelsey."

He sat back down, energy just draining out of him. This, thinking about it, always left him feeling tired.

"Losing him must have been so hard."

"It was." He swallowed and looked down at his hands. "In some ways, I feel like I lost him twice. Lark and Cade don't know this, but a few months ago a debt collector tracked me down. My father owed some money for gambling—insane, since as far as I knew he didn't gamble. He also owed some money to a bank for a car they'd been unable to repossess. And our inheritance should have gone to pay these debts. Only, we didn't know about them. In part because my father hadn't used his real name. It took nearly four years for them to connect the man he said he was in Portland with the man who lived here in Silver Creek."

"Oh . . . Cole . . . that's . . . that's—"

"It gets worse. I also found out that my father had an affair. And that the affair resulted in a child. He bought them a house and a car—part of his debt."

"Was the child . . . I mean, was it after your mother—"

"No," he said, his voice rough. "His daughter, who I haven't met, is older than Lark. Younger than Cade and me."

"And you don't want to tell them because . . ."

"Because it doesn't change a damn thing. It doesn't fix it. I can't even yell at the old man, Kelsey; he's dead. I can't ask him why. I can't make it right. He was there for us. He taught us. What about her? He didn't teach her. He wasn't there for her."

"Have you tried to get in touch with her?"

He nodded. "Yeah. She never wrote back. She's probably angry, and she has a right to be. I'm angry."

"It must be hard. Not being able to tell anyone."

He nodded slowly. "Yeah. It is. But I told you."

"You did."

Silence settled between them, and Cole waited to feel different. To feel a weight lift off of him or something. It had been nice to say it out loud. To tell her how pissed he was. But the weight was still there. It hadn't changed the reality any.

"I normally tell all my problems to Alexa. She's good at listening. At not judging. Well, after she freaks out a little."

Thank God she was changing the subject.

"She's a good friend. Even though she hates my guts."

"Yes, she is. She was in full support of me dumping Michael when I did. Even though everyone else thought I should give him another chance. I'd lived in sin with him, after all."

That forced a genuine chuckle out of him. "Lived in sin, eh? I'm starting to get why you haven't told your parents about the baby."

She put her face in her hands. "I honestly don't know which would be worse: them thinking we hooked up, or them knowing I went and pursued single motherhood on my own."

"They can think whatever you want them to. I don't mind either way. Although, all things considered, I . . . I'd rather not tell too many lies. Leaves a bad taste in my mouth."

"You don't have to be involved with my parents. Not if you don't want to be. Yes, you're the father, but you aren't my boyfriend or husband. My family is my problem."

"I do," he said before he even realized what he was saying. "I do want to be involved. With all of it. We're talking about really making this work, about making a . . . I don't know if we're talking about a family, not in the traditional sense, but we're in this together, right?"

"I guess."

"That means I get to help you with parent things and other unpleasantness. And you have to know my brother."

She looked down. "That, um . . . seems like a fair trade."

"Are you okay?"

She looked up, her eyes glistening. "I just . . . I . . ."

"Hey." He stood up and rounded the picnic table, sitting next to her on the bench. He wrapped his arm around her, the feel of her, so warm and female and way too tempting, sending a shock of pleasure through him. "Hey, don't . . . don't do that."

"I'm pregnant. It's a pregnant thing," she said.

"I've never seen you do it."

"I don't often."

"I can tell."

"I didn't even cry about Michael. I just bitched and ate a lot of ice cream."

He laughed and tightened his hold on her, suddenly conscious of the fact that he'd crossed an invisible line. They weren't really friends. They weren't lovers. They were acquaintances, and putting his arm around an acquaintance, one he didn't intend to sleep with anyway, wasn't something he would normally do.

But she didn't pull away from him. If anything, she seemed to sort of melt against him. It was the first time she'd willingly accepted something from him without getting stiff and defensive and generally annoyed.

"Sometimes I think I must not have loved him very much. Not the way I thought," she said slowly.

"Why is that?"

"Because mostly what I took away from that relationship was distrust. I don't know that I was really heartbroken. It made me not want to pour into anyone. It made me not want to be dependent. But I think from the moment I threw him out of the house, I felt lighter. Better." She breathed in deeply. "It makes me wonder why I was still with him. What my problem was. Why it's taken me so long to . . . do something different with my life."

He didn't know how they'd arrived at this topic. He wasn't sure how they'd gotten to the point of sharing intensely personal things at all. But they had. He'd told her his darkest secret, the one that made him wake up in a cold sweat at night. All things considered, he supposed that kicked them out of the acquaintance zone and had them edging into the friend zone. Which meant his arm around her shoulders had to be okay. And that was good, because he liked touching her.

"Don't take what I'm about to say too seriously." He shifted again, and his hand brushed her breast, sending a hot, reckless sensation through him that made him doubt his recent idea that they'd entered the friend zone. "I mean, because my marriage was a disaster and I apparently come from a lineage of horribly unhealthy relationships."

"You banked your sperm for that woman," she said. "You were in the trenches."

"Actions that are born out of panic don't really count; I was desperately trying to appease someone and hold together a marriage that never should have been in the first place. So, take my advice with a grain of salt," he said. "Anyway, you didn't fall out of love with him overnight. It sounds like things lost their shine slowly, and you were comfortable, so you let it be. Him being a cheating asshole actually helped you a little."

She laughed. "Alexa thinks so too. But it did make me avoid . . . relationships. Men. Which is why thirty hit me and I found myself without a man even in sight. I kept thinking . . . I knew Michael for years before I moved in with him, before I got engaged to him. And he still screwed me over. Well . . . he screwed someone else, but you get the idea. So I'm like . . . Hell, I'm thirty, and I don't even know a guy I'd want to sleep with right now, much less marry or have kids with. And if I did meet him, it might take five years for me to be sure. . . ."

"Five years?"

"Yes. Marriage is a big deal, and people . . . they can surprise you in all the wrong ways."

"Preaching to the choir."

"Well . . . yeah, so we're both a little commitment-phobic now, right?"

"More than a little."

"And for good reason."

He flexed his fingers and fought the urge to put his hand on her stomach. It was a possessive gesture, and he felt a little bit possessive. But it wasn't right. It wasn't where they were at. "But you weren't afraid of the commitment it takes to raise a child. I'm more afraid of that than just about anything. Including marriage."

"Are you?"

"Hell yes. Parents are the reasons psychiatrists exist."

"My parents are probably the leading reason," she said. "And yours, I guess."

"I don't know. Yeah, now I'm struggling because . . . the things my dad told me . . . he didn't do any of it, so what did it mean? When we had him, when we had my mom? They were amazing. I don't know how to reconcile it. And they were gone way too soon. Especially for Lark's sake. I worry that Cade and me having such a heavy influence on her will completely mess her up."

She smiled. "You don't give yourself enough credit. You're doing a great job comforting me right now."

"Yeah, I threatened to kill Tyler the other day because I was afraid he'd slept with Lark."

"You did not!"

"I did. I mean, I didn't threaten him to his face, just in front of Lark. Just long enough for her to tell me he hadn't."

"Be careful, or she won't tell you anything."

He sighed. "I would rather she didn't. She's an adult. I don't want to know."

"But I mean you can't freak out when our . . . when our child tells you something." For some reason her words hit him with a force he hadn't been expecting.

Their child. Theirs. Someday he or she would be the one

sitting on their bed crying. He would have to offer comfort. He would have to have wisdom. He wasn't sure he had it. Wasn't sure he knew how to offer any kind of real comfort. But he would have to figure it out.

And he'd have to try to do it part-time, with his child living hours away from him. The thought made his chest burn. Would he ever get used to feeling again? Would it last?

He didn't want to be that man. The man his father had been. With a whole life away from his flesh and blood. Like he'd pushed his kid away, like he was ashamed. No, Cole wouldn't let his child feel unwanted.

He wanted to teach his child the right things, and he damn well wanted to back them up with his actions.

"I can't think that far ahead," he said, his voice rough. "How about we take it one day at a time?"

"I'm good with that."

She looked up at him, their faces so close that it would have been nothing for him to lean in and brush his lips against hers. As if suddenly conscious of the same thing, Kelsey pulled away from him, smoothing her pale hair with her hands.

Good. At least one of them was thinking.

"So . . . you really want to help me deal with my parents?"

"I do, and . . . I want you to stay longer. Can you do that?" He hadn't been aware he was going to issue the invitation until it had slipped out.

"I . . . I don't know if I should."

"Is work the problem?"

She shook her head. "No, I work at home. I just . . . I don't know. I'm sure Alexa won't be able to stay."

"You know? Somehow I'm okay with that."

She laughed. "Yeah, and somehow I'm not surprised."

"What if you stay here for a while. And when you're ready to tell your parents, they can come up here for a visit. See the ranch. See what I do. Maybe that will make them feel better about the situation."

"They won't feel better about the situation until you and

I have a legally binding ceremony that unites us in the eyes of God and the United States government," she said dryly.

He felt the blood run from his face. "Oh."

"Relax, Cole. I wasn't proposing." She put her hand on his shoulder for a second, and when she removed it, the impression of her warmth lingered. Burned.

And for a moment he wondered if marriage wouldn't be such a bad idea.

Eleven

"I'm pretty sure he thinks I proposed to him."

"Oh, Kelsey, what did you do?" Alexa was spread out on the bed in the living area of the cabin, playing a game on her phone.

"I just told him that my parents wouldn't be happy with the situation until we were married, which was . . . bad." She lifted her hand and started gnawing on her thumbnail.

"Did he scream and run away in terror?"

"No."

Alexa shrugged and pushed herself into a sitting position. "Well, you are already pregnant. And he hasn't run yet, so I think he's made of more solid stuff than most. But let the record show, I still think he's a bit of an ass."

"He's not, though." Kelsey was tempted to tell Alexa about the rest of their conversation earlier, about Cole's father. But she knew he hadn't told anyone else about it. And sharing it seemed . . . wrong. Which was strange, because normally, even if something was a state secret, she told her best friend anyway. Alexa didn't count. In Kelsey's mind, telling Alexa had always been the equivalent of writing something in a journal. It was safe, and it was necessary.

But not this. Not now.

"Fine. I'm glad you think so, since you're having his baby."

"What about Tyler?"

"Nothing."

"Nothing?"

"He barely kissed me. It was like . . . affectionate. I asked him for sex and he practically patted me on the head and sent me off with a lollipop!" Alexa's cheeks darkened. "Not a euphemistic lollipop either."

"Are you blushing?"

"No. Maybe. I don't even think I'm wired to blush. What is he doing to me?" she whined. "I wanted a fling. A literal roll in the hay. And this . . . this . . . kid who, based on his age—"

"He's six years younger than you; calm down about that already."

Alexa shot her a deadly glare. "Based on his age, he should be in that stage of life where he thinks exclusively with his dick."

"Don't all men, of all ages?"

Alexa balled her hands into fists. "Yes! So why doesn't he?"

"Because it's making you obsess. I want to congratulate him. I think he's a genius."

"He's playing me," she muttered.

"If it makes you feel better, Cole hasn't kissed me at all. Not even affectionately."

"Is that a thing? Are you thinking Cole might kiss you?"

"I don't know."

Alexa frowned. "Do you want him to?"

A week ago? No. She would have vomited into his mouth, which wasn't a commentary on his attractiveness, just on where she was hormonally. But now . . . well, now her hormones were getting . . . perky.

"I don't . . . No. I don't think I do. I mean, I'm a little

attracted, but all things considered, no. He's the most complicated man I could get involved with right now, and that's saying something, because *any* involvement would be complicated right now. But if I go kissing him, and things don't work out . . . well, we've moved ourselves into a bad position for the baby. Right now? Right now there's . . . nothing between us."

"Nothing, huh?"

"We like each other. I mean, we get along okay."

"But you also kind of wish he'd kiss you."

Kelsey growled, "He's hot. I'm pregnant, not dead."

"And very celibate," Alexa said.

"*Way* too celibate."

"But you're not going to go there."

"No. Anyway, if I did now he'd think I was trying to seal the marriage deal. Blah! I can't believe I said that. His face lost all color."

"He'll get over it," Alexa said. "Balls of steel that one has."

Kelsey snorted and sank into one of the dining room chairs. "You're a class act and a half, Alex. And that's why I love you."

Alexa puckered her lips and made a kissing noise. "Love ya back, babe."

Kelsey breathed in deeply. "He asked me to stay."

"Here?"

"Yes."

"For how long?"

"Until . . . until I want to leave, I guess. But he doesn't want me to go yet, and . . . I'm thinking of accepting the offer."

"Now *he* sounds like he's proposing marriage."

Kelsey laughed. "Totally not. But . . . I'm happy here. I mean, I feel less stress. The fact that my morning sickness is fading helps, I'm sure, but . . . I feel like my head is clear here, and I don't feel like it is in Portland. I live in the same house I lived in with Michael. The only house I've ever owned. That life feels so stuck. So the same. And I'm changing now. Here, I finally feel like I'm changing inside, not just like I'm forcing a change of circumstance."

"Heavy."

She breathed out. "Kind of."

"I still have to head back to NY, though."

"I know."

"But you're satisfied he won't . . . you know, that he's not an ax murderer?"

"Yeah, I'm pretty sure he's not."

"Then, if you're happy, stay." Alexa shrugged.

"That might be the biggest reason I shouldn't stay."

It was Sunday. And Cole realized that Kelsey had never given him an answer about whether or not she'd be staying. It surprised him how badly he wanted her to stay.

It was that male possessiveness again. Evolution. Or something. And who was he to argue with it? She was carrying his baby. He felt connected to that fact more and more every day.

The realization that he was going to be a father hit him in waves. Sometimes so intense, so strong, it was enough to make his legs shake. And then it receded for a while, the idea back to being a simple concept. A baby that was coming in months. A shadowy picture.

Then there were times when that picture became so vivid . . . a little boy with blond hair just like Kelsey's and his own dark eyes and stubborn expression. Or a girl with brown curls, like his sister had had when she was young.

It was unnerving. And far too real.

"I assumed you were getting laid. I guess I was wrong." Cade walked into the kitchen and leaned back against the counter, his eyes trained on Cole, his expression smug. Obnoxious, as always.

"Why exactly did you think that?" he asked. He was more curious about what had changed Cade's mind, but he wasn't going to play his brother's game.

"I figured that's what Kelsey was here for. I didn't believe you when you said you hadn't slept with her."

"Well, I told you the truth." He wouldn't have to ask why Cade had changed his mind, because he knew that Cade would tell him. He was looking far too smug and self-satisfied not to let Cole in on his revelation.

"I knew it. You're way too grumpy for a man experiencing regular orgasms from a means other than his right hand."

Cole's lip curled up. "Come up with that all by yourself, did you?"

"I did."

"Great show of deductive reasoning. But if you think your work is done for the day, you're wrong. Gimp on over to the barn and muck a stall."

Cade didn't even flinch as he was hit by the carefully aimed dig. "You ever figure out the money thing? And I mean, did you find it or figure out where it went for sure?"

"Let's not talk about this now," he growled.

"See? Grumpy. And defensive. If you need help, ask me, you stubborn asshole."

"Right, like you ask for help or time off when your leg hurts?"

"My leg is fine."

"What a coincidence," Cole said. "I'm fine too. I'm so damn fine it's not even funny. Everything's great. The ranch is great."

"Seems like it."

"Obviously. You're as screwed up as I am," Cole said, jerking the fridge open and pulling out two bottles of beer, handing one to his brother. "So stop standing there with that look on your face. Like you have me figured out. Like you have life figured out. You don't."

"I didn't say I did. But you sure as hell don't, and if your problems, whatever the hell they are, are starting to bleed over into ranch business, I think I have a right to say something. You would say something to me."

"Since when do you care about the ranch at all?" Cole asked, delaying the inevitable by arguing.

"Since it became all I have left. Since you, Lark and Amber became the only people who seem to even want to talk to me. I can't ride anymore. I can't compete. This is my future. This—this dirt clod that I spent my life avoiding is all I have anymore, and if it doesn't succeed . . . well, then I'm a cripple with nothing, and I don't want that."

It was the most passionate, true thing Cole had ever heard come from his brother's mouth. Cade lacked sincerity. It just didn't seem to exist in him. He'd hobbled back onto the ranch after the rodeo injury had blown out his leg and back and he'd done it with a self-deprecating grin plastered on his face. All through physical therapy, he'd joked. Even when the limp hadn't gone away, he'd joked. He'd been joking about it for two years. He wasn't joking now. And he wasn't wrong.

Cole owed him. Owed him at least a measure of honesty back. But he didn't want to give it.

"I'm trying here," Cole said slowly. "I am. I'm trying to keep things going and I'm trying to . . . I'm trying to protect you and Lark. From the truth. I've been lying to you."

"What about, Cole?" Cade crossed his arms over his chest.

"I know where the money went. It was a payment. I've been making payments on a gambling debt of Dad's."

Cade nodded slowly. "Got down to it, did you?"

"What do you mean?"

"To the truth. I wondered if you would. I hoped you wouldn't."

"What do you know?"

Cade shrugged. "Not details. I mean, nothing certain. But . . . but I knew he wasn't all we thought. All he tried to show us. I think maybe he let it slip more around me because . . . because he thought I was most like him. Not sure how I feel about that."

"Damn it, what do you know?"

"About the affair. And . . . all that."

"What the hell, Cade? You knew, and you never thought . . . 'Hey, maybe I should tell my brother'?"

"No, Cole, I never thought that," Cade said, stuffing his hands into his pockets.

"And why the hell not?"

"Because. As far as I was concerned, I was privy to the world's worst secret. And you . . . Damn, Cole, you'd been through enough. You shouldered everything. All the responsibility. And things just got so hard at home. Mom died and . . . and then your marriage was hell and dad died. Then what was the point?"

"I don't know. I'm sorry." Cole rubbed the back of his neck, a sick feeling spreading through him. He knew how Cade felt. Because he'd felt that way from the moment he'd found out. Like the keeper of this thing, this horrible beast that had the power to shatter everyone's lives.

"Don't apologize. It's too nice. Makes me nervous."

Cole snorted a laugh, then sobered. "Did Mom . . . ?"

"Not as far as I know. I overheard . . . I eavesdropped on a call once. Forever ago. I was in high school. They were talking about the house and money and when he'd visit. And a kid."

"You knew all that time and you didn't tell anyone?"

"To what end, Cole? Why? So everyone could be as disappointed as I was? Why do you think I wanted to get out of here so bad? Hypocrisy burns like a son of a bitch."

Cole let out a breath he hadn't realized he was holding. He wondered if he'd been holding his breath for the better part of a year. "We have to pay his debts off or we're in danger of losing the ranch, basically because we reinvested all the inheritance money. But I have a plan."

"How bad?"

"Not too bad."

"What kind of debts?"

"Gambling. A car."

A muscle ticced in Cade's jaw. "He bought her a house and stuff, didn't he?"

"Yeah. That stuff they could repossess, though. And they did. He never saw the kid. Not more than a few times."

Cade looked out the window. "I figured. And that's where the fifteen grand went?"

"Yep."

"How much is left? How much do we have left to deal with?"

"Some more." He named a figure that made Cade's eyebrows shoot halfway up his forehead. "I know. But everything is looking promising with these horses, and I have buyers interested in them, rodeo officials who want to pick some of them up for the finals in Vegas. As long as this keeps going, everything's going to be fine."

"And you're sure this is going through?"

"Wouldn't hurt if you used your connections to grease the wheels."

"I can do that. But damn, Cole, how hard is it to just ask?"

"Hard," Cole said, pushing his hand through his hair. "Especially when you're afraid asking is going to blow up the family."

Cade nodded. "So we both know."

"Yeah."

"And Lark doesn't."

"Nope."

"Keep it that way?"

Cole tapped the side of his beer bottle. "I don't know. I don't like being a part of the deception."

"We didn't lie, Cole; he did."

"But we know the truth. Do we keep covering for him?"

"He never covered for us. He'd tell Mom on us, and then she'd whup our asses."

Cole laughed. Sometimes the memories were still good. They still seemed intact and not just like a facade that hadn't meant a damn thing. "Yeah, he did. But he's not alive to answer for it or learn from it."

"How about we drink alcohol and make no decisions?"

"I'm cool with that."

Cade took the bottle opener off the fridge and popped

the top off his beer, taking a long drink. "And you really aren't sleeping with Kelsey?"

"No."

"Why not?"

"What the hell kind of question is that? Why aren't you sleeping with . . . Amber Jameson?" He chose the name of Cade's oldest friend on purpose.

Cade took a step back. "She's my friend—that's why."

"Well, fine. Kelsey's a friend, then."

"You don't know her that well, do you?"

"I'm getting to know her."

Cade raised an eyebrow. "With the intent of . . . *not* sleeping with her?"

"Women are just people, Cade. People who are worth getting to know."

"People with breasts. Which means it's rare to make friends with one just to be friends with one."

"And Amber?"

Cade looked stricken at the mention. "I knew her before she had breasts, so she doesn't count."

"I'm sure she'd love to hear that."

"She won't." His eyes narrowed in warning. "Ever. Now seriously, what's the deal with you and Kelsey?"

"Shit, Cade, can't we just hug it out instead of standing here talking about feelings?"

"I'm curious."

"And I'm not telling you anything. I'm not even sure why you care."

"Because don't think I haven't noticed you've barely talked to a woman since the debacle with Shawna, the ex-wife from hell."

Cole studied his beer bottle. "You don't know everything about me."

"I wish that were true. I wish you weren't so easy to read, so I didn't have to feel worried about you. Or so aware that you're still punishing yourself for that epic fail of a marriage."

"Like you've been dating up a storm for the past year."

"This isn't about me."

Cole angled his bottle in Cade's direction. "But it could be."

"Fine. You win. Enough with the Dr. Phil crap." Cade took another long drink of his beer. "Does this mean I can hit on Kelsey?"

"Still a firm 'hell no.'"

"Great. When you're ready, you tell me what that's about."

He'd have to eventually. But not until he'd talked it over with Kelsey. "Yeah, I will. Why do you care so much all of a sudden?"

Cade shrugged. "I don't have anything else to do. And like I said . . . you and Lark and this ranch are all I have. Makes you cling to things tighter when you realize how easy it is to lose them."

Not for the first time, Cole felt a twinge of pity for his brother, which he knew would get him punched in the face if he voiced it out loud. Cade's injury had cost him his passion. The revelation about their dad had cost them both their memories. They were pros at experiencing loss.

"Well, we're honored. Why don't you go bother Lark? I'm sure she'd love to tell you all about the new social media project she's working on to make our ranch a world-famous destination."

"Thanks for the warning," Cade said, backing out of the kitchen. "I'll avoid her."

Cole shook his head and turned, slapping the top of his beer bottle on the counter and popping off the cap.

"Hi." He turned and saw Kelsey standing in the door of the kitchen looking . . . Well, she was glowing. That pregnant-woman glow, maybe? Or just the sun hitting her face at the right time. Either way, she looked hot, and he noticed.

"What brings you down here?"

"I realized I didn't give you an answer about staying," she said.

He shook his head. "No, you didn't."

She stood, rocking back and forth on the balls of her feet,

her hands in her back pockets, her eyes not meeting his. He found himself fighting the urge to reach out and take her chin between his thumb and forefinger. To tilt her head so that she had to look at him. So that her lips were so close to his, a slight movement would—

"What did you decide?" he said, cutting off his thoughts.

"I'll stay. I don't know how long, but I'll stay."

"I'm leaving, you know. *Tonight*," Alexa said, putting heavy emphasis on the word.

Tyler felt a sharp pang in his gut. Something close to regret. But he wasn't going to change tactics, not now. Alexa had stormed to the back of the barn, her cheeks flushed, a few minutes earlier, and she'd been loitering while he'd been working on transferring a manure pile from the dirt to the bed of a pickup. Not the most romantic setting, but such was life on a ranch.

"I'm sorry to hear that," he said, throwing one last shovelful into the pickup bed and driving the head of the shovel down into the dirt, then leaning against the handle.

Alexa breathed heavily, an overdramatic sigh. She didn't say anything. She only looked at him, her annoyance and confusion so obvious, it would have been funny if she didn't have him so tied up in knots.

"What is it, Alex?" he asked, knowing full well what it was.

"I'm leaving . . . and . . . and nothing happened between us."

He wouldn't go that far. But he got that in her mind, it was nothing if it hadn't made it into the bedroom. And that just wasn't the way he did things.

"A lot has happened between us," he said.

"What? You kissed me once."

"And I enjoyed it. Did you?"

"If I didn't, I wouldn't be a ball of sexually frustrated energy right now."

"I'm not really that sorry for you," he said.

"Why is that, you cheeky bastard?"

He chuckled. "I'd rather you leave wanting more of me than have you leave feeling done with me."

"I live in New York," she said blandly.

"So?"

"And I'm not ever going to move to a ranch to be a housewife for a man with muddy boots."

He couldn't picture Alexa as a housewife. Couldn't picture her baking or scrubbing anything. "I know how to cook, and I know how to clean my own boots. So I wouldn't worry too much."

"Why are you saying things like that? We hardly know each other."

"You're the one who brought up being a housewife."

"Oh." She bit her lip.

He reached forward and cupped her cheek. Her skin was so soft. So perfect. She was perfect, and he knew—absolutely knew—she had no idea just how perfect. "I like you. I'd like to get to know you better. I'd like to do that outside of the bedroom."

He'd like to do it in the bedroom too, but not yet. It just wasn't how he did things. It wasn't how he had been raised to treat a woman. Wasn't how he believed relationships should work. And he could tell that it was exactly what she thought should happen, that it was what she did.

"Let me take a wild guess at how your relationships usually work," he said.

"I wish you wouldn't."

"I'm going to anyway."

She sighed. "Fine."

"You think you have a connection with someone. You sleep with them, and then you get to say it reached its conclusion but wasn't a lasting kind of connection. Am I right?"

"I . . . I . . ." She frowned. "I'm never at a loss for words. How do you do this?"

"It's a gift, I guess. Do you want to know why your connections are never the real thing?"

"No way in hell. But I bet you're about to tell me."

"Yep. They're never anything because you don't give them a chance. Sex is great—I like it as much as the next guy—but it's not going to help you get to know someone. Not really. And if you're looking to make something stick by using sex as the glue, without even trying to have conversation or emotion, it's not going to work."

"I'm not trying to make anything stick," she said. "Maybe I don't want love and marriage and all that crap."

"Maybe you don't. But I doubt it. Either way, I'm not someone who can do casual sex. I've tried it, and I don't like it. I need feelings first."

"Why?" she asked, practically exploding, her petite frame vibrating. "No other guy ever in the world needs feelings for sex. They just need sex."

"That's bull. And why are you so desperate to pretend it's true? Because you want to sleep with me so you can scratch the itch and call it done. Because that's what you do. But not with me, Alex."

"I'm going back to New York," she said tightly. "And I won't think about you again. You're just a guy I knew for a couple of weeks."

"That's a bigger pile than I have in this truck," he said, taking his gloves off and throwing them on the ground, letting the shovel fall with them.

He hooked his arm around her waist and pulled her up against him, his lips hovering above hers. "I'm going to kiss you now. And you're going to think of it the whole flight home." He dipped his head and kissed her.

Not sweet like the other night. Not even close. She parted

her lips for him and he slid his tongue against hers, the soft slide sending a shot of heat straight to his cock. He knew the moment she felt him hard against her, because that was when the game changed. When she decided she would beat him. He could feel it in the shift of her movements, could feel her trying to take control.

She bit his lower lip softly and soothed the sting away with her tongue, her hands sliding down his chest, gripping his belt buckle. And she just about undid all of his good intentions with those actions. Just about.

He wrenched his lips from hers and took her hands in his, raising them to his mouth and pressing a soft kiss to her knuckles.

"I know I'll be thinking about you," he said. "I'll definitely call you."

She narrowed her eyes and reached into her purse, tugging a business card out and thrusting it into his hand. "You have forty-eight hours. Call by then or lose my number. I'm not playing your game."

He took the card from her and tucked it into his pocket. "I'm not playing one."

Alexa was gone. Which was a little sad, and also a little scary, since, in some ways, her friend had felt like a great source of accountability. Now she was alone with Cole and all the warm feelings he produced in her. And she had no one to remind her why it was a bad idea to act on impulse and do something about them.

Kelsey wandered through the main area of the lodge and sat on an expansive couch by the window. There weren't any other guests at the ranch, and the house seemed cavernous with so few people in it. She pulled her laptop out of her bag and opened it, waiting for it to wake up. Her column was just as she'd left it. Unfinished and uninspired.

She couldn't leave it that way. She did still have a job. She took a deep breath and opened a new document. She stared at the blinking cursor for a moment. Better to just start writing and see what comes out.

I'm discovering that pregnancy is a series of health challenges.

It was a personal way to construct the article, but maybe she could just be honest for now and edit it later.

On the one hand, you need to eat healthy, as always. Food is fuel, and the better the fuel, the more superior the performance of the vehicle—in this case, your body. But I've discovered that even healthy food can feel like an enemy when there's a baby involved. Chicken has always been my go-to lean protein, until recently, I couldn't go anywhere near it. And don't even get me started on salad.

Kelsey heard footsteps and looked up to see Lark standing at the foot of the wooden staircase, frozen with her hand on the rail.

"Sorry," Lark said, lowering her head, her dark hair shielding her face.

"You're fine. Come in." Kelsey shut her laptop and put it down on the rough wooden end table. She felt weird extending the offer in the other woman's house, but she seemed to be the one who felt like an intruder. "I was just sitting here letting my mind go blank," she lied.

"That never works for me," Lark said, coming a little farther into the room.

"Too much going on in your head, huh?"

"At the very least, I have code running behind my eyelids after staring at the computer all day."

"I work on the computer too, but I don't do any kind of programming or web development. Just writing."

"Sounds fun."

"Challenging sometimes. I'm a columnist, and I always

have to have something to say on my given topic . . . even when I don't."

"Do you do any social media? Twitter, that kind of thing?"

"I have Twitter linked to my blog." Her neglected blog.

"I could take a look at it. I'm working on getting the ranch on social media. I think it would be good to get out there, give away some free vacations. That kind of thing. We're not exactly a hotbed for tourist activity at the moment. Though it's better in the summer."

"Well, I'll be here for a while, so . . . yeah, if you want to take a look at my blog and stuff sometime, that would be great."

Lark cocked her head to the side. "You're staying longer? I mean, that's great, but Cole didn't mention—"

"I just told him this morning."

"Oh."

"Alexa left," she said, saying the words she knew Lark really wanted to hear.

"Oh . . . too bad," she said, her words completely false. But Kelsey would let her have her pride and her attempt at civility.

"Yeah, but she had to get back to New York. Work. I'm going to work here for a while. And I already told Cole I'd be happy to mention the ranch in some upcoming columns. I want to talk about the importance of taking time out for yourself."

That earned a genuine response from Lark. "That would be great!"

"He's been nice to me. Anything to help out. You've all been great."

"So . . . how exactly do you know Cole? You're his . . . friend?"

"Um . . . it's complicated. I mean, it's not complicated, because we aren't dating or anything, but . . . Yes. We're friends." She could feel her face getting hot, and she could tell by the skeptical expression on Lark's face that she'd been unconvincing.

"Either way, I'm glad you're staying," Lark offered. "It's nice to have another woman around. I'm caught in a wave of testosterone most of the time."

Kelsey could think of worse fates, especially since her life had been lacking in testosterone until Cole's arrival. "Well, I'm glad to offer you a feminine ear."

"I appreciate it. I'd better . . . I have work to do." She gave a small wave and turned to walk up the stairs. Kelsey put her laptop in her lap again and leaned back, her fingers resting on the keys.

Being pregnant has forced me to reevaluate my idea of what feeling healthy means. Usually, I feel healthy when I exercise. Right now I feel healthiest when I'm lying down eating chocolate.

Okay, that would have to go. But it was true.

"Working?"

She looked up again and her heart climbed into her throat. Cole was standing in the doorway, all lean hips, worn denim and general sexiness.

"Making an attempt," she said.

"What are you writing about?"

"I'm trying to write about health and pregnancy and realizing it's really hard to do when you never feel very healthy and you generally want to tear your skin off to try to escape from your personal prison of misery."

He arched an eyebrow. "Evocative."

"Dramatic, I know. And I feel just kind of . . . blerg. Not myself, really."

"Yeah. I know the feeling. At least yours is temporary."

"Until it gives way to the sleepless nights of parenthood."

Cole crossed the room and sat next to her on the couch. "You wanted this, though, right?"

"I did. I do. I . . . Having a baby, the thought of it, makes me feel like everything is coming together. Like I'm finally becoming who I'm supposed to be. I know it's not what everyone wants, but for me? For me finger-paint art and the

sound of little feet pounding down the hall at five a.m.—
that's what I want. But it hits me off and on what a big deal
it is. I mean, I made the decision, I'm confident in the decision. But it's not like getting a puppy, you know? It's big.
And there are a lot of parts of it that are really scary, even
though I know I made the right choice."

"I understand that, and I'm not the one who has to give
birth."

"You won't really be doing the sleepless nights either.
I'll be breastfeeding"—she was proud of him for not flinch-
ing at the statement—"so the baby will have to stay with me
all the time."

He frowned. "I could come over to Portland a couple
times a week. Sleep on the couch. Be on hand to . . . change
a diaper."

"That's silly, Cole. You don't have to do that."

"I don't want you to handle all that alone. You were talking about things hitting you a little at a time, and I'm kind
of in the same boat. I keep realizing all the little things you'll
have to do on your own. All the things I'll miss."

"It wouldn't matter to a lot of men."

"I can't seem to make it not matter to me."

He looked at her stomach. He did that a lot. "Can I . . . ?"
He moved his hand, let his palm hover over her stomach.

She nodded slowly, her heart starting to beat a little faster.
He rested his hand on her. "You can kind of feel a bump," he
said.

"Can you?"

"A small one."

"Maybe that's normal for me. You never touched my
stomach before I was pregnant."

He laughed. "True."

"Maybe it will feel more real when I can feel the baby
move. Right now I keep expecting to wake up and find none
of this is actually real."

"It was all just a dream," he said softly, sliding his thumb
across her stomach, the little movement sending a flash of
sensation through her. Then he shifted his hand, his fingers

edging beneath the hem of her shirt. Still just feeling the baby bump. That was all.

But she could hardly breathe, not with him touching her like that. His hand was hot, his skin a little rough, and it was so wrong, but she wanted him to keep going.

"It would be less complicated," she said, sounding as dazed and breathless as she felt. "But I think it would break my heart."

"Maybe mine too," he said, his voice soft, reverent. "The idea of being a father is really starting to grow on me."

"A *what*?" The words, not said by either of them, were spoken in a shriek that echoed in the empty room.

Their heads snapped up in unison. Lark was standing at the bottom of the stairs again, her computer in her hand.

"What . . . did you hear?" Cole asked, clearly not willing to give up any more than had been overheard.

"She's *pregnant*?" Lark's eyes were comically round. At least, it would have been comical if anything were funny about the situation.

He moved away from Kelsey, his hands sliding to his lap. "Yes," he said slowly, his eyes trained on Kelsey.

Kelsey shifted, knowing her face was bright pink. It had to be. This wasn't exactly how she'd seen this going. Actually, she hadn't seen it going any way because she'd done her best to block out that there would be other people involved in her and Cole's insane circumstances. It was hard enough with just the two of them.

Lark's jaw slackened. "Wow."

"What now?" Cade walked in, trailing mud on the glossy wood floors.

"Get the hell out if you can't remember to wipe your feet," Cole said.

"I was practically born in a barn," Cade said. "Now why are we all looking shocked and awkward? Is this an intervention? Are we finally addressing the amount of time Lark spends in front of a computer?"

"Kelsey's pregnant," Lark said.

Cade's eyebrows shot up. "Okay."

"Cole's the father," she added.

Cole looked at Kelsey. "I think we can leave, since Lark seems to have this covered."

Lark scowled. "I don't have it covered. That's as much as I know. I don't know why you didn't tell us you were in a relationship."

Kelsey felt her face flush all over again. "We're not."

Lark's eyes widened. "Oh."

"It's not our business," Cade said, surprising her with the hardness in his tone. "It's their business."

Cole looked at his brother. "Thank you."

"Now that we know, though, some details would be nice," he said.

"Not many details to give," Cole said.

Cole purposed to keep the story vague, because he and Kelsey hadn't decided exactly what they were going to tell her family. They'd both decided nothing when it came to telling people. Probably because they'd both been avoiding it.

"We met in Portland." True enough. "And when Kelsey found out she was pregnant, I invited her here to get to know me a little bit better. So we could decide how we're going to do this. Obviously we were going to tell you. It's not the easiest secret to keep. But we had a few things to figure out with each other first. And that's the most important thing for both of you to remember. This is between Kelsey and me, and your opinions don't come into it. Neither does your judgment, Lark," he said, giving his sister a pointed look.

"I'm not judging," she said.

"Yes, you are."

"Well, you came into my room and threatened to kill a guy you thought might have slept with me. And who, you assumed, had maybe gotten me pregnant or something due to extreme carelessness. So, maybe I'm taken aback by the hypocrisy." His sister was making broad hand gestures now, her speech getting faster. She was about to go into full drama mode, and he didn't have the time, or desire, to deal with her.

"I was trying to figure out why you were acting like your

heart had been pulled out through your chest," he said, standing up. "Turned out, it was nothing." She nearly objected to that, but his glare put a stop to it. "Like I said, this has nothing to do with you. For once, Cade is right."

Cade assessed both Kelsey and Cole for a moment, his arms folded over his chest. "Congratulations. Guess I'm going to be an uncle. And I'm not the first one to have a child out of wedlock, which I find a bit shocking," he said.

"No one's more shocked than I am," Cole said.

"It wasn't irresponsibility on Cole's part," Kelsey said, her voice muted. "It was the clinic."

"Clinic?" Cade and Lark spoke in unison.

"Long story," Kelsey said. "And it contains a lot of my own issues and hang-ups and a very loud biological clock that was ticking in my ear. But skipping to the important part, I decided to have a baby on my own."

Cole found he wanted to stop her from telling the story. He found that he preferred the assumption that they'd made the baby together. That he'd been involved. Really involved, and not just a contributor of necessary materials. That, and he didn't really like displaying the evidence of just how much his ex had owned his balls.

He curled his hands into fists and took a long, slow breath while Kelsey continued to speak.

"So I went to a fertility clinic to be artificially inseminated. And after a few tries . . . I got pregnant. And then we—well, Cole—found out that there had been a mistake. And his . . . his sperm was used when it wasn't . . . it wasn't supposed to be used. So, he came to find me, and the rest is history."

Now even Cade was openmouthed.

"That is unsettling," Cade said finally. "It used to be that a cheap motel and a faulty condom had to be involved in these kinds of surprises. Now it can happen without you even getting off? Well, clearly you got off at some point, but not in the preferred way."

"Write that one down, Cole. We'll put it in the baby book," Kelsey said.

"Well, I'm sorry, but that's enough to give a man nightmares," Cade said.

"It's not like they stole my sperm in the middle of the night," Cole said. Lark's face had turned purple and she was biting her lip—likely holding back a scream of mortification. Oh, well, she'd wanted to have the conversation, so she was in it now. "Shawna talked me into banking it. I didn't want to have kids yet, but she'd done some research about paternal age and she got all shrill about me denying our child their best chance at life by conceiving with potentially old sperm. Yes, her charm went deeper than either of you witnessed. So I did it. For her, because I was trying to make it work. And I preferred not to even remember that I did that for the woman, so I just . . . let it go, paid the bill via auto debit from my account every month and mainly forgot about it. But when I"—he looked at Lark—"when I went to Portland, I figured I'd have them get rid of it. Only when I got there, they didn't have it. Then it turned out it was gone because"—he looked at Kelsey—"it had been used."

"The man I picked was supposed to be a software developer," Kelsey said. It was the first he'd heard of that.

Cade laughed. "That's funny. Cole doesn't know how to check his email without freezing his computer."

"That's not true." Close, but still.

"I'm good with computers," Lark said. "So it's in your baby's genes. Just . . . if that helps."

"I'm over the computer thing," Kelsey said. "But . . . that's why we said it was complicated. Because we don't even know each other. We've never even . . . Well, that's too much information. But we haven't."

"I'm going to be an aunt!" Lark said, brightening. "I know it's a crazy circumstance, and I know neither of you planned it, but . . . now our family is going to get bigger. We've lost so much. So many people. It's . . . it's nice to add to the Mitchells instead of taking from them."

Cole looked at Kelsey. The color had drained slightly from her face, the flush in her cheeks receding. Now she looked . . . stressed. And a little bit sad. He felt the same way, and he wasn't really sure why or what it meant. Only that there was nothing straightforward about the situation. Which, in some ways, made it nice that Lark saw her glimmering positive in the middle of the mess.

Cade was quiet. His reaction had been honest. And appreciated. Even more appreciated was the fact that he wasn't offering a bunch of congratulations he didn't mean.

A rare show of perceptiveness from his younger brother.

"You still have to go wipe your boots, moron," Cole muttered.

Cade offered him a half smile and backtracked to the entryway rug. That was as close to hugging it out as they would get.

"You tired, Kelsey?" Cole asked.

She nodded, and Cole extended his hand to her. She looked at it for a moment before reaching up and grasping it, allowing him to help her up from her position on the couch.

"I'll walk you back up to your cabin. And you two—don't you have work to do?" he asked his siblings.

Lark shook her head, an expression of cheerful oblivion on her face. "I don't."

"Then go ogle Tyler," he said.

She flushed. "Jackass."

"I love you too," he said.

She narrowed her eyes, but he could tell her anger wasn't genuine. Or at least it wasn't lethal. "See you at dinner," he said to Lark's retreating back as she took the stairs two at a time. Back to her room. Back to her computers.

"I'll see you later," Cade said. He shook his head as he walked out, muttering something about guarding his sperm.

"Well, that was . . . eventful," Kelsey said.

"Yeah, I know. That's my family."

"My baby's family," she said as if she was just realizing it.

"Yeah," he said. "Come on, I'll take you back."

She nodded, her pale blue eyes wide in her ashen face. He wished he could kiss her. Not just because he thought she was beautiful and he wanted to. But because he wished there was a more solid connection between them.

One that might keep her, and their baby, close to him.

Although he doubted that a kiss, even a good one, would make it worth the trouble of putting up with him.

Cole didn't say anything until the cabin door closed behind them, which was a relief to Kelsey, since she suddenly felt sick and more than a little bit overwhelmed.

"Are you okay?" he asked.

"No. Yes. I don't know." He just looked at her, arms crossed over his broad chest. "Stupidly, I just realized that it's not just you and me. I mean, really realized it. That Lark is going to be my baby's aunt and that Cade . . . Cade is his uncle and . . . and they'll want to see him, or her, and it's . . . it's not just me anymore. It was only supposed to be me," she said, her words ending flat, as defeated as she felt.

He still didn't say anything. Which was fine, because if he wanted to let her word-vomit all over him, she was in the mood to do it.

"I wanted something that was mine. Outside the expectations of my family. Something that was for me. And . . . I didn't get it. I still have to figure out how to do this without hurting other people and I . . . I have to make decisions I don't feel like I can make."

He could relate.

"So, don't make them right now," he said.

"That's . . . that's fine in theory, but . . . but . . ."

"But what? This is our life. *Our* baby. I know having me involved is more than you really want, but right now we can leave Cade and Lark and your family and the town out of this. It's not anyone else's business."

"I don't mind having you involved," she said, her heart pounding as she made the rushed admission.

"You don't?"

"No. I like it. I'm relieved. I don't want to do this alone. Now that I have the option, I really don't want to do it alone. And I feel horrible about that. I made this decision, and it turns out I'm way too big of a wimp to stand behind it. I'm so . . . glad that I'm going to have you as the father of my baby, and that scares me. It scares me how much it matters. How I'm almost . . . happy about having Lark and Cade as aunt and uncle. It makes for a nice picture. I'm just not sure if it's reality."

It hurt to say the words. To admit that she was pretty weak when all was said and done. That part of her craved the traditional family thing, as much as she'd wanted to pretend it didn't matter. It had been fine to be all "balls to the wall, I'll do it myself" in theory, but with another option on the table? It was hard to pass up.

But they couldn't be a traditional family, not really.

"You're not a wimp," he said. "Some things . . . you don't realize what they're going to be like until you're in them. You might think you can handle them, and maybe you even can. But if you have the option of help . . . you'll take it."

"Like you've ever taken help?"

"I talked to Cade today. About my dad. You helped me do that."

"Oh. Well . . ." Heat bloomed around her heart. Dangerous, dangerous heat. "Is he okay?"

"Yeah. He . . . knew. Which makes me feel like an idiot. But . . . I was the oldest. I idolized our dad. Cade was the rebellious one. The one that's always been more cynical. I actually get why now."

"When did he find out?"

"When we were in high school. I can't believe he carried it that long. The past year has been hard enough for me."

"I guess people surprise you sometimes. I surprised me. How . . . how not strong I feel. How tired I am."

"You're allowed to be."

A half smile curved his lips, and her heart skipped a little bit. What she really wanted to do was reach out and touch his face, feel his stubble beneath her palm. She wanted to sit on the bed with him, have him touch her stomach, like he'd been doing when Lark had walked in.

She wanted to do more than that. Suddenly, she wanted it so badly, she felt restless. Achy. A little bit shaken.

What would have happened if they had just met in a bar? A man by himself drinking a beer, looking all sexy in his tight jeans and cowboy hat. Probably nothing. Because she didn't go to bars and she didn't flirt with men. She had disastrous half dates that she lied to escape from.

Maybe for Cole she would have made an exception. Maybe.

She wanted to make one now.

She put her hands in the back pockets of her jeans. Because if she didn't she might do something really stupid. Like reach out and touch his chest, just to see if it was as hard and muscular as it looked.

She swallowed hard and took a step back. Stupidity insurance. For when you're so horny, you don't trust yourself not to jump the poor, unsuspecting father of your baby. How had emotional exhaustion morphed into this? Damn hormones.

Although she had a feeling half the problem was that she suddenly needed a vacation from reality. And Cole, naked, would be a very, very nice vacation. Except he was all tangled up in her reality, and there really was no extricating him for a little naked fun and acting like it would have no implications.

"I think I'm going to take a nap," she said.

He looked at the bed and she felt a blush flood her cheeks, heat prickling her scalp.

"Sounds like a good idea."

"Yeah," she said, edging backward. "So, I'll . . . I'll come to dinner."

"Why don't I take you out to dinner?" he asked.

"What . . . like a date?"

He shrugged. "I knocked you up. I ought to buy you a meal."

She took her hands out of her pockets. "I don't know if a cheap steak is fair compensation for carrying your child in my womb."

"It won't be a cheap steak."

She snorted. "That changes everything."

"Six. I'll pick you up at six."

She should have said no. Because there was no point in them having a date.

Except it's that vacation from reality you were wanting.

Yes, it was. And she would just ignore the little panicky voice of reason in the back of her mind that was saying it was a bad idea.

"I . . . Do you really think we should go on a date?" she asked.

"This has been . . . a lot of stress, and a lot of thinking, and a lot of . . . I don't think it's been easy for either of us. So, just for a few hours, why don't we let it go and go have a meal together?"

Kelsey nodded slowly. "Yeah. Okay. Sounds good."

"See you then."

He turned and walked out of the cabin, and she couldn't help but watch him leave. The sight of the back of him had become one of her great pleasures in life. Not because she couldn't wait for him to be away from her, but because of how the, uh . . . back of him . . . looked in a pair of jeans.

"I am not going to obsess over my outfit," she said to the empty room. She turned and wandered over to the wooden dresser that housed most of her clothes. "I'm not." She rifled through the contents of the top drawer and let out a long breath. "I'm going to obsess only a little."

* * *

Cole nearly swallowed his tongue when he saw Kelsey. She was wearing a slinky black dress that hugged her curves and reminded him that she was so much more than simply the woman carrying his child. She was a woman. An attractive woman. One he was having a very hard time keeping his hands off of.

"I'm ready. So is there a local greasy spoon we get to go haunt? I brought a cloth napkin to spread out on the bench. I can use it in your truck too."

"You're funny, city girl," he said. "But we're not driving my truck. And this is a tourist trap, remember? We have a lovely bistro that serves locally grown organic cuisine, and I am taking you there."

"So, no steak? I was promised steak." They stepped off the cabin's porch and started down the trail, back toward the lodge.

"Organic, grass-fed local steak," he said, putting his hand on her lower back, his fingers tingling as the heat of her body seeped through the dress and into him.

"Fancy," she said. "Not unicorn meat or anything, but fancy."

"I didn't think you'd want unicorn. The glitter gets caught in your teeth."

"Mean," she said. "You *would* eat a unicorn. You're the kind of guy who names his ranch a haven for elk and then eats them."

"But then, you could pick the glitter out of your teeth with the horn."

"Cole . . ."

"Unicorn bacon seems like it could be some kind of rare and magical delicacy."

"Great, now you have me craving unicorn bacon. Do you know how cruel it is to make a pregnant woman crave something that doesn't exist?"

She stumbled slightly on the crooked path, and that was

when he noticed her shoes. Spiky and black. The kind of thing that gave a man very interesting fantasies. And made him want to call a woman "mistress" and say yes to whatever she asked of him. He shifted and tried to relieve the pressure in his jeans. He'd never had that particular fantasy before.

"Those shoes probably weren't the best option," he said, his voice rough.

"I love these shoes. They've pretty much been languishing in my closet. This is my first date in . . . a long time."

"How long?"

"Too long."

"Me too," he said, tightening his hold on her when the trail sloped downward before turning into a flat, open expanse of dirt.

He wasn't going to think about anything right now. Nothing except how good Kelsey felt pressed up against him. He was on vacation from logic tonight. Just for a couple of hours.

"So, what vehicle are we taking?"

"Cade's premature midlife crisis. He bought it with some of the money he got from his insurance after the accident. He came out of that pretty nicely, since one of the organizers was potentially liable for the dangerous situation."

"Poor guy."

"Yeah. It's been hard on him. He jokes about . . . well, about everything. But I don't think he finds much about the situation very funny."

"I can imagine."

"But"—Cole pulled a set of keys out of his pocket and hit the unlock button; the headlights on Cade's imported Italian sports car blinked—"we get to use his car."

"Very nice. I am impressed. He has taste. Garish, obvious taste, but sometimes a girl likes that."

"He spent most of his money in one chunk. But I think he was a little too pissed at life to care. I occasionally wonder if his original intent was to drive it off a cliff."

"I can imagine that too. Sometimes I wonder if that was

part of why I . . . No. That wasn't it." She waved a hand and walked to the passenger side of the sleek yellow car.

He reached past her and opened her door, holding it until she got inside. When he got into the driver's seat, she was buckled, facing forward, a serious look on her face.

"What do you wonder?" he asked, turning the key over, a little thrill racing through him when the engine started to purr. He loved this car. He loved it even more with Kelsey sitting in it. Kelsey and her long, sexy legs . . .

"I wonder if I was just so mad at life that I pushed back. That I wanted to laugh at fate and say, 'I don't need a husband, see? I can do this by myself.' See where my taunting got me? Ass bit, that's where my taunting got me."

"You consider me a bite in the ass from life?" he asked.

"A little bit."

"I don't think I've ever been more flattered. I need a T-shirt that reads, 'Cole Mitchell, Ass Bite.'"

"My mom could embroider it on a pillow for you. Of course, she could never, ever embroider the word 'ass,' so it would lose its impact. You'd become a tushy bite or something."

He laughed, and then silence settled between them. "I don't think that's why you did it," he said, throwing the car into drive and inching off the dirt and onto the paved portion of the road. Even a little dust would be frowned on by his brother.

"Oh, you don't?"

"No. I think you wanted a baby and you didn't want to wait. I get that."

"Well, that's true. But I also think . . . I think part of me feels like I've been punished for my bad decisions, and this was me trying to prove that I could work around the punishment. And it turns out that I really . . . can't."

"Why do you think you're being punished?" he asked.

"I don't know. For moving to the big city. For getting a job. For having sex with my boyfriend and living with him before we got married."

"Scandal," he said dryly.

"Yes, they won't let me into Almack's for the season now," she said.

"What?" The reference was lost on him.

"I read a lot of Regency romances in my spare time. It's . . . Never mind."

"Do you really think you're being punished?"

"I don't feel terribly punished right at the moment," she said, sliding her hand over the leather seat.

An arrow of heat shot to his groin, like she'd been running her palm over him instead of the lucky, lucky car. His cock pulsed and he winced, trying to keep his focus on the road.

"You aren't anyway. You aren't being punished, I mean. That's stupid, and I mean that in the nicest way. Crap happens. It happens to good people and it happens to bad people."

"And it happens to women who are idiot enough to drag their lazy-ass boyfriends around just because they're a habit. To get engaged because there hasn't been anyone else and there might not be. To deal with the fact that the sex is mediocre and the housekeeping skills are downright abysmal. Yeah, those women have crap happen to them because they don't ask for better."

"Well," he said, his mind stalled back on the line about mediocre sex, "now you're asking for better. You have been. You've been so successful, and now you're having a baby."

"I am," she said slowly. "And I should own it. And other people can suck it if they don't like it."

He laughed at the absurdity of the statement. "Yeah. They can suck it." He ignored the uncomfortable twinge at the apex of his thighs.

"Because it's my life," she said. "I'm the one who has to live it."

"Damn straight."

"Yeah, damn straight!" she echoed.

"Glad to see you're feeling empowered."

"It comes and goes."

"Yeah, that kind of thing does."

She sighed loudly. "Why is that?"

"I don't know. One of those things. Keeps us from getting cocky?"

"No danger of that. Every time I think I have it together, life pulls a Tonya Harding on my kneecaps with the metal rod of reality."

"This might be great, you know?"

"Yeah. It might be."

"And tonight let's forget about the pesky future, huh? Let's just be on a date."

She nodded. "I'm good with that. So tell me, would you have asked me out if we would have met when I didn't have your bun already in my oven?"

"Probably not. Not because you aren't hot; you are. But because I haven't asked anyone out since my ex left town with my balls."

"You get them back?"

"Yeah. Working on it."

"Right. Good to know. Well, I wouldn't have asked you out either. Also not because you aren't hot but because I haven't had a real date since Michael. Well, I have had dates. But they've been dodged, ended early, and self-sabotaged. I once played Angry Birds on my phone during dinner and barely spoke to the guy. Don't worry; I paid."

"Why did you do that?"

"Another one of life's mysteries. Mainly because I always think I'd like to date again, and then I realize how much I kind of hate the dating thing. Which is another huge reason I stuck with Michael despite the lackluster. I just like to be comfortable. Settled. I don't like having to try to meet someone new. I don't want to be in that stage where you fall crazy in love with someone ever again."

"Why is that? Isn't that the part everyone likes?"

"Sure. But the disillusionment is so bad. It's such a high that the low is . . . the low is horrible."

"Yeah, I know something about the low. Hell of a thing."

"She really knocked you on your butt, didn't she?"

"Unfortunately. I did crazy stuff for her. Made an idiot of myself. Taking off to Vegas to marry her because it seemed spontaneous and romantic. I jacked off—sorry—in a semipublic bathroom with dirty magazines on the rack so I could give the woman children conceived with sperm that was in its prime. I was insane, Kelsey. Insane. Mainly because I loved the idea of commitment more than I loved the woman I committed to. Because I wanted to have what my parents had. Permanent and solid. And then it turned out that was as real as my marriage. Love blows."

"Well, it's clear neither of us should get into the greeting card business. We would kill Valentine's Day for millions of Americans."

"But it's nice to know we're both on the same page."

"True."

Cole turned from the unlit two-lane highway and into town. The streetlights were bright, the lanterns strung between them adding further illumination and that old-world charm the town was so proud of. Cars already lined the streets, with the little restaurants filled mainly by tourists and local retirees.

And probably people on dates.

He pulled up to the curb and killed the engine, pocketing the keys and getting out of the car. Kelsey was already standing on the sidewalk by the time he got over to the passenger side.

"I was going to open your door for you," he said.

"No need."

"This is a date. That's how it works."

She laughed. "Really, is there a point in us dating, since we're anti-love?"

"I'm sorry—did you want steak or not?"

"I so do. I am anti-love, but I am pro-steak. But it's been so long since I went on a whole date, I can't really remember the protocol. Though, now that you mention it, Michael might have done that for me on prom night. But he was, um . . . after something."

"Did he get it?"

She shot him a deadly glare.

"It just seems like he might have made a habit of the door thing if it worked so well."

She sniffed. "Either way, I can open my own door."

"You're just being difficult."

"Yep. Get used to it."

"I find I am, and that concerns me a little bit."

"It's not so bad if we get used to each other, is it? I mean, all things considered."

He studied her face, her hair backlit by the glowing lanterns, a golden halo that gave the illusion of sweetness and light. "I don't know if 'used to each other' is the right phrase for it." A little kick of desire hit him in the stomach. No. He definitely wasn't used to her.

"Comfortable, then."

She took a step toward him, grasping his arm, her breast brushing against his biceps. No, "comfortable" wasn't right either.

"I don't know about that," he said, voice tight.

They walked down the sidewalk, the night air clear and crisp, quiet, like it always was in Silver Creek. It was one of the attractions. Right now he found it inconvenient. There was no steady sound of traffic, no other pedestrians. Nothing to distract him from the woman at his side.

To distract him from how incredibly gorgeous she was. And how incredibly hot he was for her.

"Let's talk about other things tonight," she said.

"I'm fine with that. What do you normally talk about on dates?"

"I'll have to dredge up a distant memory. Um . . . if I'm trying to chase the guy away or if I like him?"

He laughed. "I want to hear how you chase them away." He had a feeling it had to be pretty bad, because he knew he would endure a lot for the chance to kiss those perfect pink lips of hers. He'd put up with even more to have her in his bed. To have every inch of her bare, soft skin pressed against his . . .

"Well, sometimes I ignore them. Sometimes I make up

work emergencies. I once told a guy I needed to know if I was going to marry someone before I seriously dated them."

"Did you really?"

"I really did. Actually, it's a line one of my sisters used on a guy. It worked for her, though."

"Wow."

He opened the door to the restaurant. It was dim and a little more crowded than he would have hoped. Especially since it seemed to be crowded with a few people he knew. He hadn't been counting on that. What was it, local date night? They should have all been drinking beer and watching football in the bar.

"Yeah, well, Sadie has a way about her. And she's beautiful. All of my sisters married their very first loves. And they're all younger than me. Did I mention that?"

"You did."

"Hi, Cole." He looked down at the hostess, a petite brunette with the kind of hourglass figure that made most men look twice. Amber Jameson, Cade's lifelong friend and an honorary member of the family.

Just what he didn't need.

"Hi, Amber. I didn't know you were working here."

Her face fell slightly. "Yeah, well, I haven't been for very long. I needed to bring in a little extra. My grandfather's not doing very well right now."

"Sorry to hear that." Amber had been brought to Silver Creek as an angry foster child and had been raised by her grandparents from then on. "Is that why I haven't seen you out at the ranch lately?"

"Mostly," she said, biting her lip. She wanted to say more, but wouldn't. Amber was cagey and prickly. Which was probably why Cade got along with her so well. "I suppose you need a seat."

"It would be nice."

"Who's your . . . friend?" she asked.

"Oh, Amber, this is Kelsey. Kelsey, Amber."

Kelsey stuck out her hand, her expression slightly cool. Amber's was friendly, and she shook Kelsey's offered hand before grabbing a couple of red leather menus and leading them to the back of the restaurant. They sat in a booth with red pleather that matched the menus. Class was in short supply in Silver Creek, though at least an attempt had been made.

"Okay, Jessica will be your server, and she'll be by soon. Good to see you, Cole," Amber said, offering him a smile, one that looked sadder than usual. He would have to tell Cade so he could call and harass her. Lord knew Amber wouldn't ask for help, not even if she needed it.

"See you around, Amber." He picked up the menu and opened it.

"Is she . . . an ex?" Kelsey asked, pale eyebrow arched.

"No." His chest warmed with a little satisfaction. The coolness in her demeanor had been jealousy. Interesting. "She's one of Cade's best friends. One of his only friends. I don't know if you noticed, but he's a difficult bastard to like."

"*I* like him."

"Well, women do. He's charming, but he's a flake. Not so much these days, though. He can't get around fast enough anymore, which means he can't disappear into the night as efficiently as he used to."

"He has itchy feet, huh?"

"He always has." Though, recent revelations regarding their dad considered, Cade's itchy feet made a lot more sense now than they had in the past. Cade had always seemed like he was running from something, because that was exactly what he'd been doing.

"What about you? You just . . . You always wanted to stay here?"

"I don't know. I never thought about an alternative. My mom died when I was a kid. This is the only place where I have memories of her. My dad . . . well, he was my hero and he was a rancher. I was trained from an early age to run it, and it was all I knew. It doesn't make a lot of sense to go out and take a gamble when you have resources right at your fingertips."

"But is it what you want?" she asked, opening her menu and perusing it.

"It's what I do. It's a part of me. I don't know if I could do anything else. For me, it's always been about doing what was . . . right." He'd never really put it into words before, but then, he'd never really given it a lot of thought. He'd always been expected to take over Elk Haven, and so he'd always worked toward it.

It was his piece of the world. His place. It was in his blood. He didn't have a burning passion for it, but he doubted he could leave it and be happy. But then, he'd always considered it to be a legacy. To be part of the Mitchells. But his dad hadn't really had his whole life there. He'd had another life. So maybe he was wrong about all of it.

"So you were the good son. What's that like?"

"I don't know if I'm the good son."

"Trust me. You are. My sisters are all the good sister. I'm the black sheep. The one out of five. The 'can't win 'em all.' I'm the one that gets whispered about at every family gathering. Such an odd duck. Unmarried. Career. At a certain point, I either had to embrace it or try to fit back into the fold."

"I take it you embraced it."

"Well, yeah, the unwed-mother-by-choice thing kinda gives that away, doesn't it?"

He laughed. "Yes, that it does."

"If I worried too much about what they thought, about their ideals . . . I wouldn't be able to get what I wanted."

"What do you want, Kelsey?"

"I think the steak is probably a good idea," she said.

"Not from the menu. From life."

She laughed. "Oh. I thought you were talking food, not getting philosophical. See how bad my dates have been recently?"

"At least they've existed," he said.

She shrugged. "I lied to escape them, so I'm not sure it's better. Uh . . . what do I want? I want to be happy. Doesn't everyone?"

"I guess."

She paused, looking down at her hands. "And I sort of wish that someday . . . my family could be happy for me. Happy that my choices have been right for me. I don't know if they ever will be."

"Is it important?"

"I don't know—mostly because it hasn't happened yet."

Their server, whom Cole knew from high school, came by and took their order. Kelsey ordered a steak—an expensive one—and handed her menu back to the waitress.

She couldn't explain the little bubble of jealousy that had ballooned in her chest and had seemed to expand with every word Amber had spoken to him when they'd first walked in. It hadn't helped that the other woman was different from her in appearance. Petite, curvy, with glossy brown hair and eyes.

She hadn't really felt any better when he'd dismissed her as a friend of Cade's. Because the biggest problem wasn't who Amber was but why it had mattered to her.

Fortunately, the interruption by the waitress had put a halt to the deep conversation, and they surfaced to make small talk until the meal arrived.

"It is a nice steak," she said.

"And you feel up to eating it?"

"Beef is agreeing with me. Anyway, I feel so much better. Hardly sick at all now."

"I'm glad. I didn't like seeing you like that."

The caring admission made her stomach feel warm. Another feeling she didn't want to analyze too deeply.

"Yeah, well, I didn't really enjoy being myself when I was like that."

"I don't know that their approval would make you happier," he said slowly.

"What?"

"I'm not sure it's been my experience. I did everything that was asked of me, and things haven't been a whole lot easier, even with the approval of my parents."

She traced lines over her mashed potatoes with her fork tines. "I was afraid of that."

"I'm not really a self-examiner. But going through life, I've had a lot of things change. So in my experience, nothing is ever really done and settled. You don't reach the finish line until you die, and until then, things change. My mom died. Then I got married, my dad died, I got divorced, and Cade got injured. It always changes. And you always keep going."

"So, you're saying I won't reach a magical place where I know I've made it?"

He shook his head. "Sorry."

"I was expecting to hit a place in my life where it would be . . . perfect. Confetti would rain down. The band would play. I could go stand on the big pedestal that read 'Number One' and hold a big trophy over my head."

He laughed and shook his head. "Did you?"

"No. Well, yeah, without the fanfare. I mean, I thought I would get somewhere and I would have it all figured out. I've been waiting for my aha moment."

"I don't think those exist. You just have to keep putting one foot in front of the other."

"I like my version better. It's a lot more exciting."

"It also has confetti."

"There would be a cake too. With 'Congratulations, Kelsey! You no longer suck at life!' written on it."

"Vanilla?"

"No. What's wrong with you? No. A congratulatory-life-achievements cake is only ever going to be chocolate."

"Fair enough. But if the confetti doesn't rain down and no one bakes a cake?"

"Then I guess one foot in front of the other works."

She was planned out. Planned to near death. She was trying to map out the future, and she couldn't, because the variables were too numerous and too large. Anyway, her plans had a way of going awry in a pretty huge way.

One foot in front of the other, she could do. For now. It wasn't how she did things, but the temptation to do it now was just too great.

Right now Cole was the sexiest guy in the room. If a

random sampling of other rooms had been taken and brought into the restaurant, he would probably still be the sexiest.

He made her heart race. He made her body ache. He made her want to have that amazing, uninhibited rebound sex she'd never had after her breakup. That part was inconvenient.

Or maybe it wasn't. She was on vacation from reality tonight, after all. And all her good intentions about keeping things uncomplicated were starting to get shoved way off to the side.

Fourteen

In the spirit of being on vacation from reality and not thinking too far ahead, Kelsey didn't decide for or against kissing
Cole at the end of the date. She was just going to see what
happened.

He walked her from the car back to her cabin, his flashlight illuminating the path just enough to see immediately
in front of them. A grand continuation of the evening's
metaphor.

When they were both on the porch, in front of the door,
her stomach tightened, her heart rate increasing. It felt so
juvenile, so immature, so amazing, to be standing there at
the end of a date wondering if she'd get a kiss.

It seemed a lot simpler than focusing on reality. And a
lot more fun.

She took a step toward him. Then another. She watched
his breathing speed up, watched his chest pitch sharply. She
took another step. He was right; this was easy.

And she wasn't going to wonder about getting a kiss. She
was getting one. She decided on that while she was leaning

in, had committed to it completely only when her lips touched his.

The feel of his mouth against hers shocked her, rendered her motionless and then boneless. Thankfully, Cole was quick. He wrapped his arms around her and kept her buckling knees from sending her to the ground in an undignified heap.

She put her hands flat on his chest, the only movement she could manage with him holding her so tightly, and angled her head, letting him deepen the kiss. Welcoming the hot sweep of his tongue against hers.

A shiver worked its way through her body, leaving behind an unsatisfied ache. His big hands slid down her back, stopping just before the curve of her butt.

Oh, just a little farther.

She wanted his hands on her. Everywhere. She wanted him naked and pressed against her and naked. Because it had been too long. Even longer since she'd wanted someone this much. It was entirely possible that she'd never wanted anyone this much.

And it had happened so fast. Just the touch of Cole's lips and she'd caught fire. And now the flame was dangerously close to burning out of control.

She wiggled just enough to get her arms free and move to cup his face, her thumbs skimming his stubble-roughened cheeks, fingers lacing through his dark hair. She pulled him closer, pulled them both backward so that they stumbled. The wall of the cabin kept her from falling, her back pressed against it, Cole's hard chest solid in front of her.

She felt trapped in the very best way. A willing captive, for sure.

His hands moved back up and she just about growled with disapproval until they migrated lower, one hot hand resting on her rear.

He couldn't be the only one who was allowed to explore.

She slid her hands down his chest, the heat and hard muscle beneath his shirt evident and a big, enticing tease.

When she reached his belt, she pushed her fingertips beneath the shirt. It was sensory overload. Hot skin, the ripple of abs and, up farther, crisp chest hair. He was so masculine. Everything she wasn't. Everything she'd deprived herself of for far too long.

He leaned into her and she took her hands out from beneath his shirt, anxious to close any distance between them. She could feel his erection, hard and thick against her hip. She arched into him, wishing she was a little taller so she could move against him *just right* and satisfy some of that hollow, painful arousal that was threatening to take over her body and brain.

He lifted his head, wrenching his lips from hers, stumbling backward. "Damn," he said.

"Right. Do you want to come . . . in?"

She realized how lame that sounded, but not until after she said it. She was breathless, and it was obvious. She was desperate too. For him. For fulfillment. She was afraid that was pretty obvious as well.

"I shouldn't."

"I know you shouldn't, but will you?"

He looked like he was seriously considering it. And while he considered it, she let her eyes drift downward, to the very obvious bulge in his jeans. Oh, she wanted him to come in. Badly.

"I . . ." She'd never seen Cole look more conflicted, not even when he was trying to decide between fatherhood and running from her and never looking back. He shifted, his eyes focused on a spot just to the left of her head. "I don't think I can."

"What?"

He looked just as shocked as she felt. "It's too complicated, Kelsey."

"Damn it," she said. "I know that. I really do know that. I just . . ." How did she explain, without terminally embarrassing herself, that he was the only man who'd seemed worth the risk in longer than she could remember? There really wasn't a way to do it. And if she was being honest, he wasn't worth the risk.

Because they had a good thing now. Now they could do holidays and birthdays and Sundays together if they wanted, because they had no real attachment to each other. And none had been broken either. They could meet and be friends, and their child could have parents who were civil to each other.

But introducing sex . . . well, that would screw everything up. At least it had the potential to. There was no chance of no-strings sex with him because she and Cole had nothing but strings.

She swallowed heavily, ignoring the ache in her core. "Good night."

He frowned, his expression pained. Regretful.

Good.

"Good night." He turned and walked down the steps. She stood and watched him until he melted into the shadow of the path.

"Why is there no more beer?" Cole growled to the empty kitchen.

"You sound like you need more than beer." Cade walked in and opened a cabinet, reaching up to the top and moving some glasses aside until he produced a bottle of whiskey. "This is what you sound like you need."

"It hardly seems fair," he said, taking the bottle from Cade's hand.

"Why is that?"

"Kelsey can't drink this problem away for a few hours. I can, though, and I intend to do it."

"A man after my own heart." Cade took two small glasses down and set them on the counter. "So, other than the surprise pregnancy"—he took the bottle back from Cole and poured a decent portion into each glass—"what is driving you to drink?"

"I took her on a date tonight." He picked up the glass and knocked back the contents, grimacing as they blazed a trail of fire from his throat to his stomach.

"Yeah, I know. I let you out of here with my car. Wait . . . Nothing happened to my car, did it? Is that why you're drinking? If that's the problem, get drunker, because I'm going to bust your—"

"Nothing happened to your car."

"Well." His brother shifted. "Good."

"She asked me in."

"Like she asked you in as in she wanted to offer you coffee? And by that, I mean sex."

"I believe so."

His brother slapped both hands on the counter. "Then why are you here?"

"I said no."

"Why?" Cade looked almost comically incredulous. As if the idea of refusing sex had never occurred to him as a possibility.

"She's pregnant with my baby."

"Yeah, so?"

"So casual sex is out of the question. If we sleep together and things go south, we're introducing a whole lot of crap into the mix that we don't need."

"I don't see how sex could screw things up."

"Because you don't stay long enough to talk to a girl after you screw her—that's why you think that. I happen to have experience with relationships. And they aren't easy."

"Sex doesn't mean you're in a relationship, does it? If so, I need to make a call."

"Stop bullshitting for a second, will you?"

"I'll do my best."

"I have to figure out how to . . . make this work. We have to share custody of this kid, and I want to be involved. I'm not going to let the whole thing fall down around me because I let my dick do the thinking."

"Not that uncommon, is it?"

Cole shook his head. "Not at all."

Cade frowned and took a drink of his whiskey, his expression turning serious. "You're after a guarantee, Cole, but you aren't going to get it. You can't tell what's going to happen. You can't see into the future."

"I of all people know that. Life has thrown me enough crap out of nowhere that I've given up guessing what might happen next." Still, Cade's warning hit close to home. Maybe he wasn't after a guarantee, but a little bit of control would have been nice.

"The only way to secure things is— Well, hell, you'd have to marry her. Then at least she'd be stuck with you. And you could get some too."

His brother's tone was light, as though he were making the world's most ridiculous suggestion. Cole wasn't so sure.

"Marriage vows can be broken," he said.

Cade shrugged. "Not as simple with a kid."

No. No, it wasn't. And the alternative was separate lives. A child who would never know a united family. It made marriage seem not quite so scary.

"I . . . I could ask her to marry me."

Cade's eyes widened. "I know you aren't drunk yet; you barely touched your whiskey. What are you saying?"

"That I could ask her to marry me."

"Why?"

"I think that's pretty obvious. She's pregnant with my baby."

"But you don't even know her, you dumbass."

"Wouldn't you ask a woman to marry you if you got her pregnant?"

Cade shrugged. "I don't know. Yeah, I probably would. But only because if *I* got a woman pregnant, I would feel responsible. You shouldn't feel responsible. You didn't get her pregnant. Maybe the doctor at the lab should propose to her."

"That was my justification for not asking from moment one, but the thing that's starting to get harder and harder to ignore is that no matter how she got pregnant, the results will be the same. She's having my baby. It doesn't really matter how."

Cade shook his head before knocking back his own drink. "I don't know, man. Marriage . . . marriage."

"I know."

"You really want another wife? I'd call Shawna a bitch, but it's insulting to dogs everywhere."

"Really? Marriage scares the hell out of me. Shawna was . . . It was a disaster. My marriage was horrible, and the marriage I held up as the gold standard was a lie. But Shawna and Kelsey are nothing alike. I was stupid over that woman because I was nuts for her. Kelsey . . . I like her. I'm attracted to her, but it's not stupid like it was with Shawna. And I want Kelsey to be with me, especially now. I want the baby to be with me when he's born. I can't just leave the ranch. There's always work to do. And she can't come back and forth all the time."

"Why can't she? She's not having any trouble taking as much time off as she needs to be here."

"Well, she works from home. But she has a home. Not everyone's comfortable living out of a suitcase."

"I prefer it," Cade said, eyeing the bottle. "One more?"

"One more." Cole held his glass up, and Cade accommodated him.

"So, you'd rather get married than work out shared custody?"

"I'd rather have an intact family than a scattered one," he said. He swallowed the new whiskey, biting his lip as it went down.

"But a lot of people just deal with it."

"Sure. And some people are like Dad, and they say one thing, even maybe believe it, but they don't back it up." He let out a breath. "Dad had a kid he never saw, Cade. Ever. What if that happens? What if Kelsey marries someone else? Has more kids. What if I do? And it leaves this one in limbo. With nothing. The thought of that . . . I can't do that. The Shawna thing, this stuff with Dad, it kinda messed me up, but I think I still assumed deep down I'd have a family someday."

"I don't think that," Cade said.

"You didn't think that I would or that you would?"

"Me. I don't think I'd make a great family man. I always thought you would. You've taken great care of Lark. And if you can deal with a teenage girl, I have no doubt you'll do fine with a baby."

Cole sighed. The liquor had only increased the slight melancholy he felt. "Maybe it's not an ideal solution. But the alternative isn't ideal either. Maybe asking her to marry me is my best option."

"Then you'll have a wife *and* a baby to deal with."

Cole nodded. "Yeah, that's true."

"Don't do it just because you want to . . . do it with her. If you want to have sex, fine, but that's no reason to go and get married."

"That's not why, Cade. I've made that mistake. This is deeper than that. Bigger. And yeah, I mean, attraction figures in, but . . . mainly . . . this whole thing is a complicated mess, and the more we build lives apart from each other, the more complicated it will be. If I marry her? In my head, it just makes everything make a lot more sense."

"Does anything scare you, Cole?" Cade asked, suddenly serious. The liquor must have gone to his head too.

"Yeah. A lot of things. I just do them all anyway."

Cade nodded slowly, put his glass on the counter and walked out of the room.

"I have a doctor appointment," Kelsey said. She leaned against the marble bar in the lodge's common area, her face pale, her hair pulled back into a ponytail.

"Here?" Cole asked.

She nodded. "I went ahead and made it yesterday, after we talked. I decided that I should have someone in Silver Creek. Since I'm staying here for . . . a while longer." She looked away when she said that, clearly unwilling to specify a time frame. Or say anything that might be misconstrued as a commitment.

"Not a bad idea."

"I thought you should come. I just . . . I know you want to be involved."

"I appreciate that." He found he was more than willing. Especially since he'd gotten the marriage idea in his head. He wanted to spend more time with her. Wanted to seem more like a couple.

He was test-driving it, which shamed him a little bit. He should be able to just do it. He felt like it was the right thing, the best thing. He swallowed, his throat suddenly tight. Of course it was the right thing.

"I bet it's too much to ask to take the sports car again?" she asked, the hopeful tone of her voice dragging a slight laugh out of him. "I think every woman deserves to have an OB appointment in style. In exchange for open-backed gowns and . . . stirrups."

"Not the kind you use for horse riding?"

"No."

"I doubt Cade will relinquish it again so soon. He has to do a twelve-point inspection on it and make sure we didn't do any damage while driving it last night."

She grimaced. "Too bad. We can drive my car."

"You don't want to go in the truck?"

"Hmm . . . not really."

"All right, fair enough. When do you need to leave?"

"An hour."

He nodded slowly, a strange squeezing sensation in his chest. "I'll see you then."

Cole waited outside during the beginning of the exam. The part that dealt with internal examinations and other things she really didn't want him privy to. For the last part she was able to minimize the embarrassment of the hospital gown by putting her jeans back on, with the fly open and rolled down, the gown pulled up over her stomach.

Cole walked in slowly, the expression on his face almost comical. She would have laughed if she hadn't felt just as nervous.

Dr. Long greeted Cole with a smile and shook his hand. She seemed to know Cole too. Everyone here seemed to know him. Kelsey thanked God for laws prohibiting doctors from spreading information about patients. The woman took a bottle of gel from a warmer on the counter and squirted the substance onto Kelsey's stomach. "We're going to use the Doppler to hear the baby's heartbeat today," Dr. Long said.

"Have you done this before?" Cole asked. He looked a little pale.

Kelsey shook her head. "No. The only time I went to the

doctor was to confirm the pregnancy and check viability, but it was too soon to hear anything. I took like . . . four tests before I went. Just to be sure."

He laughed, some of his nerves seeming to dissipate at her admission.

"What?" she said. "I had to know."

"I don't blame you."

"Then the vomiting started and I was very sure."

That earned her a laugh from both Cole and the doctor.

Dr. Long put the Doppler on Kelsey's stomach and started moving it slowly. It was quiet in the room. Kelsey held her breath, waiting for a sound. For something. The silence seemed endless, dread filling her as it stretched on, nothing more than a faint crackling, watery sound.

Then the doctor found it. The sound, like wind through a tunnel, beating a steady rhythm, filled the room.

Kelsey giggled, a nervous bubble that climbed up her throat and escaped her lips. She'd never heard anything so incredible. "It's so fast."

"It's perfectly normal," Dr. Long said.

Kelsey looked up at Cole. He looked like he'd been hit with a two-by-four. "That's the heartbeat?" he asked.

"That's the heartbeat," Dr. Long said.

Too soon, she removed the Doppler and wiped the gel from Kelsey's stomach. "Everything looks good, Kelsey. I'll see you back here next month. Make an appointment out front before you go." She smiled and left, but not before offering Cole a quick pat on the shoulder.

Kelsey rolled into a sitting position, letting the hospital gown fall down over her stomach. "Wow," she said.

"Yeah. That makes it feel . . ."

"Much more real," she said. "Much more."

"His heart is beating," Cole said. "We could hear it. He's really there." He just stood there for a moment before shaking his head. "I'll go. . . . I'll let you get dressed."

She waved a hand and slid off the table. "It's fine. Just turn around for a minute."

He obeyed and she bent down, shrugging her shoulders to let the hospital gown fall to the floor.

She picked her bra up and slipped it on. "I'm glad you came," she said.

"Me too."

She took her shirt from the floor and pulled it over her head, her stomach still tacky and a little bit cold from the gel. She buttoned her jeans and turned around. Cole was facing away from her, just as she'd asked. Ever the gentleman.

Her mind flashed back to the kiss they'd shared the night before. Ever the gentleman, except when he wasn't. She liked it better when he wasn't. It was easy to remember the feel of his hands, rough and masculine on her skin. Yes, she liked that Cole better.

"I'm ready."

He turned and faced her. The impact of his sex appeal seemed more pronounced now. Maybe because she felt scrungy, while he was looking amazing in his cowboy hat, snug jeans and black T-shirt.

"Do you want to go walk with me for a while?" he asked.

"Where?"

He shrugged. "Somewhere."

"Well, how can I resist?"

They walked out of the exam room, and Kelsey deliberately avoided the front desk. She didn't know if she'd be staying long enough to make another appointment. She had no idea what she was going to do.

The small clinic was set just outside of town, next to the creek, with a path winding around the building and around behind it, following the line of the water.

Cole's heart kicked into gear. Pounding hard, fast. He couldn't remember the last time he'd felt so nervous. Maybe not since he had been waiting to get confirmation on whether or not the man in Portland who ran up those debts was really the same man he'd called "Dad."

That had been out of his hands. Something he had no

control over. Here—here he had the control. There was no waffling. No room for nerves.

Hearing the heartbeat, his baby's heartbeat—it had made the decision for him.

"Kelsey . . . that was amazing," he said, opting for unguarded honesty. To let her see how much it meant to him.

She smiled, the first smile he'd seen on her face that wasn't tinged with worry, or sickness, or sadness. Just pure joy. He was certain he'd never seen a more beautiful woman. That made his next move easier, in some ways.

"It was," she said. "I don't think I've ever felt more connected to it all. To the baby. He's really there." She looked like she might cry now, and he wasn't sure that was in his best interest.

"It made it more real for me too," he said, again going with honesty. "And it made me think about how hard it would be to be . . . hours away from you. While you're going through this. When the baby is born. To be away from him."

"We don't know it's a him," she said, neatly sidestepping his comments. He wasn't going to allow it.

"No, we don't." His throat tightened; the thought of a little girl was somehow even more . . . striking in that moment. "If it's a girl . . . I'd still miss her."

"We'll figure something out. We will." She put her hand on his arm, and a shot of electricity jolted him, from his arm straight down to his groin.

Good thing he had it worked out. He cleared his throat. "I'm sure we will."

She took her hand away as suddenly as she'd touched him, and he felt cold where her fingers had rested. "This could have been the nightmare from hell, and surprisingly, it's been okay."

He frowned. "It's not that surprising, is it?"

"Yeah, it is. Random guy shows up informing you you're pregnant with his baby? That could be scary. We're lucky in our freakish circumstances, I guess." She smiled again, and the expression on her face effectively stalled the words he'd been about to speak.

He didn't want to do anything to erase the smile.

"I would say so."

"Want to grab some lunch?"

"That sounds good."

The proposal could wait until later.

Cole looked at the ring nestled in the wooden box, surrounded by tissue paper. Not the most elegant place for a wedding ring to be stored—but the ring itself was perfection.

His mother's ring.

Strange, but it was the one he wanted to give Kelsey. Not because his parents' marriage had been so great but because it meant something to him. It was something he hadn't offered Shawna. It was something she would have spit like a cat about if she had discovered its existence and discovered that he hadn't, even for one moment, thought of putting it on her finger.

But this was different. Kelsey was different. He was making a family with her, and that was what the ring meant to him. More than asking her to be his wife, he wanted to make her a part of his family.

He didn't need love from her. He didn't even want it. Security and commitment were much more important. Much more permanent. His child would have rights to the ranch—real, familial rights that his half sister had been cut out of.

He would do it right. He would be committed. A man of his word. The man his father hadn't been. Family was what mattered, the most important thing in the world. No child of his would ever feel locked out of the family they should have.

But first, he had to talk to Lark.

He knocked on his sister's door and received a muted grunt in response that he was sure signaled permission for him to come in.

He opened the door and stepped in. Lark was sitting at her computer, leaning forward so that she was way too close to the screen.

"Hey, can I talk to you?" he asked.

She turned to look at him for the first time, her expression unbelievably sad for a moment before she remembered to smile. "Sure."

"I can wait until another time."

"I'm fine," she said, the lie so obvious that they were both aware of it.

"So . . . I wanted to ask you about Mom's rings." He held the box out and showed his sister the platinum band and the solitaire engagement ring.

"What about them?"

"I'm going to ask Kelsey to marry me. I wouldn't feel right about offering her the rings without talking to you first because . . . I thought you might want them."

Lark's dark eyes glittered. "I'm never going to get married, so I don't know why you even need to bother asking me."

"Why do you say that?"

"Nothing," she said.

"Tyler again?"

"She's gone and he still hardly talks to me." She paused, then clapped her hand over her mouth. "Sorry," she said through her hand before lowering it. "You're going to propose to Kelsey? I'm so lost in my own pathetic problems, I totally skipped over that."

"It's okay. I understand." He didn't, mostly because he'd

never felt whatever had made Lark look like someone had forced her to listen to a succession of sad country songs.

"It's not okay. I'm sorry. I . . . I'm happy for you, Cole." She stood up and hugged him. "Please give her the rings."

"Are you sure?"

"I'm not anywhere near getting married, Cole. I have way too much to do." She drew in a shaky breath and lifted her chin. "I don't even want to get married. Not now. Maybe not ever."

"Thanks, Lark."

"I'm glad Kelsey will have them."

"I haven't asked her yet."

"She'd be stupid to say no. You're a good man."

"Not any better than most. But I am the father of her baby, so I'm hoping I'll look like the convenient choice, if not the best one."

"Do you love her?" His sister's expression was so hopeful, he almost hated to tell the truth.

"I like her," he said. "I like her a lot. And we're having a baby."

"And that's enough of a reason?"

"It is for me. Romance is fine, but mostly it's a lot of drama."

"Especially a one-sided romance, I'm discovering," his sister muttered.

"Right," he said, feeling uncomfortable with the topic. "Or really any kind. I'm happier finding common ground and building a commitment from there."

"You're good at commitment, Cole," she said.

"Am I?"

"You've never let me down."

A strange tightness invaded his throat. He hoped he never would. "Glad to hear that, kid."

"She's lucky to have you. The baby is lucky to have you."

"Shucks, Lark, you're going to make me get sentimental."

She smiled. "I doubt it. You don't know how to be sentimental."

He'd thought so too. But now he was starting to wonder.

And maybe he wouldn't be the worst father in the world, after all. Maybe he would be a decent husband the second time around. If he kept his head on straight, remembered commitment over everything else and kept his emotions out of it, maybe it would be fine. Maybe.

He found Kelsey in her cabin later, sprawled across the bed, typing on her laptop and eating red licorice from a big plastic tub.

"What are you doing?" he asked.

She looked up at him from her position, her ponytail flopping to the side as she took another bite of red candy. "I'm writing about health and wellness during pregnancy."

"I'm going to call hypocrisy."

"Shut up." She reached out and grabbed her tub of licorice, hugging it to her chest. "Health is about how you feel."

"And about little things like blood sugar levels and cholesterol."

"Don't judge me."

"I wouldn't dare."

And he knew then that he was doing the right thing. He did like Kelsey. A lot. And what he really wanted to do was lie down next to her and see if he could taste some of that candy if he kissed her lips. That had to count for something. In his book, sexual attraction counted for a lot. It made the idea of marriage seem bearable. More than bearable. He hadn't gotten any from his ex. But then, he truly hadn't liked her in the end, so he wouldn't have wanted it anyway.

Kelsey was now up by two. He liked her, and he wanted to sleep with her.

But he didn't give in to the temptation; he just stood at the foot of the bed.

"Good. Fear my hormonally charged wrath," she said.

"I do."

"What's on your mind? And don't get all paternal on me. I ate dinner. I'm just also having the licorice. Now that I'm not puking my guts out all the time, eating is all I think about."

"I came to . . . Could you stand up?"

"Can I sit?"

"Sure."

She moved into a sitting position, swinging her legs over the edge of the bed. He took a deep breath and walked to where she was. He considered getting on one knee. He changed his mind quickly. Getting down on one knee was what drunk idiots did before they took their girlfriends to Vegas. It was what they did to make grand gestures. This wasn't a grand gesture. He wasn't drunk. He was just trying to do what was best.

"Kelsey, I've been thinking a lot about us. And the baby. And how it will work out."

"I'm willing to bet that's about all either of us have thought about."

"I'm sure. I think I have a solution."

He reached into his pocket and fumbled for the ring box, such as it was. The wood made a clattering sound and the lid fell off. He reached inside and took the engagement ring out from its position in the tissue paper and held it up, the diamond catching the light.

She dropped her licorice. "Are you . . . Do you . . . You aren't asking me to . . . are you?"

He nodded and sat down on the bed beside her, the ring still offered up. "I want you to marry me." It felt right to say it. It felt like glue—a solution. One he badly needed.

"No," she said, jumping up. "No. Just . . . no. Why would you ask me that?"

He nearly dropped the ring. "What do you mean, why? You're pregnant with my baby, and I think it solves a lot of our problems."

"Are you freaking kidding me? You think marriage is going to solve our problems?"

"Of all the reactions I imagined, getting yelled at wasn't one of them."

She let out an exasperated breath and crossed her arms beneath her breasts. "Tell me why you want to marry me."

"Because it will be convenient," he bit out, pocketing the

ring, not bothering to put it back in the box. "Because it makes sense. It's the right thing to do."

"Well, shit, Cole, that's the most romantic thing I've ever heard."

"Nothing about this situation is romantic, and I'm not pretending that it is. But we do have to figure out what we're doing. I'm offering a solution. You certainly haven't."

"What? Just . . . what? I don't think I heard you right. I have offered nothing but solutions from moment one. Haven't I come to stay here to get to know you? Haven't I made an effort? Gone to a doctor in town? I could have slammed the door in your face the minute you showed up, but I didn't."

"Because you need me, and you know it," he growled.

"Oh, I do *not* need you," she said, her voice low.

For a second Kelsey thought he might back down—doing his best not to get a tub of licorice thrown at his ass, she imagined. She'd confessed her tendency toward violence, after all.

Her heart was pounding, her head swimming. The worst part of it all had been the gut-wrenching moment of temptation. It had been only a moment, but it had been so real, so tangible, she'd nearly grabbed on with both hands and clung to it.

And then reality had come to her rescue.

"You don't need me?" he said, taking a step toward her, his expression dark.

This was a different Cole from the one she'd seen. This Cole was intense. Determined. Sexy as hell.

He hooked his arm around her waist and drew her up against him. His body was hard and hot, and it went a long way in proving his point.

"I think you're a liar," he said, leaning in, his lips a whisper away from hers. "I think you do need me."

"You don't need to propose just because you want sex," she said, hoping to outmaneuver him. Hoping to shock. "For you? I'd come a lot cheaper."

He lifted his hand and traced the line of her jaw. "I don't

want cheap, babe. I want lasting. And for that? I need to propose." He released his hold on her and stepped back. And she was disappointed. And she didn't want to admit it, not even to herself. "Sex is way too much of a risk without it."

He was right about that. And she was mad at him, so she shouldn't care. Right now she felt like a kid who'd had a piece of candy taken from her.

"I'm not going to marry you just because you got a bad case of the chivalries."

"Is that even a thing?" he asked, arching one eyebrow.

"Apparently. It causes otherwise sane men to propose marriage for no logical reason."

"You're pregnant with my baby. Under a circumstance that didn't involve a lab, I would have asked you the day I found out."

"Me or any other woman pregnant with your child. Am I right?"

He tightened his jaw; a muscle in his cheek jumped. "Yes."

"No."

"Why are you being so stubborn?" Spoken just like a man who couldn't fathom that anyone would think his logic was wrong.

"Because you want a perfect picture. You want to somehow cram this into a traditional ideal, and I hate to break it to you, but you can't do that in this case. You can't make 'I got a girl pregnant on accident because of a lab mistake' into traditional. You can't do it. Why you would even try is beyond me."

"Because it makes sense. When two people have a child together . . ."

"They've usually slept together first. We hadn't even met. And even then, the couple that slept together doesn't work out more than half the time. Why would you think we would?"

"You can't pretend we aren't attracted."

"Attraction isn't a good reason to get married either."

"Then what is, Kelsey? Love? How does that work out for most people? It didn't work out for me. Love made me an idiot. It was a roller coaster, and the minute it slowed down, I begged to get off that ride. Speaking of, how did that love thing work out for you?"

"Uh . . ."

"Marriage is a commitment; it's not about feelings."

"The romance keeps coming, but I'm going to go with my original answer."

"I thought we both established we didn't want love. This isn't about romance."

"No. It's about you trying to satisfy some male code of honor, but that is not a good enough reason for me to say yes to someone."

"Are you going to leave?" he asked. His expression was stoic, blank, but it didn't fool her.

"No." She knew when she said it that there was no way she was leaving, especially not now.

"Why not?"

"Because we're going to make this work. And we don't need marriage to do it, but we do need to be friends." The word stuck in her throat. She liked Cole, but her feelings for him seemed way too complicated to call him a friend.

His lip curled. "Friends?"

"Yes. Friends. I think that's our best bet. Like it or not—and right now it's edging toward not—we are in this together."

"I'm not denying that."

"Obviously. But I disagree with your methods."

"So you think 'friends raising a baby' is the way to go?" He leaned in again, and she was assaulted by his scent. Clean, a little spicy and under that . . . his skin. She missed that. Being so close to someone she could smell their skin— just them.

It made her want to close the distance between them. But she wouldn't.

"Yes," she said, her throat tight.

He leaned in a bit more and her breath caught, her stomach turning. "That means no kissing," he said, his breath hot on her lips.

"Naturally not."

"Because if you don't want marriage, then that means it has to stay platonic. Sex introduces . . . issues. And neither of us can afford those issues."

"I think I can handle that," she said, going for snarky but hitting breathless instead.

He tilted his head to the side, dark eyes glittering. He didn't believe her. Cocky bastard. "All right, then. I'd like you to consider moving into the house, now that Alexa's gone." His lips curved, a smug smile.

"This is all very Big Bad Wolf, you know? Now that my protector is gone, you're luring me into your den. . . . I don't know if I like it."

"You like it. A lot. But because we're just friends, it doesn't matter."

Her cheeks burned. "I do not. Like it. Like that. I like it as a friend." Yeah, she liked tall, dark, dangerous and alpha as a friend. Right.

"Will you come to the house?"

"In the interest of friendship?"

He moved away from her and she could breathe again. "Of course."

"Sounds fine to me." Better than fine, in many ways, since bunking out in the wilderness on her own was a little disconcerting. Though the idea of bunking in his domain was a little scary; but his brother and sister were in there.

"Good."

"I'd like to move my things over tonight." She was ready to try to take the upper hand in the situation. To put him off, since he'd so thoroughly managed to knock her off-balance.

The corners of his lips turned upward, and she found herself thinking how nice it would be to kiss the creases that bracketed his mouth. She blinked.

"Good. Do you need help packing?"

"Nah, I think I can pack my own underwear."

He arched one brow. "Are you sure?"

"Perv. Let me pack my own panties," she said, finding it hard to hang on to the anger she'd just been feeling toward him. She didn't know why it was hard.

"It was an offer of platonic underwear packing. We're just friends, after all. I'll just let you get ready. Do you want me to come back and help you carry anything?"

"Sure. I'll text you when all the unmentionables are packed."

He nodded once and walked out of the cabin. She listened to his heavy footsteps on the wooden porch, then on the steps, until she couldn't hear him anymore.

She flopped back on the bed, and as suddenly as the little bubble of amusement had appeared, it vanished. Her eyes stung, and a tear rolled down her cheek. He'd proposed. She'd turned him down. Because all he wanted was to make her fit his idea of what a traditional family looked like.

Having refused him, she didn't feel very happy either. But she didn't have another choice. She wasn't going to marry him just for the sake of the baby. It was silly. Pointless.

She wiped away another tear and stood up, taking a deep, shaky breath. She wasn't going to waste time worrying about it. They would make this work. They would make the friendship work. There wasn't another option.

Seventeen

She put her last pair of underwear in the top drawer of the armoire and pushed it closed. She was officially moved into the big house. Private family rooms were on one end, upstairs and well away from any guest services.

She'd been put with the family. It felt good, secure in some ways. Except for Cole. No matter what had been said, things didn't feel even remotely settled with Cole.

There was a knock on the door and she froze, hoping she didn't have to face him just yet.

"Come in."

"Hi." It was Lark. Kelsey felt a wave of relief wash over her until she saw Lark's frown.

"So, Cole told me you turned him down."

"It wasn't, um . . . personal, as such. Which was the problem. He just wants to do the right thing. I'm not going to marry someone just because he thinks asking me is the 'right thing to do.'"

"I . . . I understand that. But Cole is really wonderful, and . . ."

Kelsey's stomach pitched slightly. Of course Lark idolized Cole. Which actually made it even harder—because he really was that good of a guy. But it still didn't mean marrying him was the smart thing to do.

"Yes. I know. And I like him." She thought back to the intense expression on his face when she'd turned him down, and the way it had tightened her body, made her ache and even tremble a little. "Like" seemed an insipid word. "But that's not a great reason to get married. That doesn't mean I won't stay. Or that I won't be here a lot. Just that I'm not going to up and marry him when we . . . we hardly know each other."

"Sorry. I know . . . I know that. But . . . I was looking forward to having you. To having a sister."

Ouch. Now Kelsey felt even worse. "I know. I know your house is a little short on female influence," she said.

"My mom died when I was nine. Then it was just me and Dad and the boys. And then just me and the boys."

Kelsey couldn't even imagine. She'd had a house full of women. She hadn't been able to escape them, even when she wanted to. Lark didn't have anyone. Hopefully she'd at least had good friends. But it hadn't escaped Kelsey's notice that while beautiful, if a bit plain, Lark was awkward in some ways, and it had probably been hard for her to make friends.

"It's hard to do the teenage thing with brothers," Lark continued. "Especially brothers like mine. They're pretty liberal in their . . . behavior. But their views changed sharply when it came to me and my dating life, such as it is. Or such as it's not."

"Yeah, that's a brother thing." Kelsey couldn't help but wonder just how liberal Cole had been. It wasn't her business, and because she was a friend, it did not fall under her jurisdiction. Even so, her mind went there.

"I know. While you're here, though . . . I'd like to get to know you better."

"Of course."

A small, sad smile curved Lark's lips. "It would have been nice to have a sister."

"I can still be your friend. And you'll be my baby's aunt."

"True. I like that."

"Did Cole seem . . . okay . . . when he told you I turned him down?"

Lark frowned. "It's always hard to tell with him. But he told me because he gave me the ring. My mom's engagement ring and wedding band. That was what he offered you."

"Oh." Now Kelsey felt bad. "But he wasn't . . . upset?"

"No."

"That's good." And it sort of irked her.

"Of course . . . he had that look. The kind he gets when he's about to take on a particularly big problem." Lark scrunched her nose. "I kind of don't envy you."

"Yeah. Thanks." Being Cole Mitchell's problem, she knew, would not be a very happy place to be.

"I'll see you in the morning," Lark said.

"Yeah," she said, watching Lark walk out the door with a sense of foreboding closing in. She really didn't need a determined cowboy out to try to convince her to marry him.

Although the idea of what that might entail was tempting . . .

Another knock interrupted her reverie. She was going to have to get used to dealing with people. This wasn't the isolated cabin or a house to herself. She was surprised by how accustomed she'd grown to living alone.

"Come in," she said.

This time it was Cole, looking tall and broad and generally like fuel for her dearest late-night fantasies. She'd heard about this. About pregnant women getting . . . urges. Animalistic, sweaty, hungry-type urges. It had just seemed laughable to her when she'd been spending twelve of the twenty-four hours in the day with her head in the toilet. Now, though . . . now she was feeling differently.

"You settled okay?"

"Yes. And I unpacked, so you're not going to be able to get any illicit thrills via an accidental sighting of my drawers."

"That's too bad. I've been short of thrills the past few years."

"But not for most of your life?" she asked, remembering Lark's earlier comment.

He frowned. "Meaning?"

"Oh, your sister mentioned something about you being quite . . . free with your favors."

She was almost sure she saw a dull blush spread over his high cheekbones. "She doesn't know what she's talking about."

"I don't know, Cole. Little sisters tend to be pretty observant. One of mine almost got me grounded for my entire senior year, thanks to some unwanted observation."

"Does it bother you?"

"What? Your loose morals? Hardly."

He laughed. "'Loose morals'?"

"Sorry, something my mom would say. Scary." She frowned. "This experience had better not turn me into my mother."

"What's your mother like? If you tell me, I can better look out for you and make sure you don't morph into her."

"Um . . . she's strict. She didn't like us to date. But she couldn't wait for us to get married. She gives good hugs. She can make me feel like I'm about three inches tall. But she can also make me feel better when things go south. She's my mom. It's complicated."

"I guess."

Kelsey cleared her throat. "If she found out I turned down your proposal, it would be the three-inches-tall thing."

He rubbed his chin. "So, she would be my ally."

Kelsey narrowed her eyes. "I thought we had a deal."

"Did you?" He smiled.

"I said we'd be friends."

"Yes. And I asked you to marry me, because I think marriage is the best thing for us. I didn't change my mind."

"You did. You *so* did. You agreed with me, and then I agreed to move in here."

He chuckled. "I don't remember that."

"You tricked me."

"I can't force you to marry me, Kelsey, so the only reason

you have to look like that," he said, probably indicating her open mouth and red cheeks, "is if you're afraid I'll be able to wear you down."

"Never."

His smile broadened and her stomach plummeted. Cocky, sexy bastard.

"We'll see. Good night."

"Good night," she bit out.

He turned and walked out of the room, and she growled once the door closed. She wasn't worried. She knew exactly what she wanted. Exactly.

"Stupid cowboy."

Kelsey missed breakfast the next morning, really on accident, but she wasn't too broken up about it. She hadn't relished the idea of sitting around the table with Cole's friends and family while they all glared at her over her refusal to marry him.

She grabbed an apple out of the big ceramic bowl placed on the check-in counter and wandered out onto the porch. Lark was hiding in her cave, working on her computer, and the men were all out working.

It was warm, the sun hitting the porch, soaking into her skin. She closed her eyes and lifted her face toward the sky, relishing the warmth, the quiet of her surroundings. It was so different here. She was starting to love it. Which was good in a way, since this would be a place where she would spend a lot of time.

She tried to imagine it, coming here on the weekends with her baby. Braving insane snowfall to make it at Christmastime. Summer vacations later. Maybe sometimes her son or daughter would come without her.

She wasn't going to think too much about that now.

She breathed in deeply, relishing the cleanness of the air, the faint scent of hay and horses. She'd never given a lot of thought to those smells before. It had been a part of her home, and home had never brought her any comfort. She'd felt too out of place.

Maybe the sudden enjoyment of it came from so many years of living in the city. Or maybe it was some sort of nesting instinct.

Except she wasn't going to nest here. She was going to do that back in Portland. And she was excited about it.

She kept repeating the mantra in her head as she dodged puddles on her way down to the paddocks.

She saw Cade and Tyler standing against the fence, leaning over the top rail, watching the rider in the outdoor arena as he took a horse through a simple barrel course. Kelsey headed in that direction, her eyes on the horse as it wove between barrels, dodging them closely without knocking them down.

The rider lifted his head, lifting the shadow his hat had cast on his face. It was Cole, his muscles shifting as he directed the horse.

Her thoughts scattered, a coherent syllable impossible to grasp as she watched the way his body moved with the horse's. He rode the animal up to the fence and tugged the reins, dismounting in a smooth motion. Sweat beaded on his brow, darkened the back of his T-shirt.

"Hey," he called, lifting his chin in greeting as he took a water bottle from a fence post.

She waved and Tyler and Cade turned, offering her a greeting. Neither of them seemed to be scowling at her, so maybe Cole hadn't mentioned the whole her-rejecting-his-proposal thing.

"What's up?" she asked, lifting her foot and resting it on the bottom rail of the fence.

"Giving the horses some exercise, keeping them sharp for when we have visitors," Tyler answered.

"Cole drew the short straw," Cade said.

Cole raised his eyebrow. "And I can still ride."

Cade flipped Cole his middle finger while still smiling at Kelsey. "How are you feeling this morning?"

"Great," she said.

"Have you heard from Alexa?" That question came from Tyler.

"Uh . . . not recently. Have you?" The smug smile on his face told her he had. "Good for you," she said. "I fully expect you to make an attempt at taming her."

A faint blush colored his cheeks, and he looked down. "I don't want to tame her. I just want to try to keep up."

The quiet admission made her throat get all tight and painful, emotion getting her in a stranglehold. If Cole had proposed with a line like that, she would have been a goner. Well, maybe not. Because the real beauty in Tyler's words was that they weren't a line. And if Alexa weren't a huge idiot, she would give him a serious chance.

"You should tell her that," Kelsey said, her throat still constricted.

Cole took his hat off and set it on the fence, then gripped the hem of his shirt and tugged it up over his head, his muscles putting on a fantastic show with the motion. "Hot work," he commented, straightening and resting his hand on the top rail.

Her mouth dried.

Dear. Lord.

She'd known he was hot. The cut of that cowboy denim did nothing to disguise the round, muscular, sexy firmness that was his ass. But his chest, his abs . . . he was like a statue come to life, perfectly formed, every line, every muscle moving in harmony and making her feel shivery.

He was gratuitous, was what he was. It wasn't even that warm. And there he was, shirtless, with well-fitted, low-riding jeans that showcased a big, distracting . . . belt buckle.

She cleared her throat. "I can see that. That it's . . . hot." She bit her lip. "Hot work."

He arched a brow, his mouth curving up into a half smile. He knew. He knew just what he was doing. Cocky bastard. "Well, I'm just about done."

"Good. I mean . . . that's fine. Don't women usually barrel race?" she asked.

"In rodeos? Yeah. But if that comment was meant to imply it might be easy or wimpy, I welcome you to give it a try." His smile widened.

"What? No. I wasn't implying that. Why would you think I was implying that? Because I said women did it? That's . . . well, that's sexist, is what it is."

"Is that what you call it?"

"Yeah."

"Hey, Cade," Tyler said, straightening from his position. "I have to go check that thing? Did you want to go check?"

"Yep." Cade pushed off the fence and followed Tyler, his gait uneven as he made his way toward the barn.

"I see what they did," she said. "I see what you're doing," she called after them.

"What are they doing?"

"Either they're leaving us to fight, or . . ." She turned to face him, and her eyes met one very interesting nipple, covered with just the right amount of chest hair. She raised her focus. "Or fight."

"I see. Are we going to fight?"

"I don't know. Are you mad at me about yesterday?"

"Nope."

"Oh." That was almost disappointing. Although, really, it just reinforced her feelings on the subject. If he wasn't even mad about her refusal, that said a lot about his feelings. Not that feelings mattered. Because they didn't. At all.

"Did you want me to be mad?" he asked, leaning over the fence. She was grateful to have it between them. Her hands itched to touch his chest, to find out if it was as firm and hot as it looked.

She'd never, ever touched a chest that looked quite like that. Her ex had been pale. And his chest had been sort of concave. Nothing like the broad expanse of drool-worthy flesh that Cole possessed.

Egad. She needed a cold shower.

"No. I don't want you to be mad."

"Yes, you do," he said, nodding his head, that maddening smile still in place. "In fact, you're a little pissed that I'm not."

She sputtered. "What? What would give you that idea?"

"It's a woman thing, right? You want me to feel rejected."

"No."

He shrugged one shoulder and turned, taking his horse's reins in his hands. The big, glossy animal followed him as he headed toward the barn. She stared at his back for a moment. Broad shoulders, trim waist, narrow hips, and his butt . . . oh . . .

She shook her head and followed him along the outside of the fence. "Okay, maybe a little bit. A woman wants to have her refusal mean something. That seems normal, right?"

"And how about my ego?" he said, tossing her a look over his shoulder. "How am I supposed to feel about you seeming completely at ease turning me down?"

"Um . . . I don't know. A little annoyed, I guess."

"I don't know if 'annoyed' is the right word." He bent down alongside his horse and lifted her leg, pulling it back and taking a plastic tool from his pocket, then using it to clean out her hoof. Then he moved and did the same to the rest of her hooves. And Kelsey couldn't help but stare. He showed so much care for the horse, so much gentleness.

He undid the girth on the saddle and slid it off her back, hoisting it up over his shoulder and carrying it to the tack room. Kelsey leaned against the door, feeling like she was privy to something personal. It seemed so much a part of him, the barn, the horse, the work.

She wasn't sure if anything had ever felt that natural to her. Writing, maybe. It was easy for her to spill her thoughts out onto the page. Easy when she was able to think it all out, change it around and perfect it before anyone saw it.

A lot easier than dealing with people, family, boyfriends, in person.

She wondered what it would be like to feel like a part of where you came from, instead of like a tenant in every place you went.

She watched him finish with the horse and put her back in her stall. He was still shirtless.

She swallowed. "So, now what?"

"Do you want to look around a little bit?"

Strangely, she did. "Yeah, that would be great."

"So, in this barn, we have the tack room."

She followed him, puffs of dust rising from the dirty floor with each footstep. He indicated the open door. The room was clean, with a cement slab for a floor and everything organized to the extreme.

"If you can't find it, you waste time," he said, explaining the order.

"And this is where the older rodeo horses are kept," she said. "So where are your other horses?"

"Do you want to head over to the other barn?"

"That would be great."

"It's a short walk. I didn't realize you hadn't been to see them."

"I haven't spent that much time down on this side of the property. I've been getting over being sick, and then trying to get back into the swing of working again."

"How is that going?" he asked.

"Better. Although I still find myself in the awkward position of wanting to eat junk food while I spout the importance of lean protein."

"Have you had elk?"

She curled her lip. "What? No."

"That's lean protein."

"I'll pass."

"You might like it," he said.

"Ech. Show me the horses." She followed his broad, sexy back across to another structure that bore the name of the ranch across the top in wrought iron letters. "Seriously, that's kind of ironic. Elk Haven Stables. You were just talking about eating them; what kind of haven is that?"

"Don't be so literal," he said.

"The elk would appreciate it if you were a little less confusing."

"You speak for the elk now?"

"I am the Lorax," she said.

He laughed. "Okay, then, come over here. This is where we have the horses we breed for the rodeo. We used to do a little more training before we sold them, but with Cade out of commission, it's just not practical."

"And he really can't ride?"

"Not without a lot of pain. He tries sometimes, but he's an idiot."

"He doesn't want things to be different," she said softly.

"I know that feeling," Cole said.

"I'll bet." She leaned back against the wall and looked at the line of stalls.

Cole stopped and turned to her, resting his palm flat by her head, his eyes intent on hers. He smelled good. Like sweat and hard work and man. Like so many things she hadn't been around in a long time.

He lifted his other hand and brushed her hair back from her face. Her heart started to beat faster, and her lips felt suddenly dry. He lowered his head, his nose brushing against hers. Her breath stopped, freezing in her lungs.

She searched his face, trying to see what he was thinking. Trying to guess what he might do next.

He closed the distance between them, and she sighed in relief. His lips were hot and firm, everything she remembered and more. She raised her hands and pressed them flat against his bare chest, a shock of attraction hitting her, immobilizing her for a moment.

All she could do in that instant was take and enjoy. The feel of him, the taste of him. He wasn't like any other man she'd kissed; he wasn't like any other man she'd met.

She wanted to melt into him. Wanted to lean on his strength.

His arms came around her, strong, perfect. He drew her against him and she slid her hands up to his shoulders, around to cup the back of his head, weaving her fingers in his dark hair.

He tilted his head and slid his tongue over the seam of her lips. She opened to him, inviting him in. His tongue moved against hers, and a groan rose in her chest. He tightened his hold on her, and she arched into him. She felt hyper-sensitized. Everything that touched him felt good. Her lips, her breasts. She felt even better when the hard ridge of his erection pushed against her hip and one large hand came down to cup her butt and bring her in even tighter.

She wanted him. She couldn't remember ever wanting anyone like this before. Couldn't remember feeling the desperate need just to have someone then and there, against a wall, on the floor, without any thought to who might walk in.

She couldn't remember it because it had never happened. Not with anyone but Cole.

He pulled his lips from hers and spread kisses down her neck, to her collarbone.

"Oh, yes," she said, her hands moving to his belt buckle, logical thought down for the count.

Cole jumped away from her and she stood frozen, her brain fuzzy from arousal, her body still demanding that he get back up against her right this instant.

She was almost afraid to follow Cole's gaze, but she managed to. Cade was there, in the doorway.

"Are you going to work these horses next?" he asked, showing a completely uncharacteristic amount of grace by not asking why they'd been about to get it on against the barn wall.

"Yeah," Cole said. "So, I'll catch up with you later?" He directed the question at her.

Cole could feel the relief radiate off of Kelsey when he gave her the out.

He needed to be hosed down. The presence of his younger brother had gone a long way in cooling his arousal, but he was still uncomfortably hard.

Kelsey offered a short smile and scurried out of the barn. She was probably going to hide in her room for the rest of the afternoon. Maybe he could join her. That thought did nothing to lessen the problem that was making his jeans feel like they were too tight.

The kiss had started out as manipulation. Just like the removal of his shirt. Conceited that he was using his body as a tactic to seduce her, maybe. But it had worked.

The kiss hadn't ended as manipulation, though. At least not for him. He had a feeling that she could snap a leash on him and lead him around if she wanted to after that.

"Go ahead and make your lewd quip and let's move on," he said.

Cade raised his eyebrows. "Lewd quip? What the hell does that mean?"

"I know your deep, dark secret, Cade. I know you got As in English, so don't even pretend."

"I'm not going to say anything. I think you're damn smart."

"Do you? I question that myself."

"You want her to marry you, right?"

"Right."

"So, that seems a good enough way to go about it to me. In my opinion, sexual attraction would be about the best enticement for marriage. Really good, blinding sexual attraction, not your common, garden-variety kind. You know, the special kind. The kind that has you so out of your mind, you just about do it in the barn during work hours."

Cole grunted. "I'm not overly familiar with that last kind."

"Really? I assumed you had to feel some kind of crazy for Shawna. Well, I assumed she must have had magic powers beneath her—what I am sure were sequined—panties."

"There was the lewd comment. Just not where I expected it. Yeah, I was nuts about her. And about . . . sex with her. When I got it. But it still wasn't like . . . that. Kelsey's . . ." He let out a breath he hadn't been aware he was holding. "She's something else."

"She is. Hell, I'd be tempted to propose if you hadn't."

"You wouldn't."

"Sorry. I didn't mean 'propose.' I meant 'proposition.'" Cade offered him his best lopsided, devilish smile.

"Now that sounds more like you."

"How are you doing?" Cade asked, his tone suddenly serious.

"How am I doing? Do you really want a play-by-play? It could become a case of too much information real quick."

"I don't mean now, specifically. I mean in general. With the dad shit."

"Oh, that. I don't know; I'd kind of like to run away and join a rodeo, but I'm not a dumb teenager, so I don't have the luxury."

Cade nodded slowly. "Yeah, I wanted to run away to the rodeo too. And as soon as I was old enough? I did."

"Lucky bastard."

"But you're going to have a kid. No running from that."

Cole shook his head. "I don't even want to."

Cade cleared his throat. "Look, I know you think I'm a screwup and a jackass, and basically, you're right. I am. But I can do more than I have. I'm not going back to the circuit," he said, the admission heavy. "I know it. You know it. I hadn't admitted it fully to myself, so I've been holding back around here. Not wanting to get too involved. But there you go. I should start taking on more responsibility around here, and I can. I should start helping you clean up Dad's mess."

"Thank you," Cole said, his arousal completely doused now. "I appreciate it."

Cade stuck out his hand, and Cole grasped it. "Anything. Whatever you need. You know that."

"I do." Cole clapped his brother on the back. "You're still an asshole."

Eighteen

"He proposed, Alex," Kelsey said into the phone. She was stretched across her new bed, trying to ignore the fact that her pulse was still racing, her body still on red alert. All systems were completely go.

"What?" Alexa screamed into the phone.

"Yep. There was a ring."

"And you said no, right?"

"I said '*Hell* no.'"

"Good girl. I'm proud of you. Why does he want to marry you? Does he think he's doing the right thing?" The last few words were dripping with disdain.

"Basically."

"Typical. Old-fashioned male possessiveness. You start gestating and they get all caveman. Drag you back to their cave by your hair."

Kelsey couldn't stop the whimper from escaping.

"What?" Alexa asked, her tone flat.

"I would love to be dragged back to his cave," she said, the admission rushed. "By the hair. Oh, even that sounds hot."

"Oh, would you?"

"I want him so much." Kelsey covered her mouth after the words escaped as if that would make them less spoken. Or less true.

"Join the club. I still want that pantywaist cowboy who was too chicken to take me on in the sack."

Kelsey knew from experience that the more hostile and dismissive Alexa was about something, the more she wanted it.

"It sucks. And the thing is, I think he's dangling a carrot."

Alexa snorted. "Oh, geez. Dangling carrots. There's an image."

"Har-har. I mean, I think he's withholding sex so I'll agree to marry him."

"What a bitch!"

"I know, right?" Kelsey let out a breath. "The thing is, though, that I can't really sleep with him, because it would complicate things."

"Right, because things are sooooo simple right now. With him proposing and you being pregnant and also dying of the wanting."

Kelsey growled. "No. Things aren't simple. They've never been simple, but say we . . . hook up. And then we break up. And then we have this big bad thing between us and it turns us into a bitter couple sharing custody and then . . . and then we've just sent it all to hell, all so we can get off."

"You wouldn't be the first people to do that."

"I know, but it doesn't make it right. Other people don't have the option of starting out with the blank slate we have. We should take advantage of the blank slate, not . . . scribble on it."

"Maybe you aren't giving yourself enough credit. Maybe you could burn off the attraction between the two of you and then put it behind you. Maybe it would be better."

"Alex, you are my shoulder devil. You make being bad sound so good. And so easy."

Alexa laughed. "It's a gift."

"So, what are you going to do about Tyler?"

"There isn't much I can do. Except keep calling him and telling him all the wonderful, dirty things I want to do with him."

"Poor guy."

"I like him, Kelsey," Alexa said, sounding subdued. "I like him, and it scares me. I haven't actually cared for anyone in a really long time."

"Don't let fear keep you from something good, Alexa. You deserve to be happy."

There was a long pause, and Alexa sighed deeply. "I'll do my best. And maybe you should take your own advice."

Kelsey put her thumb up to her lips and started chewing her nail. "Yeah, maybe."

"Not maybe. Definitely."

"If you say so," she said. There was a knock at her door. "Oh, hey, I have to go. Talk to you soon?"

"Yeah. I'll call Tyler now."

"Heh. Don't blister his ears." She hit the END-CALL button and tossed the phone onto the bed. "Come in."

It was Cole, and it didn't surprise her. She was starting to know him by his knock, which was strange and sobering. She didn't want to know him that well.

He was so big that he filled up the room, made it seem smaller. More intimate. It was so very dangerous for him to be in a room that contained both her and a bed. It gave her very wicked thoughts. Or, rather, it heightened the wicked thoughts she already had.

"Hey, sorry about before. About . . . Cade catching us."

"I'm sure he had a million extremely off-color comments."

Cole scrubbed a hand over his hair. "Surprisingly . . . no. I think he must like you. He's less of a jerk where you're concerned."

"Well . . . that's flattering."

"I don't know. He's not the best judge of character."

"You were the one making out with me, Mitchell. I'm just saying."

His expression turned serious—smoldering, almost.

"And so you know, I'm just saying, I don't let go of things I want easily."

She took a deep breath and stared him down. "If you want me, you can have me." Her words were so much bolder than she felt. Inside, she was a quivering mass of jelly. "You can have me now, right here on this bed. I think we're both up for it."

"That's not what I want," he said, his voice rough.

"Liar. You want it. I felt how much you wanted it."

She swallowed hard, not sure where this boldness was coming from. She felt like she was channeling Alexa. Channeling some woman who wasn't her. One with savvy and sophistication and some idea of how to seduce a man.

It seemed to be working, though. Because he looked paler, and his eyes looked intense.

She took a step toward him, and this time she had no intention of keeping her touch platonic. She raised her hand, ready to put it on his chest, but he caught it.

She stared at where his fingers, dark and strong, wrapped around her arm, so pale and delicate-looking in his hand. He raised it slowly to his lips and turned it so that the sensitive part of her wrist was exposed. He pressed his lips to her skin, and she felt the impact through her entire body.

"I won't lie," he said, his breath hot against her skin. "I do want you. And not tumbling you back onto the bed is taking a hell of a lot of willpower. But I want more than that. I want you to marry me, make a family with me. I don't just want sex. I want more."

She pulled her arm free and took a step back. "You say that like you're offering the moon and the stars. You don't want more. You want to keep me with you. You want to have control. You want to have me with you, in your bed and by your side, so you don't have to suffer any kind of separation or inconvenience. No, thank you, sir. I'd rather just have the sex."

Something deadly flashed in his eyes, something dark and sexual that tugged at her, called to her, and for a moment, she thought he might tumble her back onto the bed.

Then he turned away, and she was tempted to try to goad him to touch her again. Because he was on the edge of control, and it wouldn't take much to push him over. She could sense it, could feel it echoing inside of her.

His kisses had been a taste of a kind of sexual paradise she'd never experienced. In her mind, Cole knew how to push all the right buttons. He was the man who could take her to that peak that authors wrote about in romance novels and that women rhapsodized about. The kind of peak she'd never found herself on.

There was the other option too. That he was a hot guy who was used to knocking a girl on her back, spreading her legs and getting his way. There was the possibility that sex with him wouldn't be the amazing thing she was fantasizing about.

Yes, there was that possibility.

She looked at his face, felt the heat in his eyes burn into her. She didn't really believe that. And if it was true . . . well, it would be a waste of a lot of potential. Cole was a man who could light a woman on fire. Just thinking about him brought her to the peak. How was that even possible? Frankly, she was used to being responsible for her own orgasm. What she wasn't used to was a man with the ability to just look at her and get her halfway there. And his kiss . . . She was a lot more than halfway after that.

"That's really all you want?" he asked. "Then find it with someone else. Someone you don't have to deal with on a more complex level. Because like it or not, we can't have simple. We can't have just sex. We're having a baby, and we have to be parents together. I don't think we can do both."

"What if I do?" she asked. She wasn't sure if she did. She never had before. She'd found one guy and stuck with him through all kinds of stupid crap because she'd felt so bonded to him. She wasn't sure if she was capable of sex without . . . well, attachment, at least. But it felt good to spit those words out at Cole. To defy him, and herself, with them.

He looked at her, lifted his hand and brushed his thumb

along her cheekbone. "I don't believe it, sweetheart, not for a second. If I did . . . if I did, it might be different."

The last words were rough, strained. She knew how he felt.

He dropped his hand back to his side and turned away from her. He was going to leave again. Walk away and leave all this sexual attraction burning between them and do nothing to satisfy it.

"You're being such a . . . such a girl," she said.

It was stupid, but she was desperate to keep him there for just a few more seconds. She regretted she hadn't pushed him over the edge when she'd had the chance. Because she had had the chance. She'd had him raw and on the cusp of losing control. And now she'd given him a chance to regain it. Rookie mistake.

He stopped, but he didn't turn. "It's not consideration for myself that's stopping me. And that's what you call being a gentleman."

He walked out the door and closed it behind him.

"Well, touché," she muttered.

It became abundantly clear over the next few days that Cole was trying to seduce her into marrying him. He took his shirt off while working a lot. And he didn't have the decency to have an ounce of fat on his broad, muscular frame. He didn't even have the decency to have back hair.

Not only that, but he smiled at her a lot. And his smile was so sexy, it made her knees weak. Literally. Weak knees. Who actually got weak knees around a guy?

She did, apparently. At least around this guy.

Was it pregnancy hormones? It was really convenient to have them to place blame on. Anything else was just too scary.

She leaned over the porch railing and clutched her mug of tea tight as Cole came into view. He was walking up from the paddocks, shirtless again, jeans low on his hips, cowboy hat on his head. He looked ridiculous and stereotypical. And good enough to eat.

She watched his abs as he got closer, the way they moved. She was really messed up. And a lot horny.

He tromped up the steps, his boots echoing on the porch. "Good afternoon." He leaned in, and her heart stopped as his lips brushed her cheek.

And then, stupidly, she wanted to cry. Because he was manipulating her. Trying to get her to agree to his marriage-and-perfect-family plan. And the all-out "check out my sexy bod" seduction was annoying, but it was so over-the-top, she could deal with it.

This, the show of tenderness—*that* she couldn't handle. It was too close to feelings. And when she started having feelings about Cole, she started wanting, longing for things she really shouldn't want or long for.

Not now. Not with him.

That was just convenience stuff. Forced proximity and the intense connection they'd had to find, quickly, while they dealt with the reality of being parents together.

Really. That was all.

She pulled away from him, her hold on the mug reaching death-grip status. "How has your day been?" she asked, her voice stilted. She wanted to scold him for touching her, for kissing her like he had a right to. Like they were a happy couple. Like he was going to make good on the tease and get her naked later, when they both knew none of that was true.

But that would have been giving too much away. There was no reason for him to know he affected her at all. She would get over it.

"Fine," he said. "I managed to go a day without gambling in a casino or conceiving another secret child."

"Ha," she said.

"Hey, at some point I have to learn to laugh at it, right?" he said dryly.

"I don't know. Do you?"

"Seems better than sulking about it."

"Or dealing with it?"

"Maybe this is how I'll deal with it," he said.

"And then you'll tell Lark?"

He shrugged. "Someday."

She could tell the subject was closed. "Speaking of, Lark told me you had a huge booking. It's for midsummer. Some kind of work retreat. Like one of those trust things where they stand on a stump and fall back and their coworkers have to catch them."

"Oh, good. My favorite sort of clientele. Well, not really, but any kind that fills up the cabins makes me happy. In just a couple of weeks, we should start having guests. They usually show up in June."

"That'll be interesting."

"Doesn't change much for me. I am not guest services."

"I'm not entirely surprised by that. But if you walked around like that while they were here, or if you put that in the brochure, I bet you'd get more women to come out."

The corners of his lips turned up into a real smile, not a smirk, not some self-satisfied, controlled expression. "Are you flirting with me?"

She shook her head. "No." Yes, she was. And why in the world was she doing that?

"I think you are, sweetheart."

"I think it's been so long since a woman flirted with you that you're grasping at straws."

"Hasn't been that long."

A little flash of jealousy assaulted her. "Oh, really?"

"Last time I went to a bar with Cade, in fact."

"When was that?"

"A couple months ago. I've been busy since." He looked at her pointedly.

"I see. And what was the result of the flirtation?"

"Nothing. I bought her a drink and talked with her for a couple of minutes. And then I remembered how I met my ex in a bar, and let me tell you, fantasies about my ex are sort of the equivalent of a cold shower. With scorpions. In other words, not sexy. So I went home alone."

"Oh." She was annoyed at the idea of a woman hitting on him, which was stupid. But she also felt . . . sad. Because she could imagine how he'd felt. Sitting there talking to someone, something that should have been normal and easy, and then having it all go south.

It sounded like the story of her dating life.

"I never think about her when I kiss you," he said softly.

"I appreciate that." Her words barely came out a whisper. "I, um . . . don't get flirted with very often. I think it's because I work at home. And when I go out, I tend to have that whole hostile, 'don't talk to me' thing going on."

"You do?"

"Yeah. Well, I haven't wanted to date."

"You've got to stop letting that guy have so much power over you," he said.

"What? Michael? He doesn't . . . I mean, I don't—"

"Yes, you do. You think you're quite the revolutionary. All independent and doing what you want. But I think a lot of what you do is to spite your family, and the other part is to protect yourself from getting hurt again. Everyone has power in your life. Everyone except you."

He opened the door to the house and walked in. She followed.

"Excuse me, Dr. Phil, but where the hell do you get off psychoanalyzing me? You're an angry, bitter, sexually frustrated man who hasn't dealt with the facts that his old man ended up being a douche and his ex was a nut. You've internalized it. All of it. You're like a big ball of tense. Angry at her, angry at him and trying to hold it all in so no one else has to deal with it. Even though you aren't dealing with it. And you want to armchair-psych me?"

"Okay, I might be all those things, but at least I know I'm screwed up. You seem to think you have a plan for everything. And you walk around acting like you have it all figured out, when it's pretty clear that you don't."

What was it about this man? How could he bring her from aroused to tears to rage in a matter of five minutes? "And you do? You're the man with the plan?"

"No. But I don't claim to be."

"I've never claimed to be either."

"Sure you have. You think we're going to just 'work this out.' You think things aren't already complicated between us. You're delusional."

"Nothing is complicated. I feel nothing for you."

"Nothing?" He put his hands on his slim hips, his chest and stomach on show for her.

"You're hot. So what? A lot of guys are hot."

"And you're afraid of them. You don't seem to be afraid of me."

"Because you are just an ass."

"And you want me," he said, the cocky smile returning.

"Well, you want me, so that seems fair."

"I do," he said, his voice getting rough. He closed the distance between them, standing just close enough to touch, close enough for her to feel his heat. "I want to taste your lips again, but I don't want to stop there. I want to taste every inch of you."

She started shaking. Her thigh muscles shivering, her hands trembling. She couldn't do anything. Not anything but keep listening and hope, pray he kept talking.

"I want to take that top off you and see what color your nipples are. I've been thinking about it."

This was what she wanted. Him out of control and wanting her. Just her. Not marriage or anything else. And maybe it was stupid, but it was healing something in her. Beyond any grander purpose, she just wanted him.

She stretched her hand out and put it flat on his chest, letting it drift down, her fingertips skimming his abs. "Oh . . ."

Heavy footsteps on the stairs broke up their moment of intimacy, and Lark appeared a moment later.

"Oh, hi," she said, clearly oblivious to having interrupted anything. "Cole, we got a huge booking for July."

"I heard," he grunted, his eyes never leaving Kelsey.

"Is it hot outside?" Lark asked, probably due to Cole's state of undress.

"Not especially," he said.

"Shameless hussy," Kelsey said, her eyes trained on his chest. She directed her focus to Lark. "He's just showing off."

Lark frowned, a clear indication she thought they were both insane. "Um. Okay. You might want to shower first," she said.

A statement made by a woman who clearly didn't understand the appeal of a man with a little sweat and dirt on him. Kelsey got the appeal. Big-time.

"Maybe take a cold one," Kelsey said.

"You're funny," he said.

She grinned, big and cheesy. "I know."

"I could take a hot shower and you could join me."

"Ah!" Lark made a very indignant sound. "Could you please keep a muzzle on it while you're in front of me? Men are so gross."

Kelsey had a feeling she was looking for a little bit of female backup, but Kelsey couldn't find anything about the proposition gross. Mainly enticing. Potentially slippery.

"What's this about the booking?" he asked, obviously attempting a subject change.

"I thought you'd heard about it."

"I have, but I thought you could give me the details."

Lark brightened. "Oh, well, we'll have all the cabins full. And they want some ropes and harnesses set up in the woods."

Cole grimaced. "Please tell me this isn't a kinky-sex thing."

Lark made a face. "What could you even . . . ? Never mind. No, it's part of their trust exercises. I figured we could find out how to accommodate them, and then we'd have it set up in case any more corporations out of Portland or Seattle wanted to come have wilderness experiences."

"Good idea," he said.

His sister beamed. "And we'll do a big old-fashioned barbecue-type thing. And have them learn low-speed barrel racing."

"As long as the insurance is fine with it."

"I checked."

"Good job, kid."

Cole seemed so much less cagey now. Like he was opening up a little, letting go a little. Rather than holding to everything so tight, like if he gave an inch, it would all break apart. Kelsey didn't know what had brought the change on, only that she liked it. And Lark obviously did too.

It made Kelsey feel warm and fuzzy about him. Of all the conflicting emotions she had about him, that was her least favorite. Anger or arousal was much safer. Much less challenging.

And when they were all mixed together—well, that was lethal.

Her body still ached, and her mind was spinning with the possibilities of what they could get accomplished if there weren't so many people crawling around the ranch. He could have bent her quite nicely over the back of the couch and had his way with her while she looked out the floor-to-ceiling windows at the majestic view. . . . Yes, there could have been that. She'd never done anything like that before, but it suddenly seemed like a very good idea.

"I think I am going to take a shower," Kelsey said. A cold one. A freezing-cold one that would shock some sense into her and numb her body.

Cole nodded. "I'll see you later."

Kelsey waved at Lark as she headed up the stairs to her room and into the bathroom that was connected to it. She let out a breath and turned on the water, changing her mind about the temperature when she felt a few frigid drops on her fingers.

She cranked up the hot water and pulled her shirt up over her head. She unhooked her bra and took her jeans and panties off in one motion. She reached into her makeup bag for some hairpins and started pinning her hair in place to keep the water off of it.

She looked different. Her eyes were bright, her cheeks flushed. Her face looked a little bit fuller too. She wouldn't be surprised if she was gaining weight. She hadn't paid attention to the doctor, and she hadn't really bothered to examine herself visually recently, not closely.

She put her hand on her bare stomach. It was starting to really stick out now. It seemed so much more real. She looked down and moved her palm over the bump. It was real. The baby. And it was there. She was going to have a baby, and she was planning on doing it alone. Going back to her house in Portland. On not being here with Cole. She turned and shut the water off and grabbed a towel off the rack, wrapping it around herself.

She moved to the bed and sat, holding the terry cloth against her chest.

"Kelsey." Cole walked in without knocking.

"I just told you I was going to take a shower. You might have knocked."

"I didn't hear water."

"Well, I'm naked."

"I see that," he said. "You are covered, though." His words sounded strangled.

"You put a shirt on," she said, looking at the tight black shirt that hugged his torso like a second skin.

"Yes. It seemed appropriate."

"What do you want?"

He closed the door behind him. She tightened her hold on the towel. "To . . . to say something about what happened downstairs. About what keeps happening."

"Then say it."

"Strangely, I don't really want to talk anymore." He crossed to the bed and paused. He was waiting, she realized, for permission. Or to be yelled at.

She drew in a shaky breath. "Show me what you do want, then."

That was all the permission he needed. He sat down on the bed, next to her, his arm curling around her waist. His lips crashed down on hers, hot, hard, insistent. Everything she wanted from him. She slid her tongue into his mouth, and he sucked gently.

She whimpered, wrapping her arms around his neck and letting the towel fall to her waist. His hands slid up over her bare back and she arched into him, her nipples grazing the fabric of his shirt. He moved his hands around slowly, thumbs brushing against the sides of her breasts.

"Oh, please, yes," she whispered against his lips.

Then he brought his hands around so he could palm her breasts. His skin was rough, calloused from so much manual labor. She loved it. She loved everything about his hands and about what they made her feel.

He shifted and pulled her up onto his lap. She could feel his hardened erection beneath her thigh, could feel his heat through the denim. The towel slipped, now just covering the top of her legs and the *V* at the apex of her thighs.

He pinched her nipple lightly between his thumb and forefinger, moving his lips against the side of her neck, his tongue sliding over the sensitive skin. She moved her hands beneath the back of his shirt, pushing the fabric upward until it caught on his arms. She moved back and he bent forward, allowing her to tug the black T-shirt over his head.

"I like you this way," she said, planting her hands on his chest. "I like you this way a lot."

"I like you this way too," he said, eyes glittering, wicked, as he let his fingers drift over her tightened nipples.

"Oh, you're so good at that."

"I'm good at a lot of things."

"I look forward to discovering your list of talents," she said, shifting in his lap so that she was straddling him, the denim rough and amazing between her thighs. She kissed him, hard, her hands bracketing his face.

He wrapped his arms around her, his kiss devouring, drugging. Perfect.

She pressed lightly on his chest and he went backward onto the bed. She leaned forward, her lips still pressed against his. She moved again, and his flashy belt buckle hit her in the stomach.

"Ow. Let's get rid of that," she said, sliding to the side, working at the ornate metal closure of his belt.

He moved away from her, and she rolled neatly from him to the bedspread. He sat up, his legs swinging over the side of the bed. "Kelsey, this can't happen," he said roughly.

"Um, I think it very well can. It's about to."

"It shouldn't. Not like this. It's all or it's nothing." He stood, looking down at her, his expression blank. "Either you marry me or . . ."

She scrambled for the towel and tugged it over her naked body. "Oh, for heaven's sake, you aren't that irresistible," she spat. "You think you're going to bribe me into marrying you by tempting me with your body? That's . . . low. And demeaning. And it won't work."

Shame heated her face. It was less that he'd turned her down and more that he'd had the presence of mind to remember why their sleeping together was a bad idea. She couldn't remember anything when he kissed her. And when he'd touched her breasts . . . logical thought had become a thing of the past. She had barely known her own name, and he'd just . . . stopped.

He was so controlled. So maddeningly immune to the beast of desire. He was able to keep it on a leash, and she . . . she was in danger of being consumed by it.

She should be used to it, she supposed. She just wasn't the kind of woman who drew that out in men. She'd witnessed her ex doing things with another woman that he'd never wanted to do for her. And then Cole was ready, every time they touched, to just walk away. To serve the greater agenda. If that wasn't proof that she wasn't the sort who unleashed animal passions, then . . . she didn't know what was.

"That's not it, Kelsey," he said, interrupting her thoughts. "I'm not trying to manipulate you. I'm being logical here. I'm being realistic."

"I already told you, just because we have sex doesn't mean you'll break my heart."

It didn't mean he wouldn't either. And she could not believe she was egging the guy on to have sex with her. And yet she was. And she couldn't seem to stop.

"I don't believe you."

"Your ego is amazing," she said. "You think we'll have sex and I'll fall in love with you, and you'll leave me utterly devastated with the loss of you in my life and bed. I'm not looking for love; I never was. I think my life choices have made that pretty obvious."

"Even if it's not an issue of falling in love, how will you feel if I end up with someone else?"

"And how will you feel if I end up with someone else?"

"I'll want to cut the bastard's balls off—that's how I'll feel."

"Oh." That hadn't been the answer she'd expected. "Well . . ."

"I can see it working only two ways," he said, his voice rough.

"That's kind of a flawed argument, though," she said. "Because that assumes that there's nothing in between those two options already. That assumes that we can't just feel nothing, or be friends, or whatever."

"We can control this. It doesn't have to control us. I'll let you take your shower." He walked out of the room, closing the door hard behind him.

Control. He was so controlled. And she hated it. Why were men able to be so controlled around her? And why was he the one man who seemed to keep her from having any of it?

She growled and stalked back into the bathroom. She gripped the edges of the vanity and looked at herself in the mirror, at her swollen lips and pink skin.

"It's time Cole Mitchell lost his control," she said.

Nineteen

Cole cursed a blue streak all the way back down the stairs and out the door. He had half a mind to stick his head in a bucket of freezing-cold water. He was an idiot, and he was an asshole. And he absolutely felt like both.

He'd hurt her. Which was about the worst of it. Worse even than the constant throbbing in his cock. The entire idea of denying his desire for her was to keep from hurting her. To keep from making things awkward and painful.

And a little bit to manipulate her, you jackass.

Yes, there was a little bit of manipulation at play. How much of an egotistical bastard did a man have to be to withhold sex as a means of getting a woman to marry him?

A big one.

He growled and hit his hand against the porch railing.

"What are you doing?" Cade asked, walking out of the house at just the wrong time.

"Screwing up my life, and Kelsey's, to the best of my abilities."

"How?"

"I hurt her feelings." He wasn't going into detail. He

wasn't adding "sharing his near conquest with his brother" to his list of growing sins.

"Well, stop doing things like that."

"If only it were so easy."

"What's the problem?"

"I don't know. I don't know what to do with women. Not anymore. If I ever did. I screwed up my only attempt at commitment."

"You screwed it up because you picked the wrong woman. That was your real problem, man. Nothing you did could have worked after that initial bad decision."

"True." Cole looked down at his hands. "If I had met Kelsey without all this . . ."

"You would have slept with her."

"I don't know. I think so now, but maybe not."

"Why not?"

"She's not the kind of girl you just sleep with. She seems like she's the kind of person who wants more. And I wouldn't want to hurt her."

"And you like her," Cade said.

"That's a good thing. You should like the woman you're having a baby with."

"The woman you proposed to."

"Well, she's sticking with no, so I'm not sure the proposal matters," Cole bit out. "It's for the best. I'd be a bad husband. I already know that about myself. I'm selfish, and I don't really get female emotion. I can't give her what she wants."

"What makes you think you don't get female emotion? And don't say 'Shawna.' Understanding Shawna would have required you to understand . . . I don't know, the subtle nuance of the velociraptor. Her emotions had very little to do with a normal woman's emotions."

That pulled a reluctant laugh from Cole. "Fine. All right. That's true."

"You've always done well with Lark."

Cole shrugged. "Yeah, well, she's my sister. And it's . . . different. I feel protective of her. I feel that way about the baby, especially since we heard the heartbeat. But as far as . . . as loving someone, like a husband is supposed to love a wife . . . I don't even know if that's real. If it can last."

"Why? Because of Dad?"

"Yeah. And Shawna. And yeah, I know she was . . . I know she wasn't who I thought she was, but I still didn't have it in me to make it work. Those feelings I had for her? They burned hot like a brush fire, and when there was nothing left to keep it going? Nothing. Not even a spark. And my whole reason for keeping it together, for being the man I am . . . it's all a lie, Cade. Is it even possible to be that man?"

"So you're worried . . . what? You'd stop loving her if you started?"

"I'm worried I never could. I don't . . . I've loved too many people who are gone. And one who was never there to begin with. I don't want to depend on anyone like that, not again."

"Are you worried you won't love the baby?"

Cole frowned. "No." He wasn't sure why he wasn't worried; he just wasn't. He'd felt an attachment, almost supernatural in strength, from the moment he'd found out about Kelsey and the baby. He hadn't been able to walk away, not from moment one.

"Well, maybe you aren't quite as hopeless as you think."

"Maybe."

"You don't believe me."

"It doesn't matter. The love thing doesn't matter. I just want to do what's right. That has to be enough. She won't let me."

Cade shifted the weight from his bad leg. "She doesn't think it's right. She's not a pushover. That's what you need, man."

"I don't *need* her. That's not the point. She needs me. And anyway, if she gets her way, I'm not going to have her."

Except he could have had her in bed today, could have taken care of the physical desire he had for her. But that wasn't enough with her. Because of the baby. Just because of the baby.

"If you say so. You have to decide if you're willing to try to have her on her terms, even if you screw it up. Or if you're going to stick to yours." Cade shrugged and turned away.

"When did you turn into some relationship guru?"

Cade turned back to him. "I'm good at breaking them up. It seems like if I give the opposite advice to what I do, I might be able to help you keep this one together."

Cole flashed back to his time in the bedroom with Kelsey. "We don't have a relationship."

"Because you're doing the wrong things." Cade frowned. "Stop doing the wrong things."

"Great. Good plan."

"I thought so."

Cade went back into the house and left Cole standing there. The bucket of water still seemed like a good idea. But it would only help ease the heat in his body. It wouldn't deal with the turmoil that was swirling in his chest.

Which meant he should probably just work until he was too exhausted to think. He let out a breath and headed to the paddocks.

It was dark when Kelsey emerged from her room. She'd managed to avoid Cole for the rest of the day while she considered her next move.

She couldn't think too far into the future. She knew that much. She also couldn't just be his friend. She couldn't forget that he'd touched her, kissed her, held her naked body against his clothed one. There was just no way.

For her, the line had been crossed already. It had been such a slow crossing that she hadn't realized it until she'd been way on the other side of the line. Too far over to go back.

So the only logical solution she could think of was to take things to their conclusion. And that would require him losing his mind, losing his control, even if it were only temporary. Which was her intent tonight.

Maybe the best thing to do was to just do it. Get it over with. If they were fighting a losing battle, getting the drama out now might be the only thing to do.

You're just horny. You're using horny logic.

She pushed that snarky voice aside. If it was going to happen, better it happen now. Early. Lots of time to recover from it all. Yes, that was it.

"Third room on the left," she whispered as she padded down the dim hallway.

She would die of embarrassment if she sneaked into Cade's room. Or worse, Lark's room. At least Cade would just laugh it off. Lark would look at her like the horrified virgin that she undoubtedly was and shriek with offended morality when she found out Kelsey had been intending to seduce Cole.

Oh, was she really going to seduce him? She paused midstep, worrying her lip between her teeth. She'd never seduced anyone in her life. She wasn't really seductress material. The best she'd ever gotten was that she was cute. And that wasn't really good enough when you were aiming for making a man lose every last bit of resistance.

"Just get over yourself," she whispered, starting to walk again.

Her heart pounded harder when she reached Cole's door. She took in a breath and wrapped her hand around the door-knob. Like ripping off a Band-Aid. But naked.

She turned it quickly and opened the door, stepping into the room and shutting it silently behind her. She leaned against the wooden frame, hoping he couldn't hear her heart-beat in the silence of the room.

He was lying in bed, his arm thrown up over his face, the covers riding low on his hips, dangerously close to giving away the secret of whether he wore boxers, briefs or nothing.

She didn't even feel guilty that she hoped it was nothing.

"Cole," she said, the word coming out a voiceless whisper. He didn't move. She cleared her throat and tried again. "Cole . . . are you asleep?"

He made a grunting sound and rolled over. "What?"

"Are you asleep?"

He pushed up into a sitting position. "I'm not now. Kelsey?"

"Yes. Unless . . . You weren't expecting another woman to sneak into your room in the middle of the night, were you?"

He laughed. "Uh . . . no. Can't say that I was. But then, I wasn't exactly expecting you either."

"Good. I live to be unexpected."

"I've noticed."

She took a deep breath and a step toward his bed. "I have a little bit of a problem."

"What's that?" he asked, his voice rough.

"Well"—she took another step toward his bed—"you're about the most entitled, autocratic man I've ever met. You think you can seduce me into marrying you. You think your way of doing things is the only way of doing things and that I should just fall into line."

"You're no different."

She took another step. "I admit, I can be stubborn. But you shouldn't get to make all the decisions." She came to the edge of the bed and leaned forward, resting her knee on the edge of the mattress. "It's not all about you, you know."

She exhaled the breath she'd been holding and put her hand on his shoulder, sliding farther onto the bed so that both knees were on the mattress. "And it wouldn't kill you to loosen up a little bit."

Cole's face was hidden in shadow, but the moonlight filtering through the window let her see impressions of his expression: the glitter in his dark eyes, tension in his mouth. He was frozen, his muscles tense beneath her hand.

He was like living stone, hot but completely solid, uncompromising.

"Cole," she whispered, leaning forward, "this isn't loosening up."

He lifted his hand and placed it on her hip. She wanted to whimper with relief. He wasn't pushing her off the bed. And he hadn't proposed. So things were going well.

"I'm out of practice," she said, her voice shaky.

She leaned forward and pressed her lips to his. He was still beneath her mouth for a moment before he opened for her, letting her explore him, taste him. When he slid his tongue past her lips, she sucked it, and both his hands came up to grip her hard at the hips.

Any semblance of passivity ended there. He straightened, wrapping his arms around her, drawing her tight against his body. She could feel his heat, and she was pretty sure he was naked beneath the sheet. The thought made her dizzy with desire. She wanted him so much, more than she could remember wanting anything. Sex *or* chocolate. His mouth was rough on hers. He didn't ask; he took. And she loved it. This wasn't a controlled burn. This was the wildfire she'd been waiting for. The one she'd been certain existed beneath all that rigid self-restraint.

He pushed her robe off her shoulders and wasted no time tugging her flimsy nightgown over her head. She was thankful that she'd remembered to put on a pair of sexy underwear before she'd made her trek down the hall, because it was all she had on now.

He slid his hands down her back, kneading her bottom. If there had ever, in the world, been anything better than the feeling of his rough hands on her sensitive skin, she couldn't remember it.

"Oh, yes," she said against his lips.

He chuckled and tightened his hold on her. She shrieked as she found herself deposited on her back, Cole positioned above her, a feral grin on his face. She couldn't help but smile in return.

She moved her hands over his arms, then down his back, putting her hands on his bare, muscular butt. "Very nice," she said.

"I'm out of practice too," he said, his voice sounding ragged. Out of breath.

"That's okay. If it's quick, it works for me. I'm used to quick. And anyway, I'm on edge."

"Oh, no," he said, "this isn't going to be quick. I'm going to take my time." Some of the playfulness left his expression.

"I should stop." He let the back of his hand drift over the curve of her breast. He closed his eyes. "I should. But I can't. Not now."

"Good. I think I would die if you stopped. Well, maybe not die, but burst into flames."

That brought his smile back. "We can't have that."

He lowered his head and ran the flat of his tongue over her nipple before drawing it into his mouth. She grabbed the back of his head, holding him to her, only releasing him to allow him to give the other breast the same attention.

"Five years," he growled. "Way too long."

He pressed an openmouthed kiss to the valley between her breasts, then lower, the tip of his tongue tracing a line down to her belly button. His hands skimmed her back as he traveled down her body, rough palms gripping her hips tight, holding her in place as he kissed her just above the waistband of her underwear.

"Oh, yes, please," she said, closing her eyes tight.

"You don't have to ask twice," he said, hooking his fingers in the sides of her panties and dragging them down her legs.

He cursed, short and sharp and crude. And she liked it.

"You're beautiful," he said, leaning in, kissing her inner thigh.

She should have been embarrassed. Or something. Only one man had ever seen her naked, and he'd never been that interested in looking at her too closely. It was dark, but Cole's attention was definitely on a very intimate part of her, fully and completely.

She wasn't embarrassed, though. Not at all. She was just excited, shaking with anticipation, wondering what would happen next. He was clearly a lot more experienced at this than she was. And she was ready for him to show her everything she had left to learn.

He moved his hand between her thighs. An involuntary whimper escaped her lips as he slid one finger inside of her, then two, drawing the moisture up to her clitoris, sending a shot of heat and pleasure through her body.

He lowered his head again, his lips on her thigh, then on her clit. She let her head fall back, her hands grasping for something, anything, to hold on to. She gripped the sheet hard, her fingernails pushing against the thin fabric, digging into her palms, as Cole continued to lavish attention on her.

He held her hips, his tongue and lips working magic on her. He was relentless, in the very best way. And there was no control. Not for him, and definitely not for her. She couldn't think; she could hardly breathe. There was nothing else, only this, only Cole and what he was making her feel.

He released his hold on her, moving his hand down and sliding a finger back inside of her as he continued to move his tongue over the bundle of nerves at the apex of her thighs.

Everything in her tightened, and for one moment, she was sure she couldn't handle any more. Was certain there was no way her body could contain all the sensations that were rioting through it.

Then it all released, pleasure pouring through her in waves. When it was over she was spent, panting.

Cole moved to lie beside her, kissing her deeply on the mouth, his hands drifting over her curves. She could feel his erection pressing against her stomach, hard and hot, a reminder that while she had been satisfied, he hadn't been.

"I've never done that before," she said, dazed.

"What?"

"I've never had a man . . . do that for me."

"Oh, baby, you know stupid men. You make it sound like it was only for you," he said. He took her hand in his and guided it down to his cock. "I enjoyed it."

She wrapped her hand around him and squeezed him gently. "I can feel that."

He groaned and kissed her again. She'd thought she was satisfied by her earlier orgasm. She'd thought it would take her days to be able to be aroused again. After all, a woman could take only so much.

But she'd underestimated Cole. And herself. She wanted

more already, wanted everything. With him. As soon as possible.

His hands shook as he brushed her hair back from her face. A rush of power filled her. Cole was a rock. And he was shaken. Because of her.

She put her hands on his shoulders and urged him closer to her. She parted her thighs and he settled between them, the head of his shaft testing the entrance to her body.

"I'm ready," she said, putting her hands on his butt and guiding him into her.

He filled her, stretched her. It was so much better than she remembered. Probably because it was better than it had ever been. He thrusted hard, grunting as he entered her to the hilt. She wrapped her legs around his calves, holding him hard against her.

He pressed a kiss to her neck, her collarbone, unsteady fingers lacing through her hair. "This was worth waiting for," he said.

"I agree."

He started to move inside of her, his action measured, controlled. It wasn't what she wanted. Not now. Not when they'd come so far together.

"Come on, Cole," she said. "Don't hold back."

He seemed to take it as a challenge, his tempo increasing, his thrusts less careful, harder.

"Yes," she said. "Like that."

She'd never asked for what she'd wanted before. She'd never felt brave enough. Had always been afraid it would be rejected. She wasn't afraid of it now. She didn't have any room for fear, no space for insecurity.

There was only the deep, driving need inside of her to have satisfaction. To have all of Cole. She flexed her hips, rising up to meet him, bringing her clit up against him, sending sparks of sensation along her nerves, the familiar, tightening sensation starting low in her pelvis.

Kelsey met him thrust for thrust, each meeting of their bodies bringing her closer to the peak. She gripped his shoulders tight, her fingernails digging into his skin. He didn't seem to mind.

When his control slipped entirely, when he gave over to his need, the same blinding need that filled her, she knew it. Could feel it, in the raging of his heart, in the shortness of his breath.

His pace quickened, the muscles in his arms shaking. And she clung to him, riding out the storm with him. Her orgasm crashed over her and she bit down on his shoulder, unable to hold back the groan that had climbed up her throat.

He thrust hard into her one last time, freezing above her as he found his own pleasure.

She pulled him down against her, holding him to her. His back was slick with sweat, his breathing heavy. She closed her eyes, and she felt like she was falling.

A lump of emotion swelled in her chest. Impossible to ignore, impossible to identify.

She tried to speak but couldn't. She couldn't form a thought, much less a word. She didn't have words for what had just happened between them.

Her mind was a fuzzy, pleasant blank. Reality was trying to intrude, but she wasn't letting it. She was deliberately ignoring reality, even as it pressed in on her pleasant post-orgasmic haze.

One thing she wasn't going to do was remember her adamant statement that she could have sex with him and leave it at just sex.

She wasn't going to think about how close she felt to him. How much she wanted to hold him all night.

No. She wasn't going to think about any of that. Not right now.

Twenty

Cole couldn't catch his breath. His body felt like it was on fire, his heart ready to burst from his chest. Five years of abstinence was a long time. And having it come to an end like that, with the best sex of his life, made it hard to do normal things like think and breathe.

It wasn't just the long time without that had made it so good. He hadn't forgotten what sex was like. He was a man; he remembered every woman, every time. Nothing had ever been like this.

She was intoxicating. Her smell, her taste, the feel of her tight, wet heat around his cock. He felt his body stir again at the thought. He wanted her again.

But Kelsey was asleep, her face resting against his shoulders, breasts pressed tightly against his chest. He moved his hand over the indent of her waist, down the curve of her hip. She was so smooth, soft as silk. And he was so hard, he was sure he was going to explode.

He groaned and tightened his hold on her, dropping a kiss onto her head.

He tried not to think of how badly they might have

messed things up. He was willing to marry her—that much he'd decided—but he hadn't agreed to the strange, over-powering feeling of possessiveness that was roaring through him. This wasn't something he'd counted on. He'd done the nuts-out-of-his-mind-for-love thing. It was something he never wanted to repeat. Something he never would. Because that only ended in fighting and pain and the loss of your mother's quilts.

All right, he knew it wasn't that way for everyone. But after Shawna, if he could have gone out into the shop and with a jigsaw cut out whatever part of his heart that had ever been there for the purpose of his loving a woman, he would have done it. Failing that, he'd just choked it off. He was too cynical to feel it again. More to the point, he didn't want to feel it.

That was what concerned him. Because Kelsey was all heart and emotion. She might think she was hard and world-weary, but she just wasn't. If Kelsey loved someone, she would do it with her whole heart. And he didn't have his whole heart left to give. It was too chewed up. Had been stomped on too many times.

The moonlight illuminated Kelsey's face, casting a glow on her cheek, her lashes pale and glistening.

Panic—the kind of panic he hadn't experienced since he'd found out his little sister's care was falling to him, since he'd first found out about his dad, since he'd gone to the clinic and found out a stranger might be pregnant with his baby—filled his chest.

He had to keep Kelsey with him. It had nothing to do with . . . needing her. But how would he keep her safe, the baby safe, cared for, if they weren't with him? She was going to leave. Leave and take his baby. What if she gave birth and he couldn't make it to the hospital in time? What if something happened? His head felt like it was spinning, or maybe that was the room. So much for postorgasmic bliss.

The need to keep her with him was so strong. Almost as strong as the need to push her away.

He gritted his teeth and closed his eyes.

*   *   *

The next morning his bed was empty, which didn't surprise him too much. He doubted Kelsey wanted to broadcast the change in their relationship to everyone in the overcrowded house. He was a bit resentful of the high population on the ranch at the moment.

But with the alone time, which included a lukewarm shower, he came up with a plan. One that eased the panic that had tightened his chest into a knot and helped him start breathing again.

The sex could be separate. Sex and friendship. Perfect and detached. Detachment was a good plan. He'd been detached from women and relationships for years. And yes, that had meant no sex at all. But why not add the sex and keep the detachment? And yes, during sex with Kelsey, it was hard to find it, but after . . . it would work. He could marry her, protect her, keep her with him. They could live together but keep a good amount of space between them, which Kelsey would like, and then at night . . .

He still had to get her to agree to marry him, but he was feeling a bit better about his odds now that they'd slept together.

Married friends. A hell of a lot better than married strangers, like his parents had been without his mother even knowing. And a damn sight better than married enemies, which had been his own personal experience with the institution. Commitment and companionship, that was the way to go.

He ignored the twinge of discomfort in his chest. Kelsey was the kind of woman with the capacity to love big. She'd chosen this baby. The way she loved the baby more than her own life when it was no bigger than an avocado pit was the most amazing thing he'd ever seen. And he was going to offer lifelong friendship?

Maybe the baby would be enough. And having family surround them. Yes, because what Kelsey loved more than anything was the baby. He knew the baby trumped romantic love for her. Obviously it did, since she'd chosen to be a single mother.

He was offering her the best thing for their child, and he knew she would be on board with that.

When he went downstairs, there was no one in the house except for Kelsey, who was curled up on the couch by the big windows, her laptop positioned on the armrest.

"Good morning," he said, approaching with caution. He wasn't entirely sure what kind of mood she would be in, and reading complex female emotion, especially from a distance, wasn't his strong point.

"Morning," she said, her voice muted.

When she raised her eyes from the computer screen, her cheeks flushed pink. Just looking at her felt like a punch in the gut.

"Did you sleep well?"

She looked around. "Yes."

He crossed to the couch and sat down beside her. He leaned in and pressed a light kiss to her lips. "Really?" he asked, brushing his thumb over her cheekbone.

He couldn't remember what his plan was, just for a second. Like it had evaporated, turned into a fog. And everything was replaced, filled, with Kelsey. Her smell, the softness of her skin.

"Well, I was a little sad I had to get up and brave the cold hardwood floor so I could get back to my room, but yes, other than that."

He was supposed to ask her again about marrying him. He remembered now. But the words stuck in his throat. He didn't want her to get angry at him. He didn't want to ruin whatever this was between them.

He ignored the pang in his chest. It was the logical thing to do anyway, waiting for the right moment. She would just get mad at him if he asked now. She would accuse him of using sex to get what he wanted. That was one thing he didn't want her to think. He'd tried to avoid using actual sex, had tried to avoid sex at all costs. And it certainly hadn't been for his own well-being.

"There are definitely better ways to wake up."

"I see you're not a novice. Which is good, because you may have noticed that I am," she said.

"I definitely wasn't thinking you were a novice last night."

"That's a relief. As is the fact that you were better than I imagined." The pink in her cheeks spread.

That was a bigger turn-on than it should have been. "You imagined how it would be?"

"Well, yes. And in my experience, sex is *pretty* good, but a lot of the time it's really fast. And also men don't usually like foreplay."

"They don't?"

"No. They want the main event."

"You're basing this off of how many guys?"

She coughed and looked away. "One."

He tried to mask the shock on his face, because she really didn't need that. She was embarrassed, which she shouldn't have been. But it was surprising. "Oh. Well, that's not a very good cross section of the male population."

"Well, no, but it's also based on a survey of friends who have told me about their lame sexual escapades. And . . . anyway, I just was a little worried that since you're so . . . nice-looking, you would just try to ride on that instead of actual skill, but . . . color me pleasantly surprised." Her smile turned a little smug.

He felt something strange bloom in his chest, a feeling that hurt and warmed him at the same time. "Glad to know it worked for you."

"It did. And it worked for you?"

"You have to ask?" He watched the expression on her face, saw the insecurity in her blue eyes. "You do? I swear, if I ever meet your ex, I'm going to punch him in the face."

"It's not his fault. I mean, I just wasn't . . . everything for him. Obviously, if I had been, he wouldn't have cheated."

"No, if he hadn't been a dick, he wouldn't have cheated. It has nothing to do with you."

"I appreciate that."

"I have some work to do," he said. He resented it, because at the moment all he wanted to do was drag her upstairs and have a repeat of last night.

"That's okay, so do I. I've used up my store of emergency columns, so unless I want to run repeats, I need to get this out."

"Then I'll let you get to it."

He hesitated, thinking about kissing her again. He thought better of it. If he did that, he'd never leave.

Kelsey watched Cole walk out of the room. She sighed, laying her head back on the couch. She turned her attention back to her column, which was starting to take shape. And look less like an homage to the junk food that made her feel so good and more like what she was actually paid to write.

Her phone vibrated in her pocket, and she retrieved it, holding it out in front of her so she could read the number. Her stomach sank a little when she saw MOM flash up on the screen. She hadn't talked to her mother in weeks, so she should have known the reprieve was over.

They didn't talk very often, but if she went too long without calling, her mother would take the initiative. And she would be mad.

She pressed the TALK button. "Hi, Mom," she said, wincing.

"Kelsey, I'm glad you answered."

Kelsey looked down at her nails. "Of course I answered."

"Did Kailey call you?"

"What? No."

She had talked to her youngest sister only a couple of times since her wedding. The overt starry-eyed bliss put her off a bit, and frankly, she bet her sister noticed. It didn't make her feel very good to know that she was probably mainly to blame for the silence.

"She's pregnant!"

"Oh. Good." Kelsey put her hand on her stomach, her heart pounding hard.

"Yeah, not very far along. She's due in January."

Two months after Kelsey. The words stuck in her throat.

They weren't words you said over the phone. Except her mother had just said them. She didn't know how she was supposed to, though. To tell her mother that she was single and pregnant.

Why was she such a coward?

"I'm so happy for her," Kelsey breathed.

"Well, you should come down and visit."

Kelsey thought about her house in Portland, and how she was due to go and take care of whatever she might need to take care of there. Forwarding mail. Checking to see if anyone had stolen her TV. Or her old Hanson posters.

"I should be able to head down that way in a week or so."

"Well, your father and I would like to see you."

For the first time, Kelsey wondered if she imagined some of the criticism she'd always heard in her mother's tone. Right now she sounded like she missed Kelsey. And when Kelsey's baby grew up, she didn't want him or her to ignore her for weeks at a time. She'd be pretty pissed. And hurt.

And that was what she did to her mother—a lot.

"I'm sorry that I don't keep in touch as well as I should."

There was silence on her mother's end, and Kelsey waited, her eyes glued to her fingernails.

"I always like to hear from you," her mother said finally.

"Good. Well, how about if I come up next Wednesday?"

"The door is always open."

"I'm glad about that." She was. Because she was having a baby, and as rocky as things were going to be when she told them, her baby deserved to know all of its family. Even Kelsey's parents. Even when they drove her nuts.

The baby was why she did anything. It was why she was here with Cole.

She ignored the little kick in her stomach that said otherwise.

Kelsey wasn't sure what would happen after dinner. Everyone was there: the ranch hands, Cade and Lark. They lingered over coffee and pie, then filed out, headed to bed or, in Lark's case, to play a game on the computer.

That left her and Cole sitting at the table. For a second. Cole stood up, his coffee still in his hand. "Want to go sit out in the living area?"

"Sure." The living area–lobby–common area was divided into a few seating sections, and she took her usual position on the couch by the windows.

She didn't really want to sit. She wasn't exactly sure what she wanted. That was a lie. She knew what she wanted; she just wasn't sure what she should do.

Cole joined her, keeping a respectable distance between them, which meant she had a hope of stringing together a coherent sentence. And not jumping him.

"Did you get your article done?"

"Yes. And I talked to my mother."

Now was as good a time as any to bring up the fact that she was going to take care of her house and visit her parents in the next week. The subject of her mother might also kill any lingering lust that was between them.

"Did you tell her about the baby?"

"Uh . . . no. Turns out my sister Kailey—the one who got married at the end of summer—is pregnant. So I didn't want to steal her thunder by announcing I was about to birth a test-tube baby with a stranger and spend my days as a single mother."

"Yeah, no one can top that," he said dryly.

She made a short whining noise. "She was nice to me. If she'd been dry and disapproving like she can be, it would have been easy. I would have felt justified. But she said she missed me. Things seemed so normal. And now I'm going to have to wreck it. I'm starting to actually look pregnant."

"You look beautiful," he said.

"I'm roundish."

"Stand up." She cast him a withering glare but obeyed the command. "Turn to the side for me. Let me see."

She pulled her stretchy top tight at the back, molding it over her stomach. "See?"

A strange smile crossed his handsome face and he leaned forward from his position on the couch, resting his palm flat on her midsection. "Beautiful," he said.

His touch was tender, and she imagined it should evoke feelings of tenderness in her. But Cole's touch was never that simple. He made her feel warm, made her feel cared for. He also made her feel like her blood was rushing close to the surface of her skin, like she might lose every rational thought in her head if he would just keep touching her.

He was always too many things. A stranger, in some ways. The father of her baby. Now her lover. Her jilted suitor.

"I'm glad you think so."

"Beautiful doesn't quite cover it. It's too simple."

She laughed. "Funny, I was just thinking the same thing about you."

"What's that?"

"That there's nothing simple about this. There never will be, will there?"

He shook his head. "I doubt it."

"That . . . might be okay."

She put her hand over his, and he turned his palm so that it was facing up. He grasped her fingers in his. "Well, it has to be. It's all we have."

"Good point." She lowered their hands and released his, sitting back down on the couch, sure to keep some space between them. So she could think. "So, I told my mom that I would come and visit. And that works out because I was going to go make sure my house was in order anyway."

"You're going to go by yourself?"

"Uh . . . yeah. You have work to do here. I know you can't take a lot of time. And anyway, it's not going to be any fun."

"I said we'd do the thing with your family together, and I meant it. Unless you changed your mind."

"I . . ." She laughed. "Well, what am I going to tell them?"

"What do you need to tell them? We're having a baby. They don't need to know anything else unless you want them to. The baby will be their grandchild. You'll take care of him. I'll take care of him. What else is there?"

"There's that whole traditional family unit you're so big on. It's something you have in common with my parents, actually."

"I don't think I explained myself very well when I asked you. It's not about being traditional or even necessarily doing the right thing, though that is a factor for me. It's about taking care of you. Taking care of the baby to the best of my ability."

"Do we really have to be married to do that?"

"I . . . I think we might." She opened her mouth to disagree, but he held up his hand to stop her. "If we aren't a couple, that means . . . dating, possibly marrying other people. That means having separate households and lives."

"But we have no reason to believe we shouldn't have separate lives."

His dark eyebrows shot up. "None? Because I think last night is pretty compelling evidence that we have some reason to be together."

"Sex? That's the best you've got?"

"When it comes to sex, I've got the best you've had, so that has to mean something."

She narrowed her eyes. "Bastard. That's not remotely gentlemanly."

"I proposed to you, so let's figure that erases my more ungentlemanly comments."

"Except I don't really consider your proposal overly gentlemanly either."

"Because you're stubborn," he said.

"Yep. I am."

"You're also incredibly sexy."

"Low. That's not going to work. Not even a little bit."

"Yes, it is," he said, leaning in. "It's working already."

She leaned back. "No, it's not."

"If you take me with you to talk to your parents, you won't have to sleep alone."

She laughed. "Oh, yes, I will."

"We could sneak."

"My mom has ears like a collie's. You'll never get away with it."

He leaned in. "I still might go with you."

She moved closer to him. "No way."

"You going to stop me? Because I think that could be fun to watch."

"I need some alone time," she said.

"Answer this, then. Do you want to sleep alone tonight?"

No. She absolutely didn't want to sleep alone. She wanted to get naked with Cole again and feel his hot skin against hers. Run her fingers over every inch of his delicious, muscled body, then collapse in an exhausted, sweaty heap against his chest.

She shrugged. "Eh."

"Oh, you are a liar," he said, leaning in, his breath fanning against her cheek. "You want me," he said, his lips hovering just above hers.

"I could take you or leave you," she whispered.

A wicked smile curved his mouth. "I don't think so, Kelsey."

Her heart was pounding so hard, she was dizzy. "I'm cool as a cucumber."

He lifted his hand and traced her lower lip with his thumb. "No. You're burning up, baby."

She nipped his thumb. It was supposed to make him stop. Supposed to defuse the tension. It did neither. Instead, a heat flared up in his eyes, his expression intensifying. And she felt an answering flame burn bright and hot in her belly.

"Sorry," she said, putting her hand over his, not quite sure what she was thinking. She pulled his thumb back to her lips and pressed a light kiss to his skin.

He rubbed his thumb over her tender skin and she shivered. She wanted him. No use pretending otherwise. He was right. She'd never had sex like the sex she'd had with him. She'd thought sex like that was a unicorn. Wonderful enough to write it into books, put it in movies and on posters, but completely and thoroughly made up.

But it was real. And Cole had shown her that. And damn it, she wanted more.

"Kiss me," she said.

"Changing your mind?"

"No. I could resist if I wanted to. I just don't want to."

"Not convincing."

"I am in complete control," she said.

"Really? I'm not."

Her heart squeezed tight. "You aren't?"

He shook his head. "Not even a little." He leaned in, closing the distance between them, his lips capturing hers. Finally. And it was perfect. He was perfect.

She leaned into him, deepening the kiss, her heart rate increasing, her nipples tightening as his tongue stroked against hers. She grabbed the front of his shirt and pulled him closer. Subtle? No. But there was no time or room for subtle. She'd lied through her teeth when she'd claimed control, and at this point she wasn't in the mood to cover it up.

He wrapped his arms around her and pulled her tightly against him. She had to fight the urge to climb onto his lap, straddle him and find the rhythm that would get her there now. Fast. Still in her jeans. She didn't care. She just needed.

"Sorry!"

They snapped apart like spooked cats and looked in the direction of their intruder. Lark was standing there, her face beet red, her mouth slack.

"Why did you say sorry?" Cole asked. "We didn't hear you come in. You could have sneaked back out. No one would have known."

"I . . . I was surprised," Lark said, her eyes owlish.

"Join the club," Cole grumbled.

Kelsey felt like melting into the couch cushions and sliding through the cracks in the wooden floor. If it were an option . . . she would have grabbed it with both hands.

"Game over?" she asked Lark.

Lark edged away from the couch. "Just going to the kitchen to get a snack."

"What are you doing?" Cole asked.

"Killing zombies," Lark said.

"Neat," said Cole, his tone dry.

"Nazi zombies," Lark said as she backed out of the room.

Kelsey raised her fist. "Give 'em hell."

"Right."

Lark turned and scampered out of the room, and Kelsey collapsed against the back of the couch, a giggle rising in her throat.

"That was ridiculous," she said.

"This house is too crowded," Cole said.

"It's probably better we were interrupted."

"Why?" Cole asked, his eyebrows locked together.

"Because we haven't decided anything. And . . . and maybe . . . I'm just not sure if it wasn't a mistake. It seemed smart, but now it seems . . . confusing."

He frowned. "I don't think sex confuses anything."

"Ah, look at you. Not arguing the abstinence side anymore. Give a guy an orgasm and his tune changes quickly."

"I'm not looking!" Lark passed through the room, her

head angled away from them, a can of Diet Coke in her raised hand, covering her face.

"Nothing to see anyway," Cole growled.

"I'm tired. I think I'll go to bed." Kelsey turned and headed toward the stairs, and she heard Cole's heavy footfalls behind her. "Alone."

He groaned behind her, and a very sick, illicit thrill went through her. She liked that she was the one in charge now. That he was the one dying a slow, sexually charged death. Not that she was unscathed. She was in dire need of, at minimum, a shower and some time to herself to resolve the ache between her thighs.

Still, she felt like she finally had the upper hand. And that, she liked.

Even if that meant she would now have to apply said upper hand to herself so she could have some modicum of relief.

"Good night, Cole," she said, heading up the stairs.

"We'll see," he countered.

"And that means?"

"We'll see if you can keep from coming to my room tonight."

She paused. "Now that you said that, you can guarantee I won't come to your room."

"Cutting off your nose to spite your face."

"Maybe," she said, starting up the stairs again. "But I win."

"Sort of."

Damn him, he was right. But she wasn't giving in now. Not to the desire that was coursing through her body, and not to his marriage proposal.

Kelsey wiggled beneath the covers and hoped some of the excess heat would burn off her skin if she rolled over the cool sheets enough. No such luck.

There had been no luck satisfying herself either. She'd tried. But it was futile. She wanted Cole's hands. Big and rough and masculine. Her hands weren't Cole's hands, and she couldn't even pretend. Not when the memory of them was so clear in her mind.

She let out a breath and stared sightlessly at the ceiling. She was going to die of sexual frustration. How was it she'd managed to be celibate for so long and not care, and now twenty-four hours seemed like an impossibility?

Stupid, freaking cowboy.

There was a heavy knock on the door, and she sighed with relief. He'd given in. Thank God.

She rolled out of bed and padded to the door, opening it a crack. She saw a sliver of Cole's face through the opening.

"You're weak, Mitchell," she whispered.

"You're wide-awake, Noble."

"So? I didn't come to your room."

"Are you going to let me in or not?"

She opened the door wide. "Come in."

He swept her into his arms and closed the door in one fluid motion, walking her to the bed as he devoured her lips.

He laid her down on the soft mattress and she moaned with relief. *Yes. Yes. Yes.* This was what she wanted. This was what she wanted so badly, her entire body ached.

She tugged his T-shirt up over his head and ran her hands over his chest while he made quick work of her shirt and pajama bottoms.

He kissed her deeply while she clawed at his pants, tugging them and his underwear down and kicking them to the floor.

"You want this?" he asked.

"Yes," she breathed, running her fingertips over his back, relishing the feel of hot skin and hard muscle.

"Good." He hooked her thigh up over his hip and entered her in one smooth stroke.

It was fast, and it was amazing. She was so close to the edge that the combination of a few deep, hard thrusts, his breath on her neck and his muscles beneath her hands was enough to make her come in record time. And he wasn't far behind, shuddering out his own pleasure just as the last intense waves of her orgasm trailed off.

She held him against her chest, her heart pounding hard, their breath sharp and broken in the silence of the room.

"I feel so much better now," she said.

He laughed. "Yes. So do I."

She smiled. "Okay, you're right about the sex. It's great."

"As much as I like hearing you say I'm right, can we just enjoy this?" He rolled to the side and took her with him, drawing her tight up against his chest.

"You mean, without a fight or snark or . . . anything like that?"

"Yes. That."

She turned her face into his chest and inhaled the scent of skin and sweat. And Cole. He was starting to seem so familiar. So important.

"Okay."

"Did you just agree with me?"

"Yes. I would like to lie here in postorgasmic bliss for as long as possible."

He moved his hands, letting his fingers drift over her curves. She felt her nipples getting tight, felt that little tightening of arousal low in her stomach. "Until you're ready to have some real-time orgasmic bliss," he said, his voice rough. He leaned in and pressed a kiss to her neck, and she shivered.

"Don't you have to . . . recover?"

"There are a lot of things I can do while we wait."

There was no smart remark at the ready for her. There was nothing but need. "Show me," she said.

And he did.

Restraint wasn't their strong point, it turned out, but Cole didn't mind. He slept in Kelsey's bed every night for the rest of the week. Well, most of the night. He still left before everyone in the house woke up. It was too complicated to broadcast that they were now sleeping together, having a baby together, but still not getting married or even committing to dating.

He'd never imagined such a screwed-up situation could exist, much less that he would be involved in it. In his mind, marriage was the best solution. The way he could be there for her. Protect her. Kelsey didn't agree.

And today was the day they left for Portland, and then her parents' house. Cole was making good on his promise to come, whether she wanted him to or not. She'd done crazy things for their baby, including coming to the ranch in the first place. It was time for him to be a little crazy. Even if he had to follow her in his truck, he was going. Because he was in it. And he would be a part of their son's or daughter's life, which meant that her parents had to at least get to know him.

Plus, the idea of what her parents might do or say when they found out made him feel slightly sick. Kelsey was a beautiful, unique, amazing woman, and she didn't seem to realize it. Not fully.

Some of that was the rat-bastard-ex factor, he was sure. But some of it came from her parents. And that made him feel pissed. And protective.

Kelsey emerged from her room carrying a duffel bag, and he held out his hand. "Can I take that?"

She looked up at him. "Um . . . sure." She handed him the bag, and he slung it over his shoulder. "What are you doing?" she asked.

"I'm coming with you."

She rolled her eyes and started walking down the hall toward the stairs. "I know."

"No argument?"

"Is there any point?"

He shook his head. "No."

"I didn't think there was. So, I figured I would just bring you."

He caught up to her and descended the stairs beside her. "A pity inclusion?"

"If you want to think of it that way." She let out a sigh. "No. Okay? No. I'm scared. I have to go and face my parents and tell them that their heathen, job-possessing daughter went and got knocked up, and I don't want to. I'm scared of what they'll say, and . . . and yeah, I want you there, so they can get mad at you. Can you pretend you took my virtue?"

"Sure. But you'll have to tell me if I'm projecting the proper stealer-of-innocence vibe."

"You sort of exude that, actually."

"Do I?"

"Well, I mean, I'd have given it up for you. If I hadn't already. I mean, I've slept with you. Lots. So clearly . . . I find you somewhat irresistible."

A shot of heat went straight down to his groin. "Really? Irresistible?"

"Oh, don't let it go to your head."

She pushed open the door, and he reached over her head and held it open, letting her go through first.

"Too late. Irresistible?"

She blew out an exasperated breath. "Have I resisted you once this week?"

She turned away from him and walked down the stairs, heading across the gravel lot to her car. "Nope," he tossed back.

"So, there's my point."

He followed her down to her car, watching her shoulders bunch, her irritation clear.

"I mean, clearly I was powerless to resist."

"The lure of the fertility clinic," he said.

She growled and opened the door to her car. "I'm a wimp."

He leaned in and hit the button for her trunk, then deposited the bag in the back. "No, you aren't. Parents have a way of making people totally crazy. If I remember right."

She looked down at her hands. "What happened to your parents?"

He walked over to his truck and took an overnight bag out of the bed, then threw it in beside Kelsey's before slamming the trunk shut. "My mom . . . my mom had an accident on the ranch. She was trying to drive a tractor through some mud. It was too deep, but you know, she'd done it a lot of times before. She was . . . she was a hell of a woman, Kelsey. Strong and . . . strong. Anyway, she rolled the tractor onto herself, and it was too late by the time anyone found her."

"Cole, that's . . . I'm so sorry."

"It was horrible," he said. "But . . . we all survived. We sort of stuck closer together. Come to think of it, my dad went out of town less often after. I always thought it was just because he had more to take care of. The ranch and the kids. But I wonder now if he felt a little guilty too."

"Trying to atone?"

He shrugged and rounded the car, opening the passenger door. "You want to drive?"

She nodded, and he got in, buckling up while she made her way to the driver's seat.

She started the car and sat for a moment. "And your dad?"

He frowned, closing his eyes against the wall of anger and grief. Just intense, strong emotion that he couldn't seem to sort through or get a handle on. "He had a heart attack. He was that guy, you know? Bacon and steak all the time, and damned if the doctors knew what they were talking about. He was a stubborn cuss."

"A little like you."

"Yeah. I always thought so. I always wanted to be like him." He shook his head. "I don't anymore, Kelsey. That's the biggest thing I lost. Not just my dad but . . . who I was going to be. I was so torn up over the divorce, because I knew that my dad, if he'd been alive, would have been disappointed. Would have told me a real man owned up to his responsibilities. To his mistakes. A real man didn't quit. Well, he wasn't a real man. He wasn't the man I thought."

She reached over and put her hand on his. "I . . . Is saying 'I'm sorry' worth anything?"

He nodded slowly. "Yes."

"Maybe he believed what he told you, Cole. He just couldn't live it. Not perfectly. But it doesn't mean that he didn't mean what he told you."

He dragged a hand over his face, his chest heavy. "Maybe. Maybe that's true."

"And I don't think he would have been mad at you for getting divorced. If he had seen your ex yelling at Lark?"

"He would have thrown her out himself."

"He loved you." Kelsey stuck the key in the ignition and tapped on the little plastic key chain that hung from it.

Cole nodded. "I know."

She turned the car on, the engine rumbling, swallowing some of her words. "I think he probably loved your mom too."

He cleared his throat and looked out the window. "That's one of the things that scares me."

Cade came out onto the porch, looking toward the car, his hands in his pockets.

"Does he know you're going?" Kelsey asked.

Cole welcomed the subject change. "Yeah, I told him last night."

"Ah. And yet, you didn't tell me. Not even after we—"

"I was planning on having to fight you. So, I figured I'd spring it on you at the last minute."

She snorted a laugh, then waved at Cade as she put the car into reverse. "You always have a plan, Cole Mitchell."

"Except when I don't. Except when I feel completely at a loss."

"Do you ever?"

"Every moment of the past month." And basically for the past few years of his life.

"You seem like you always know what you're doing."

"I have you fooled."

"Yeah, you're pissed at life, but you move through it like you're ready to bar-punch it if it gets too mouthy with you. You just don't seem as . . . flail-y as me."

He laughed. "I never thought you seemed that way. You always seem like you're the one with the plan. The one with the guts to take over your life."

"When I'm not quaking over the fallout of my decisions, yeah, that's me. My family scares me, though. Still . . . I'm grateful that I have them."

"Family is complicated. And just because you feel bad

that I lost mine doesn't mean you can't resent yours sometimes. I resent the hell out of my dad right now, and he's
dead. So, go on and complain all you want."

"I appreciate that."

"We might actually get along on this trip."

She laughed. "Yeah, maybe. We'll see. If you get too
tough to deal with, I have some cables—I can always tie you
to the roof."

"If you don't need them to tie me to the roof, maybe save
them for the bedroom."

"Don't tempt me, Cole."

"But I like to tempt you."

She tossed him a quick look. "Then it's a good thing I
enjoy being tempted."

Her house looked small. It had never looked small to her before. But it could easily fit inside the common area of the big ranch house, and it was crammed up against the neighbor's fence. No wide-open spaces here.

She'd always thought it was cute and quaint. On the edge of the city without really being urban. Not one of the new clone houses that had no character or personality.

But it didn't look as inviting as it always had. It looked cold. And old.

She let out a breath. Probably because it was both of those things. Especially since she'd been away for a month. It was out of the way, as in it added hours to their trip, but she really had to go check on her house in person. Anyway, maybe one night spent there would provide her with some magical life answers. Maybe it would make her feel less drawn to Silver Creek and the ranch.

"Home sweet home," she mumbled, digging her keys out of her purse and marching up the uneven cement walk. She jammed the key in the door and swung it open, walking into her familiar little kitchen. Thankfully, it was clean. Which was mostly Alexa's doing—her contribution before their road trip, since Kelsey had felt too much like garbage to accomplish anything even remotely productive four weeks ago.

Had it been only a month? It felt like forever.

She felt Cole behind her. It really did seem longer than that. Had he really been a stranger the last time they were here together?

"Does it feel good to be home?" he asked, setting their bags on the floor by the door.

"Meh," she said, leaning up against the counter and looking around. "I mean, yeah, it does, but . . . weird too."

It didn't feel like home. She'd expected a rush of emotion. Happiness. She'd expected the wonderful sense of being in surroundings that fit her. But there was none of that. This felt like a part of someone else's life. Like a place she'd visited once. Not like her home.

"But you know"—she bent down and opened up one of the drawers set into the cabinets, rifling until she found a paper take-out menu—"I can order dinner, and someone will deliver it. You don't have that in Silver Creek."

"Not so much."

"Takeout. Glorious takeout. Will Chinese do? I seem to recall you eating it."

"Anything will do."

"Great, okay." She punched in the numbers and rattled off her typical order without thinking. So there were some things that felt normal, some things that were easy to slip back into. "It'll be here in thirty. Do you need a . . . shower or anything?"

His eyes darkened, his gaze raking over her body. And just like that she was totally hot for him.

"Only if you want to join me."

In her house. Her house, which she'd shared with her ex. The idea seemed weird. Not that her ex mattered, because he didn't. But . . . it seemed domestic, maybe. She was trying to avoid domestic with Cole. She was trying very hard to avoid it.

Yes, Kels, and taking him to meet the parents is the way to do that.

"Not right now. I need to go . . . flush the toilets and stuff." She wrinkled her nose. "There's probably algae in them."

"Pleasant."

"Not in the least."

"You get the upstairs. I'll get the down," he offered.

"My hero," she said, clasping her hands beneath her chin.

"Damsel in distress . . . yeah, I don't believe it for a moment."

She batted her eyes and made her way up the narrow staircase. Everything was as she had left it. Clean and utterly unlived in.

She scurried quickly into the bathroom and flushed the toilet, hoping things weren't too musky and disgusting. She wandered into her room and looked at the bed. She'd bought it a couple of years ago. It was big enough for two.

And yeah, she was going to share with Cole. No point in *not* sharing with him.

Even though it was going to feel very couple-ish. But that wasn't really a bad thing. She could give it a chance. Maybe see how things went.

And then what? Marry the guy and be a happy family?

For one glowing second, her answer to that was yes. But she knew that wasn't reality.

It would be more like strapping themselves to the same ball and chain. It wouldn't solve anything. Wouldn't make anything easier. Not in reality. And she would be another wife who wasn't what he wanted or needed.

Except sometimes she felt like it would be great. Like things would be magically easier. That was just dumb girl-ishness. Marriage wasn't easy. Marriage to Cole wouldn't be easy. She would always wonder if he felt . . . well, if he felt leg-shackled, and that was the last thing she wanted.

She let out a breath and walked out of the bedroom, closing the door behind her.

She wasn't going to worry about it now. For now she would go downstairs and have dinner with Cole. When she was with him, things might not seem simple, but she was happy.

She tried not to dwell too much on what that might mean.

"I don't really have a guest bed made up. I hope that's not a problem." Kelsey stood at her bedroom door, Cole in front of her, looking down at her, his expression hungry. And since they'd just finished dinner, she was sure he wasn't hungry for food.

"I don't have a problem with that at all."

She pushed the door open and went and sat on the edge of her very feminine bed.

"Everything in your house is . . . floral," he said, surveying the decor.

"Yeah, I know. I like flowers." She smoothed the blue fabric of her bedspread. "Another compelling reason you might want to rethink your offer of marriage. Think of how feminine your house might become."

"It is a risk."

He tugged his shirt up over his head, and her mouth dried.

"Yes . . . Yes, it is."

She watched with rapt interest as his hands went to his belt and worked the leather through the loops. Then he undid the button on his jeans. She licked her lips.

"Kelsey, the way you're looking at me is enough to make me blush."

"I doubt you know how to blush, Cole."

His lips curved into a half smile and he shoved his jeans and underwear down his legs. And now he was very naked, very aroused and unashamed.

Great. She could be that way too. Bold and naked. And just . . . all out there. That was one of the many good things about Cole. She didn't feel unexciting with him. She didn't feel average. Cole made her feel like a goddess. The way he looked at her, the way he touched her, like he couldn't get enough . . . he made her feel like a woman.

Enough woman for him. And he was all the man she could have ever asked for.

She tugged her top over her head and reached around to unhook her bra, yanking it down and throwing it onto the floor before she stood and took her jeans and panties off as quickly as possible, hoping it might minimize the embarrassment of total nudity with the lights on.

"Now you, Kelsey," he said, taking a step toward her, running his thumb across her cheekbone, "are blushing."

She shook her head. "No way."

"You are." He leaned in and kissed her on the cheek. "I think it's cute."

"Cute, huh?"

"I mean that in the best way."

He bent and kissed her. And his kiss was most definitely not cute. It was pure, raw sexual need. And it was exactly what she needed.

She wrapped her arms around his neck and pulled him down onto the bed with her, reveling in the feeling of his skin against hers.

"You're . . . you're just so hot," she moaned, running her hands down his back, gripping his tight butt.

He chuckled and dipped his head, tracing the outline of her nipple with his tongue. She arched into him, needing to be closer to him. As close to him as she could be.

When she was in his arms, it all seemed to make sense. Everything else faded away. Worries. What-ifs. The expectations of other people. When she was with him, it was like the world was reduced to Cole and Kelsey. Like nothing else mattered.

She slithered away from him and sat up, looking at the picture he made. So masculine and big, spread out on her flowery bed. She ran her hand down his arm, over his well-defined biceps. This felt like playtime. A chance to explore a body that was as close to male perfection as existed, she was sure.

She leaned in and pressed a kiss to his chest, and his muscles went taut beneath her lips.

"What are you doing?" he asked, his voice strained.

"I'm about to have my wicked way with you." She pressed a kiss to his abs. "I think you should let me."

"Kelsey . . ."

"What? You don't like this?" She ran the tip of her tongue down below his belly button. "I think you do."

"I'm close."

"That's fine. If I have my way, you'll be finished."

She lowered her head, flicked her tongue over the head of his cock. His body jerked beneath her, and a rush of power flooded through her. Right now he was her captive. She was in command.

She wrapped her hand around his shaft and guided him into her mouth, gratified by the raw sound of need that escaped his lips.

He put his hand on the back of her head, tangling his fingers in her hair, holding her to him.

"Yes," he whispered, his voice broken.

She slid her tongue down the length of him, then back up, before taking him deep into her mouth again.

"Careful," he said, pulling away from her.

"What?" she asked.

"I'm right on the edge, baby."

"That's fine. Let's go over together."

"Really together, though," he said. "Not like that."

"I was fine with it being like that."

"Later. Come here."

He leaned back against her headboard, extending his hand. She took it. He tugged her to him so that she was draped over his body, her thighs on either side of his, and he kissed her deeply, guiding her so that the head of his erection was poised at the slick entrance to her body.

She lowered herself onto him, loving how he stretched

her, filled her. She held on to his shoulders as she started to move over him.

Her release flooded her, sudden, fast and hard. She held on to him while she rode out the storm, while she shook with the aftermath of her orgasm. He followed her a second later, tensing beneath her, his fingers digging into her hips.

She collapsed against him, her head resting on his chest, his heat raging beneath her cheek.

"I don't think I'll ever get tired of that," he said, his voice rough.

"It's not possible," she mumbled, wrapping her arms around his waist.

He shifted, lying down and bringing her with him, drawing the blankets over them.

"Cole . . ." She knew he wasn't the kind of guy who did pillow talk. He didn't talk about himself very much at all. But he'd shared some very personal things with her since she'd met him, and they'd done some very personal things in bed. So she was willing to give it a shot. "Why haven't you found any other women? Since your divorce, I mean. You were with women you didn't marry before your wife. Why not after?"

He tightened his hold on her, his heart rate slowing. "I haven't wanted to."

"But you seem to want to. I mean . . . you really seem to want to."

He stroked her hair, his touch firm. Comforting.

"I do with you. Honest, Kelsey, I wasn't interested before you came into my life. I didn't even want to find someone to sleep with. It seemed like too much work. But you make it . . . you make me want to work for it."

"What made me so special?" she asked.

She regretted the words as soon as they left her lips. She wasn't special. She was the screwup. The black sheep. She'd proven it by the way she and Cole had met. A mistake. A big mistake. And the only reason he wanted her was for the baby. It had nothing to do with her. But she hoped he'd lie. Lie and make her feel good.

"You just are," he said. He tilted her face up so that she was looking at him. "You really are."

Her heart tightened, a strange heat spreading through her chest. It didn't matter if it was a lie. It was the prettiest lie ever. "Well, thank you."

He laughed, a sound she was hearing more often lately. "You don't need to thank me for that."

"It seemed polite. Hospitable."

"I see. Is that what this was? Your hospitality?" His eyes glittered with humor.

"I'm an excellent hostess," she said, deadpan.

"It was also very hospitable of you to lay me down and offer to suck my—"

She put her hand over his mouth, laughter bubbling out. "Stop! You're ruining the moment by being a guy."

He laughed under her hand, then gripped her wrist, peeling her palm off his mouth and giving her a quick kiss. "Sorry. I won't be a guy anymore."

She'd never laughed like this after sex. Ever. "I like it when you're a guy."

"I'm glad to hear it."

She curled up against him, his heartbeat steady and soothing against her cheek. She let her eyes flutter closed. For tonight, she wasn't going to worry about why they were together. She was just looking forward to spending the whole night wrapped in Cole's arms.

Cole could feel Kelsey's tension heightening the closer they got to Bonanza. Gone were the smiling, the laughing, the joking. The touching. She had both hands on the wheel, her shoulders shrugged up by her ears, her jaw set tight, her expression focused.

Ten miles out of town and she shut the radio off. By the time they pulled onto the dirt road that led back to her parents' two-story farmhouse, he was afraid she might burst a blood vessel.

She put the car in park in front of the house and then

put her hand back on the wheel. She didn't shut the engine off.

"Are you okay?" he asked, putting his hand over hers.

She didn't turn to him. "Fine," she said.

"Yeah, honey, that's not a real convincing way to demonstrate how fine you are."

Her head whipped in his direction. "What's not?"

"You're . . . clenched. Your entire being is clenched."

"I am not."

He uncurled her fingers from the steering wheel slowly, then held her hands, still formed into little claws, in both of his. "You are."

She pulled her hands back and shook them out. "I'm fine. It's just my . . . family." She put her head back on the seat. "Aw, damn it."

"What?"

"I didn't really tell them you were coming. And also I didn't really work out the sleeping arrangements in advance, and now it's going to be a thing."

"It won't be a thing. I'll sleep in another room."

She blew out a breath. "The fact that you even know that that's what my mom would make you do . . . it's like you get them."

He shrugged. "In a way, I do. I was raised to respect women and to respect the parents of the woman I'm dating. Seeing. Having a baby with."

"Yeah, well, normal people would just show us to our room. We're in our thirties, for heaven's sake. But they won't. And they're going to raise eyebrows at you because, well . . ." She indicated her slightly rounded belly.

"And just last week you could have said we weren't sleeping together."

Her cheeks turned pink. "Times change."

"People get laid. Ready to go in?"

She let out a heavy breath. "As ready as I'll ever be." She leaned forward and hit the button that popped the trunk, then straightened.

"Hey," he said. She looked up at him. "Before we go in."

He leaned forward and touched his lips to hers. He felt the tension drain from her, and his heart swelled in response. That he'd had a hand in relaxing her. That his touch meant something.

They parted, and she offered him a weak, unconvincing smile. "All right. I'm about as ready to do this as I am to get stabbed in the eye with a fork."

"So not at all."

"Astute," she said, deadpan.

"Come on, chicken."

"Asshole."

"It's been said. Repeatedly."

She opened the car door, and he got out with her, holding out his hand. She looked at it and chewed on her lip, then shook her head slowly. "Better not. Not yet."

He put his hands in his pockets and followed her up the muddy walk to the front door. It was white with blue-checked curtains in the windows. Quaint and shabby, but neat.

Kelsey knocked.

"You're going to draw blood on that lip," he said.

She stopped biting it for a second and shot him a wide-eyed look. He hadn't seen her look scared before. Not really. Sick? Yes. Pissed? Yes. Annoyed and uncomfortable? Sure. But not scared. She was scared now. He hated that her parents had that kind of power over her. But then, he supposed everyone's did, really. He'd been a young adult when his mom had died, but when she'd been mad at him, even when he'd been taller than her by a foot, he'd felt like a grubby five-year-old with his hand caught in the cookie jar. And his dad . . . the fear of disappointing his dad had kept him in a marriage after the old man was dead. Parents had power.

The door swung open to reveal an older woman who looked a lot like Kelsey. Her blond hair was faded, her face lined. But she had the same petite frame and the same vivid blue eyes as the woman at his side.

He wondered if the blue eyes were a strong trait. If their baby would have them.

Kelsey's mom looked from Kelsey to him, her expression questioning. "Kelsey. I didn't know you were bringing a guest."

"If it's a problem, I can get a room in town," Cole said, feeling like the interloper he was.

Kelsey's mother shook her head. "Not a problem."

"I'm sorry, Mom. I didn't . . . think. I didn't realize he was going to . . . Mom, this is Cole."

She extended her hand to him, and he shook it. "Lisa Noble. Very nice to meet you."

"Nice to meet you too," he said.

"Come on in," she said, her eyes never leaving Cole. "Your dad and sisters will be here soon. And the grandkids."

He noticed that made Kelsey smile. "Great. I've missed everyone."

"You should visit more."

He could sense Kelsey tensing beside him. "Sorry. I know. I've been . . . busy. With . . . things."

Like vomiting, he mused.

"You're always busy," her mother said. There wasn't a lot of venom in the words, but Cole could still tell they stung.

"Sorry, Mom."

He looked at Kelsey, who seemed to have shrunk a little. He also noticed for the first time that the top she was wearing was very loose fitting. It covered the bump completely while she was standing. Probably a good thing.

Kelsey fought the urge to start pacing. She was so nervous, she thought she might explode. She felt awkward, she was sure Cole felt awkward, and her mom probably felt awkward because Kelsey had shown up with a great, hulking cowboy without giving any explanation as to who he was or why he was with her.

"Would you like something to drink?" her mother asked. She was a good hostess, even in situations like this. Kelsey had to give her that.

"Just a soda," Kelsey said, sitting on the faded blue couch

that she'd sat on so many times. She had a strange sense of déjà vu wash over her. Probably because she'd sat on the couch so many times while keeping a secret from her parents, while gearing up to tell them something they weren't going to like.

"Same," Cole said, sitting next to her.

She wanted to push him away. She was a chicken; he was right. She wanted him to sit across the room from her and pretend to be her best friend. Her gay best friend. And she wanted to leave out the part where she told them she was pregnant.

Unfortunately, that would be pretty pointless. Because the longer she kept it from them, the more hideously awful it would be.

"Don't get too handsy," she whispered.

"I'll do my best," he said.

She looked at him and saw a glitter of humor in his eyes. She hated it. Hated that he could be relaxed or see any humor in any part of this situation. She also needed him to have a sense of humor, since she was so brittle, she was ready to snap in half.

"Wait till my dad gets here. He's big. You won't look so cocky then."

"The worst he'd probably do is instigate a shotgun wedding. And that kind of goes according to my plan."

She shot him a deadly look. "That's not the worst he could do. You're a rancher—you're familiar with burdizzos, I assume."

He had the decency to look slightly pale at the mention of the very efficient castration tool. "I'm familiar."

"Yeah, I thought you might be."

Her mother returned a moment later with three Cokes in glasses, with ice, on a tray. She set the tray down on the coffee table in front of the couch, her expression expectant. For an explanation, Kelsey assumed, and not for her reaction to the drink. Still, she stayed true to her chicken roots and took the coward's way out, taking a long drink to keep from having to talk for as long as possible.

"So . . . I have news . . ." Kelsey said, clicking her fingernails on the glass, looking at a spot on the rug. The same spot she'd looked at when she'd told her parents she was going away to college. The same spot she'd looked at when she'd told them, oh yes, hadn't she mentioned? She and Michael were living together.

She'd been on the fence about waiting until her father got home. But she really didn't want to run the risk of her sisters, and their children, being around. She wasn't in the mood to have the whole clan explode around her in one big ball of scandal.

Her mother's eyebrows shot up, and she looked from her to Cole again.

"I'm, um . . . expecting a baby," Kelsey said.

Her mother sank down into a chair slowly, nodding as she did. "Okay."

"In November."

"Oh. So you're a bit along, then."

Kelsey looked down into her soda glass and watched the bubbles rise to the top, her heart pounding hard. Her mother wasn't talking anymore. Her face was set like stone, and Kelsey could feel the disapproval sinking into her, could feel it wrapping around her heart and squeezing tight. She shot Cole a panicked look. But Cole wasn't moving either.

And what could he say? She'd never told him what she wanted him to say.

Her mother looked pointedly at her hands, clutching her soda glass tightly. "And you're single?"

"Well . . . no. Not . . . I mean . . . Cole and I . . ." She shot him another desperate look. She wasn't sure what she expected from him. "We're getting married." The words just sort of fell out of her mouth. She hadn't planned them. She hadn't even thought them. They'd just sort of appeared.

"Oh."

Cole didn't miss a beat. "I'm sorry things happened out of order like this. Ideally, I would have spoken to her father first. Ideally, I would have met you all." He left out anything about the baby not being conceived before the wedding, but otherwise, he was saying just what her mother would have wanted to hear.

Damn him. How did he do that? She could never do that. Ever. All she ever did was put her foot in her mouth.

"Well, naturally, things happen," her mother said slowly.

"What? Things happen?" Kelsey blurted. "Really?" Where was the fire and brimstone? The outrage?

Her mother stood. "Kelsey, you're thirty years old. I hardly thought you were a virgin." Kelsey nearly swallowed her tongue. "I'm so pleased that you're giving us another grandchild!" She leaned down and embraced Kelsey, who felt like she was going to implode from the onslaught of unexpected emotion.

"Oh . . . good?"

"You're happy, aren't you, Kelsey?" she asked.

Kelsey nodded mutely.

"We both are, Mrs. Noble," Cole said, offering her mother a winning smile.

Mrs. Noble, even. He was like a Stepford future son-in-law. And he was saving her bacon, so she couldn't even hate him for it. No matter how much she wanted to.

"Well, how can a baby be a bad thing?" her mother asked, treating Cole to the kind of smile Kelsey had never once been on the receiving end of.

"Great," Kelsey said.

"I'd be happy to speak to Mr. Noble when he comes home," Cole said. "To try to start things off right."

"That's . . . very thoughtful of you."

"Mom, I'm not . . . feeling that well," Kelsey said. It was a lie that wasn't really a lie. Her mom would think morning sickness. She was just pissed, really.

"Why don't you go upstairs and rest? I'll let you know when your dad comes home."

Kelsey nodded. "Cole . . . can you bring up my bags?"

Cole nodded and stood up, preparing to head out to the car. Feeling dizzy, Kelsey watched him walk out.

"Even though you are engaged, and pregnant, he's not sleeping in your bed while you're here," her mother said, that tone that was so familiar to Kelsey emerging.

"I know, Mom. He knows too."

"Good. As long as you understand."

"I do." She understood it was what her mother had to do. But that was as far as it went.

"Well, then, have a nice rest."

Her mother started clearing the glasses from the coffee table, and the intense normalcy of it hit Kelsey square in the chest. It was so normal, it was abnormal. Because nothing felt usual about the moment, and yet nothing had really changed either.

She made her way up the stairs to her childhood room. There was one queen bed in it now, instead of three twin beds, but otherwise, it looked a lot the same. Faded pink paint, white curtains dotted with roses.

She sat down on the mattress and sighed. She'd just managed to take a mess and make it messier. It was sort of becoming her thing.

Cole appeared a few seconds later, bags in his hands. "Well, she didn't yell at you," he said, setting her bag down at the foot of the bed.

"No. But that's just because I lied. The big mother of all flipping lies."

"So it was a lie? I was hoping you'd changed your mind."

She let out a long breath and put her face in her hands. "Oh . . . I don't know if it was a lie." She looked back up at him. "I'm making a huge disaster of this."

"It's not like there's a guidebook."

"Stop it," she groaned. "Stop being so nice. Be . . . vaguely disapproving, at least. It's what my mother would do."

"Is it?"

This subject was a tiny bit easier to deal with than her impromptu acceptance of his proposal. "She's happy about having a grandbaby, and I believe that, but she hates the idea that I'm pregnant without being married. And I don't even think it's morality with her. It's just . . . There's a way things should be, a way they should look, and that's the most important thing. I've never, ever fit her idea of what one of her daughters should be like. And I never will. This just sort of . . . confirmed it."

"She didn't say anything horrible when I left, did she?"

"She didn't have to. It's just . . . there. I mean . . . she loves me. I know that. But she wishes I were different too. And I don't really know what to do with that."

Cole sat down next to her on the bed. "I don't wish you were different."

"You don't?"

"No. I like the way you are. Stubborn and independent. Headstrong."

"Hey now."

"I meant it as a compliment."

"Even when you don't get your way with me?"

He nodded. "I like that you have your own mind."

Kelsey felt something in her chest melt, like butter. It was disconcerting. Everything Cole made her feel was wonderful, and terrible, and scary. She wasn't sure what to do with any of it. He'd asked her to marry him, but he'd never once mentioned having feelings for her.

And she really didn't want to be in . . . feelings alone. More than that, she didn't want to trap a man with her because she was having a baby and then have to wonder if he'd lost interest in her yet. She and Michael had, supposedly, had this real, true emotional commitment. Even that hadn't kept him faithful.

What would keep Cole faithful?

Though, really, she couldn't imagine Cole being unfaithful. He was too good. He would just stay in abject misery with her for the rest of his life.

She didn't really want to be a part of that either. Which meant no feelings. But what about the marriage proposal? She could always make her parents believe she'd said yes for a while, then changed her mind. But then, what would that do to their perception of Cole? And of her?

He was the father of her baby, and he would be in her life. And likely in her parents' lives. The last thing she needed was for them to hate him.

"You really do?" she asked.

"Yes."

"And do you mind so much that I just kind of . . . accepted your proposal?"

"You really want to marry me, Kelsey?"

"I don't know," she whispered. "I so don't know what I want. What I'm supposed to want. I feel like . . . I feel like every route I take is so confused and tangled, there's no way I can see the outcome. I don't know what the best thing is. I don't know what I'm supposed to do. And I'm a chicken, like you said. I just caved as soon as my mother gave me that look. And I told her what she wanted to hear. Well, the closest thing I had to what she wanted to hear. She really didn't want to hear that I was pregnant out of wedlock."

"'Wedlock.' Do people even use that word anymore?"

"My mother does. In that context."

"So, will you marry me, Kelsey? Really?"

Kelsey's throat felt too tight, and so did her chest. "Yes," she said, the word a strangled nothing, even in the silence of the room. How could she say no? How could she say no when, no matter how crazy her family made her, the fact remained that she had her family? All of them. Together. She'd had it growing up; she had it now. And being here made it clear, so blindingly clear, that she needed to do this for her child.

"You sound thrilled."

"I'm scared to death. I don't know if it's the right thing to do. . . . I don't—"

He leaned in and caught her lips with his.

He broke the kiss and rested his forehead against hers, his breathing broken, ragged. "I'll do my very best to make you happy. To make sure you never regret marrying me."

In that small moment, when she wasn't thinking too hard about the future, she could believe it. Believe that everything would be fine. They would live in the big ranch house and raise their child. Sleep in the same bed. It would be fine.

She willed away every intruding thought, every concern. Just for a moment, things were clear. They made sense. She wanted them to stay that way.

"You'll be faithful to me?" she asked, hating how insecure she sounded, but knowing she had to ask.

"Always." The conviction in his eyes burned down to her soul.

"Then that's all I need."

A small ache in her chest made her wonder if that was a lie. If she might need more. She looked into his eyes: dark, beautiful, so sincere. And she wished she could ask for more. Wished they could have more.

And she prayed he would never feel like he was stuck with her, like he'd been sentenced to life in prison.

"I shouldn't stay in your room for too much longer. We might give your mother gray hair."

"Ha!" she said, not really feeling like anything was funny.

"And I have to figure out what I'm going to say to your father."

"You don't really have to talk to him."

"I do. We both know I do."

"Ah, Cole, it's just . . . You don't have to play the game. They're going to be pissed at me no matter how we do this."

"I want to. For you. For later. Right now this is hard, but if we do it right . . . if we do it right, this won't matter, not in ten years." He turned and walked out of her room, closing the door behind him.

Ten years. Dear Lord. They would be together that long. Or longer. She waited to panic. But there was no panic.

She flopped back on the bed and crushed a pillow to her chest. This whole mess was almost starting to make sense.

Dinner with the Noble clan was interesting, to say the least. Kelsey looked pale. Her sisters—Kailey, Jacie, Alesha and Tara—and their husbands were oblivious to the tension, and her nieces and nephews were shrieking and passing food back and forth. Through the air.

Cole hadn't had a chance to talk to her father, and he was sort of looking forward to putting it off. He hadn't had to talk to a girl's dad about anything since high school. And that had just been prom. And while there had been sex involved, he hadn't asked for permission. His wedding to Shawna had been untraditional; she'd been estranged from her parents, and he'd never once met them. He was a novice at this.

His main goal was to get through it without getting killed. Or without having his balls separated from his body.

"So, Cole, what is it you do?" This from Kelsey's mother.

"I own a ranch in Silver Creek. We raise horses and we have guest accommodations. It's nice. You should come and stay. All of you. On the house, naturally." Lark wouldn't be happy, but oh, well.

Kelsey's sisters nodded enthusiastically.

"A ranch, huh?" Kelsey's father, who had been introduced to him as Chuck, spoke now. "That surprises me. Kelsey isn't so into country living."

"Things change," she mumbled, looking down at her food.

"You can hardly be bothered to come back and visit here. You looked like you were on the verge of hives through my whole wedding," Kailey said, treating Kelsey to a dagger glare.

"It was a pollen . . . reaction. Thing. Nothing to do with the wedding," Kelsey said. "Anyway, you can make changes when you—"

"Fall in love," Jacie finished, a dreamy expression on her face.

Kelsey nodded, her lips curving into a smile that looked more like a sneer to Cole.

"Uh-huh. Yeah. Love."

An uncomfortable tightness hit him in the stomach. He chose to blame the meat loaf. And the fact that he still had to tell Kelsey's father she was pregnant with his baby.

"Love, huh?" Chuck gave Cole a pointed look.

"Yeah," he said, offering a smile and taking another bite of the meat loaf. It was awful. If it had come straight out of a Purina can, he wouldn't have been surprised. Thank God he had a chef at the ranch. Just in case Kelsey had inherited her mother's cooking skills. Though, knowing Kelsey, she'd become a world-class chef just to be different.

The rest of dinner was filled with talk of Kailey's baby and the due date and morning sickness. He could tell Kelsey was biting her tongue.

He reached under the table and put his hand over hers. She squeezed it, and he felt a strange sense of satisfaction that he'd connected with her. That he'd managed to make her feel better.

"Dessert?" Lisa stood from the table with a bright smile on her face.

He shot Kelsey a look, and she shook her head slightly.

"No, thank you," Cole said. "But, Mr. Noble, if you have a moment, I'd like to speak with you."

The older man looked at him and nodded slowly. "The living room okay?"

There was a low chance Chuck would shoot him inside the house, so it suited him fine. "Works for me."

He stood, and Chuck followed his lead, letting Cole direct them into the other room. He could feel Kelsey's sisters watching them, their eyes glued to his back. They were guessing, he imagined, that he was going to be asking their dad about a proposal. And they were right. Sort of.

"Have a seat," Chuck said.

"I'll stand, thank you." Because while he respected that Kelsey's parents were traditional, there was going to be a shift here and now. "I would like very much to marry your daughter." He found that the words were true as he spoke them. It surprised him just how very true.

"I see. Does she want to marry you?"

"She seems to." That was less true. She seemed more trapped than eager. "There's another thing. We're having a baby. I thought I should be the one to tell you."

The lines in Kelsey's father's face hardened, and for a moment, Cole really did fear for his life. If not his life, his testicles.

"A baby?"

"Yes." Cole crossed his arms over his chest.

Chuck shook his head. "I shouldn't really be surprised. She never did see the point in doing things the right way."

Cole gritted his teeth. It wouldn't do him any good to explode at her father, but there were certain things he wasn't willing to let slide. Not now, not ever. "And this is where we'll have to disagree, Mr. Noble. It would be nice if you could be involved. You're her father and I respect that, but only as far as you respect her."

The silence was deadly. Cole thought he really might have pushed it too far. That he might end up buried in a Bonanza field, never to be heard from again.

Kelsey's father assessed him, gray eyes glinting in the dim light of the room, and then he extended his hand. "You just might be able to handle her."

He clasped the other man's hand and shook it. "I don't want to handle her. I just want to be with her."

Chuck nodded. "All right, then. You're going to marry her fast, right?"

"As fast as she'll let me. Which means I have no idea. She may want to wait, but that's up to her. And I'm absolutely serious about one thing. If I hear anyone making comments about her doing things wrong, or if anyone makes her so much as tear up, I'll step in. I'm not letting her get hurt like that. If I could protect her from ever getting hurt again, I would."

He got another nod of grudging respect from Chuck.

"I'm glad we had this talk," Cole said, backing out of the room. He was not going to turn his back on the older man. No.

He turned and saw Kelsey at the dining table still, sitting in front of a big piece of pie that looked like a pickax was necessary to break through the crust.

Her sisters looked at him expectantly.

"I'm alive," he said, sitting down next to Kelsey.

"Why don't you go have a beer with the men?" Jacie asked, her look pointed.

Kelsey resisted the urge to elbow her sister. "You don't have to, Cole."

"He probably wants to, though," Kailey said.

Cole stood again. "Suddenly, I want a beer."

"They're out back in the yard watching the kids run around," Jacie supplied as Cole turned and abandoned Kelsey with the barracuda.

She suddenly wished her mom would come back in—a panicked response if ever there was one.

"So, what's the deal?" Jacie asked, leaning in.

"Spill it. Where'd the sexy cowboy come from?" Alesha asked.

"And what are you doing with him?" This question from

Tara. "And please, if it's good, give details so I can live vicariously through you."

Kelsey almost choked. "Excuse me? You're married."

"Yeah. I know. And things are very missionary position, so I want to hear about your wild singleton sex with Buffalo Bill."

Kelsey put her head in her hands, then popped back up. "Listen to yourselves. Bored, horny housewives. You're like the live contents of a spam email."

That brought snickers from Jacie, Tara and Alesha and a scowl from Kailey.

"You're still pretty newly married, Kailey," Alesha said, patting her hand. "Give it time."

"Nice," Kelsey said. "Well, now that you've ensured I'll never be able to look my brothers-in-law in the eye ever again, maybe we can move on—"

"To headboard-rattling nooky stories?" Jacie asked.

"It's not like that." She was treated to blank stares. "Fine, it's totally like that. But also we're getting married." The collective scream was deafening.

"Holy frack, Kelsey, I didn't think you would ever get married," Tara said.

"What? Why? I . . . shower every day. I'm not repellent."

Tara let out a long breath. "Not because there's something wrong with you. Because you didn't seem interested. Not for a long time."

"Well, I wasn't. But then I met Cole." *Fudge that truth.* "And I'm going to marry him."

"Head over heels?" Jacie asked.

"And a little pregnant."

The second scream was louder than the first.

Tara shook her head. "Do not marry him just because you're pregnant. You have no idea how permanent marriage is. They are . . . there, at your house. All the time. Squeezing the toothpaste tube in the middle and leaving the toilet seat up. Nope. Don't get married because of that."

"I won't. I'm not." That felt true, and it surprised Kelsey.

"I suppose there's the headboard rattling," Alesha said, her tone slightly wistful.

"Yes. There is," she said, feeling a little smug now. "He's great. And hot."

"Where's your ring?" Kailey asked.

"At his ranch. He . . . wanted to talk to Dad first."

Jacie stretched her hand across the table and put it over the top of Kelsey's. "Is this what you want, though? I mean . . . are you happy?"

"I'm getting married. Isn't that the important thing? Isn't that what everyone wants me to do?"

All four of them shook their heads. Jacie frowned. "No, what we want is for you to be happy."

"Oh." Kelsey looked down at where her sister's hand covered hers. And for the first time, she really felt like it was true. Like they weren't just judging her or thinking she should do what they did. Like maybe she'd been the one who made herself feel that way.

"We're proud of you, Kelsey," Tara said. "You're . . . brave. You moved away and you went to school and you have this crazy-awesome job. And the best shoes. You're my older sister. I've always looked up to you."

A thick sheet of tears welled up in her eyes, and she blinked. Wow, pregnancy was making her sappy. "Well . . . I've always been proud of you. All of you. I've always envied you a little too."

"Join the club," Jacie said. "I think we've all envied you at some point in time."

"Me? Why?"

Alesha shrugged one shoulder. "You've always been free to do what you want. To be who you want."

"And you aren't?"

Alesha shook her head. "I'm happy. I never regret what I chose to do. But sometimes I envy how easy you make it look."

"How easy I make what look? Everything in my life is an overcomplicated nightmare."

"You just make it look like being you is the easiest thing. Like you're never trying to please anyone but yourself. I've never been able to do that," Alesha said. "I've always been too afraid of the wrath of Mom."

Kelsey snorted. "Well, I've never felt free. I've always felt like a ball of neuroses."

Jacie smiled. "You never looked like one."

Kelsey felt her chest expand. "Thank you."

"Congratulations, Kelsey," Kailey said.

"Now I almost forgive you guys for all the hideous bridesmaid dresses you all made me wear. Almost."

The next morning, Kelsey woke up in a cold bed. It was strange how quickly she'd gotten used to sharing with Cole, but she supposed that was a good thing. They were going to be sharing forever.

Now that was a delicious thought. A lifetime between the sheets with Cole, having the best sex ever. Yeah, she could deal with that.

A little smile curved her lips, and she walked out of the kitchen and into the yard, inhaling the crisp, damp air, her eyes on the familiar horizon line.

She felt at home suddenly in a way she'd never felt there before. Not that she wanted to pack up and move back, but it was a nice difference from wanting to climb out of her skin every time she came here.

She zipped up her jacket and stuffed her hands in her pockets, wandering across the yard, the wet grass hitting her jeans and sending waterdrops flying.

"Morning."

She turned and saw Cole walking toward her.

"Where have you been?"

"The long morning walk was supposed to help the cold shower."

She laughed. "You did not take a cold shower."

"I did. I had to. It was either that or invade your room at five this morning."

Her heart rate went up. "I'm not a morning person, so I doubt that would have helped."

"I missed you last night. That was my thoroughly male way of saying that."

She stopped walking. "You missed me?"

He shrugged. "Yes."

He meant the sex. Which was great. And flattering. Because it was nice to be missed in any capacity. Also, she'd missed him too. His body mostly. But also him.

"Good to know. We only have one more night here."

"I may die."

"For a man who went—what . . . four, five years without sex?—you don't seem to be handling a couple nights of celibacy very well."

She started walking again, headed toward the old white barn that had seen some way better days.

"I blame you," he said.

"Really?"

"I didn't know what I was missing. Actually, I wasn't missing anything. Until you."

"That's just a little too smooth, Cole. It concerns me."

"You don't want smooth?"

She walked through the open door and into the dark barn. There was hay, damp and musky on the floor, cushioning their footsteps as they made their way inside.

"We used to have a couple of horses in here. But not anymore," she said. "Not like Elk Haven at all."

"What does your dad do?"

"He's a mechanic. For farm equipment, so it's kind of specialty. Nothing that ever interested me. I was never very interested in any of this."

"And you're willing to come and live in Silver Creek with me?"

"It's a better place to raise a child," she said, gripping a rung of the ladder that went up to the hayloft.

"Your house seems like a nice enough place to raise a child."

"It is nice. But . . . Silver Creek is growing on me. So are you."

"I would hope you liked me at least a little bit at this point," he said, his lips curving up into a lopsided smile.

He was so handsome. She wasn't sure she would ever get used to that. Or to how he looked at her. Like she was the most fascinating thing he'd ever seen. No one had ever looked at her that way before. And she hadn't realized how much she wanted someone to.

"You know I do."

He made his way over to her and tucked a strand of hair behind her ear. "Really?"

"Really."

He looked up. "Did you ever get into any trouble in here?"

"Trouble?"

"Yeah. Sex."

She laughed. "Nooo. That was reserved for backseats. I have class, you know."

"Clearly." A wicked smile curved his lips. "It's very quiet back here. And I bet no one notices we're missing yet."

She shook her head. "Cole, no way."

He leaned in and kissed her neck, angling his head, nipping her ear. "We won't get caught."

The words sent a little thrill through her. "We might."

"It's worth the risk."

Heat pooled in her stomach, her internal muscles clenching tight. "We can wait until tomorrow."

"Can we?" He took her hand in his and put it flat on his stomach.

She bit her lip and moved her hand down to his belt buckle—down farther to the hard ridge of his erection, pushing against the front of his jeans. Then she ran her palm over his length, her breath hissing between her teeth.

"Nope. No, I can't wait." The words left her mouth in a rush, and as soon as she'd spoken them, he captured her lips, wrapping his arms tightly around her, pulling her against him.

When he pulled away, they were both breathing hard. "Good. I don't want to wait."

"Back there," she said, tilting her head toward a shadow that fell across the back wall of the barn.

He took her lips with his again and walked her backward. She clung to him, kissing his mouth, the hard line of his jaw, his neck, until her back came into contact with the smooth wooden wall.

He pushed his hands under her top, his fingertips teasing her nipples through the thin fabric of her bra.

"Oh, yes."

She put her hands on his belt and opened the buckle quickly, tugging at the button and fly on his jeans until she had them loose around his slim hips. Then she pushed the tight fabric of his underwear down over his erection. She squeezed him, loving the feel of his heat and hardness, all for her, in the palm of her hand.

He unbuttoned her jeans and shrugged them down to her hips.

She leaned back and tried to lift her leg to bring him in closer, but the denim restricted her movements. "How do we do this?" she asked.

He looked around for a second, the expression in his eyes hard, purposeful. Sexy. "Like this. Turn around."

She obeyed him, her heart hammering, her body on fire. "Hang on."

She bent down slightly, taking hold of the beam that ran across the barn wall. "Like this?" she asked, her voice breathless, her stomach tight.

"Just like that." He moved his hands over her curves, from her breasts, down her waist, gripping her hips and pulling her tight against him.

She felt the blunt head of his shaft against her slick entrance. She tightened her hold on the beam and arched back. He pushed inside her, and she felt something shift into place inside of her chest. He was hot behind her, in her. She felt surrounded by him.

His hands were strong on her hips as he thrust into her. He slid his hand around and cupped her, moving his thumb over her clit in time with his movements.

She turned her head, and he leaned forward and kissed her, deep and hard. She leaned back against him, one hand still on the beam, the other on his cheek. His movements intensified, and pulsing waves of pleasure started moving through her.

Each thrust, each movement of his thumb, sent a streak of heat through her.

"Yes," she said louder than she had intended. But she didn't care. She didn't care at all. Because nothing else mattered but this. Nothing mattered more than what she was feeling, than what Cole was making her feel. "Oh, yes, Cole."

He thrust into her one last time, and her orgasm crashed over her. A low moan escaped her lips, echoing in the otherwise silent barn. And she didn't care.

He groaned and stilled against her, finding his own release, his fingertips digging into her hips.

Her thighs were shaking and she put both hands back on the beam, bracing herself, trying to catch her breath. And she realized how ridiculous she must look. With her jeans pulled halfway down and her legs about to give out.

And she didn't care. Not even a little bit. Because she felt more like herself than she'd ever felt in her life. It hadn't been about putting on a facade, or protecting herself, or trying to be different from or contrary to what her family thought of her. Or trying to be perfect for them.

It had been about pleasing herself. About feeling. About grabbing what she wanted and running with it. And it felt good. Better than good.

"Damn," Cole said, the curse sounding nearly reverent.

She laughed and pushed her hair off her face, trying to stand up without melting. "That good?"

"That good."

She tugged her jeans back into place and cast a wary glance at the open barn door. "I can't believe we did that."

He was adjusting his own clothes, his expression unconcerned. "I don't have a whole lot of control with you."

"I like that," she said. "I don't think I've ever made anyone lose control before."

"Well, you've got me losing it on a regular basis."

She inhaled sharply, words hovering on her lips. Words she could hardly think, let alone say.

That's what I love about you.

Thankfully, she didn't say them. But just thinking them made her heart stop cold in her chest. The thought seemed so natural. The feeling almost seemed natural. As she stood in the barn, her heart still beating fast from the best sex of her life and feeling like she'd pushed free of prison bars, like she'd found a new piece of herself she hadn't known about—it seemed as natural as breathing.

To love Cole. To admit she loved him.

But she knew if she spoke it out loud, he'd turn and run. She didn't know why she knew it, only that she did. It was as inexplicable as the feeling itself.

"Cole . . . I . . . I'm glad that we're doing this. Well, not"—she gestured around them—"not this. Although I liked this. A lot. But I mean, you and me. I'm glad we're giving it a chance. Glad we're getting married."

"Nice to know I didn't scare you off with . . . that. The proposal. Such as it was. Not my smoothest moment."

"I would rather have real than smooth. Every time."

"I'm not going to do what your ex did. I'm not going to do what my dad did. I'm not going to cheat."

"I know. I actually really believe that. Anyway, the ex was not smooth. The ex was a dumbass who forgot my schedule and let his bimbo come over and get naked about the time I got home from work. This was back when I worked in real clothes and not in my pajamas."

"Yeah, your ex was a dumbass."

"So, I'm not afraid of smooth; it's just that . . . I don't need it. I like this." She moved toward him on impulse and wrapped her arms around him, resting her head against his chest. Just a hug. A chance to be close to him again.

He put one arm around her, rested his chin on her hair. "I'm glad."

Cole felt like his heart was going to claw its way out of him. He was on fire. From making love to Kelsey, from the need that was still coursing through him. As if he hadn't just had the most mind-blowing orgasm in history a few minutes earlier.

And now she was hugging him. Her touch so sweet, so much more than lust. It scared him.

She inhaled deeply, her fingers curling around his shirt. Then she released him, stepping back and looking at him like no one ever had before. Like he was the best thing she'd ever seen. Like he was Christmas morning or something.

Something in his chest expanded, his heart stalling for a beat as a huge emotion started to fill him. He took a sharp breath, pushed it away.

"We should go back," she said. "My mom probably made breakfast."

"What is the deal with your mom's cooking?" he asked, glad for a subject change.

"Oh. I don't know. She's terrible. I think my dad's taste buds and hers must have died thirty-five years ago or so, because they don't seem to notice."

"You don't cook like her, do you?"

"No way. I don't cook at all."

He laughed, trying to ease the constricted feeling that was binding his insides tight, and followed her out of the barn. Soon they would be back in Silver Creek. And things would get back to normal.

Whatever that was.

Cole breathed a sigh of relief when they walked into the house at Elk Haven Stables. Now he could get the ring and put it on Kelsey's finger. Now she could sleep in his room, in his bed, all night. Forever.

Now he could get back to feeling like he had some form of control in the situation. Limited though it might have been, since Kelsey was one hell of a variable.

"I have no rules about us keeping to separate beds," he said, turning to face Kelsey when she walked into the living room.

"I appreciate that. And I'm looking forward to sharing."

"You're agreeing with me too much. I'm starting to get concerned you're sick."

She laughed. "Maybe I am."

Cade came wandering in from the kitchen, his timing completely imperfect, as always. "You made it back without Kelsey killing you. I was afraid you might mysteriously disappear."

"Sorry, Cade. I couldn't do it," she said. "I'll return the money later."

"Nice," Cade said. "Everything good at your house? And with your parents?"

"House is still standing. Parents still are who they are. But it wasn't as bad as I thought. Well, exhibit A is that Cole didn't hobble in here."

His brother shot him a meaningful look. "True."

Lark came down the stairs, a broad smile on her face. "You're back!"

That she smiled like that when she saw him always made Cole feel like he'd made less of a mess of everything than he usually assumed he had. "Yeah, and . . . well, we have something to tell you."

Her eyes widened. "What?"

He felt Kelsey get tense beside him. He couldn't blame her. He felt tense too. "I'm going to need the ring again. Kelsey's agreed to marry me."

Cade's mouth dropped open. "Really?"

"Don't look so surprised," Cole said.

"I can't help it. I am. Kelsey, I thought you had better taste than that," he said. "I would have married you."

Cole felt an unreasonable surge of jealousy shoot through his veins. "She wouldn't have married you. Anyway, you have the sexual attention span of a horsefly. You couldn't stay faithful if you tried."

"I'm wounded," Cade said, his tone sounding anything but.

Lark made a face. "You guys suck." She leaned forward

and gave Kelsey a hug. "Congratulations. I'm really happy for you."

"Thanks," she said.

Lark started backing toward the stairs. "I just came down to say hi. You can come up and get the ring later."

"Why are you disappearing to the tech cave, Lark?"

She grimaced. "Avoidance. Can you send dinner up?"

"No, you can come down and get it."

She made a face and walked up the stairs.

Cole turned to Cade. "Her problem?"

"Alexa is back."

Kelsey's eyes widened. "What?"

"Yep. She came back the day you left. And she's been glued to Tyler, which, of course, Lark finds objectionable."

Cole sighed. "Of course."

"Where is she?" Kelsey asked.

"Alexa? In the same cabin you were staying in."

"I should go see if I can find her."

She leaned in and kissed Cole on the cheek, and heat rushed through him. The control he'd felt when he walked in was definitely tenuous.

"See you at dinner?"

"Yeah," he said.

He watched her walk out of the room, and he wondered why he felt like part of himself had gone with her.

Alexa slid her hands beneath Tyler's shirt and felt his muscles tense beneath her fingertips. His mouth was hungry on hers, but his hunger could not be anything compared to hers. It wasn't possible. She wanted him badly enough that she'd flown in from New York to seduce him. That was pretty bad. Pathetic even, considering there were plenty of guys to sleep with in New York.

But none of them were him. And he was all she could think about.

She tugged his shirt over his head and pulled him down onto the bed. And thank God, he didn't object. The taking-it-slow crap was still a happening thing with him, and she'd barely gotten to second base since she'd arrived four days ago.

But today would be different. Today he'd wandered into her domain. And today, she was going to get hers.

He lowered his head and pressed a kiss to her neck, his thumb sliding over her cloth-covered nipple.

Yes. Yes. Yes.

"Alex?"

No. No. No.

Alexa popped up and shoved Tyler to the side just as Kelsey walked in through the door of the cabin. There was no way to make it look like what was going on wasn't what was going on. Why bother anyway? Now she was horny *and* mad.

"It's exactly what it looks like," Alexa said, bending down and grabbing Tyler's T-shirt from the floor, throwing it to him. He looked like he'd just been kicked in the head.

"I'm sorry," Kelsey said, her face pulled into a grimace.

"Yeah. Right. I know. Tyler? Catch you later."

He nodded and shrugged his shirt on, and she felt so much bone-deep regret over every covered inch of skin. He leaned in and kissed her before nodding to Kelsey and walking out of the cabin.

"You just cockblocked me," Alexa said, trying to be nice since her friend was in a delicate condition and all. But wasn't being terminally horny a delicate condition?

"I'm sorry." Kelsey winced again.

"You have no idea how sorry *I* am. He still hasn't given it up. But he was going to. Oh, he was about to."

"I'm sure you'll get him tonight."

Alexa whined. "Maybe. But I want him now."

"What are you doing here?"

"Burning through my vacation leave to have sex with a guy who seems to want a relationship and is also six years my junior. In other words, I'm making crappy decisions and owning it. What's up with you?"

"I told my parents about the baby."

"Smashing. Did your mom's head explode?"

"Nearly. Until I told her I was marrying Cole."

Alexa inhaled a breath and choked on the air. "You what?"

"I told her I was marrying Cole."

"You aren't, though. You aren't. Kelsey, Kelsey, you aren't, right?" She looked at her friend's face and her stomach sank. "You're marrying him?"

Kelsey looked sheepish. "Yeah. Kind of."

"Why?"

"I'm . . . I'm in love with him."

Alexa exploded. "You're what?"

"I'm in love with him."

"When did . . . when did that happen?"

Kelsey crossed her arms and cocked her hip to one side. "When did you start taking vacation time to fly cross-country and try to connect with a guy who works on a ranch?"

Alexa frowned. "Touché. Seriously, though? You love him?"

Kelsey frowned and nodded, her expression miserable. "I do. I don't know what happened."

"You slept with him, yeah?"

"Several times."

"And you didn't tell me?"

"I didn't want to brag, considering your celibate state."

Alexa gave her the evilest glare she could conjure up. "I was about to be uncelibate. Keep talking, Noble."

Kelsey frowned harder, lines creasing her forehead. "It wasn't supposed to happen. It just did. And it turns out, he's fantastic. But it's not just that. It's . . . everything. It's how he makes me feel."

"How does he make you feel?"

"Like me. And I don't mean that in a vague, general sense. I mean . . . he makes me feel more comfortable with who I am than I've ever felt in my life. He makes me feel like I'm . . . I'm okay. Like I don't need to change. I don't need to try to fit in with my family. Or try to be different from them. I can just . . . be. He makes me feel that. Not in the way, like, he validates me and makes me more important or more special, but . . . he makes me feel like being me just like I am is good enough. And . . . and I love him."

Alexa's stomach tightened. "I . . . I kind of know that feeling. The one where you feel like you. That's not really love, though, is it?"

"It is for me."

"Well, damn. I'd really like to avoid that whole 'love' noise myself."

"And you think you might love Tyler?"

Everything in Alexa recoiled in horror. "What? I haven't even banged the guy. I can't be in love with him."

"You can love someone without ever . . . sleeping with him."

"Maybe *you* could."

"I think you do. And I think it freaks you out. Because you feel things for him even without the sex. Oh, and once you do sleep with him—"

"Shut up! Don't ruin the sex fantasy with all this emotion talk." Alexa's heart was fluttering like a bird trapped in a cage. And not because what Kelsey was saying was true. But because it was crazy and she was worried for her friend's emotional health. That was all.

"I think the sex is better with emotion," Kelsey said. "Loving Cole is . . . nice. And terrifying."

"Because he doesn't love you back?"

Kelsey shook her head. "I don't think so."

"He's marrying you, though. So . . . he'll be with you."

Kelsey nodded. "Yeah, and I hope that's enough. I really hope so. Because I want to be with him. You know . . . without him feeling like he's serving a prison sentence."

Alexa felt an unwelcome, unfamiliar surge of emotion. "If he's smart, then he'll feel lucky to have you."

"Thanks, Alex."

"Now, I'm going to hang a necktie on the door tonight. So, for heaven's sake, if the cabin's rocking, don't come knocking."

Cole put his hand in his pocket, over the ring box. This was the second time he'd prepared to offer Kelsey a ring. The first time hadn't worked in his favor. But this time he was sure she'd say yes. Even with the assurance, his palms were sweating.

What was it about her that did this to him? That turned him on when he'd been off for so long? That made his heart beat faster? That made him feel like he was standing on the edge of a cliff, thinking about jumping off?

She was standing out on the deck, facing the mountains. He just stood in the living room for a moment, looking at her through the windows. She was beautiful. It was more than just her looks. It was something that reached out and grabbed him deep inside.

He wasn't sure he liked it. Because the truth was, these feelings took all that control he was so attached to and gave it right to Kelsey. And he wasn't sure he wanted that. Not again.

He walked out onto the deck and closed the door behind him. She turned, offering him a soft smile. "Hello."

"How are you feeling?" he asked.

"Great. I've been feeling great."

"Did you and Alexa have a chance to talk earlier?"

She frowned. "Uh, yes. I . . . interrupted something."

He laughed. "Is that why Tyler couldn't hold still at dinner?"

"Probably. I think he has unfinished business."

"Well, as it happens, so do I."

She looked around and gestured to the windows and the lit-up living room. "Uh . . . I think we need to be a little more discreet than that."

"Not that kind of unfinished business. Although we can make time for that later. Just . . . this." He reached into his pocket and pulled out the ring box. "Kelsey, please marry me. Wear this ring."

She looked down at the closed box, then up at his face.

"Don't say no again," he said.

She shook her head. "I wasn't going to."

She didn't make a move for the ring. He thought about getting down on one knee, but the idea of doing that made him feel exposed. Made him feel like it was . . . real.

It would be real. He knew that. But not yet. Not like that.

He opened the lid on the box and took the ring between his thumb and forefinger. She extended her hand, and he noticed that it was shaking. He took it in his and rubbed it gently. Her fingers were freezing.

He bent his head and kissed her knuckles, then slid the ring onto her fourth finger.

She looked down at her hand, flexing her fingers. "It's . . . beautiful. And huge."

"It's funny, because my mom lived in Levi's and flannel. She could rarely wear the thing because she worked on a ranch. She didn't want to lose a finger if it got caught on anything. I used to think . . . I used to think it was nice he bought it for her. Now I wonder if he just bought it because it was what he thought she should want. I wonder if he wanted something she would never be. But . . . that's not why I'm giving it to you. And if you want something else, you can have something else."

"I'm really happy to wear it. I"—she leaned forward and pressed a kiss to his lips—"I feel more like myself when I'm with you. . . . You make me feel so comfortable. Like I can just be me. Like I don't have to try so hard. I . . . I think I love you, Cole."

Cole felt like he'd been punched in the stomach. "You what?"

"I love you. I mean, I'm pretty sure."

For one brief moment, he felt like the walls around him had cracked, letting in shafts of light, fresh air, freedom. A glimpse at life, a glimpse at the bigger world, when he hadn't even been aware that he'd been caged.

Then it felt like his chest was caving in. It hurt to hear her say the words, and he wasn't sure why. Because he couldn't respond to them. Because fear held him on a leash, and he couldn't, for the life of him, slip out of it. In fact, he was clinging to it.

"You don't need to say that. That's not what this is about."

"But I do."

He tightened his jaw, grinding his teeth together, his heart pounding heavily. Not this. He didn't need this. He couldn't do this. "You think that, Kelsey, probably because we're sleeping together. Or because of your hormones."

Her eyes narrowed, her expression turning fierce. "Did you just tell me that my hormones are keeping me from knowing what I feel? Because that is just bastardy, is what that is."

"Kelsey, it's just . . . I don't want you to get hurt." That rang false. It was about more than that. It was deeper than that. But he wasn't going there.

She threw her arms wide. "Do I look like a child to you?"

"No."

"Did I just finish telling you that when I'm with you, I can be me?"

"Yes."

"Then please, assume that I know who I am. And that I'm comfortable with how I feel. If you don't love me, Cole, well . . . that sucks. But you know what? It's okay. Don't ever say something you don't believe or don't feel. But never, ever tell me what I feel."

She brushed past him and walked into the house. He put his hands on his head and growled, then stalked into the house behind her.

"Kelsey . . ."

She whirled around. "Don't take that tone with me."

"Tone?"

She pointed her finger in his direction. "You had a tone."

"Yeah, well, so do you."

"Why did you have to ruin the proposal?"

Anger burned in his chest. "Me? I'm not the one making declarations that weren't agreed upon."

"Oh, now we have to agree on everything? Including how I feel?"

"Kelsey, I can't . . . I don't . . . I can't love you." The words felt torn from him. "Every love in my life has turned to hell. And I can't do it again. I don't . . . I can't have you depending on me like that."

"Who says I'm depending on you for anything, Cole Mitchell? I'm loving you. That means giving to you. So take it. Enjoy it."

"I can't do that," he said, his stomach so tight, he could barely breathe.

"Why? Why not?"

"Because in my experience, love isn't sweetness and flowers. It's screaming and crazy, and it fades faster than a sunset. It's lies and betrayal. I don't want that. I want solid. I want commitment."

"I am giving to you, you dumbass. I'm not taking. I'm not even asking."

"I can't give it back."

"So?"

"What do you mean, 'so'?"

"I didn't stutter. I said, 'So?' I don't care."

"Kelsey, you don't understand," he said, the words raw and rough.

She put her hands on her hips, her expression fierce. "No.

I don't. I just told you I loved you, not that I kicked puppies. Calm the hell down."

"You think this is a joke?"

"No. I think you're overreacting. I didn't ask you for anything. And I won't. I offered. I'm giving. Though you're making me rethink the offer."

"Good. This is . . . a partnership, Kelsey. That's what I can see working. A partnership. None of this passion shit that makes people crazy. That makes people abandon their family and live a secret life half the time."

"So this is about your dad?"

"And me, Kelsey. Me. I have to find a way to . . . to be better. Than him. Than I was. I need . . . I don't need love for that; I need a partner."

"Is that what we've been doing in bed every night? Shirking passion? Being partners? Because if you want a partner, I can do that. But if you want a wife, then you have to accept that certain things come with that."

"But I can only give what I can give."

"Then give that."

That was when he realized it wasn't enough. He didn't have enough to give her. Not what she deserved. She was looking at him with big, earnest eyes, sincerity written into her expression. He felt like she'd just handed him a priceless pearl, and he'd shown up with only a cheesy fairground stuffed animal as an offering.

He was broken. And she didn't deserve that. She was the strongest woman he'd ever met. The most special woman he'd ever met. She made him feel like he was on fire, made his heart pound faster and his chest ache.

He felt like that part of him was gone. The man who'd been able to give trust and love as easy as he breathed. The people he'd loved most, trusted most, had screwed him over the worst, and he just couldn't do it anymore. He couldn't give any more only to have it taken away.

"I don't want to take from you," he said.

"It's not taking. It's a gift."

He shook his head. "We'll talk tomorrow."

"We damn well won't talk tomorrow. We'll talk now. What is your problem?"

"Did it ever occur to you that I just don't care?" he asked, his stomach tightening. "That I don't need or want you to love me? That was never what this was, Kelsey. You know it. It was for the baby. So we could make a family for our child."

"And you don't think more love will help?"

"I think it confuses things."

"I'm not confused. But I can see you are. I'm sleeping in my room tonight."

"Kelsey—"

"No. Don't. You're right. We'll talk tomorrow." She tugged the ring off her hand and held it out to him. "Can you keep this? For a while."

His heart stalled. "Yeah."

She dropped it into his upturned palm and stalked up the stairs. Cole sat down on the couch and lowered his head. He'd managed to mess up what had started as the most beautiful moment of his life. He laughed, mostly at himself. With more bitterness than humor. Yes, that moment of handing Kelsey the ring, that moment when she'd looked at him and said she loved him, or she thought she loved him, had been the best moment ever. For just a second.

The light had broken through. And everything had seemed simple. Like it didn't matter what else had happened because it just didn't exist. There had been only her.

And then fear had grabbed him around the neck and refused to let go. Because he knew what love cost. What trust cost.

His eyes stung and he tightened his grip on the ring, letting the stone dig into his palm. He was afraid. He was afraid of being hurt, and so he'd stabbed his own damn self in the chest. But what was he supposed to do? Just let it all go? Put it on the line again? He couldn't do it anymore.

He doubted he'd ever really be comfortable with Kelsey. Passion wasn't comfortable. It burned. He burned whenever he looked at her, whenever he touched her.

He could hardly breathe. There was fire in his chest burning him from the inside out.

And he had two choices. He could walk through it—embrace the flames, the pain, the pleasure and everything she had to offer. Or he could go back behind the walls. Where it was safe. Where he didn't have to depend on anyone else. Ever.

He had been an idiot. He'd thought that he could marry Kelsey, add her to his . . . existence . . . and keep going as he had been. That nothing had to change. That he didn't have to change. Or feel. Or give her more than a place in his bed.

But he did. She was inside him. Wrapped around every part of him, in his blood, his heart. But if he was going to be with her, to make a life with her, he would have to start living again. Not just existing. Not just going forward, putting his head down and protecting himself.

He'd shut himself down for the past five years. Until Kelsey had woken him up. That had been like living again. Like breathing clean air after being locked in a box. When he'd held her in his arms. When he'd looked into her eyes. When he'd put his hand over her slightly rounded stomach.

She was passion. She was love. She needed his trust. She was everything he'd been running from, hiding from, protecting himself from.

He didn't think he could do it. She wasn't taking; she was giving. But the thing was, if he didn't give back—things he wasn't sure he could ever give—he would end up making her miserable.

He put his head in his hands and stared at the floor, trying not to focus on the incredible emptiness that was echoing through him.

"Want to come in?" Alexa put her hand on the doorknob and gave Tyler her very best come-hither look.

"I don't think I should."

Her stomach hit her shoes. "What?"

"Things got out of hand earlier."

"No . . . things were never in hand. If we hadn't been interrupted, some things would have been firmly in my hand. And you and I would be in much better moods right about now."

Tyler gave her a look that was . . . sad. She wanted to kiss it off his handsome face. Tell him to stop thinking so much. Stop feeling so much.

"We've gotten to know each other pretty well over the phone the past few weeks."

"Right." She didn't like where this was going.

"I have feelings for you. Very strong feelings. I won't go labeling them, because intuition tells me you'll run from me. But just know that I do."

Her hands felt shaky. "Great. Fine. But what does that have to do with you not coming in?"

"I still think it would be a mistake right now. I want to build something real with you."

"How can we have anything real?" she said, her chest aching. "I live in New York. I have a great job. I am not moving back to this dirt clod. Not for you. Not for any reason." When his blue eyes met hers, she wondered if she was lying.

"Then I'll move there."

"You're a cowboy. New York already has a cowboy. He plays his guitar bare-ass naked in Times Square. I don't really think that's your gig."

"I can do other things."

"Don't you love ranching?"

He shrugged. "If I have to lose one thing that I love, it would be ranching in a heartbeat." Those eyes, so full of sincerity, the kind she'd never seen before, stared straight into her. "I would never choose to lose you."

"Gah. Don't. Don't say things like that!"

"It's true."

"Tyler . . . this isn't what this was supposed to be."

"You just wanted a fling with a hot younger man," he said, a half smile curving his lips.

"Yeah, yeah. You flatter yourself."

"Sorry I disappointed you."

She looked away from him. Tears. Damn—she was welling up with stupid tears. When did that even happen to her? Ever? "I don't know if I'm disappointed or not. Maybe freaked out."

He took her chin between his thumb and forefinger and redirected her focus back to him. "Alexa, you're the most amazing woman I've ever met. I don't need to sleep with you to know that. But I do need you to know, to understand, that I'm different. That what I feel for you is different. That you're worth every ounce of restraint, even though it's killing me."

She smiled an evil little smile. "It's killing you?"

"You like that?"

"Misery loves company."

"I am in your company." He bent and kissed her lips. "Tell me tomorrow. If you want me to, I'll fly back to New York with you. We'll see about making this work."

"You would really come to New York?"

"I don't want a night, Alexa. I want everything."

He turned and walked down the porch steps. She leaned against the wooden support and watched him, feeling like the stupid, twitterpated idiot she was.

Kelsey crossed her arms around her midsection, like it might hold her together. Or at least keep pain from taking her down to her knees.

She walked up the winding trail and prayed that Alexa wasn't getting lucky. It was mean, and she knew it. But she needed her friend.

She tromped up the steps and knocked twice before she heard Alexa cross the cabin. The door swung open and she was greeted by her friend, who looked way too unhappy for someone getting lucky.

"He's not here?" Kelsey asked.

"Nope. Come on in."

"Where is he?" She stepped inside and crossed to the bed, sitting on the foot of it.

"Still proving to me how much he lurves me by not satisfying my more carnal urges."

"Love?"

Alexa nodded mutely. "Yeah. So he says."

"Did you tell him you didn't want his love? Because that's mean," she said, trying to ignore the constant pain in her heart.

"No. I just . . . didn't really know what to tell him."

"Do you love him?"

"I don't know him very well."

"That's not what I asked."

"Yeah. Fine. I do a little. Are you happy?" Alexa started pacing. "He's not like any guy I've ever met. Which pisses me off, because I know that's what he wanted, to be unlike any other guy. And he . . . he likes me, not just my boobs, and that's . . ."

"That's something you should hold on to."

Alexa frowned. "Why are you here? What's wrong?"

Kelsey felt like she might break apart. She tightened her hold on her midsection. "Cole doesn't love me. He doesn't want me to love him. And all I can think of is that we're going to have one sad, cold house."

"He actually said he doesn't want your love?"

Her throat threatened to close on her. "Yep."

"Well . . . what are you going to do?"

"What do you mean what am I going to do? Nothing's changed. I'm still having his baby. We were prepared to marry without love in the first place. . . . Maybe nothing has to change."

Alexa let out a long breath and pushed her hand through her dark hair. "Kels, you've changed. Your feelings for him have changed. That matters."

"It shouldn't."

"So you're going to accept less than what you deserve just to try to preserve an idea that you think is nice?"

Kelsey shook her head. "But if I leave, I don't get to be with him at all."

Alexa moved to the bed and sat next to her, laying her head on Kelsey's shoulder. "You do have it bad, don't you?"

"Really bad."

"Listen, honey, if you don't ask for better for yourself, then Michael was for nothing. All that junk he put you through? If you learn nothing from it—what was the point? Don't you know by now that you don't have to settle?"

Kelsey let out a breath. "I can't stay with Cole. I want to. But I can see us getting dissatisfied and bitter with each other. Him resenting me for tying him down or something. And honestly, if you don't love someone, what's going to make you stay with them when they end up with stretch marks and a stomach that will never be flat again and deflated boobs?"

Alexa sighed. "Got me."

"Well . . . that's just it. He likes sleeping with me now. He's willing to marry me to try to make a family, but the thing is, the lust stuff will fade. Well, not on my end, but . . . on his. And then our child will be in this tense, loveless household, and I don't want that."

"I'm leaving tomorrow, Kelsey."

Kelsey nodded, her stomach clenched so tight, she could barely breathe. "Then I think I'll leave too." A tear slid down her cheek, and she didn't bother to wipe it away, didn't bother to stop the sob that climbed up her throat and shook her shoulders.

Alex put her arms around Kelsey and squeezed. "You have to do what makes you happy."

She laughed, a shaky, watery sound. "Unfortunately, what would make me happy isn't going to happen. It wouldn't make him happy. And that matters to me. I won't let him be miserable just so he can do what he thinks is the right thing. He's had enough crap in his life without me adding to it. And he's too freaking honorable to do it himself."

"For what it's worth, Kelsey, I don't think you've ever added crap to anyone's life. You only make it better. I'm sad for him, because he obviously doesn't see it."

"Are you drunk?"

Cole looked up at his brother and poured himself another tumbler of Jack. "Not yet. But I'm close." He held his glass up in a mock salute and downed the contents, the burn a welcome relief to combat the pain in his heart.

"Why are you drinking?"

"I am an asshole."

"I've been telling you that for years."

"But you were right."

Cade frowned and walked forward, tugging the bottle away from Cole. "You must be drunk."

"If I were drunk, I wouldn't be in this much pain."

"What did you do?"

"Kelsey told me she loved me. I told her I didn't care."

"Why did you do that?"

"Because. Because I am a coward."

"Damn straight you are," Cade said. "And you know what else? You've been shutting down slowly since Dad died. Shutting us out, shutting everyone out. I thought you would be smart enough to realize you'd have to give her something if you wanted to hold on to her."

"I do realize that," Cole growled, standing and snatching the bottle back from his brother. "But I can't do it anymore. I can't. I'm not even the man I thought I was."

"Bull."

"What? You think you know what I've been going through?"

"A little, jackass, since he was my dad too."

"So you think I should put on a fake smile like you do?" he asked, knowing he would regret the words later.

Cade snorted. "No, Cole, I think you should live the rest of your life bitter, angry and alone."

"What does that mean?" he asked. He knew. He knew full well what it meant.

"All this stuff . . . Shawna, Dad . . . it changed you."

"This from the guy who ran like hell when he found out about Dad."

"I was a teenager. You're a grown man; act like it. Stop acting like a hurt boy."

"That's what I feel like, damn it. Everything he taught us was bullshit. He didn't live any of it. I tried. I would have stayed married for the rest of my life trying to be the man I thought he'd want me to be. I was devastated having to end it, because living up to his standards was what I aimed my whole life at."

"So, now you're going to give up and just be a jerk because a couple people let you down?"

"Just the woman I married. Oh, and my father. No big deal. You're right. I should get over myself."

"Fine, ruin your life because you're too afraid to care."

"It's safer when you don't care," Cole ground out.

"What's the point of being safe if you don't even enjoy

it, Cole?" Cade leaned in and took the bottle out of his brother's hand again and headed up the stairs. "Because clearly, this . . . this thing you're doing is not the magic combination for a happy life. I'm going to take this. You're going to sit here and think, not drink."

Cole sank onto the couch, his stomach ready to reject everything he'd just ingested. He laid his head back and let his misery wash over him. Then he saw Kelsey's face. He held on to that, on to her. Just for a while, he would think of her and nothing else.

Because nothing else seemed to matter.

Cole woke up with a cramp in his neck and a pounding headache. A rush of cold air hit him in the side of the face and he sat up straight, his eyes locking with Kelsey's. She had a suitcase in her hand.

"What the hell?" he said, his voice rusty. He ran his hands over his face and stood up.

"I don't see the point in tying either of us down in a relationship that just isn't going to work. Wanting to do the right thing isn't enough, Cole. There has to be more."

"You didn't think there had to be more when you said yes. Why do you need more now?" he asked, terror streaking through his veins, pain streaking through his head.

"Because things are different now."

"Not for me," he said, striding across the living room.

"That's the problem."

He shook his head and fought off a wave of dizziness. "That's not what I meant."

"Cole, I don't want you to feel—"

"I won't."

"Why? Because your honor will keep you warm at night?"

"No," he grated. "You will."

"That's sex. And that's great and fine, but it's not enough to build a life on."

It felt like it. The thought of being with her, being in her, consumed him. The way she smelled, the way she tasted.

She was everything. It wasn't just sex; it was her. Being with her.

"Why not?" he asked, his tongue thick.

"Because lust fades. I'll get lines on my face. I'll gain fifteen pounds. My hair will get gray. And one day you'll look at me and wonder why you thought it was a good idea to marry me."

He could imagine her like that. Older. Even more beautiful.

"I'll never wonder why," he said, his tone fierce.

He took another step forward, the sun hitting his eyes. Pain lashed him, and he closed them tight. And it was her face he saw. The same image he'd held in his mind all night. The same image that was imprinted on his heart.

He didn't feel dizzy now. Everything was clear. Clearer than it had been in a long time.

"I"—he blinked and took another step toward her—"I've been breathing for five years. And that's all. Just going forward. Going through the motions. But then you came into my life and you reminded me that there were reasons to breathe."

Her mouth dropped open, a tear sliding down her cheek. "Cole . . . I'll never keep the baby from you. You'll always have him. I won't use him as a pawn. I swear I won't."

"That's not what I meant, Kelsey. I'm thrilled to have a baby with you. Thrilled that we're having a child. But *you're* the reason things are different. You. And it's you that I want, not just a vague idea of family or a satisfaction of duty. It's you."

"But you said you didn't want—"

"I was scared. Because the people I've trusted most in my life have abandoned me. Betrayed me. My mom died, and it wasn't her fault, but I lost part of me, Kelsey. And my dad . . . everything he taught me, everything I believed about him, about me . . . it was a lie. It was more than a marriage that didn't last two years that chased me away from love. I could have gotten over that, over her. It's the fact that I felt like I wasn't really the man I thought I was. Because the man I patterned myself after was a fake."

"I understand that. I do."

"I know you do. But it doesn't mean I was right. You told me you loved me. And it was like . . . like I suddenly realized that I was hiding. You offered me something new. Something real. I saw the possibility in it. That if I would just trust you, let my guard down, I could have every emotion, every triumph and every heartbreak possible. And I ran from it. From you. Kelsey, those losses almost broke me, but it's nothing compared to what it would mean to lose you."

He drew closer to her, his heart pounding, his hands shaking. He put his hand on her cheek, wiped the moisture from her skin.

"Kelsey," he said, "safety is worth nothing to me without you. Every risk is worth taking if it means I'll have you in my life. In my arms. If I have your love."

Her lip wobbled and he leaned in and kissed it. "You have it," she whispered. "Always."

His breath released in a rush. "Oh, I am so thankful to hear you say that. I'm so thankful that me being such a big, cowardly ass didn't kill it."

"It would take more than that," she said. "I just didn't want to . . . It's pathetic to think of staying with a guy who doesn't want you."

"I do want you," he said, and the truth of it filled his entire body. "Kelsey, I love you."

Her blue eyes widened. "You . . . love me?"

"So much. I have loved you for a while now. I think that's why you scared me so much. I was all shut off, trying to keep from being hurt more. I thought if I didn't trust anyone, didn't depend on anyone, then I would be safe. But I wasn't really living. You said that you felt like you could truly be yourself when you were with me. You do the same for me. You brought me back to life. And that's just you, Kelsey. It's not the baby or satisfied honor. It's you. I didn't know who I was anymore, who I wanted to be. You led me back to myself."

She wrapped her arms around his neck and held him close. "Oh, Cole, I do love you."

He hugged her back, his chin resting on her head. "I won't be perfect. I'll let you down. But I will love you with everything I have. If I make a promise to you, I swear I'll move heaven and earth to keep it. And I will never, ever betray you. I will be a better man than I am, so that I deserve you."

"I'm not perfect either, you know. I hog the blankets. And my temper is quick. I get absorbed in writing projects and forget to shower."

He laughed. "You're not scaring me away."

"I'm not trying to. I'm just saying that we both have flaws. I don't love you in spite of what you've been through, Cole. I love the man you've become because of all the crap you've been through."

He laughed and pulled her closer, kissing her lips, embracing every ounce of emotion that filled him. He would never turn away from it again.

"I love you," he said again.

"I love to hear you say it," she said, her lips turning up into a half grin. "And I love you."

"And when we get married and you make Alexa your maid of honor, I won't even fight with her."

Kelsey threw her head back and laughed. "I'll tell her you said that."

"I hope you do." He walked back over to the couch and pulled the ring off the coffee table. "Kelsey, I'm going to offer you this ring for a third time, with the disclaimer that if you refuse, I'll only offer it again. And again and again. Forever."

She smiled, her eyes glittering. "Well, I'm not going to make you work that hard for it."

Kelsey extended her hand, so ready for this now. So ready to share her life with him. Not because of the baby but because of them.

He slid the ring onto her fourth finger, and it didn't feel heavy or strange. It felt right.

"I thought this mistake would ruin . . . everything," she

said. "I didn't know what I would do when you showed up at my door. How I would manage to incorporate you into my life. And now I can't imagine it without you."

"Maybe we should send a thank-you note to the fertility clinic."

She laughed. "I don't know about that. I've always tried to plan and organize. I've never liked the unexpected, but I'm rethinking. Maybe the unexpected isn't so bad."

"Me too, Kelsey."

He leaned in and kissed her, and heat spread through her, melting her, making her want to drag him upstairs and have her way with him.

But there was the small matter of telling Alexa she wouldn't be leaving.

"Just a second," she said, slinking out onto the porch. "Hey, Alex?"

Cole followed her onto the porch, wrapping his arms around her waist.

Alexa, who was leaning against the car looking bored, suddenly looked much more attentive. "You're staying, aren't you?"

"Yeah. I am."

"You," Alexa said sharply. "Do you love her? Because she's my best friend and she deserves someone who loves her more than anything."

"I do," Cole said, holding Kelsey more tightly against him.

Alexa nodded, a smile teasing her lips. "Great. Then, Kelsey, if you put me in yellow, I will make your life a living hell. So, choose the bridesmaid dresses wisely."

"Ready?"

They all turned and watched Tyler come from the direction of the bunkhouse, his suitcase in hand. He turned to where Kelsey and Cole were standing. "I need some time off," he said. He looked back at Alexa. "At least, I think I do."

She sighed heavily. "You do." She turned back to them. "He does."

"How long?" Cole asked.

Tyler shrugged. "I'm hoping I'll be calling with a long-distance two weeks' notice in a few days."

"Don't get cocky, Tyler," Alexa said. "But get in the car." Then she ran up the steps and threw her arms around them both. "I'm happy for you," she said.

Kelsey hugged her friend back. "I'm happy for you too."

"Keep me up-to-date on wedding and baby. I need to be here for both."

"Will do."

Alexa trotted back down to the car, and she and Tyler waved while they pulled away from the house. Cole and Kelsey watched them until the car was gone.

"Do you think they'll make it work?" Kelsey asked.

"Stranger things have happened," Cole said. "Look at us."

Kelsey laughed. "Well, that's true."

"So, when do we need to have this wedding?" he asked.

A little thrill flipped Kelsey's stomach. "The wedding . . . Well, it's really important. And we'll need lots of planning. And rehearsal."

"Okay," Cole said slowly.

"But right now . . . I'd rather practice for the wedding night."

He swung her up into his arms in one fluid movement and dropped a kiss onto her lips. "I'm all for that."

She snickered. "Ride 'em, cowboy."

Cole rewarded her with a laugh. "Hang on, cowgirl."

She kissed his cheek. "Forever."

Epilogue

"So, Kelsey, when are you two having another baby?"

Kelsey looked from the well-meaning wedding attendee to her husband and then to her nine-month-old daughter. "We haven't thought that far ahead yet. But I promise we'll send out announcements when the time comes."

That seemed to satisfy the nosy guest, who moved on to another table. She and Cole had talked about other kids, in that distant-future kind of way. Even though Madeline was a mighty stealer of sleep and could projectile vomit with the best of them, they were agreed they wanted more.

At least a year after Maddy started sleeping through the night.

"The bride wore black," Cole muttered, looking at Alexa and Tyler, who were holding each other close on the dance floor.

"Yes, she did. But are you really that surprised?"

He shook his head. "I was just surprised she wore that lavender dress you chose for *our* wedding."

"It's what friends do. It's why I'm sitting here looking like an angsty teenager's closet threw up on me."

"I think you look pretty cute."

"Well, then, that makes up for it."

She and Cole shared a smile, and Kelsey felt like she would burst with happiness. But then, she felt that way at least once a day. Life on the ranch with Cole and Maddy and Lark and Cade was busy. And it was wonderful.

Cole reached out and took Maddy off her lap, settling her in his arms. The love that Cole had for their daughter never failed to amaze her. Never failed to make her teary-eyed.

Cole lowered his head, his cheek resting against Maddy's hair, and took a deep breath. "It's a beautiful day," he said, his eyes meeting hers. "Of course, every day has been beautiful since you've been in it."

"Life is pretty beautiful," she said, putting her hand over his.

He looked from Maddy to her, a smile on his lips. "Yes, it is."

Read on for a sneak peek
at the next Silver Creek romance
from Maisey Yates

UNTOUCHED

It wasn't like she even wanted any of this for herself.

Lark Mitchell looked around the completely unconventional wedding being thrown in her yard and fought the urge to cry.

Which was as dumb as rocks, because there was no reason to cry. Seriously, the bride was wearing a black wedding dress. It was ridiculous. And okay, the bride was also marrying the man Lark had spent the better part of two years completely fixated on, but that was no reason to cry.

It wasn't like she *loved* Tyler. And in the year since he'd started dating Alexa, his new wife, and moved to New York, Lark had completely gotten over him.

No, this wasn't heartbreak. She was just in the throes of that left-behind kind of melancholy that she was more familiar with than she'd like to be.

She'd felt that way when most of her friends had gone off to college and she'd stayed in Silver Creek to help out on the ranch. She'd felt it all through high school when other girls had gotten dates and she'd gotten the chance to tutor cute boys in English.

Just this sort of achy feeling that other people were going somewhere while she stood in the same place.

Or, in this instance, sat in the same place. At one of the florid tables placed around the lawn. This little wedding had come to Elk Haven Stables because Tyler had once been a ranch hand and because the bride in black was best friends with Lark's sister-in-law, Kelsey.

Lark adored Kelsey, but she could honestly do without Alexa.

Which might have been sour grapes. Maybe.

But damn, woman, marry a dude your own age. Tyler was in Lark's demographic, and he hadn't known her in high school, which helped, because as awkward as she was now . . . high school had been a biotch.

"Hey, sweetie."

Lark looked up and saw Kelsey holding baby Maddy on her hip and looking down at her with overly sympathetic blue eyes. "Hi," Lark said.

"Are you okay?"

"What? Yeah. I'm . . . so okay. Why wouldn't I be okay? I had a crush on this guy for like two seconds a year ago. I never even kissed him."

"I remember how much you liked him."

"Thanks, Kels, but I'm a grown-up, as much as Cole doesn't like to acknowledge it. I've moved on. I have another man in my life now."

Because she was sure three rounds of cybersex six months ago with a guy she'd never met counted as having someone in her life. And if not, it at least bolstered her lie. She needed the lie. It was so much better than admitting she was pathetic. And that she spent most days in her room doing tech support for various and sundry people while eating Pop-Tarts and streaming *Doctor Who* through an online sub-scription service.

Yeah. Saying she was involved was better than admitting that.

"Oh. Do you? Because Cole . . ." Kelsey narrowed her eyes. "Cole doesn't know."

"No. And it's okay if it stays that way." The idea of her brother finding the transcripts from those little chats she'd had with Aaron_234 was ever so slightly awful.

Almost as bad as admitting that the closest she'd ever come to sex was a heavy-breathing conversation. Over the net. Where you couldn't even hear the heavy breathing.

The very thought made her cringe at her own lameness. It was advanced geekiness of the highest order.

At least she excelled in something.

"I'm not going to keep secrets from Cole," Kelsey said, sitting down at the table. "I mean, I won't lie to him if he asks."

"He shouldn't ask. It's not his business."

Of course, Cole wouldn't see it that way. To Cole, everything in Lark's life was his business. Thankfully, Kelsey and Maddy had deflected some of that, but then there was Cade. Cade, who was the more wicked brother. The irresponsible one. The one who should have been cool with her doing whatever and finding her way in life by making a few mistakes.

But Cade was even worse than Cole in his way. The hypocrite. She always figured it was because while Cole guessed at what debauchery was out there in life, Cade had been there, done that and bought the souvenir shot glass.

She'd considered ordering the shot glass online. So to speak. But she'd never done a damn thing. So all her brothers' overprotective posturing was for naught, the poor dears.

Although Cole had nearly torn Tyler a new one when he'd suspected they might have slept together. Alas, no such luck.

She'd have loved to have a mistake that sexy in her past.

All she had was a greasy keyboard and a vague, stale sense of shame that lingered a lot longer than a self-induced orgasm.

"Yes, well, you don't want to keep your boyfriend from us, do you?"

"He's not my boyfriend. He's not. I exaggerated a little. It's not like that."

"Oh, so . . . is he someone in town, or . . . ?"

"He's on the computer. He's not . . . I haven't talked to him in a while." Like they'd ever really chatted about anything significant. It was more like a straight shot to "What are you wearing?"

"Oh . . . okay."

"But the bottom line is that I'm fine. With this. Right now. Alexa and Tyler are welcome to their wedded bliss. I'm not in the space to pursue wedded bliss. I have other things to do." *Like sit on my ass and shoot zombies?*

No. Real plans. To travel someday. To have adventures. Maybe a meaningless fling here and there. In Paris? Paris seemed like a good place for a meaningless fling. Silver Creek certainly wasn't. She knew all the idiots here.

Worse, they knew her. They knew her as a bucktoothed nerd who would do your calculus while you did the cheerleader. It was a poor set of assumptions to begin a relationship, so she just never tried.

It was better than doing the guy who was doing the cheerleader. Doing math was way less painful. Keeping it virtual was a lot less painful.

Otherwise you ended up watching the only guy you'd ever really thought you might have a shot with marrying another woman. Not that that was what was happening. Because she didn't love Tyler, damn it.

But if she had married him, she wouldn't have done it in a black dress. She was a gamer geek with limited social skills, but even she knew major life events were the time to drop your freak flag a little bit. Wear some lace. A pair of pumps. Ditch the Converse All Stars for a couple of hours.

Not that anyone had asked her, of course.

"I'm glad. I was a little worried about you."

Worry for Lark's well-being was apparently a virulent contagion at Elk Haven Stables. Cade and Cole had a bad case of it, and Cole had clearly infected his wife.

"No need to worry. I'm golden. I'm not in a picket-fence place right now."

"Yeah, neither was I," Kelsey said, shifting Maddy in her arms and looking pointedly at the little bundle of joy.

"Unless you can get knocked up driving by sperm banks now, I'm not going to be in your situation anytime soon."

Kelsey laughed, the motion jiggling Maddy and making her giggle. "Yeah, steer clear of those clinics or you might find yourself shackled to an obnoxious alpha cowboy for the rest of your life."

"Already am, Kels. Two of them. We're related, which means I can't just ditch them. I'm not marrying a cowboy." She looked back at Tyler. "I'm sick of cowboys, in fact. I'll find someone metropolitan who knows that high fashion isn't a bigger belt buckle and your Sunday-go-to-meetin' clothes."

"Nothing wrong with wanting something different," Kelsey said. "I guess Cole is my something different, so I can see the attraction to something you aren't used to. I still rent out my house in Portland. If you ever want to go try something a little more urban . . ."

For some reason, the idea made Lark's throat feel tight. "Uh . . . maybe another time. Cole is just getting all his social media stuff going for the ranch and you know he needs close help with that. He's death to computers." All true enough, but in reality she could do most tech help remotely.

She would leave someday. Just not today. Or next week. Or next month. But that was fine.

"Well, that's true," Kelsey said. "But I'm not illiterate, so I can help him a little. I do work on my computer, so I'm pretty familiar with everyday glitches."

"But who would optimize your blog?" Lark asked. "It's just starting to get huge."

"True. The modern world is a wonderful thing."

Kelsey was a health-and-wellness columnist, and she still had her column published in papers across the country, but since moving to the ranch, she'd started doing a lot of humorous posts about acclimating to life in the sticks, and thanks to her already established audience, they had become an instant hit.

And Lark was in charge of design and management of the website and its community.

Which was nice. It was nice to feel important. Nice to be needed.

"So, you're really okay?"

"Yes," Lark said. "Stop giving me your wounded-puppy eyes. I'm fine."

"Great. I'll be back in a minute. I have to go grab Cole."

"Neat," Lark said, reaching down beside her chair and pulling her phone out of her purse. She was itchy to check her email, because it had been a couple of hours and she hated the feeling of being disconnected.

She keyed in her pin and unlocked the screen, her email client immediately loading about fifty messages.

She opened up the app and scrolled through the new mail. She had another one from Longhorn Inc. She'd been negotiating with the hiring manager, Mark, for a few days now. She hadn't told anyone in her family about the offer, because she knew her brothers would get all proprietary and think they had to do it all for her.

Like she wasn't smart enough to handle her own job opportunities in her own field. And yes, she worked for the family by and large, but she'd also done websites for several local businesses and had become the go-to IT tech for Silver Creek residents.

This would be her biggest deal by far. And the first time she'd be signing a contract for a job, but she was ready for the challenge.

She'd be setting up computers, servers, firewalls and web filters at a ranch for troubled boys. And then doing a little bit of tech training too. It was a big undertaking, especially with everything she already did at Elk Haven, but honestly, she could use something to mix up her life.

Something that wouldn't take her too far from the safety of her bedroom.

She had a little bit of a complex. She could admit that.

But she'd lost her mother so early and then her father. Cole, Cade, the ranch—they might drive her nuts, but they were all she had. All she knew. Life felt horribly insecure outside of that. Terribly fragile.

Life was safe in games. When you had armor and you could collect health right from the ground. Along with an AK to take care of anyone or anything that might threaten you.

She skimmed the email and typed in a hasty reply, asking for more details on the time frame and payment, then hit SEND.

"Is that thing welded to your hand?"

Cade walked over to her table and sat on the edge of it, his friend Amber in tow. Amber gave her an apologetic look. She would be annoyed with Cade silently, but Lark knew if push came to shove, Amber's allegiance was with Lark's obnoxious brother.

That was one relationship she had no desire to ever figure out.

"Nope, detachable." She tossed the phone down into her purse. "Unlike your stupid face, which you're sadly stuck with."

"Very few people have a problem with my face."

"Oh, dear, the tone of this conversation is lowering already," Amber said.

He turned to Amber. "Women really like my face."

Amber's forehead wrinkled, her brows drawing together. "Do they?"

"If not my face, they like my—"

"No!" This came from both Amber and Lark in unison.

"My personality," Cade said. "Sick people. You are sick people."

"Yeah, we all believe that was going to be the next word out of your mouth, Cadence," she said, using a name she'd assigned to Cade in childhood to piss him off.

Her brother hopped down from the edge of the table, wincing when his foot made contact with the grass, then freezing, a pained expression on his face as he waited for what Lark assumed was a wave of pain to pass through him.

"Hey," she said. "I didn't think your leg was bothering you as much now."

"It's not," he said.

"Lies. Dirty lies. What's up?"

Cade gave her a hard look. But she knew he'd tell her, because he knew she had no problem harassing him until he did. "Nothing," he said, his tone hard. "It's nothing new. Just the same shit. It's like there's this nice little highway of pain that goes from my knee up to my spine. Not any worse."

Just not any better. Not really.

She hated that. Hated that Cade couldn't ride anymore. Hated that he hurt all the time. That day had scared years off her life. She'd been convinced, when they'd gotten the call about Cade's fall, that he was going to die too.

That she was really destined to lose everyone she loved. All of her family. That she would be left alone.

She blinked and tried to pull her mind back into the present. Cade wasn't dead. He might be surly, and he might have a limp, and he couldn't compete on the circuit, but he wasn't dead. She really appreciated that, since as much as he drove her crazy, she needed him.

"Well, glad it's not any worse."

"Me too."

"So, want to get hammered?" she asked, not that she made a practice of getting hammered, but it seemed like it might be a good idea.

"Hell yeah," he said. "And Cole bought a lot of booze. His wedding gift to the newlyweds."

Amber's lips twitched. "You're going to get hammered drinking champagne? Because Cole bought champagne. For the toast."

"I have a talent where alcohol is concerned."

"I know," Amber said dryly. "I've held your hair, so to speak, while you puked off a hangover or ten."

Lark made a face. "Sick. I've never had a hangover."

Cade shrugged. "That's because you live timid. I don't."

"And you're all busted up to prove it," she said, knowing Cade would rather joke about his condition than say anything weighty about it.

"But I've lived. Bless me, Father, for I have sinned. Indeed."

"STFU, jackass," Lark said.

He put his hand on her forehead. "You're starting to speak lolcats. Get off the computer once in a while."

"You don't even know what lolcats are."

"Something to do with cats and cheeseburgers. Amber texts me crap like that all the time."

"At least she tries to modernize you," Lark said, shaking her head.

"How did this become a commentary on me? At least I come out into the light every day."

"Look," Lark said, holding her admittedly pale arm out in a shaft of sunlight. "I don't even sparkle!"

"Suspicious. I'm suspicious. Seriously," Cade said, "I worry about you in your cave all the time. You've got to live life, Lark, or it's going to pass you by."

"Are you seriously giving me advice?" she asked. "Name one thing in your life that's organized, or settled, or . . . aspirant."

"Fun, Lark, I have fun. With real people. Outside. Look around you. It's in high-def."

"You're an idiot, and also, I have a life."

"Virtually."

And if that didn't count as having a life, she was screwed. She bit the inside of her cheek. "Annnnd?"

"And maybe you should get hungover, is all I'm saying."

"But maybe have enough class not to go drinking all the champagne at a wedding to accomplish it," Amber said somewhat pointedly.

Yeah, if Lark did that here, she really would look lovelorn and pathetic.

"Then I'll hold off. Anyway, you don't know everything about me, Cade."

"Beg to differ."

"You don't."

"If I checked your browser history, I would."

"Nuh-uh." No one touched her computer but her, but even so, she didn't leave certain things lying around on it. Secret shame was secret.

"Witty comeback," he said. "Witty indeed. Why don't you go talk to someone? Meet a guy."

"Right. Meet a guy. Cole would be interrogating him before a full greeting exited my mouth."

Cade shrugged. "You take the good with the bad."

"You're both mostly bad," she said, not meaning it at all.

Amber rolled her eyes. "Have fun," she said to Lark. "And catch up with us later maybe? You can help me haul his drunken ass to his room."

"I say we leave him on the lawn."

"Fair enough," Amber said, turning and following Cade down to the table laden with drinks.

Lark bent back down and took her phone from her bag, trying not to think too much about her brother and his comments. Look what "living" had gotten him. And anyway, a hangover was hardly her definition of living.

She didn't have to drink herself into a stupor to feel like she'd reached the heights.

She opened up her mail app and saw another one from Longhorn HR. She opened up the message.

The money offer had doubled; the length of the contract was for six weeks, with the possibility of an extension. And attached was a contract to be returned as soon as possible.

She knew exactly what her answer was.

She fired off a quick reply and the promise to fax the signed contract over that night.

There. It wasn't much. It was a local contract, and she would still be able to live at home while she fulfilled it. But it was something. A decision made on her own. A step toward meaningful independence.

She put her phone back in her bag and stood up, taking a deep breath. Then she headed over toward where the bride and groom were standing by the cake.

She was going to offer her congratulations and sincerest well wishes. She wasn't feeling quite so left behind anymore.

Two

Quinn Parker was mean when he was pissed. Okay, he was mean most of the time, but especially when he was pissed.

And he was currently pretty pissed.

"You don't have anything?" Quinn asked Sam, his right-hand man and basically the only person who could put up with his shit.

"Nothing concrete. It's pretty tough to prove you didn't do something, Quinn, barring a confession from someone else."

"Beat a confession out of someone else."

"Who?"

"I don't know." Quinn rested his elbows on the granite countertop and stared across the bar at the empty living area. The cabin was almost completely done now. Though "cabin" seemed like a misleading word for the place.

Five thousand square feet. Huge kitchen, a dining room big enough to seat twenty. A living room made for the same number. And a section of private living space for himself.

The rest of the grounds had a kitchen that stood alone, along with outdoor dining, classrooms and cabins that were much more like actual cabins. Small and rustic. Just right for boys who needed to get their heads on straight.

His new role as a philanthropist didn't sit too well with him. Especially because a few local news outlets were wanting to do a piece on the ranch, and that was the last thing Quinn wanted.

Because if they started looking at his present, they'd look into his past too. And that was a minefield. It would start with his family background, onto his arrest record, straight down to his being barred from the Rodeo Association.

No way in hell was he issuing an invitation for someone to open that Pandora's box.

But he could just keep hanging up on reporters. The important thing was the ranch. And messing with Cade Mitchell's head.

"I was thinking Cade was the guy we might nail, in truth."

"Really?"

"Yeah, really. I don't know. You think he's as injured as he said he was?"

"He got trampled pretty good. I saw the video."

"Yeah, he got the hell beat out of him. That's for sure."

It had been an ugly sight. Quinn had been there, watching from the gates, when Cade had taken a fall on his horse, which had been spooked beyond reason, stomping and bucking. And unfortunately, Cade had been trapped beneath the animal at the time.

It was the worst injury he'd seen in his years on the circuit. It had left everyone there with a sick feeling in the pits of their stomachs.

And Quinn's had stayed. Because when the spike was found beneath the horse's saddle and inquiries were made, Cade pointed his finger at Quinn.

True, he'd never liked the bastard. Cade had been the golden boy on the circuit. Mr. Good Time. Every buckle bunny had been on him after events; every sponsor had been after him for an endorsement. And all that had been fine, because Quinn attracted his own women. The all-American good-time boy was nice for some. But some women liked dark and dangerous, and he wasn't above catering to that. And as for endorsements, he frankly had a fortune on his hands now that his father was dead.

The man commonly billed as his father anyway. Though Quinn and everyone else in his family knew differently. Whether they'd ever speak it out loud or not.

He didn't need any of what Cade Mitchell had, no matter what anyone thought. And while he'd never been a particularly nice son of a bitch even, he had his limits. If Cade had taken a swing at him in a bar fight, Quinn would have knocked his teeth out of his head and made that million-dollar face a lot less valuable.

Even he had enough . . . pride? Conscience? Something. He wouldn't just ambush a man, especially when the move would injure an animal like this one had. The horse was fine, but it had been reacting to pure, biting pain.

Quinn might not like Cade, but he'd had no beef with the horse he was riding.

Bottom line, Quinn was a bastard. Cade knew it. The Rodeo Association knew it. Hell, the man commonly called his father knew it too, though he meant "bastard" in the more traditional sense of the word. Everyone else just thought he was a prick. But no matter how big of a prick he was, he wouldn't do what he'd been accused of.

And the accusation had damn well ruined his life. Taken his credibility, taken the only thing he'd ever cared about.

Barred from competition. For life.

Damn it to hell, he had to fix that. He had to prove it wasn't his fault. All of his appeals so far had been denied. Apparently, he needed evidence. He closed his eyes and felt a cold sweat on his back, the memory of his last hearing playing through his mind, more terrifying than the times he'd stood trial in court as a teenager.

I need evidence? Show me your evidence.

This ain't a court a law, Mr. Parker. We don't need

evidence. All these men here, bein' of sound mind, have come to a unanimous decision based on the testimony of Mr. Cade Mitchell.

He opened his eyes again and looked around at the cabin. Things were definitely starting to come together. A whole lot of things.

"I'm going to have a little job for you coming up, Sam," he said.

"Oh, really?" The other man straightened and crossed his arms over his broad chest.

"You and Jill, actually."

Sam's expression tightened. "All right."

"I'm going to send you on an all-expenses-paid vacation to Elk Haven Stables."

"That's the Mitchell ranch, yeah?"

"Yessir. If Cade Mitchell has exaggerated his injuries in any way, it will be pretty clear pretty quick. If I show my face over there, he won't drop his guard."

"I thought you wanted him to know you were here."

"I do. And he will. But he doesn't need to know you work for me. And on his ranch, he's bound to be relaxed. Just for the first week, at least, I want you and Jill there pretending you're on an anniversary trip."

"Won't we need a reservation?"

"You have one. Mark called it in."

"He's a helpful son bitch, ain't he?"

Sam was obviously irritated with the directive, but Quinn couldn't figure out why. A little all-expenses-paid alone time with his wife should have made Sam happy. Although Quinn couldn't see the appeal, personally, since he had no intention of ever having a wife. Though Jill was a nice enough woman. Not his biggest fan, but he did monopolize a lot of her husband's time, and even more of it since Sam had been in Silver Creek helping him get things together.

"Yes, he is. He's also arranged a contract for me that will prove very useful indeed."

"Aw, shit, man, what did you do?" The lines on Sam's face looked more drawn.

"You say that like you think I did something bad, buddy. I think I'm offended."

"Did you?"

"Depends on your perspective."

Sam shook his head and pulled his cell phone out of the front pocket of his shirt. "I'll have to call Jill and see if she's up for this. Otherwise it'll be me staying in that cabin by myself, looking like a nutjob."

"Mark might be willing to come down and stay with you."

Sam flipped him off on his way out of the room, grumbling as he dialed his wife.

Quinn braced himself on the counter, palms flat on the granite surface. Yeah, he was pretty sure Sam would think what he'd done was a very bad thing.

Cade would think so too.

And that made Quinn feel nothing but good. Because Lark Mitchell had signed a contract to come and work for him for the next six weeks.

It was a good thing to keep your enemies close. But it was better to keep their little sisters closer.

Because there was nothing on God's green earth that would piss Cade off more than having Lark in close proximity to Quinn. Like sending your lamb to bunk with a wolf.

Quinn smiled and pushed off from the counter. Oh, yeah, if Cade Mitchell had secrets, Quinn would find them. If Cade had a weakness, Quinn would damn well exploit it.

Quinn Parker was mean when he was pissed. And Cade had sure as hell pissed him off.

ACKNOWLEDGMENTS

I owe huge thanks, as always, to my wonderful agent, Helen Breitwieser. To my editor, Katherine Pelz, for her insight and enthusiasm. My critique partner and soother of my neuroses, Jackie Ashenden. The makers of Lucky Charms, for providing me with the sugar rush I so desperately needed. And huge thanks to Lisa Hendrix, who pushed me to write these books in the first place.

Ready to find
your next great read?

Let us help.

Visit prh.com/nextread